"I cannot become a man's property.

"I fear being trapped and powerless more than anything else in this world."

Ethan knew better than to reassure her. He appealed to her instead with logic. "Is it better to mete out your time in tiny increments to avoid commitment? Would you rather sell yourself by the minute or hour? Think, Sadie. One man instead of many. A certain financial security?"

Tears filled her eyes and she pulled away from him, just as she had pulled away from Cedric Broxton. "I must not lose myself, Mr. Travis. I cannot give myself up to a man. I cannot...surrender."

Ethan dropped his hands to his sides. Of course she would not want to depend upon a man who had a reputation of being ruthless and dangerous. She'd be a fool to trust him. And whatever else Sadie was, she was not a fool...!

* * *

Saving Sarah
Harlequin Historical #660—June 2003

SAVING SARAH

GAIL RANSTROM

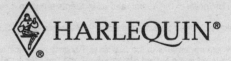

HARLEQUIN®

TORONTO • NEW YORK • LONDON
AMSTERDAM • PARIS • SYDNEY • HAMBURG
STOCKHOLM • ATHENS • TOKYO • MILAN • MADRID
PRAGUE • WARSAW • BUDAPEST • AUCKLAND

ISBN 0-373-29260-0

SAVING SARAH

Please address questions and book requests to:
Harlequin Reader Service
U.S.: 3010 Walden Ave., P.O. Box 1325, Buffalo, NY 14269
Canadian: P.O. Box 609, Fort Erie, Ont. L2A 5X3

For my mother, Shirley,
who taught me more than she even realized, and for the
subtle ways those lessons manifest themselves day after
day. And for my beautiful sister, Cheryl, who has been
my best friend and staunchest supporter.

Special acknowledgments to Cynthia,
who made me do it, and Ann Leslie, who made it better.
And always, a nod to the Wednesday League:
Margaret, Rosanne, Cynthia, Joy and Joanne.

Prologue

London, April 1818

What could possibly be serious enough to merit such a desperate measure as summoning Ethan Travis, the Demon of Alsatia? He couldn't imagine, but it was worth the trip to Lord Kilgrew's office at half past one in the morning to find out.

A steady drizzle penetrated his black wool coat as he strode down the unlit cobbled street. He wished he could have turned his back on the formal summons, but honor required him to at least hear Lord Kilgrew out.

Ethan entered the government building and climbed the two flights of stairs to a door lettered in gold with Lord Kilgrew's name. At his soft rap, a muffled voice bade him enter. He took a deep breath, squared his shoulders and opened the door.

Lord Kilgrew, considerably grayer since the last time Ethan had seen him, glanced up and waved to a chair in front of his desk. "Good to see you again, Travis," he said. "Sit down."

This could not be good news if he needed to sit for it. He took a chair across from his former commander. "What is this about, sir?"

Kilgrew frowned as if Ethan had wounded him. "What? No time for pleasantries? It has been—what—two years, since last I saw you? How have you been, lad?"

Ethan gave him a sardonic grin. "You know how I've been, sir. I see your operatives around, watching me."

Kilgrew had the grace to look abashed. "Not watching, lad, just keeping an eye on you. I like to keep tabs on my friends. I haven't given up on finding the real traitor, you know."

"That's not likely to happen after all this time."

"Sooner or later, he'll slip. When he does, we shall deal with him. Surely you want to clear your name, Ethan."

"More than anything." God, what would he *not* give to have his life back, his good name and reputation. His honor.

He felt the familiar chill invade his vitals, settling somewhere in the region of his withered heart. His anger rose in the form of a heavy dark substance that clung to him and was such that he could not face the man. He stood and went to the window, looking into the dark street below. Rain glistened on the cobblestones like slick oil and reflected the light from the window where he stood.

"Why have you summoned me, sir?" he asked. He heard the clink of a bottle against a glass and the trickle of liquid being poured. The silence lengthened, but he waited. The past two years had taught him to be a very patient man.

Kilgrew brought him a glass of claret. "I, ah, have a favor to ask. Discretion. That's what I need. Paramount. Will you hear me out?"

"Is it a personal favor, sir, or for the Ministry?"

"Personal."

Drat! He'd do nothing for the government that had left him dangling in the wind. Honor required him to help Lord Kilgrew. "Tell me about it, sir."

"There is a small matter of blackmail—" Lord Kilgrew paused, seeing the frown on Ethan's face.

Ethan could not imagine Lord Kilgrew doing anything worthy of blackmail. No one who knew the man would believe it. "Deny it, sir."

"The problem is more complicated than that."

Ethan took the glass and sipped. "Go on."

"The matter is extremely delicate. The blackmailer has got his hands on some sort of evidence. Letters, I believe. He has hidden them in a secret place, leaving instructions that, should anything happen to him, the evidence is to be made public."

Ethan arched an eyebrow. "Own the error. Admission renders a blackmailer impotent. 'Tis the only sure way to be rid of him." He tried not to think of the fact that simple denial had not helped him. It had made matters worse. It had ruined his reputation completely.

Kilgrew sighed deeply. "I hoped you would help. I need a man of your…talents."

Ethan shook his head. He knew the rumors. Hell, he'd encouraged them. "I will not kill for you."

"Quite the opposite, lad. I want you to follow the blackmailer and keep him safe. Nothing must happen to him. We are searching for the letters but, meantime, he must be kept safe so the letters will not be made public."

Kilgrew rose to his feet and leaned across his desk, his palms down upon it. "Ethan, do not make me beg. If I hadn't held off charges until the damned rumors died down, you'd be on the gibbet—hanged for treason!"

"I know, sir. I haven't forgotten how much I owe you." Though his former commander did not seem to know it, he'd won the argument. He had made it a point of honor. When everyone in London thought the worst of him, Kilgrew believed the best. He had even interceded on Ethan's behalf.

"I refused to bring you up on charges. I knew we could wait the whispers out, but a trial would have spelled your end. British lives were lost because *someone* sold information to the Dey. You were the target because you were in charge of the advance reconnaissance. It was a witch hunt, Ethan. I was lucky to keep you out of court. You're alive, lad.''

Alive, perhaps, Ethan thought, but a pariah in his circle. Most of his former friends did not speak to him. The scandal killed his father, his fiancée had jilted him and his own brother had disowned him.

Lord Kilgrew cleared his throat and looked pained. He sank back into his seat like a man defeated and stared into his glass of claret. "They call you the Demon of Alsatia for a reason, Travis. You have a legion of minions at your disposal. You have eyes in every dark squalid corner of London, and you, yourself, could follow our man into the highest drawing rooms where your spies cannot go. I can arrange invitations to every event this season. Our man must not know he's being followed, even if it is for his protection. He'd bolt, or do something foolish. We need those letters, but until we have them, he must be kept safe. No matter the cost.''

Yes. Ethan had the connections to make such an undertaking possible. He had entry, if not welcome, in society, if he chose to use it, and he could command any number of ruffians and street urchins. He *was* the man for the job.

And Kilgrew was right. When all was said and done, Ethan was trapped by his own sense of honor. He was a man who paid his debts. No theatrics, just conviction. "Very well, m'lord. You have my word. What is his name?" he asked.

Lord Kilgrew's relief was obvious. He nodded and gave a grimace of a smile. "Mr. Harold Whitlock. Keep him safe, no matter the cost.''

Chapter One

London, May 1818

Tension thickened the air in Lady Sarah Hunter's private parlor. The cheery blue and yellow decor and the light streaming through the tall second floor windows did nothing to brighten the mood. Four women seated around a low tea table glanced at one another anxiously. The decisions they made at such times were never easy. And rarely pleasant.

The fifth woman in the room was a virtual stranger to them. Gladys Whitlock, an agreeable but unremarkable looking woman in her mid-thirties, had been referred to them by Madame Marie, the ton's premier modiste. Periodically throughout telling her story, she would touch a thin scab at the base of her throat.

When she finished, Mrs. Whitlock dabbed a linen hankie at the corners of her eyes. "I feel so foolish telling you all this, but Madame Marie hinted that you might be able to help. In fact, you are my *only* hope."

Sarah placed her teacup back on the saucer with a sigh and tucked an unruly wisp of hair behind her ear. She feared she was becoming quite jaded and wondered if all twenty-four-year-olds felt as world-weary as she. She returned her attention to the group as Grace Forbush, an elegant widow in her mid-thirties who disdained the curly hairstyles of the day in favor of sleek chignons, attempted a précis of the problem.

"In summary, Mr. Harold Whitlock has hidden the three children and continues to abuse and assault Mrs. Whitlock. As he spends more and more time in the opium dens, he grows more and more unpredictable. Mrs. Whitlock fears for the safety of her children, and for her own life. Time, I collect, is not in her favor."

Sarah glanced at the other women and shrugged. Someone had to say it. "'Tis time he is put out of the way."

"We could petition the court—" Charity Wardlow began, her deep blue eyes wide with earnestness.

Grace shook her head. "The courts are at fault here. Mr. Whitlock is a highly placed bureaucrat, not to mention a man of considerable influence. He may abuse his wife and stepchildren at will and no one will say him nay. He has every legal right to take the children away to punish his wife—or for any reason whatsoever. Furthermore, as her marriage contract has no provision for a separate estate, he may take her inheritance from her father's death and use it as he pleases."

"He has likely squandered it all," Gladys Whitlock sighed, waving one hand in the air. "But I do not care about my inheritance. 'Tis the children. I cannot find them, and I cannot pry, cajole, beg, trick or seduce their whereabouts from him. You see, he knows I dare not leave or show any defiance as long as my babies are missing."

The ladies glanced around the circle again. "He would not…that is, surely he would never actually harm—" Charity ventured. She shook her head in disbelief, setting her blond curls bobbing. "Would he, Mrs. Whitlock?"

The woman's reddened eyes filled with tears again. As she wiped at them, a coating of rice powder came away to reveal a greenish-yellow bruise beneath the eye. "I would put nothing past him. He is completely void of natural affection. Why, last week he beat a small sweep for becoming lodged in the chimney. I had sent for masons to remove mortar and brick to free him, but when Harold arrived home, he said 'twas the sweep's fault for being stuck. He said I should have lit a fire and the boy would have freed himself fast enough.''

"We must take action at once," Annica Sinclair, Lady Auberville, said. The petite brunette's eyes flashed green fire and Sarah knew for a certainty that Gladys Whitlock's cause had become their own.

She nodded to Annica, recognizing that they were in complete accord on this issue. "Mr. Whitlock must disappear without a trace," she said.

Charity's blue eyes widened. "Sarah! You cannot be suggesting what I think you are. You…" She lowered her voice. "You would not 'do away' with him, would you?"

Sarah glanced at the man's wife. What must she be thinking of them? "Mr. Whitlock held a knife to her throat last night and drew blood. He threatened to kill her and the children, wherever they are hidden. He must be dealt with quickly and completely. But, I am not advocating assassination."

Mrs. Whitlock nodded, now twisting her handkerchief in her hands. "I have wondered if the children may be dead even now. If they are…" She fell silent, her gaze dropping to her lap.

Knowing she would never have children of her own made Sarah's heart ache. She resolved that, no matter what the outcome of the meeting or how the Wednesday League voted, she would begin hunting for those children at once.

"We must not be rash," Lady Annica warned.

"To the contrary, I am not rash at all. I have carefully considered it," she defended. "I am thinking a voyage around the world might give Mr. Whitlock sufficient time to reevaluate his behavior. Give him a fresh perspective, as it were."

Grace squeezed a lemon wedge into her cup. "You would send him on a grand tour?" she asked.

"Of sorts."

"What would prevent him from returning and carrying out his threats?" Charity asked.

"Ah, there's the rub." Sarah smiled. "But if he were conscripted by the Royal Navy, he would not be able to return for a good long time. At least two years. By then, we will have located the children, Mrs. Whitlock will have liquidated their assets and, together with the children, will have disappeared. I hear many 'widows' are making a new start in Australia. The Americas might be better, though, as it is a different country independent of England's laws. Mr. Whitlock would be less likely to find her, were he to go looking, or be successful in gaining the cooperation of the authorities there."

"No," Mrs. Whitlock said, her manner as firm as her voice. "Nothing must happen to Harold until I have my children back. I cannot risk that they will not be found, or that he would retaliate against them for my actions if he learns of our plans."

Though patience was not Sarah's strong suit, she nodded her agreement. "Very well, Mrs. Whitlock. But once we have located the children we must act quickly and decisively in putting him out of the way. He must have no opportunity to gain the upper hand again."

"I agree," Mrs. Whitlock said.

"I've never heard of an official being conscripted," Charity mused. She looked at Sarah for clarification.

"One is apt to claim anything if one is attempting to avoid conscription. Mr. Whitlock will appear to be just another deserter claiming position or consequence to save himself."

Lady Annica smiled. "How very clever of you, Sarah. I like the idea of conscription. I am certain Mr. Whitlock could benefit from two years at sea. Shall we employ Mr. Renquist to handle the details?"

"Yes," Sarah confirmed. "He still has friends in the Royal Navy who, for a price, will swear that Mr. Whitlock is a deserter. In fact, I believe he knows of an excellent forger who could provide Mr. Whitlock's Last Will and Testament to facilitate Mrs. Whitlock's claim."

"Yes, I believe we could produce witnesses who will see Mr. Whitlock fall into the Thames," Lady Annica said.

"Shall we ask Auberville's assistance?" Grace asked. "He must have connections in both government and military."

Annica shook her head. "If we involve him in any aspect of this, he will insist upon knowing everything. He has only agreed to ask no questions so long as he has my promise that I will do nothing illegal and will tell him if there is imminent danger. We have always agreed that the Wednesday League's dealings are of the highest confidentiality."

Sarah waited a moment but there were no further objections. She put the issue before them as a silent Mrs. Whitlock held her breath. "Those in favor of sending Mr. Whitlock on a 'grand tour'?" she asked.

Four hands went up. Unanimous, as always.

"Sarah, will you lead this particular cause since you have such an excellent grasp of the situation?" Lady Annica asked.

"With pleasure. I shall begin immediately." She gave Gladys Whitlock a reassuring smile. "I may look insignificant, Mrs. Whitlock, but let me assure you, I am tough and tenacious."

"A woman to be reckoned with," Lady Annica confirmed.

Sarah very much feared she had lost her conscience, along with her innocence, on a darkened path in Vauxhall Gardens two and a half years ago. Pray she found Mrs. Whitlock's children before they lost *their* innocence.

Snuffing the candle on her bedside table, Sarah turned toward her window and pulled the woolen jacket closer about her. She pushed stray chestnut tendrils beneath her cap, wondering why she could never make her unruly hair behave.

The clock on the upstairs landing struck the hour of twelve and then fell silent. Nothing, not even a servant, stirred in the cavernous manse. All four of her brothers would be deep in the gaming hells, and when they returned home shortly before dawn, they would not dream of checking her apartments on the second floor at the rear of the house. The stable boy and groomsman would report that she had returned home before midnight and had immediately retired for the night. None of them knew she never slept till dawn, and hadn't since…well, since that night in Vauxhall Gardens.

There was one advantage of having only brothers, Sarah thought as she lifted the sash of her bedroom window. They provided an endless supply of outgrown lad's clothing and never suspected their little sister of any form of deviousness. To them, she was simply a sweet but inconsequential inhabitant of the same house. Only Reginald, her oldest brother and guardian, considered her as more.

Since her father's death last year, Reginald had been plotting how he might marry her off to advantage. She knew he had affection for her, but he rarely thought of her as having preferences.

Reginald had begun, very gently, to urge her to be more flirtatious. More receptive to interest. Less particular in her choice. Sooner or later, he would have to know why she could not marry. But not yet.

She sat on the windowsill and swung her trousered legs out, scooted along the tile slope to the eaves, then edged along to a trellis by the kitchen door. Wedging her boot toe into one opening of the latticework after another, she gained the stone path that led around the house to the street. She entered the lane and hurried toward the Thames, blessing the fog that hid her from close scrutiny.

Sarah was not a fool. She knew, too well, the vulnerabilities of being born female and that when she was dressed as a woman, she drew attention—dangerous attention. But when she secretly dressed as a lad and prowled the lanes and alleys to conduct investigations, she lost all her fears, all her inhibitions. No one noticed a lad. On the streets she was without note, free of the rules, restrictions and vulnerabilities of being female.

Blackfriars was her destination, and a tavern within sight of Saint Paul's Cathedral. The Wednesday League's chief investigator, Mr. Renquist, would be waiting at his usual table. She had sent him a note last week, detailing all the pertinent facts. By now he would have set his investigation in motion and would already have something to report. Mr. Renquist was extremely efficient.

Feeling especially bold tonight, she tagged a ride from a passing coach by catching hold of the luggage straps and swinging herself up to sit on the empty rear rack. Her weight was so slight that the driver did not feel the sag of coach springs that would betray an unpaid customer.

Just past St. Paul's, she alighted and darted down White Lion Hill toward the river and the King's Head Tavern. She ducked her head, pulled her soft cap down about her ears and walked through the door, heading directly to a table in the dimly lit back of the large public room.

Francis Renquist, a short, powerfully built man about Reginald's age, gave her a discreet wave and nodded to a chair opposite him at the table. Had there been trouble, he'd have waved her off and she would have disappeared into the street again. Tonight, however, all was well.

She slid into the chair and wrapped her hand around a waiting pint of ale. *Lord,* she thought, *I must be some mistake of birth. Truly, I was meant for the low life.*

As if to contradict her thought, Mr. Renquist bobbed his head deferentially. "Evening, Lady Sarah."

"Good evening, Mr. Renquist. What have you got for me?"

"Not much. I set Sticky Joe and Dicken on it," he said,

referring to two of the young street lads he employed on occasion. They lived in the lanes and alleys of the walled city and could appear and disappear at will. "They are looking into boarding schools and workhouses. Mayhap the little ones have been put in orphanages. Dicken should have something soon."

Sarah sighed. "Very soon, I should hope. There is no time to waste."

She had memorized the list, and now she felt as if she knew the Whitlock children. Araminta, the eldest at ten years of age. Theodore, second born and six years old last week. And Benjamin, the baby at age five. Their welfare was her chief concern now. She had to find them quickly. Their lives, and their mother's life, depended upon it.

Mr. Renquist recognized her impatience. "I'll have Dicken meet you at the steps of St. Paul's tomorrow at midnight. He's sure to have news by then."

She nodded. "Thank you. I fear patience has never been one of my virtues," she admitted, still keeping her voice low. "But with so much hanging in the balance, 'tis difficult to say *'anon, anon.'*"

"We are not saying 'anon,' Lady Sarah. We are strategizing. We are planning and putting affairs in order."

"Are we, indeed?" She smiled at his attempt at encouragement. "Whose affairs?"

Renquist grinned. "Within the month, a certain ship is leaving for Java. The first mate is anticipating the delivery of a 'Mr. White,' a deserter from the Royal Navy, as a deckhand. The ship will not make port until Capetown. If we've got the children beforehand, we'll lock him up in the hull. If not...we'll snatch him off the street and force their locations from him by any means necessary. Meantime, I've hired a forger to draft the Last Will of Harold Whitlock. Seems he's going to leave everything to his wife and stepchildren."

Sarah laughed outright, finally believing they could succeed in saving the children and securing their future.

She realized her mistake when Mr. Renquist's smile faded and he muttered "Bloody hell" under his breath.

"Well, Renquist. What's this? Feminine laughter? I thought you were a married man."

Sarah froze, not daring to turn and look at the owner of that deep, amused voice. His speech was not that of the working class, but that of the ton. And what in God's name would a member of the ton be doing in this part of town after midnight?

"Yes, er, well…" Mr. Renquist hedged.

"Where are my manners?" the intruder said. He moved around the table to face Sarah. "Ethan Travis, at your service, Mistress…?"

Mr. Renquist looked at her helplessly.

"Sadie," she supplied as she lifted her face to meet the stranger's eyes. "Sadie Hunt."

"Miss Sadie Hunt," he repeated in softer tones and added a lopsided smile and a courteous bow.

Sarah's insides liquefied. Mr. Ethan Travis was tall, dark and decidedly handsome. His hazel eyes held a little more green than brown, and his hair was a dark polished brown that was an inch or two longer than fashionable. In all, he was unforgettable.

That came as a relief, since she realized he could not possibly be a member of the ton. She would have noted him had he ever been in the same room—even a crowded room. In fact, she wondered how he could have been in the same city without her knowing it.

"I'd say well done, Renquist, were you not newly wed," Mr. Travis said, a hint of cynicism in his voice. "What would your wife say, I wonder?"

Sarah was amazed to see Francis Renquist color the shade of an apple. How unusual. She supposed she must rescue him again. "I perceive your comment as a warning to me, sir, and I thank you for it, but it is entirely unnecessary."

"You know he is married?" The man arched an eyebrow, a smile curving his sensual mouth.

"Know it, and know his wife, sir. I believe you have misunderstood our meeting. We are conducting business."

The man's head tilted back in a deep laugh. "Business? I never would have guessed it. Past midnight. Darkened corner of a pub. A woman alone. Ah! I begin to see."

Now Sarah felt *her* face flood with heat. Ethan Travis thought she was a prostitute!

Mr. Renquist found his voice at last. "Here now, Travis. La—Miss Hunt has hired me to…to find her missing brooch." His hesitation gave lie to his words.

She held one hand out in a gesture of interdiction. "Do not explain, Mr. Renquist. This is none of his business. Who is he, anyway, to question us?"

"No one of consequence, Miss Hunt," Ethan Travis answered for her companion. "I was merely passing when I heard you laugh. That is not a sound common to this place. Please accept my apology for interfering in your… affairs." He offered a curt bow before turning and walking away.

Anxiety burned in her. Or was it excitement? "Have we been found out, Mr. Renquist? Will he tell?"

"Mr. Travis will not talk. He is discreet to a fault. And that is the only good thing I can say about him."

"Oh?" She turned to watch the man exit. "Do you think he might be of use to us?"

"Good God! You cannot be serious. What would we want with the 'Demon of Alsatia'? There is a high price to be paid for dealing with men like Travis."

Alsatia! That most disreputable of neighborhoods where thieves and murderers used to find sanctuary! Though cleaned up somewhat since its heyday, the area still suffered an unsavory reputation. She did not know many people who would willingly go there after dark. Mr. Travis must be a very brave, or very dangerous, man.

"High price? Cost is not a consideration, Mr. Renquist. The Wednesday League has adequate resources."

"Your soul?"

Sarah shivered. "My soul, Mr. Renquist, has already been forfeit."

Mr. Renquist glanced away, always sensitive to her past. "Remember, Lady Sarah. Tomorrow at midnight. The west steps of St. Paul's."

Ethan Travis closed the door of the King's Head Tavern behind him and moved silently into the mist with a rueful smile. What had possessed him to involve himself in Francis Renquist's personal business? That was not like him at all. What other men did was of no interest to him.

Ah, Sadie Hunt's laughter! That must have been it. He hadn't heard that sound in years. Oh, he'd heard laughter— polite, patronizing, or purchased—but not the sweet, unaffected rippling of true amusement.

The little strumpet was the most unlikely "light skirt" he'd seen since coming to Blackfriars. No exposed décolletage, no brash face paint and no hollow, empty eyes. Who could have suspected a waiflike figure dressed in trousers could be so erotic? Who could have thought curling tendrils of chestnut hair escaping a boy's cap and deep violet eyes would awaken long-dormant feelings? Certainly not he.

Was she new to the fallen sisterhood? Would it be too late to save Sadie from the soul-stealing profession? Did she even want to be saved? Ethan gave a self-deprecating smile. He was scarcely the man for such a task. The blind leading the blind? Not likely. What he could and would do, however, is remember her name. Perhaps, some night when he was drunk enough, lost, dissipated and desperate enough, he'd track her down, pay his money and see if she could still laugh like she meant it. And if he was still capable of passion.

Chapter Two

Sarah arrived at St. Paul's for her appointment with Dicken and Sticky Joe well before midnight the following night, climbed the steps and crouched in the shadows of a column. The dense fog pooled near the ground and swirled around her. She could hear the voices of vendors and prostitutes calling their wares to passing gentlemen followed by the occasional burst of laughter and a drunken reply. Near dawn the noises would change to vendors coming early to stock their carts and shops with the vegetables, flowers, fish and meat arriving by barge from the outlying countryside.

She took a deep breath and lifted her face to the cold darkness, loving the anonymity of night. She suspected she should be afraid of the night, or at least afraid to be alone, but she had conquered those demons, and now the night held no fear for her but sleep, and the relentless nightmares that came with it.

She looked forward to the meeting with twelve-year-old Dicken. She enjoyed their camaraderie. Dicken reminded her of her brothers before they entered society—funny, bright, enthusiastic, adventurous and optimistic. And he treated her like a social equal. Mr. Renquist had introduced her as Sadie Hunt, the middle daughter of a working-class family who liked to help people in need. He had taken her under his larcenous wing.

A steady drizzle began and the temperature dropped by several degrees. Dressed in her brothers' castoffs, Sarah wished she had worn a heavier coat. She was soaked to the skin by the time she saw Dicken coming up the steps toward her.

"'Ere then," the twelve-year-old said, squinting through the dark and the rain. "That you, Sadie?"

"Yes, Dicken," she said, stepping out of the shadows. She ruffled his sandy hair fondly, even though he was nearly as tall as she. "What have you got for me?"

"Nothin'." he said. "Me an' Sticky Joe have been askin' all day, and I can only tell you where they're not."

"And where are they not?"

"They're not in any private schools or boardin' 'ouses."

"That's more than we knew before, Dicken. You've earned your pay. You'll keep looking?"

"Aye. Me an' Joe'll find 'em." Dicken grinned, exposing a row of even white teeth with a gap between the front two. A sprinkling of freckles across his nose made him appear deceptively innocent. "We'll look in orphanages, work 'ouses, poor 'ouses, an' 'ospitals. Ask neighbors if they've seen any new faces, or if any of the tradesmen 'ave new apprentices."

"You are so resourceful," Sarah praised. "You will be as clever as Mr. Renquist one day."

"Am now," he replied, puffing his chest out proudly. "I'm 'eaded over to Saint Bart's Orphanage to meet Sticky Joe. We're gonna see if they got any new inmates. Wanna come?"

She had five hours before daylight, four before she had to be back in her bed. She did not even hesitate. "Lead on, Dicken."

Saint Bartholomew's Hospital was just around the corner from St. Paul's. The orphanage was down a side street, its coal-darkened stone walls holding out a cruel world. Crueler than the orphanage itself? Sarah wondered.

A single oak tree stood in the courtyard and tall iron gates were ajar. Dicken turned to her and winked. He slipped through and pulled her after him.

Sticky Joe stood by the kitchen door, signaling them with a wave of his hand. He was a year older and taller than Dicken, all arms and legs, the sort that her father would have called "a gangling youth." His grin when he saw Sarah revealed slightly crooked teeth. He laid one finger across his lips, signaling her to silence.

"Well met, Sadie," he whispered. "I've been chatting up the maid, Bridey O'Malley. She says as 'ow there's three new arrivals. One of 'em meets your description of the oldest girl. Araminta, is it?"

Sarah said a quick prayer as she took a miniature from the pocket of her vest. She handed it to Sticky Joe and ducked to let the light from the doorway spill upon it.

"Aye," Sticky Joe bobbed his head. "Shall I show it to 'er to be sure?"

"Yes, please," Sarah said. She turned toward the street at the sound of a hired coach drawing up outside the iron gates. Before she could react, Dicken seized her by the coat sleeve and pulled her through the door into the kitchen.

"Blimey! If we're caught, Bridey will have a beating."

She did not resist when Sticky Joe and Dicken pushed her to the back stairwell. The three of them huddled together as they saw the kitchen door thrown open and a stout man step across the threshold. Sticky Joe laid a finger across his lips and began inching up the stairway on his errand, leaving her and Dicken to hide in the stairwell.

"Mrs. Carmichael!" the visitor shouted, standing in the center of the kitchen. He dropped his tall hat, gloves and walking stick upon the long wooden table before going to the banked fire in the hearth to warm his hands.

Sarah frowned. The man was of medium height, heavy,

had a receding hairline, and was dressed in the height of fashion, though disheveled. His eyes were glazed and a damp sheen on his forehead hinted at more than rain.

A middle-aged woman in nightclothes and a lace-edged nightcap rushed into the room, wrapping a rough woolen blanket about herself. "Oh, sir! 'Tis you! I feared something happened to you. You said you'd be back in a week, and I haven't seen you in more than a fortnight."

"I shall come when I please, Mrs. Carmichael. I gave you enough coin to feed all three brats for a month. I know you've got rid of the boys, but is the girl still here? Have you found a place for her?"

"She is here, sir." The woman smoothed her blanket in a vain attempt at preening. "I have been keeping a close eye on her, just as you instructed. She even sleeps in my room and cannot draw a breath without my knowing it. But I have not found a position for her."

"'Twould never do to have the chit seen. Wouldn't put it past Gladys to hire runners to find her."

Sarah clutched at her heart. The man *was* Mr. Harold Whitlock! Araminta was being kept here, at St. Bart's. She glanced at Dicken and he smiled and nodded.

"I would not care if you indentured her, just keep track of her. I need to produce her if I have to. That may be the only way to keep Gladys in line—giving her the occasional glimpse of her brats."

Indenture her? His own stepdaughter? Sarah could scarcely believe her ears. What sort of monster could be so cruel to an innocent child?

"Do you want to see her, sir? Shall I wake her? She has been disconsolate, weeping herself to sleep at night."

The visitor waved one hand dismissively. "I have other calls to make this night. Have her gone by tomorrow. I cannot say what has changed, but my clever wife has grown silent on the matter. Too clever by half. I think she must have something up her sleeve. That will never do.

She will learn that I am the master here. Araminta must disappear before she can find her.''

''Yes, sir. Tomorrow.'' Mrs. Carmichael gave a flustered glance over her shoulder as if wondering if she could, indeed, be rid of the girl that quickly.

''The box, now, that's a separate matter,'' Mr. Whitlock continued. ''Bring it to me, if you please.''

Mrs. Carmichael was gone scarcely more than a minute before she returned carrying a small padlocked metal box. She placed it on the table.

Mr. Whitlock took a key from his vest pocket and opened the lock. With his back to her, Sarah could not tell if he was putting something in or taking something out. The box was relocked, and he gave it back to the woman. ''Keep that safe, mind you, and keep your mouth shut. I'll be back for it soon.''

''Yes, sir. 'Tis as safe as safe can be.''

'''Tis locked, Mrs. Carmichael, and shall remain so. Do you understand?''

The woman nodded her head and pressed her lips together.

''Good, because if I find out you've been prying, I'll tell what I know about *you*.''

Mrs. Whitlock had not mentioned a box. Likely it had nothing to do with the missing children. Sarah dismissed the thought and began to formulate a plan. She would need the assistance of Lady Annica and of her servant, Mr. Hodgeson, as well as Dicken.

Satisfied that all was well, Mr. Whitlock retrieved his hat, gloves and walking stick from the trestle table. Sarah noticed that his hands shook as he attempted to pull his gloves on. She wondered if he were ill. Would it be too much to hope that he had contracted some dread disease and would succumb? Likely. She'd heard that only the good die young.

She pulled her coat tighter around herself and gave a

nod in Mr. Whitlock's direction. Dicken's bright blue eyes grew wide and he shook his head.

"He may lead us to the other children," she whispered.

Dicken made a face. He understood her urgency and would not argue further.

Mrs. Carmichael closed the heavy kitchen door behind Mr. Whitlock, tucked the little box under one arm and retreated across the room to the door she'd come in, shaking her head and clucking her tongue.

The moment the door was closed, Sarah and Dicken dashed for the outer door, Sticky Joe fast behind them.

"Bridey says that's the new lass," he said as he returned the miniature to Sarah. "So now what?"

She pointed to the retreating figure of Mr. Whitlock and slipped into the shadows to follow. He turned down a street leading back to St. Paul's, and Sarah feared he would find a coach and disappear.

Luck was with them, and Mr. Whitlock did not find a coach. He made for the river and a prickle of misgiving went up Sarah's back. The closer they got to the river, the more dangerous the endeavor. Some of the old warehouses had been converted to hired rooms where God only knows what was done. Not even Sarah, with her reckless streak, wanted to go there.

Her hesitation cost her. A rough hand seized her by the coat collar and lifted her off her feet, much as a mother cat carries her kitten.

"What's this?" a deep voice asked, hushed, as if he did not want to be heard. "Looking to relieve the man of his purse?"

"'Ere now!" Sticky Joe shouldered the man in the stomach. "Leave 'er be."

The man might have been bothered by a gnat for all he was affected. "My, my," he said in an amused voice. "I had no idea you and your friend had taken up a life of crime, Sticky Joe."

A warning thrill of danger raced through her. She recognized that voice! The Demon of Alsatia! Mr. Renquist's warnings rang in her ears.

"S-sir, we…we was only…" Sticky Joe began.

"Who's this, then?"

Horror held Sarah's companions immobile. Her feet touched the ground as her captor released her. She made a great show of straightening and smoothing her garments, delaying the moment when she would have to turn and face the consequences.

"'Tis Sadie Hunt, Mr. Travis," she said, looking up into his eyes with a hint of defiance. *Brazen it out, Sarah,* she told herself. After all, Ethan Travis thought she was a doxie who was quite at home on the streets. One long look at him almost made her wish she were. That would be safer than lying to a man with a wicked looking knife in his hand.

"Ah," he nodded somberly. "Have you decided to change professions, Miss Hunt? Picking pockets requires a great degree of skill, is that not so, Sticky Joe?"

"Beggin' your pardon, sir, I 'aven't picked a pocket in two years," Sticky Joe defended. "I've mended me ways."

"Me, neither," Dicken contributed. "An' we'd never cut in on your mark, sir."

Sarah frowned. Sticky Joe and Dicken were brash little beggars. She had never seen them kowtow to anyone. Ah, but Ethan Travis was not "anyone." He was the Demon of Alsatia.

A veiled expression darkened Travis's eyes. "The man was not my 'mark.'"

A glance down the poorly lit street told Sarah that Mr. Whitlock had long since disappeared. She feared the chance encounter with Ethan Travis had cost her the last opportunity she would ever have to find the other Whitlock children.

Anger made her incautious. "If he was not your mark, sir, why did you interfere?"

The man regarded her with something between amusement and annoyance. She could not help but notice that Sticky Joe recoiled at her temerity and Dicken looked awestruck. What did they know about Ethan Travis that she did not? Had she overstepped some invisible boundary? What sort of man could command such fear with nothing more than a look?

"Miss Hunt," he said in a painfully polite voice, as he bent to replace the dirk in his boot top, "surely you know that I keep watch on anything that happens here?"

"Do you make a practice of interfering when it suits you?" Sarah asked. If the blackguard thought she would quail at his mere lifted eyebrow, he was mistaken. Four brothers had taught her to show no fear, even if she felt it.

"In truth, Miss Hunt, I make it a practice not to interfere with anyone or anything," he said. He cocked his head to one side, a quizzical look passing over his features. His muscles, taut a moment ago, relaxed to a state of tensile readiness.

Sarah begrudgingly approved of the respect he accorded her. After all, he assumed she was a prostitute—a pickpocket at best—yet he afforded her the courtesy of polite address. She inclined her head to acknowledge his words, though she could not help but disagree. "I have met you twice, sir, both times as a result of your interference."

"An anomaly," he assured her.

"I shall hope so," she said. She turned to Sticky Joe and Dicken and took a few steps back the way they had come, tucking stray locks of dark hair into her cap.

"I am bound to say, Miss Hunt, that I approve of your change in occupations. The streets and taverns are not kind to women."

She turned back to Ethan Travis in surprise. Why would he care what she chose to do? Some little demon tweaked her to challenge his assumption. "I have not changed occupations. Rather, I sought to supplement one with the other.''

She had to credit the man. He did not even blink. He merely inclined his head in acknowledgment. ''Then I feel it behooves me to inform you that Newgate Prison does not segregate pickpockets from murderers and madmen. Were I you, I'd develop more skill before attempting to carry it off.''

''More skill in which occupation, sir?''

Ethan Travis laughed. His gaze swept her figure as if he were assessing her value, and warmth seeped and tingled upward from her toes to her cheeks. Would he find her wanting?

''You know, Miss Hunt, if you dressed to show your wares, you'd likely make a fortune. A woman of wit and spirit commands a high price. Those are rare qualities in your profession.''

''Yet another piece of advice,'' Sarah observed to her companions. ''Can you credit my good fortune?''

Sticky Joe's mouth moved, but no sound came out. Dicken took two more steps backward, tugging on her sleeve. ''C'mon, Sadie. The game is over for tonight.''

Sarah recognized the sense in Dicken's urgency, but she could not resist one last gibe. She turned back to the Demon of Alsatia and bowed low, sweeping off her cap in a flourish. ''Thank you, sir. I thought, when my mother died, I would be deprived of maidenly advice. You make an admirable substitute. You should consider charging for your observations and advice, sir, since they are such little gems of wisdom. Then, too, those who do not want it would not be forced to listen to it.''

She was sure she saw the flash of a smile before she turned to follow Sticky Joe and Dicken. She prayed she would not run afoul of him tomorrow when she returned to retrieve Araminta. She very much feared she was at a disadvantage when dealing with Mr. Ethan Travis. The man unsettled her.

Chapter Three

Ignoring the preparations all around them for Grace Forbush's grand ball, the ladies of the Wednesday League settled themselves on the green brocade settee and damask chairs in Grace's small study. Sarah paced, ignoring the sound of the orchestra as they tuned their instruments.

"Sarah, what is amiss? Did Mr. Renquist find something?"

"Not he," Sarah told them. "But I have discovered something of import. Last night I met with Dicken and—"

"Sarah! Should your brothers discover your nocturnal habits, they'd keep you under lock and key," Charity warned, her eyes wide.

"Who will do it, then?" she rejoined. "Annica used to, but now she is married. Grace is too...too—"

"Old?" thirty-three-year-old Grace asked, arching her elegant eyebrows in warning.

"Endowed," Sarah supplied, gesturing at Grace's curvaceous figure. "You'd never pass as a male. And Charity—well..."

"Charity hasn't the desire," Charity admitted, "or the nerves. I vow, Sarah, you are flirting with danger. One of these days—"

"Sarah knows the risks," Lady Annica said with a glance in Sarah's direction. "Better than most."

Sarah continued, ignoring the interruption. "Araminta is being held at Saint Bart's Orphanage. Mr. Whitlock arrived while I was there and told Mrs. Carmichael, the headmistress, to find a position for her at once. We must act quickly or the children will all disappear. We cannot reunite them with Mrs. Whitlock if we do not know where they are."

"Are the boys with Araminta?" Grace Forbush asked.

"No. We followed Mr. Whitlock in the hope that he might lead us to them, but we were waylaid by a man who—"

Charity gasped and the entire group leaned forward in their seats. Grace paused with a wineglass midway to her mouth. "Did he learn who you are? Did he injure you?" she asked.

"Only my pride," Sarah sniffed. Her mind seized on the heat in the appraising hazel eyes as they swept her figure. She'd been horrified to realize that her breasts had tingled and firmed beneath her jacket in response to his slow grin. Such a thing had never happened to her before. But then she'd never been appraised like that before.

Struggling to recall the thread of her conversation, Sarah smoothed the purple velvet of her gown. "I…ah, I only mention him because he…he prevented me from following Mr. Whitlock. We must still discover the whereabouts of the other children, but Dicken is retrieving Araminta from the orphanage."

Lady Annica paced to the window and glanced out to the street where guests were beginning to arrive. "Sarah and I came up with a plan this morning. I've told our laundress that I am going to hire a helper for her. I sent Hodgeson to St. Bart's tonight to meet Dicken and buy Araminta's services. Dicken will retrieve her and, after Sarah questions her as to the whereabouts of her brothers, will take Araminta to my home. She will be safe enough there, disguised as a washer girl. We shall keep her out of sight until we have recovered her brothers."

Sarah nodded. "Mr. Whitlock will eventually return to St. Bart's to check on Araminta, and I shall be there to follow him. He is sure to go straightaway to check on the other children. Once we locate them, we are free to dispatch him on his voyage."

Charity shivered. "I pray it is all that simple, and that nothing goes wrong. If Mr. Whitlock changes his mind or panics, he may dispatch the other children to remote locations, or even accuse Mrs. Whitlock of treachery."

Sarah's hands tightened into fists. Here was the fatal flaw in any plan. The only alternative was to allow Whitlock to abuse his family and hold them virtual prisoners to his rage. That was unacceptable and could only end badly. "We…we must go forward and be prepared to move quickly when opportunity presents itself. I have obsessed over little Araminta all day. If she knows nothing as to her brothers' whereabouts, we will have to start from scratch again. We cannot delay any further. I am determined to search every night until we find the lads."

Lady Annica turned back from the window. "Auberville and I are hosting a grand ball on Friday next. The invitations went out this afternoon, and I made certain Mr. and Mrs. Whitlock are on the guest list. I thought we could demonstrate our friendship and support for Mrs. Whitlock, and that might prevent Mr. Whitlock from misusing her for a time."

"What a lovely idea!" Grace said. "Mr. Whitlock, the weasel, will be so ecstatic to receive an invitation from Auberville that he will not want to risk his wife arriving with bruises. She will be safe at least until then."

Sarah sighed, immeasurably relieved that Lady Annica had found some way to encourage Mr. Whitlock's nonviolent behavior.

"What can we do to help?" Charity asked.

Sarah took a deep breath. "Stand ready to absorb one of the boys into your household. I can take one without causing notice. Reggie does not trouble me over the servants as long as his creature comforts are met. I doubt my other brothers even know all the servants.''

Five hours later, the mantel clock in Grace's ballroom struck the hour of midnight and Sarah grew anxious. The crowds showed no signs of flagging and Sarah would have to leave the party soon to meet Dicken. Every minute she delayed was another minute Araminta was in danger of being snatched back by her stepfather.

She placed her punch glass on a footman's tray and edged toward the corridor to Grace's study and the bundle of men's clothing waiting there. The corridor was empty and she breathed a sigh of relief. She nearly jumped out of her skin when a hand touched her shoulder.

''Lady Sarah. I am so pleased to find you at last.''

She covered her impatience with a smile as she turned to Lord Cedric Broxton, her eldest brother's dear friend from their days at Eton together. Handsome as he was, with his fair hair and deep blue eyes, the man had been agile enough to evade the wiles of a bevy of husband-hunting debutantes. Every time she looked at him, however, she recalled the time he had short-sheeted the head-master's bed and Reggie had taken the blame—and the beating that went with it.

Lord Cedric had that effect on people. He was quite simply so charming and angelically handsome that others wanted to take care of him and ease his way. But not she. She had problems enough with her own charming brothers without adding Cedric Broxton to the mix.

''Lord Cedric,'' she said. ''How are you this evening?''

''Splendid, thank you, now that I've found you alone.''

Sarah glanced over Lord Cedric's shoulder toward the ballroom, dismayed to find that he was right. Drats! They *were* alone. She cast about for a way to evade him. ''Briefly,'' she said. ''I am on my way to find my brother. I have a crushing headache and want him to take me home.''

"Reginald?" Lord Cedric asked. "He was engaged in a rather intense game of cards with our host when last I saw him."

"Any of them will do," she hedged. "I believe I saw James and Charles near the punch bowl very recently. And Andrew was sporting with Lady Jane's younger brother. In the game room, if I recall."

"Allow *me* to escort you home, Lady Sarah. I assure you, I shall do nothing improper."

"I am certain of it, Lord Cedric, but we must avoid even the appearance of wrongdoing. You would not want to find yourself leg-shackled to me for the favor of seeing me home."

"I would not mind at all, my dear. I have come to believe that may be the only way I will become leg-shackled."

Sarah suppressed a shudder. What made any man think a woman would voluntarily subject herself to marital attentions? No doubt that was why women were supposed to remain virgins until after the vows—because once she knew what lay in store, she would shun marriage. Why, the entire fate of the species lay upon an unmarried woman's ignorance! Thank heavens *she* was neither virgin nor ignorant.

She smiled and tapped Lord Cedric on the arm with her fan. "You sell yourself short, Lord Cedric. If you wish to accomplish marriage, stop running so fast. None of the ladies can catch up to you."

He laughed. "Why is it, Lady Sarah, that none of my pursuers is worth slowing down for? It is my curse to have lost my heart to a woman who does not know how to chase."

"Good heavens! I should think that would be a tremendous advantage to you, m'lord. A still target is easier to hit, is it not?"

"So it is." He grinned, exposing two rows of perfect, even teeth.

She waited a moment, but Lord Cedric said no more, only watched her with that unnerving grin. He really was behaving quite oddly. Her impatience to be away began to mount. How could she divert the man?

"Um, m-my brother. Yes, that was it. I was looking for my brother," she muttered.

"An excellent notion, Lady Sarah. I shall take my petition to the proper person."

Petition? Ah, to take her home, of course. Fie! How frustrating! Now she would have to go home and sneak out her window. She was trapped and could see no way out.

"I shall find one of your brothers and send him to you presently. Where will you be?"

"Mrs. Forbush's private parlor," she mumbled.

Fully one hour late, Sarah arrived in the mews behind the King's Head Tavern. She whistled softly and waited for an answer. When it came, she was immeasurably relieved. She had been afraid that Dicken would leave when she was late.

He slipped from the shadows of the livery, his expression and manner betraying agitation. "Trouble, Sadie. Big trouble."

Her heartbeat sped, and her mind raced in several different directions at once. "Pray say Mr. Whitlock has taken her home again," she whispered.

"Nay. Worse 'n that," Dicken sighed. "She's been sold away. Bridey is tryin' to find out where she's gone, but Mrs. Carmichael ain't talking."

Sarah reeled from this news and crushing guilt weighed down on her. She blinked her tears back. "The poor child. She must be terrified. We must find her, Dicken, and soon."

Dicken started at a sound from the tavern. "Let's go, Sadie. We can try again tomorrow."

The back door flew open and the proprietor peered out.

"Who's there? Here now, no skulkin' about, ye thievin' rascals! Steal my customer's mounts again, will ye? I'll show ye trouble!"

A loud boom rang out and an object whizzed past Sarah's left ear before spraying splinters from the livery wall into the air. She lunged forward and pushed Dicken toward the street. "Run, Dicken!"

Sarah dashed in the opposite direction, trying to divert the tavern keeper's attention. She knew it would be a moment before the man could reload and fire again. "We're not thieves," she called. "Please, sir, desist!"

Heavy footsteps chased her down a blind alley. When she came to a high stone wall, she halted and turned to face her pursuer. He carried a lantern in one hand and his pistol in the other. A wide toothless grin split his round face like a grotesque wound.

"Got ye now," he said, slowing to a walk, menace in every step.

"Enough, Jack. Let her be. She's no horse thief," instructed a voice behind the man's beefy girth. She heard the metallic slide of a sword easing back into a sheath.

Sarah did not know whether to laugh or cry when she heard the low raspy voice. How had she made occasional forays into Blackfriars without encountering this man before, and now all of a sudden, she could not sneeze without drawing his attention?

"She?" The tavern keeper peered through the gloom. He held his lantern high to illuminate her face. "How do ye know she ain't?"

"I've had dealings with her in the past," Ethan Travis said as he shouldered the man out of his way. "Go back to the tavern, Jack. I'll handle this."

Jack took several backward steps before turning and retreating. Sarah waited for him to be out of earshot before acknowledging Ethan Travis's assistance.

"I suppose I must thank you for your interference this time, sir."

He inclined his head—an oddly elegant gesture in such a setting. "You are welcome, Miss Hunt. I do not often lie. I hope you prove worthy of it."

"You have not lied, sir. I am not a thief."

"Not a very good one, at any rate." He smiled. "Did picking pockets prove too difficult? I will grant that horses are larger and do not require you to reach into pockets, but hiding the goods is more difficult. Are you certain you wish to change your career?"

She nearly laughed, but she did not want to encourage him. "I swear I am not a thief," she repeated.

"That is not what you swore just last night. I believe you said you wished to supplement your income."

"You are impossible," she said, suppressing her smile.

"I? How so?"

"It is not gentlemanly to call a lady a liar."

"Thankfully I am not a gentleman and you, Miss Hunt, are not a lady."

Sarah fidgeted as he came closer. The scent of lime and French-milled soap seemed incongruous in a back alley in Blackfriars, and yet appropriate for a man like Ethan Travis. It intrigued her in an oddly unsettling way. Her heartbeat sped as he closed the distance between them.

"And you are a liar," he continued as he gazed down at her. "One or the other, Miss Hunt. You cannot have it both ways."

"Very well, then. I am a liar, but not a thief."

"And I am a thief, but not a liar," he confessed in a husky voice.

Confounded, she allowed him to take her arm and lead her toward the street. The heat from his hand penetrated the fine wool of her jacket, and the memory of Lord Cedric Broxton flashed through her mind. She wondered why his touch, his nearness, awoke none of the exciting nervousness this man generated in her. When his breath, scented ever so lightly with fine brandy, fanned her cheek, she nearly stumbled. She wondered if his kiss would taste of it, or his tongue bear some residue that would make her drunken with—she caught herself with a start. *Where had that thought come from?*

"Thus, since I am not a liar," he continued, smiling at her momentary distraction, "you may rest assured that I am speaking the truth when I say that you are unsuited for thieving. Stick to…your other profession, Miss Hunt. It will serve you better and may keep you out of Newgate."

"Y-you think so?" she managed.

"I do." An odd expression passed over his face as he said the words, as if he was perplexed by his own advice.

She fell silent. How in the world had she got herself into this predicament? The thought flitted briefly though her mind to tell him the truth—that she was not a prostitute—but some instinct for survival stopped her just in time. She could not imagine what a man of Mr. Travis's reputation would do with the information that Lady Sarah Hunter wandered the streets of London after midnight disguised as a boy, and gave her business as that of a prostitute. The ton would cut her dead. Reginald would kill her! She would not mind for herself, but she could not bear to bring shame to the Hunter name or her brothers' honor. She'd already sacrificed a great deal on that score.

"You seem preoccupied, Miss Hunt. Was it something I said?"

She shook her head and, failing a better plan, assumed her persona as Sadie Hunt. "I do not want to go to Newgate, Mr. Travis. There is no one whom I could call upon to buy my way out. I would rot there."

His gaze dropped to her chest, buttoned tightly into her jacket. "I am afraid there is no way around it, Miss Hunt. The streets are cruel for women in your profession. You have chosen a dangerous occupation."

"And you would know about dangerous occupations?"

There was a long silence during which he appeared to weigh his words. When he answered, it was clear that he was not inviting further questions. "Yes, Miss Hunt. I would."

"Then I shall take your word for it, Mr. Travis."

"Thieving aside, have you considered other options?"

"What other options do you think a prostitute has, sir?"

His hand moved to her jacket front and, before she could protest, undid the top three buttons. Her shirt buttons gave way as easily and allowed her flattened breasts to swell at the deep opening. Before he dropped his hand, his knuckles brushed the heated flesh and caused her to shiver. Such an action from another man would have made her flinch, or provoked fear or anger, but this man was different, and there was no imminent threat in his manner. He was almost brotherly.

"Miss Hunt, you are a great gift wrapped as rubbish. You needn't ply your trade on the streets of Blackfriars. Any number of expensive brothels would be pleased to employ you. You'd be off the streets, under the protection of an employer, and certainly able to afford better clothing than a man's castoffs. If you are interested, I'd be pleased to recommend you to some of the better establishments. They would, of course, wish to interview you as to your, er, qualifications and any, ah, special talents or proficiencies you may have acquired."

There was no mockery in Ethan Travis's manner, Sarah realized. She was both touched with his apparent concern and humiliated to her core that he believed her a woman of ill repute. What could she say to such a reasonable argument? How could she refuse such an offer? "Would I have to…service anyone with the price?"

"I believe that is the custom," he allowed.

"Thank you, but no, sir. I value my independence too highly to sell it. As things stand, *I* decide who, and what, and where. I do no one's bidding. I prefer it that way, and if I must trade it for independence, I shall choose independence. 'Tis is the last vestige of pride I have." At least there was an element of truth in that.

He smiled again, as if both disappointed and pleased at the same time. "As you wish. Should you change your mind—"

"I will not."

"Nevertheless, I stand ready to tender you an introduction to two or three of the better establishments. I believe, beneath the cap and trousers, you are comely enough, and I can vow your speech is pleasing."

She smiled to herself, then she realized what he was suggesting. "Would these be establishments at which you are a client?" she asked. She could not see a man of Ethan Travis's ilk purchasing favors. Neither could she see him with a demure wife in a cottage somewhere on the outskirts of London.

An angry flush colored his cheeks. "Miss Hunt, my personal habits are not relevant to this conversation. When they are, I will be certain to inform you of them. Unless..."

"Unless?" she challenged.

"Unless you'd like to find out now." He stepped forward and lifted her chin with his forefinger. His mouth came down to hover just above hers as he continued speaking. "That is an interesting prospect, is it not? You could learn my 'habits' firsthand whilst I test your professional qualifications."

Oh my! Nothing brotherly here! As his lips descended the half inch that had separated them, she had the answer to her earlier question. Yes, the brandy on his lips was intoxicating. Yes, she wanted more. His arms tightened fiercely around her, drawing her so close that she felt as if she would melt into him. And she wanted him to kiss her—not this tantalizing teasing with his lips barely brushing hers in contrast to his possessive embrace. She craved a deeper contact from those lips. As deep as his embrace. She wanted to feel the weight and heat of his mouth. That realization should have frightened her. Indeed, she should be shocked. She should run.

Instead she clung to his coat to keep from swooning and ran her tongue along the seam of his lips, wanting to taste more of him. She heard a little moan and realized with horror that it was hers. With a quick intake of breath, the Demon of Alsatia dropped his hands and stepped back as if he'd been stung, a look of surprise on his face.

He could not possibly be more surprised than she. She—who'd lost her innocence but never been kissed before tonight—was playing the role of a practiced wanton.

"Nicely done, Sadie," he breathed. "Very seductive. I nearly forgot myself, and I cannot recall the last time that happened. I shall vouch that you are good at your job."

Sanity returned with the chill that replaced the heat of his body against her, and she realized he had just conceded the skirmish! He must never know that she had been more at a disadvantage than he. When all was said and done, *she* had not been able to break the spell.

He gave her a little push toward White Lion Hill. "Run, Sadie, before I pay my money and take you up on that invitation. And do not let me find you thieving again."

Sarah sprinted up the hill toward St. Paul's, desperate to escape. In mere seconds a myriad of thoughts raced through her mind. That kiss. She gulped. That kiss, her first from a man she was not related to, had been the most disconcerting event of her life.

Even when she had been assaulted and raped by four men in Vauxhall Gardens, she had not been confused or unsettled. That was terror, plain and simple. That was pain and shame and grief. But Ethan's kiss was bitter *and* sweet, terror *and* temptation.

She wanted more.

She was terrified she'd get it.

Chapter Four

Ethan Travis let himself in the garden door of his home on Clarendon Square well before daylight and bolted it behind him. The address afforded him the trappings of respectability, if not the actual reputation. He had purchased the town home because of its distance from his work, not because he wanted entrée into society. He had that, though somewhat tarnished, if he ever chose to use it.

When he'd first come back to London after the scandal, he had lived down by the river, near the warehouses, knowing he would be needed close by should anything go wrong. Now, however, everything was running smoothly and there were others in his organization who could handle most emergencies.

His housekeeper, Mrs. Grant, had gone home hours ago, leaving his dinner of steak and kidney pie on the kitchen table and a fire banked in the hearth. The woman was a blessing; prompt, reliable, discreet and efficient, but she was possibly the worst cook he'd ever encountered.

He whistled for Wiley, his Irish setter, as he put the cold dish on the stone hearth next to the fire. The dog came running from the front parlor, his nails clicking on the oak plank floors. He wagged and leaned against Ethan's leg for a pat on the head before sniffing at the steak and kidney pie.

Ethan took a knife from the cutting block and sliced several slabs of bread, a wedge of cheese and an apple, and put them on a china plate from the cupboard. He carried his cold supper to the small library off the front foyer, poured himself a glass of sherry and dropped into a deep club chair in front of the fire with a weary sigh.

His mail was stacked on a silver salver beside his chair. Mrs. Grant had once again anticipated his mood. Using the small fruit knife with a deftness that hinted at a darker past, he opened the envelopes on the tray. Aside from the assorted household bills, there was the monthly accounting from his factor. Satisfied that his investments were doing well and that his import business was at least paying for itself, he folded the accounting sheets and put them back in the envelope. There were no accounting sheets for his real business.

The final envelope was linen white, edged in gold and bore an elegant *A* in the upper left corner. He stuck his thumb beneath the flap and broke the wax seal. Puzzled, he read the formal script on the face of the folded card. It seemed he was cordially invited to a grand ball at Lord and Lady Auberville's London home on Clarendon Place Friday next. The favor of a reply was requested.

Odd, he hadn't been aware that Tristan Sinclair, Lord Auberville, lived around the corner on Clarendon Place. Leave it to the Aubervilles not to forget their smaller neighbors. As an afterthought, Ethan lifted the fold. Heavy dark lines scrawled a personal note.

My old friend, Imagine my surprise to find you are my neighbor! We must take this opportunity to renew our acquaintance. I would consider it a great personal favor if you will come to our little soiree. You must meet Annica. T.S.

Damn! A personal request. He could not think of a polite way to refuse. Well, he'd make an appearance, shock the ladies to the core with his audacity to mingle in their society, endure the cold greetings of their husbands, accept Auberville's apology for his poor judgment in insisting, and then make an early night of it.

An idea began to take root. Perhaps he could make discreet inquiries about Harold Whitlock. The scoundrel's peers might be able to tell him something Ethan's hirelings had not been able to learn. He went to his desk to find a pen, scribbled his acceptance, slipped it in an envelope and tossed it onto the salver for Mrs. Grant to post in the morning.

There were other gatherings he could attend. No one would stop him at the door or tell him he was unwelcome. He still had his "position" in society. Yes, there was the crush at Webster Manor two days hence. Perhaps he'd test the waters there.

Wiley ambled into the library, still licking his jowls clean of steak and kidney pie. The dog came to him and laid his head upon his knee, the rich reddish brown of his coat awakening uneasiness in him. Why? He stroked the cool silky strands and closed his eyes.

Ah, yes. Sadie Hunt with her dark pansy eyes and the glorious glow of her chestnut locks as they spilled from her boyish cap—that was what had got his hackles up. The little coquette was far too present these days. Too much to be coincidental?

Instincts that had preserved him thus far urged him to caution. Something was not what it appeared to be. Something was "up." Sadie would bear watching, and the sooner he uncovered her scheme, the better. Tomorrow night he'd send one of his men to follow Whitlock while he would search for Sadie Hunt.

A loose shingle shifted underfoot and Ethan stepped back from the edge of the roof. Alerted to the muffled

sound, Sticky Joe glanced upward before hurrying after
Sadie. Ethan would have to put the lad out of the way. He
estimated his distance to the next intersection, then lowered himself to street level by shinnying down a drain pipe.

Sticky Joe never heard him coming. He had his hand
over the lad's mouth and was dragging him into an alley
before he could react.

"Go home, Joe," he rasped in the lad's ear. "You are
in my way. I do not take kindly to that."

He removed his hand from Joe's mouth and held him
at arm's length. Surprise and consternation replaced anger
when Joe turned to confront his adversary.

"S-sir, I cannot leave Sadie alone."

"Yes, Joe, you can. You will."

The lad looked as if he were about to argue, and Ethan
narrowed his eyes to demonstrate how useless that would
be.

"But it ain't safe, sir."

"Leave her to me," Ethan said.

"She won't come to no 'arm?"

Ethan never made promises he couldn't keep. He gave
the boy a cynical smile. "We are wasting time, Joe, and
Sadie is getting farther away. Must I find another way to
convince you?"

Joe backed away, fear clearly etched on his face. Ethan
sighed, knowing he had that effect on others. "I...no, sir.
I am trustin' you as a gen'leman to do the right thing, sir."

Gentleman? The "right thing"? Ethan nearly laughed.
He waited while Joe disappeared before resuming his pursuit.

He sniffed the heavy damp air, always sensitive to the
least little nuance, the faintest element that was out of
place. The scent of lilacs, soft but distinct, lingered. His
body responded instantly. Yes, Sadie had come this way.
He swung himself up to the eaves again, using his vantage
to see ahead, the fog heavier at street level.

No more than one hundred feet ahead, barely within

sight, was the charcoal cap bobbing along, just visible above the fog cover. He hurried after her, sprinting along the eaves and leaping from roof to roof. He kept the cap in view, imagining the sleek chestnut tendrils slipping from the confines, as they had when she had lifted her face to accept his threat of a kiss.

When he'd initiated that kiss, he'd meant to shock her, to make her understand her dangerous appeal. She had taught him something quite different—that he was still a man with an unquenchable hunger that couldn't be met with so little as a curious kiss. *She* had kissed *him*. Her little moan had been oddly innocent, and could not have been faked. She had surprised him by melting into him and running her tongue across his lips. Another second and he'd have handed over his purse for her favors. Hell, he'd have given his fortune for a night.

A dog barked and Sadie pressed herself against the wall below him as if that would make her invisible. He grinned. She really was amusing. Looking down on her from his position on the eaves above, she had the look of dilettante, as if she were a child or some society maid playing at investigation.

The little prostitute was an enigma. She had a Mayfair accent, court manners, uncommon beauty and the self-assurance of those born to money if not power. She had quite obviously been brought up for finer things than prostitution. What misfortune had befallen her to bring her so low? A wastrel father? A mother in the trade? A lover's abandonment? Starving babies to feed?

Whatever it was, he could not put her out of his mind. He was a man, after all, with all the baseness that implied. His hunger—all the greater for his denial—had awakened with the sound of Sadie's single laugh in the King's Head Tavern.

So there it was. Sadie's appeal. She might be a liar and a thief. She might sell her body to strangers. But her laughter was genuine, her teasing fearless and her spirit untouchable. He suspected she would not fake pleasure, not laugh at unfunny jokes, never say things she did not mean in order to earn more money and never pretend affection she did not feel. If he bought her favors, he would only be renting her body, and he would want all of her. Most especially the parts that could not be bought—her loyalty, her fidelity, her…love?

She rounded a corner and her silent grace took his breath away. He wanted her. Wanted her with a deep, aching urgency that he could not rationalize. My God. To have felt something so real and touching after all this time! To have experienced again that elusive thing called ''hope''! It was almost more than he could bear.

And he must never let it happen again. But how?

Perhaps he could start by not interfering in Sadie's business once he discovered her game. He would not give her advice, nor would he attempt to save her from the consequences of her profession. She could make her own decisions, determine her own future. Yes, he'd stand aside and allow Sadie Hunt to make her own mistakes. Maybe he would be one of them.

Once again Sadie stopped, moving closer to the buildings. Ah, there it was! The guilty glance over the shoulder. She had not looked before, and she was not likely to look again any time soon. It was time to make *his* move.

Sarah peeked around the corner, praying she would catch some glimpse of her quarry. Light from an open doorway formed a soft yellow glow in the fog, then went dark as the door closed. A glance over her shoulder revealed she was quite alone. She could wait, hoping Sticky Joe would catch up, or she could try to find which doorway Whitlock had gone through.

The memory of Araminta and her brothers passed quickly through her mind and the decision was made. Her boots made no noise as she pressed close to the buildings and tiptoed farther down the street.

The district was notorious for opium dens and brothels, and while Sarah had little idea what went on in such places, she was certain there must be conversation, words and money exchanged.

The fog behind her thickened. The hair on the back of her neck stood on end. She sensed movement and instinctively knew that she was in imminent danger. She braced to turn.

A hand clamped over her mouth and an arm snaked around her waist. The grip around both was unbreakable. She was lifted off her feet and dragged backward into a recessed doorway, kicking and flailing against her attacker.

"Shh, Sadie," a voice whispered. "If you do not want the local thugs down on us, keep quiet. Can you do that?"

She nodded, going weak in the knees with relief. That voice! That deep, warm, raspy voice. It could only be one person. He dropped his hand to her shoulder and turned her about. She narrowed her eyes and hissed at him. "Mr. Travis, you are fortunate you are not unconscious along the riverbank. Sticky Joe is right behind me, protecting my back."

The man shook his head grimly. "Not so, Miss Hunt. I intercepted him half a mile back and sent him packing."

"He would never leave me unprotected," she denied.

"He did not," Ethan Travis said. "*I* have been at your back since then."

"That is not possible. I would have known it."

He raised an eyebrow, and Sarah was forced to acknowledge the evidence—Ethan Travis stood before her, dark and taunting, and Joe was nowhere to be found. The man was good at this!

"What are you up to, Miss Hunt?" he asked. His tone was arrogant, as if he had a right to know her personal business.

"Me? What are *you* up to, Mr. Travis? Why have you been following me for the past few days?"

His voice lowered dangerously. "I have not been following you before tonight, Miss Hunt. All the same, you do turn up wherever I go these days. I suspect *you* are the problem.''

"I am tending my own business, which is more than I can say for you. From the moment I met you, you have been breathing down my neck. Desist, Mr. Travis. Attend to your own affairs and leave me to mine.''

He studied her through the fog-laden air. "What, precisely, *is* your business?''

His unwavering regard sent her mind darting for a logical defense. She would have to come up with a likely story. Mr. Renquist! Yes. She had first run afoul of Travis at the King's Head Tavern the night she'd met with Mr. Renquist. A story began to take shape, but she would have to think quickly.

"Ah, I…I do not exactly have…well, as you know, I have not been hugely successful at, um—''

"Prostitution?'' he supplied.

"Exactly.'' She gave thanks that she did not blush easily, even though she could feel the humiliation to her core. "Nor have I done particularly well at thieving.''

"Not even second-rate,'' he agreed.

"But, when all is said and done, a girl must earn a living,'' she murmured, shuffling her feet pathetically. "And that is why I have been practicing my following.''

"Your 'following'?'' he repeated. "Whatever do you mean?''

"You know. *Following.* Dicken and Joe put me in the way of Mr. Renquist, who has said that he would hire me if I could perfect a needed skill. I thought perhaps I could follow people. Most likely women. I could follow them where Bow Street runners could not go. Mr. Renquist said that would be a useful skill if I can become good enough to remain undetected.''

"Then you were practicing your 'following' when I thought you were trying to pick that man's pocket?''

"Um, yes.''

"And last night? Were you thieving or following?"

She cast about for an explanation for her presence behind the tavern. "I...I still must earn a living whilst I learn new skills."

"So you were trying to steal the horses from the livery?"

"Horses? That is a little ambitious, Mr. Travis. Horse. One horse." Why couldn't she resist the temptation to tease him?

"Hmm," he said, looking unconvinced.

"I suppose you are going to advise me to stick to prostitution and send me on my way?"

"No, Miss Hunt, I am not going to give you advice, nor will I interfere with anything you might choose to do."

"You just did, sir, when you dragged me from that door. Why should you care who I follow, whose pocket I pick or whose business I solicit?"

"I make it my business to know all that goes on in my district. I want to know what the activity is, Miss Hunt, not direct it."

She nodded. "Ah, yes. The Demon of Alsatia. If you do not know about it, how can you profit from it. Logical."

"I do not—" He took a deep breath and shook his head. "Be on your way, Miss Hunt. Go practice your 'following' elsewhere."

She couldn't leave. She had to follow Mr. Whitlock. But how could she defy such a direct order? If she could not shake him, perhaps she could enlist him.

"Sir? You were outstanding. I neither knew you had taken Sticky Joe's place, nor that you were anywhere close behind me. Could I convince you—that is, would you teach me?"

"Teach you?" The blank look on his seductively handsome face was comical.

"To follow," she explained. That ought to send him packing. The last thing the Demon of Alsatia would want was to be saddled with a thieving, lying prostitute in search

of a profession. He would not be able to run fast enough.
And he would keep running every time he saw her. She
smiled brightly in anticipation of his refusal.

A slightly bemused expression clouded his eyes, as if
he were looking inward for the answer. The pause drew
out interminably. A muscle in his left jaw tightened, and
his eyes narrowed with caution.

Which was worse, Ethan wondered, continuing to run
into this persistent little baggage on a regular basis, and
when it was least convenient, or having her where he could
keep an eye on her? There were pitfalls and advantages to
both.

One of the pitfalls was that his fingers burned to tuck a
chestnut tendril back under her cap and touch the soft pink
of her cheek. Bloody Hell! Next he'd be waxing poetical
on the bottomless depths of her violet eyes, or the lush
fullness of her lips, and the clean lilac scent of her skin.

For his own sanity, not to mention his safety, his resolve
to leave her be, to not offer advice or guide her decisions,
had to stand.

"At least now everything is beginning to make sense,
Miss Hunt. I wondered why Francis Renquist, whose marriage to a French modiste is notoriously happy, would hire
a prostitute. He hadn't. He was conducting a job interview.

"And why would a prostitute, whose livelihood depended upon attracting customers, wear men's clothing,
and why have I suddenly begun running into you every
night? Because, I assume, you have been practicing your
'following.'"

She tilted her head to one side and smiled. She looked
so eager, so hopeful, and those luscious lips tempted him
almost beyond endurance. Good God. He never should
have kissed her. Now he could think of nothing else but
how soft those lips were, and how they had trembled, actually *trembled,* beneath his, and the fact that, if he did not
help her, she would starve. She could not whore effectively
because of her manner and dress; she was a clumsy, inept

thief at best; and her "following skills" were more apt to
result in disaster than success.

And anyway, he did not want to think of her dropping
those well-tailored trousers in some back alley for a toff
who would never appreciate her true value, or some
drunken, diseased sod who might bruise that flawless
creamy flesh. The mere thought of such a thing set his
teeth on edge.

"Very well, Sadie," he sighed before he could prevent
it.

Those soft dark eyes widened and the impossibly long
lashes blinked several times. "Y-you will?"

"Yes," he growled. As an afterthought, he added, "I
will expect repayment in kind."

"K-kind?" she repeated.

"Tit for tat." He smiled.

"Y-you want me to teach you…?" She retreated until
her back was against the door.

He nearly laughed outright. For a woman who made her
living at prostitution, she seemed inordinately concerned
that someone might avail themselves of her services. But
that wasn't his meaning. "I may call upon you to use your
newly acquired skills for my benefit. I expect you to honor
that debt."

"Oh." She swallowed hard. "Oh, of course."

"You must swear to follow my directions—quickly and
without question. *Do not argue.* Your life may depend
upon it. If you cannot promise that, leave now."

"I assume this applies only to those times that we are
engaged in following?"

"Are you arguing with me, Miss Hunt?"

"Perish the thought," she said, the corners of her mouth
twitching deliciously.

He nodded, wondering if he had just set some karmic
wheel in motion. What would come back to him as a result
of his moment of weakness? No matter. It was done now.
"Come to the Cheese at noon tomorrow and—"

"Ye Olde Cheshire Cheese in Holburn?" she gasped. "Noon? No. I cannot. I must practice following at night. Late at night."

He paused only a moment. Between himself and five of his men, Harold Whitlock was under observation twenty-four hours a day. He did not have to take the night hours. But if he could combine the two, so much the better. "Can you meet me tomorrow night?"

"Midnight? The west porch of St. Paul's?" she suggested.

He nodded agreement. He'd have one of the others pick up Whitlock's trail.

The door next to them opened and a man stumbled out, tripped in the gutter and fell on the cobblestones. His sandy hair fell over his forehead as he tried to push himself up with his hands. A voice from within the house called after him.

"You no come back till you got blunt! You hear me? Nothing for free!"

The accent was that of an Asian. As he suspected, the place was an opium den. He glanced askance at his companion. She shook her head, denying that the man in the street was the man she'd been following.

When the door closed, he whispered, "Who are you following, Miss Hunt?"

She glanced up at him and blinked as if he had startled her with the question. She glanced away for a moment, then shrugged. "'Twas just a man who happened by when I was ready to begin. I have trailed him several miles."

"He did nothing to provoke your chase?"

"Nothing, sir. I am practicing. Just practicing."

Her reassurance strengthened him. If Sadie Hunt simply wanted to follow someone as practice, she could come along with him on the nights that he, and not one of his men, followed Whitlock. The efficiency of his plan cheered him considerably.

"Miss Hunt, if your quarry has gone in there, he is not

likely to come out again before morning. Are you prepared to wait here all night?"

She chewed her lower lip as her forehead creased in concern. "No, Mr. Travis. I must be home before long. But what if he should come out and go elsewhere? How would I ever know it? This 'following' business is more complicated than I thought."

He fought a smile. "Are you now in search of yet another profession?"

"No!" She lifted her chin resolutely. "I shall stay until the last vestige of dark."

"Please yourself, but I am going home. Tomorrow you must let me know if your prey reappears."

He must be mad! Sadie Hunt was trouble, plain and simple.

Chapter Five

Music filtered onto the terrace from the Grand Ballroom of the Duke of Beddinham's palatial London estate, and Sarah glanced toward the French doors to be certain she would not be overheard. She took Lady Annica's hand in earnest.

"Mr. Renquist's men are looking for the children night and day, scouring the alleys and orphanages. We cannot risk losing another opportunity like Araminta's again."

"I agree. We must bring all our resources to bear on this," Annica said.

"I've been helping search, too. I am haunted by the fear that something awful has happened to Araminta because of my delay."

The music grew louder as the French doors opened wider. "My dears, you must not stand in drafts. You will catch your deaths," an elderly male voice warned from behind them. His grace, Nigel Dunsmore, Third Duke of Beddinham, stood at the French doors with a concerned look on his face.

The duke was eighty if he was a day. A thin gray ring of hair banded his otherwise bald head. His posture was stooped and he was barely two inches taller than Sarah. His nose and chin were sharp, and curved toward one another, and his skin was pale and thin. His eyes, however, were a bright, clear blue and as lucid as a man in his prime.

She and Annica dropped proper curtsies. "Your Grace," they murmured.

He winked. "I've come to collect my dance. That is the only reason I host these damned events, you know. Affords me the opportunity to dance with all the pretty young gels."

Sarah gave him a fond smile. Lord Nigel had been one of her father's closest friends. In his prime, he had been devilishly handsome and a positive wag. The late Duchess of Beddinham had been a very lucky woman, if Sarah was any judge.

"Annica, do you mind?" she asked, offering her hand to Lord Nigel.

"Why yes, I do," she teased as they reentered the ballroom together. "I've not had my turn yet."

"You are next after Grace Forbush, m'dear," Lord Nigel promised with a wink. "I am working my way alphabetically backward tonight. Z to A. Variety, y'know. Do not go far. I shall be back for you."

The duke led her to the dance floor and into the steps of a waltz. His pace was slower than the other dancers, but his style was flawless.

"I do love a waltz," he confided. "In my day, men were not allowed to hold a woman so for any reason. Now I may actually converse and face my partner. Progress is a wonderful thing, is it not?"

Sarah laughed. "It is indeed, Your Grace."

"I have not seen much of you since your father died, m'dear. I hope you are keeping well."

She hesitated just a moment before thinking of the most politic thing to say. "My health is excellent, Your Grace."

"Hmm," he said.

The single word reminded her of the disbelief in Mr. Travis's voice when she had sworn she only meant to steal one horse. Warmth swept through her at the memory, and her pulse accelerated with the knowledge that she would see him again tonight. She missed a step and murmured a soft apology to her partner.

After a moment, Lord Nigel tried again. "Tell me, Sarah dear, why you are not betrothed by now? You are what? Twenty and two?"

"Four," she admitted. A sly suspicion leaped to her mind. "Has Reggie asked you to speak with me, Your Grace?"

He grinned and Sarah remembered why she had always been so fond of the man. She thought him one of the kindest men she had ever known. "You are too clever by half, m'dear. I tried to tell that young buck it wouldn't work, but he bade me try."

"I cannot think why my unmarried state should concern him so." Sarah sighed, fighting to keep her anger at bay. "It is not as if our house is too small, or that I eat too much. Papa left me my own estate, so Reggie does not pay my dressmaker or my milliner. What could possibly account for his haste to see me wed?"

Lord Nigel chuckled "He is fond of you, m'dear, and would like to see you settled."

"I could say the same of him, Your Grace. In fact, I will. Go back to him, please, and tell him that I despair he will ever find a woman who will take him on. Tell him that I am crushingly concerned that he will fail in his obligation to provide an heir for our family title, and that one of his younger brothers will have to do the job for him."

"Well, well." Lord Nigel grinned again. "Our little Sarah has teeth. That is a big bite to take out of your brother. He is apt to see that as a challenge. Are you certain you wish to issue one?"

"Your Grace, I adore them all, but my brothers will be the death of me. I can, however, guarantee that Reggie will be married before I will." She gave a single nod for emphasis.

"How can you be certain, m'dear?"

Sarah shrugged. She might as well tell him and thus inform Reggie, through Lord Nigel, of her intentions. "I fully expect to remain a spinster, Your Grace. I shall not marry for any reason."

"A dreadful waste, if you ask me. Have you looked in a mirror lately? There is not a nubile virgin here who can hold a candle to you."

Startled by the sweeping assumption, she did something she rarely did. She blushed. She knew it by the heat in her cheeks and the duke's widened eyes. She hadn't said a word, but the truth was out. Tears sprang to her eyes and her hands began to shake. She had guarded her secret so diligently that she could not believe she had betrayed it involuntarily so quickly.

The smile faded from Lord Nigel's face. He led her from the dance floor to a quiet spot near the punch bowl. "Dear Sarah, do not be so distraught. Your father and I suspected something of the sort years ago. He refused to question you 'pon it. He said you were his light and joy, and that he could not bear it if he had failed to keep you safe."

"Never!" Sarah vowed, tears coming to her eyes. "Never. He was always the kindest, most loving—" She fell silent.

"Reggie should know why you refuse to consider any offer he puts to you."

She shook her head vehemently. "No. To tell Reggie would be to tell James, Charles and Andrew. They have never been able to keep secrets from one another, and I could not bear it if they knew. I'd rather have their contempt than their pity."

"They worship you, to a man. Contempt is out of the question, Sarah. But, as the issue is a sensitive one, they may wish to deal with the blackguard who—"

"Done, Your Grace."

He patted her hand again, his wrinkled face creasing with concern. "No, my dear. 'Tis a matter of honor, you

see. The man must be *severely* dealt with. Must know that
to breathe a word would result in certain death—''

''Done, Your Grace,'' she said again. ''There is no one
left to utter those words.'' She did not want to discuss this.
She had thought it was finally behind her.

''How—''

''Believe me, Your Grace, it has been dealt with. If you
have any doubt, you may speak to Auberville. He will be
able to give you the details.''

''Reggie could be a comfort to you, Sarah.''

''I do not require comfort. I require privacy.'' She heard
the edge of panic in her voice and prayed she could contain
it long enough to elicit the duke's promise.

Her life had been turned upside-down when she had
accompanied Richard Farmingdale down the Lover's Walk
at Vauxhall Gardens. He'd lured her there so he and three
other members of a Hellfire club could rape her. Annica
had found her and helped her keep the truth from her father
and brothers. She simply couldn't face them with her folly
in having walked down that path.

Neither had she been able to permit the villains to ruin
her without paying a price. Annica and the Wednesday
League had devised a plan and, one by one, exacted justice
from each of them. By the end, the villains had been involved in more than just rape, and the investigation had
resulted in the death of one of their group. Sarah did not
like to think about those days, much less to talk about
them.

Outside of the Wednesday League, only Lord Auberville
knew the entire story, and only then because he had been
induced to aid them. If Lord Nigel wanted to know the
details, he would have to learn them from Auberville.

''Very well, m'dear.'' He gave her a look of puzzled
respect punctuated by a polite little bow. ''You have my
word.''

She expelled breath held too long, almost dizzy with

relief. "Thank you, Your Grace. Now, if you will excuse me, there is something I must do."

Still stinging from her conversation with the duke, Sarah ran up the steps of St. Paul's. It seemed to her as if her world was narrowing and crushing down on her. She had known Reggie was anxious to arrange her future, but she hadn't realized the depth of his concern. Why, he must be in absolute despair of her prospects. Perhaps she had not been vocal enough about her preference to remain single.

Worst of all was the Whitlock "situation." There was no time to waste. She had to devise some way to induce Mr. Travis to follow Harold Whitlock, but she could not think how. If she didn't think of something soon, she would have to strike out on her own again. It was all she could do to keep guilt at bay. Oh, how she wished she could have spared Araminta the terror of being passed from hand to hand and separated from her family.

As she gained the top step, she found Ethan Travis standing near one of the center columns. He could have passed as a statue of a saint, so handsome and still was he. Then she realized there was nothing saintly in that utter stillness, but a watchful awareness that was prepared for anything and missed nothing. It was a lethal stillness, and it made her shiver.

She nearly turned and ran, but he'd seen her, and she did not want him to think her a coward. She approached him breathlessly. "Sorry to be late, Mr. Travis, but—"

He stepped forward, his face devoid of expression. "Miss Hunt, there are some things we must address if we are to go forward with this plan of yours.

"First, you will be prompt. Spare me the excuses. Tardiness is inconsiderate, and I have no desire to cool my heels whilst I wait for you to complete your toilette, or whatever else delays you."

"But, I—"

"Second, you will not question me or disobey my instructions, but perform them quickly and efficiently.

"Third, in future you will knot your hair tidily on top of your head. It is disconcerting to see it always falling from beneath your cap, and also betrays your gender."

Sarah quickly pushed a long tendril beneath her cap, outraged at his arrogance yet eager to placate him so that he wouldn't change his mind.

"Fourth, exercise your talent for thieving to obtain possession of a pair of good riding boots. The softer leather will give better purchase on steep slopes and in climbing, and they are quieter on cobblestones.

"Fifth, there will be no conversing once the chase has begun. Silence is necessary if you wish to remain undetected.

"Sixth, bind your breasts. You will never pass as a lad when your chest is so obviously female."

She glanced down at her chest, noting for the first time that Andrew's linen shirt molded to her curves and betrayed small dots against the fabric. Mortified, she pulled the lapels of her jacket tighter.

"Seventh, you cannot hope to pass as a street urchin once you open your mouth. Practice another voice. I want it lower, harsher and imbued with the accents of the streets."

Reeling from this diatribe, she responded as she would to one of her brothers. "Are you quite finished, Mr. Travis?"

He nodded. "For the moment."

"You are despicable!"

"That *is* the consensus, Miss Hunt." His lips curled upward, but she would not have called it a smile.

Her confusion must have shown, because he passed her, descended several steps and glanced over his shoulder. "Are you coming, Miss Hunt? Or have you changed your mind again?"

Sarah fought the impulse to stamp her foot, bit back an angry retort, and said, "Right behind you, Mr. Travis."

What on earth had possessed him to be so abrupt with the little Ladybird? Ethan wondered. He hadn't been waiting all that long, but he had been worried, wondering if she had met with some accident or if one of her other businesses had got in the way. More and more, at odd times, unwanted images of her kissing another man, or in various postures of lovemaking, invaded his mind—invariably with swine who were unworthy of one such as Miss Sadie Hunt.

Disturbingly, the little doxie was becoming a dangerous obsession. That would never do. Ethan did not like sharing his toys. He never had.

He rounded a corner and turned to see if Sadie had kept up. Yes, she was still there, looking intense and a little breathless. He waited for her to draw closer.

"Psst," she whispered when she caught up. "Where are we going, and who are we following?"

Ethan smiled to himself, grateful that the darkness hid his amusement. Were it not for Kilgrew's secrecy and his own need to conceal his true activities, he'd simply tell her he had already selected their quarry and that they were on the way to intercept him. "We are going to choose a subject, Miss Hunt. I sent one of my men to scout a tavern."

"Is that why you were angry that I was late?"

"No, I was angry because it is rude and disrespectful."

There was a long silence, then her soft, well-modulated voice floated to him. "I apologize. I would not for the world have treated you with disrespect. It will not happen again."

Her sincerity nearly undid him. Feeling now at a disadvantage, he cleared his throat. "Rule Five, Miss Hunt."

She frowned, a puzzled look on her pretty features.

Lord, he thought, she really was a mixture of guilt and innocence. He took pity on her. "No talking, Miss Hunt."

As arranged, near the intersection of Fleet and Faringdon Streets, Ethan saw his man, Peters. He hurried ahead, anxious that Sadie not overhear their whispered communication.

"Where?" he asked as he approached.

"The Swan," Peters said.

Ethan turned left and waited for Sadie to catch up. "The Swan," he said. "We shall pick a man there."

"But I thought, perhaps, the man I was following last night might be a good test."

"Where will we find him?" Ethan asked. He had gone to a great deal of trouble to make his selection of Whitlock look natural. The last thing he wanted was for Sadie to divert him.

She glanced heavenward as if begging patience. "Lead on, Mr. Travis," she said with a sigh.

When they arrived at the Swan, Ethan directed her to a table in the back, away from the fireplace and direct light. He paid for two pints of ale and carried them to the table.

At a table next to the rear entrance sat Harold Whitlock. He had disdained the mild ale for whiskey and looked as if he had not had nearly enough. He glanced up each time the door opened. He was waiting for someone.

Sadie wore a look of contained vitality, and he was mildly surprised by her excitement. "Mr. Travis, may I pick?"

Rather than answer, he glanced around as if seeing the occupants for the first time. "Who do you favor?"

"I think it should be someone who looks as if he has something to hide, do you not agree?"

"If you say so, Miss Hunt."

"Then what of the man in the corner? The one who looks so furtive?"

Ethan glanced over at Harold Whitlock. How very perceptive of Sadie. She had a keen eye. Perhaps there was hope that she would make a decent spy. And best of all, he wouldn't have to overrule her selection. He nodded. "Done. I will find out who he is. Wait here."

He went to back to the publican and asked, "Where is the water closet?"

The man barely glanced up as he polished a glass and said, "In the usual place, gov'nor."

Ethan nodded and returned to the table. "Harold Whitlock," he announced without a single twinge of conscience. "The publican knows him well."

"Ah." Sadie smiled, excitement dancing in her pretty violet eyes. She tugged her cap down about her ears and lifted her pint of ale. "What do we do now?"

"We wait," he said, controlling an urge to touch her cheek and tuck away one of those wayward tendrils. "And then we follow."

Before long, a disreputable-looking man entered the Swan and made his way to Harold Whitlock's table. The two of them carried on a hushed conversation and Whitlock handed over a small packet. Money? Opium? Sarah could not tell from her vantage. Soon afterward, the stranger left the tavern. A moment later, Whitlock drained his glass and stood.

Sarah, too, was on the verge of rising when Ethan laid one hand on her arm. "No, Sadie. Too obvious. Try to look as if you have settled in for the night. Do not look directly at him."

Anxiety burned in the center of her stomach as she gave attention to her tankard. Ethan leaned back in his chair and stretched his legs out, crossing his ankles. Whitlock walked past them, not even glancing in their direction.

Only when the door closed did Ethan come to his feet. "The game's begun, Sadie. Stay close and quiet. Follow my lead and, above all, do not waste time questioning me." He tossed a schilling on the table and turned to the door.

Sarah could barely keep pace as they trailed Mr. Whitlock. Mr. Travis was astounding. His silence was total, his stealth envious, and his methods were nothing short of awe-inspiring. He led her down narrow streets, ducking into doorways and alleys to hide, and through taverns and inns to intercept Whitlock as he rounded a corner.

She marveled at his audacity when, having anticipated Mr. Whitlock's next turn, he pulled her into a corner pub to exit the opposite doorway just in front of Whitlock and continued to walk for more than half a block with Whitlock following them! Her heart pounded like a drum when Whitlock shouldered past them and hurried ahead. That move had allowed them to follow Whitlock openly for a quarter of a mile before reverting to hidden tactics. The ploy had been bold and impudent—and it had left Sarah breathless with admiration.

"Where did you learn such things?" she whispered.

"Rule Two, Miss Hunt. No questions."

"But—"

"Rule Five. No talking."

She narrowed her eyes. She would have to think of some rules of her own. Nothing in her experience with four brothers, which was extensive, had prepared her to deal with him. Travis was the most aggravating male she had ever met.

When Whitlock's pace slowed, Travis slowed more, dropping farther back. In the fog, she could only hear Whitlock's boot heels, but they did not lose him. How, Sarah wondered, had Ethan Travis learned to discern direction by sound? How could he possibly anticipate the other man's next move?

Finally, near London Docks, Sarah rounded a corner and ran into Ethan's back. He had halted to observe their quarry enter a dimly lit building. "That's it, Sadie. May as well go home."

"Why?" she whispered.

He turned to her, a skeptical expression on his face. "Do you not know?"

"Know what?"

"What that house is."

Sarah shrugged. "Pray, enlighten me, Mr. Travis."

"The sisterhood, Miss Hunt. 'Tis a bordello."

She gave him a bland smile, thinking quickly. "Why should I know every bawdy house in town, sir? I do not work at any of them. I am…independent."

"I am painfully aware of that, my dear." He smiled. "But it is good business to know the competition."

"I see that *you* do, sir," she snapped, hoping to throw him off the scent. She fought the annoying thought that he might have availed himself of the goods sold at such a place and gazed back at the closed door. "Do you really think he'll be in there all night?"

He tucked a tendril of hair behind her ear and the trail of his finger seared her cheek. "Faith, Miss Hunt. Has a man never purchased your services for longer than a few minutes? Do you simply drop your trousers and allow him to do his business? How long have you been in the trade?"

She was nearly undone and the soft query confused her. "R-rule Two, Mr. Travis."

He laughed and pulled her against his hard chest. "Aye, no questions. No pasts and no futures. Just here and now. Very well, Miss Hunt. Here is a question you are accustomed to answering. How much?"

"H-how much what?"

"How much to sate my hunger? How much to taste your charms? How much to…satisfy my curiosity?"

Lord! This possibility had never occurred to her! Not that she had not thought of Ethan Travis in that context—she had. Incessantly. She had wondered how he would look without his shirt, and if she tangled her fingers through his hair, would it feel as clean as it looked, and if that one little kiss had been a fluke, unlikely to ever happen again—or, if it did—would it kindle the same tenuous fire in her belly. But he simply did not seem the sort to purchase favors. He was too self-contained, too fastidious. Or so she'd thought.

"How much, Miss Hunt?" he insisted, his mouth dropping to within inches of hers.

How much? she wondered. His soul? Oh, no. Nothing so simple. She would come more dear. His heart. Not an iota less. When his lips finally reached hers, they were softly demanding, asking the question anew. The insistent demand for an answer drew the very breath from her and she lifted her arms to circle his neck. The soft curls at his nape slipped through her fingers. "Ethan," she sighed, unable to think clearly.

He moaned or growled, she couldn't tell which. "Answer me, Sadie. How much? Whatever it is, I'll pay it." His voice was hoarse now, and his hand, at the small of her back, pressed her closer. The dull thud of his heart pounded against hers, and the rhythm matched his, as if answering the question against her will.

There was a fierceness in his hazel eyes that took her breath away. Her old fears surfaced, confusing and unsettling her. How could she give Ethan what he wanted, what he needed, without letting go of herself? Without risking everything she had fought so hard to reclaim? But, oh, how she wanted to!

She pulled away, crossing her arms over her chest, as if to protect her traitorous heart. "Th-that would be a grave mistake, Mr. Travis. That would change everything."

"Yes, Miss Hunt, it would," he sighed, dropping his hands to his sides.

"If you r-really believe Mr. Whitlock will be occupied for the remainder of the night, I believe I shall be going."

"Running away, Miss Hunt?" His voice had an angry edge she had not heard before.

"Rule Two," she answered.

Chapter Six

The Hunter coach lurched as it turned the corner on Bedford Street and entered the queue for the Webster crush. Excited voices and the clatter of horses and carriages drifted to them on the soft spring breeze. Sarah reached for the door latch and smiled at her oldest brother.

"Shall we walk the rest of the way, Reggie? It seems so silly to wait our turn in the coach when the doorway is no more than half a block away."

His gentle hand on her arm stayed her. "No, Sarah. I sent the others ahead because I wanted to talk to you."

Sarah settled back against the cushions. This could not be good news. She smoothed her ivory satin gown and adjusted the pink ribbon beneath her breasts. She fastened her gaze to the posy of pink roses on the seat beside her, saying a silent prayer that Reggie had not found out about her nightly forays.

"Sarah, you must know that you are…of a critical age, and that there is not much time remaining before you are labeled a spinster. I have discussed your…situation with our brothers, and they concur with me. 'Tis time you wed. We cannot indulge further demurring. You must make a choice."

She looked up at Reggie. He was sinfully handsome, as were all the men in her family. His brow was creased with

genuine concern, and she realized the degree of thought
her brothers had given her situation. That they could agree
on anything was a minor miracle.

"Charles? Charles agreed to this ultimatum?" Charles
was sober and serious, and the world rested upon his shoulders. But he had never indicated that he was anxious over
her future. Surely *he* would support her?

"Yes," Reginald confirmed. "He thinks you will need
a push in the right direction since your only associations
are within your bluestocking group. The Wednesday
League, I believe?"

"But James would never—"

"James was the first to agree," Reginald said. "None
of us want to see you unhappy, and that is why you must
make a choice."

She shook her head in disbelief. The Hunter brothers
were famous for their rows and, as one, they had come
together to decide her future. They had reached agreement.
She must wed.

Of course she wouldn't, but she could not tell them why.
Instead, she grasped at a familiar argument. "A choice,
Reggie? Of whom? You must have noted my lack of suit-
ors."

"Indeed we have. A few discreet inquiries have yielded
the answer to that troubling question. You, Sarah, have
been turning men away at their first tenuous overtures.
Some of them are unmarried still and would welcome a
show of interest from you. James has made a list—"

Sarah gaped at this announcement. "What? Say you and
my rogue brothers have not been drumming up interest in
me! Oh, how could you humiliate me so! How could you
market me like vegetable marrow or a ham hock? I must
be the laughingstock of the season. *Poor Lady Sarah. Her
brothers must solicit suitors on her behalf. Is she so grace-
less that none will have her?*"

"Hold up, Sarah. You know we would never compro-
mise your reputation in such a way. Did I not say 'dis-

creet'? And we have suggested to the men in question that henceforth inquiries should be directed to me, not you."

"If you are all so anxious for a wedding, Reggie, what say one of *you* marry? You are all older than I, and you, Reggie, have a duty to the family to produce an heir. Go to it, I say, and leave me be."

"I will not rise to your bait, Sarah. Men are marriageable at any age. A woman has a certain…"

"Urgency? Whatever makes you think that, dear brother?"

"A woman has only a certain time to bear children, whilst men can father them at any age."

"Yet more proof that God loves the female gender best," she snapped. "Well, I want neither a husband nor children. And at this very moment, I do not even want brothers." Her heart squeezed painfully with the lie.

True to his nature, Reginald took a deep breath and refused to be diverted. "What you want at the moment is of little consequence, Sarah. Women need the protection and guidance of a husband. You will thank us later. You are, after all, an innocent, sensible to the demands on a wife. Unfortunately, you have had the rather base example of your brothers, and no softening influence of a mother, to add to your fears. I could wish we had not teased you so unmercifully, and—"

"No, Reggie. I spoke amiss. You and the others have been my salvation," she told him with a degree of sincerity impossible to fake. "I would have perished without you. It is by the love I bear you all that I can even tolerate the touch of a man. You are the example of all that is worthy in your sex."

"Tolerate? Is that not a rather strong word, Sarah?"

"I only meant that, well, having only brothers has taken a bit of the mystique of men away. Truly, because of you, I do not fear men." No, not men. It was intimacy she feared.

Reginald took her hand and squeezed it in gratitude.

''Thank you, dearling. Still, my decision stands. You will choose a husband within the month, or I will choose one for you. Lord Cedric Broxton has long petitioned me, expressing an interest in you. It would please me to cement our friendship with a marriage.''

Cedric? She could not imagine being with Cedric, lying beneath him, receiving him into her body, bearing his children. The mere thought revulsed her. Clearly Reggie would have to know the truth before the month was out. But not now. Not tonight. And not here, when the door to their coach could be thrown open at any moment by a footman. Not when she would have to smile and greet friends and pretend that nothing was amiss.

Meanwhile, how could she prevent Reginald from making plans? ''I do not think Lord Cedric and I are...suited.''

''He thinks so, but we shall leave that question for later, m'dear. For now, all you need know is that you should begin looking in earnest amongst the young men who curry your favor. I am amenable to you making your own choice, but choose you will, and soon, because if you do not, I shall choose for you.''

Her own choice? The face of Ethan Travis, Demon of Alsatia, rose to her mind. What would Reggie say to such a choice? That he was well beneath her station? That no good could come of it? Yes, but Ethan would surely be preferable to Lord Cedric Broxton, or any of the other useless self-involved dandies who sought her company. But the only favors Ethan curried were the sort one could purchase. *That* would shock Reggie to the core.

Oh, drat! She had to talk to Annica at once. Nica was the only one she could trust to understand these strange thoughts and feelings she'd been having—confusing Ethan Travis with some ideal of manhood, thinking of him every time romance or marriage was mentioned. She knew she could not—would not—marry, so why would these thoughts even enter her head?

She was saved the necessity of a reply to Reggie by the

arrival of a footman to open the door of their coach at the steps of the Websters' manor. He let go of her hand and gave her the posy of pink roses.

She and Reggie were soon separated by the crush of the crowd, and she waved to him before being swept up the steps and through the door. She wanted to find Annica and the others to report the results of her first "following" lesson and discover if they had any leads on the children's whereabouts from Mr. Renquist.

Before she could locate her friends, Lord Cedric seized her hand and pulled her toward the punch bowl, his eyes bright with pleasure. The suspicion entered her mind that he had been waiting for her. How clever of Reggie and Cedric. Catch her whilst his admonition was still fresh in her mind. Was it a conspiracy?

"Lady Sarah, I vow I am pleased to see you tonight. I have missed you at the late routs the past several nights. And did you not have a voucher for Almack's last night?"

"Last night?" She frowned, trying to recall what had been on her social calendar. "Was that last night, Lord Cedric?"

"It was, indeed. I intended to claim a dance. I was devastated that you did not come. But there will be other nights, Lady Sarah, and other balls," Cedric continued. "I am certain I will collect my share of dances."

Was there something veiled in that phrase, Sarah wondered, or was she simply being overly imaginative?

Cedric paused in the process of ladling her a cup of punch, a speculative gleam in his deep blue eyes. "May I look forward to a waltz tonight, Lady Sarah?"

She had the vague feeling that she had been rather neatly maneuvered. Deny, and she would look rude and inconsiderate. Accept, and she would have stepped willingly into Lord Cedric and Reggie's tender trap. Though she saw the trap, she could see no way out without being rude. "I believe I can make room for you in my evening, Lord

Cedric. I am to meet my friends, and then go on to another rout, but there will be time. Perhaps in half an hour?''

He took her arm as she began to turn away. ''I hear the orchestra now, Lady Sarah. If you are not committed—''

The touch caught her by surprise and triggered a panic reaction. She whirled on him and stepped back, effectively disengaging his hold. ''I am committed, Lord Cedric. Did I not tell you I must find my friends?'' The look of hurt surprise in his clear blue eyes made her feel churlish.

What, she wondered, was wrong with her that she could not warm to the man? He was deemed a stellar ''catch'' for any young woman. He was handsome, had an engaging smile, impeccable manners, an excellent family name and wealth to match. Given all that, she could understand why Reggie would want to promote him. Perhaps she should be a little gentler with the man.

''Give me half an hour, Lord Cedric. I could devote my full attention then.''

Lord Cedric proffered the punch cup again. ''I am more than content with that,'' he said. ''For now.''

Sarah's smile locked in place. She accepted the cup and her hand brushed Lord Cedric's. His touch was cool and smooth in contrast to the warm roughness of Ethan Travis's. She recoiled from the contact, not liking the sensation, and put the cup down again.

Speechless at her reaction, Lord Cedric stared at her.

She held her posy in one hand and gave him a listless wave with her other. ''Ta-ta, Lord Cedric. Keep well, won't you?''

She pressed through the crowd in the direction she had glimpsed Annica a few moments before. She needed to talk to someone who knew her and knew her history. Nica would know what she should do about Mr. Travis. She had been through something similar with Auberville.

Oh, Lord! She could even smell him—that clean scent of lime and soap! What was wrong with her? She must be losing her mind!

She was jostled by the crowd and a firm hand from behind cupped her elbow to steady her. Warm breath fanned her ear and a deep voice rasped a hushed demand. ''Meet me in the garden in a quarter of an hour.''

She did not need to turn. Dizzy with shock, she gave a single nod.

When he'd first seen Sadie Hunt in the crush of the crowd, Ethan had been amazed. She looked like an angel, all pink and white. She seemed so at ease in the surroundings—more so than he—that he wondered if it could really be her. After all, he'd never seen her in a dress before, or in the light of a thousand candles. But of course it was. He could never mistake the burnished shade of her hair, the lush, inviting cupid's bow mouth, the fan of long black lashes against her cheek and the slender, supple line of her figure. Oh yes, it was Sadie. No one else could have stirred him so instantly and completely.

But what could the little troublemaker be doing at an event hosted by a high-ranking member of the ton? Which trade was she plying tonight? Who was her target?

Now she could present an even greater threat to his plans. He must make her understand that she could not expose either of them by invading the world of the ton.

To her credit, she did not falter, turn, speak or betray his demand that she meet him in the garden as she passed him by. She continued on her way until she intercepted Reginald Hunter, Lord Lockwood. Ethan was too far away to hear what was said between them, but Lockwood shook his head and held up one hand, palm outward in denial. He gave her a pat on her shoulder and watched as she walked away, his affection easy to see.

That surprised Ethan. Lockwood, although a bit of a rake, was not known as a womanizer. Did he avoid scandal by availing himself of courtesans? High-priced, discriminating courtesans? Was that Sadie's game?

Once again he felt anger burn in the pit of his stomach.

He had bloody well get over his unwarranted possessiveness where Sadie Hunt was concerned unless he was willing to accept the full consequences of it. That thought brought him up short.

He conjured an image of Sadie, curled up in his bed, the glorious chestnut locks in stark contrast against his bed linens, waiting for his return at night. Her doe eyes, as deep a plum as pansies, opening to greet him, burning with desire. The soft scented flesh as it lay bare to his gaze. The luscious lips, swollen and wet from his kisses, or parted in the throes of orgasm. Those black lashes lying against cheeks flushed with the afterglow of lovemaking. If he bought her—made her his mistress…

He swallowed hard, suppressing the image. He glanced at the faces around him to see if anyone had noted his utter distraction. No. He was safe from that embarrassment. He downed two cups of rum punch in rapid succession and made his way through the French doors to the gardens.

He found a spot protected by a boxwood hedge. The warmth of the rum seeped through his veins and calmed his thoughts enough to wonder if he'd ever know a moment's peace again if he took on the task of saving Sadie.

"Psst! Mr. Travis." Her whispered voice carried to him from the other side of the hedge.

He slipped around the side of the hedge and seized her arm, dragging her back with him. She did not resist when he pulled her against his chest and cupped the back of her head with one hand. "Sadie," he whispered. His voice sounded harsh to his ears and he softened his plea. "Sadie…"

Her eyes were enormous as he lowered his mouth to hers and claimed it. No sweet, teasing kiss this time, but a kiss fully realized. No tentative brushing of lips, but deep and demanding more. No barely parted lips, but an open, hungry quest.

After her initial surprise, she melted into him, lifting her arms to wrap around his neck. She was oddly, innocently, unpracticed, as if such a thing was new to her. And that aroused him even more. He wanted her here and now!

Hands shaking with the effort, he held her away from him, and took in a long, shattering breath. "Sadie, what are you doing here?"

She blinked and dropped her arms. "I…I might ask you the same, Mr. Travis," she murmured at last.

"Rule Two," he grinned.

She returned his smile. "We are not engaged in following now, sir. Do the rules apply?"

"Are you engaged in your other occupation tonight?"

She glanced away. "Yes, I suppose you could say that. Are you going to give me away?"

He shook his head. "Never think it, Sadie. Need I say that I expect the same courtesy from you?"

"No, you needn't. And shall I assume that you are here in *your* other occupation? Hmm. *Demon of Alsatia.* I wonder what business such a person could have in Lord Webster's ballroom?"

"Too much curiosity is not a good thing, Miss Hunt."

"I shall try to remember that, Mr. Travis," she said as she took another backward step. "You do the same."

A small tug on her hand landed her back in his arms. "I have not seen you like this before, Sadie. I swear, you seduce my senses. Gone is the little guttersnipe, and in its place is a swan. You are sleek and elegant and self-assured and —" he smiled as a tendril slipped its pink satin cord to curl at her temple "—the more disheveled you become, the more I want to ravish you."

"You tease me, sir," she sighed.

"Not in the least. I still want to know, Sadie. How much? Not for an hour. Nor for a night. How much to be my mistress? How much to keep yourself for me alone?"

Her eyes widened and she turned away from him. "There is not enough to buy me, Mr. Travis. I cannot become a man's property. I fear being trapped and powerless more than anything else in this world."

Ethan knew better than to reassure her. His words would ring false, and there was no reasoning with fear. He appealed to her instead with logic. "Is it better to mete out your time in tiny increments to avoid commitment? Would you rather sell yourself by the minute or hour? Think, Sadie. One man instead of many. A certain financial security?"

Tears filled her eyes and she pulled away from him, just as she had pulled away from Cedric Broxton. "I must not lose myself, Mr. Travis. I cannot give myself up to a man. I cannot…surrender."

Ethan dropped his hands to his side. He had never come so close to begging in his entire life. Nor would he again. Of course, she would not want him. Of course, she would not want to depend upon a man who had the reputation of being ruthless and dangerous. She'd be a fool to trust him. And whatever else Sadie Hunt was, she was not a fool.

Still there was someone who was an even greater threat to Sadie. "Stay clear of Broxton, Miss Hunt. He is not to be trusted."

Ethan had never liked the man, never trusted him. Broxton had been one of the men who had led the gossip accusing Ethan of treason after the bombardment of Algiers. He'd also seen how Broxton's easy charm could turn to lethal rage in the space of a second. He'd watched Broxton in the heat of battle. The man was an ice-cold killer, preferring slaughter to taking prisoners. They'd had more than one fight over it. Add to that his conduct in a brothel, and Ethan's blood ran cold. Even Kilgrew, their commander, had not been able to stop his nephew. But not Sadie. Pray not Sadie.

He'd seen earlier the way the man touched her. The gesture was too familiar, as if he had touched her before. That possibility disturbed him more than he cared to admit.

He stopped himself. Theirs was not a courtship, for God's sake, and the little Cyprian could take care of herself quite well! He and Sadie had a business arrangement, which he honored for sole reason of keeping her from running afoul of his real occupation. He had no time for a dalliance, purchased or otherwise. Sadie was right. Why *should* he care who she solicited or whose pocket she picked?

Locked in the Webster library, Sarah wrung her hands and paced in front of Annica. "…and when he looks at me, I have a peculiar feeling in my stomach. Nausea, I think. The closer he comes to me, the more befuddled I grow. I swear, Nica, I do not know myself these days."

"Oh! This is dreadful!" Annica agreed.

"Yes! Yes, it is. And when he kisses me—" She pressed her forehead with her fingertips and moaned, "Dear Lord! I *want* him to kiss me. I crave it and fear it at the same time."

Sarah thought she saw a gleam of amusement in Annica's dark green eyes. "What do you think it is?" she asked.

"Love."

She stopped dead in her tracks and stared at her friend. "Do not tease me, Nica. This is serious. I think I am losing my mind."

"You are. There is nothing rational or sane about love."

"I cannot believe that. Surely you are mistaken."

"Possibly," Annica admitted. "But I do not think so. And, evidently, you have indulged in a few stolen kisses. I cannot believe you would allow just any man that liberty. What surprises me, Sarah, is that you managed to fall in love without any of us noticing. Come. Tell me. Who is it? Lord Cedric? I have long noted his interest."

"Do not be absurd. Lord Cedric is…" She shrugged.

"He is quite handsome, Sarah. There are at least a dozen debutantes who court his attention. And I think Lady Jane Perrin has something of an tendress for him."

"Well, warn her away," she snapped.

"Warn her away? What an odd way to phrase it. If you have an interest in him, I am certain Jane will step aside."

"I do not have an interest in Cedric Broxton, and neither should Jane. Mr. Travis said he is not to be trusted, and I have never much cared for him. He let Reggie take the blame for something he did at school. Reggie did not care, but I thought it showed a lack of honor. I would be loathe to see anyone tied to a man like that."

Annica's expression sobered, and she nodded her agreement. "A man reveals his true nature in the little things, Sarah. I am inclined to think you are right about Lord Cedric. But who is Mr. Travis? I do not believe I have heard that name before. Is he a new acquaintance?"

She cursed herself for letting the name slip. If Annica or her husband found out that Mr. Travis was the Demon of Alsatia, and that Sarah was prowling the dark London streets with him nightly, she would never hear the end of it. And if Annica found out it was Mr. Travis who had caused her current state, she would commit Sarah to a convent. She shook her head vigorously. "Not so new, Nica. But that is beside the point."

"What *is* the point?"

"That I am confused. Why should one person have such a devastating effect on me? Why can I not think of anyone else? Why does his name leap to mind whenever I think of...."

"Yes." Annica nodded and sighed. "I very much fear we have gone beyond infatuation and are now dealing with a rather nasty case of love here."

Sarah collapsed onto the settee and buried her face in her hands. "Oh, this is appalling! This is beyond enduring! I cannot be in love, Nica. That has never been a possibility. You know I cannot marry."

"Sarah, any man worthy of your love will not care what was done to you. He would be sad for you, or angry at the men who did such a thing, but he would not hold you responsible."

"Oh, I know well enough that men do not require virginity from women they would consort with, else how would prostitutes make a living. But for a man to want a woman for any honorable purpose…"

Annica patted her shoulder comfortingly. "Dear Sarah, do not be distraught. Love is not the end of the world. In many ways, it is the beginning."

"I do not want to begin anything," she snapped. "I want to be cured."

"There is no potion or poultice for this. I am afraid you will have to weather it, my dear. If it is love, you are stuck with it. But you will survive. Now come and tell me who your paramour is. Geoffrey Morgan? Oh, I know. 'Tis Lord Nigel!"

Sarah wiped her eyes and sniffled. "I wish it *were* Lord Nigel. He'd, at least, be kind, and I've heard it whispered that he is impotent."

Annica chuckled. "Then who might Mr. Travis be? Does he have a title, because I know your brother has his heart set on an important match for you."

A title? Important? Would "the Demon of Alsatia" qualify? Oh, no doubt, but not in any way that Reggie ever dreamed. "Bloody hell," she sniffled. How was she going to get out of this?

Chapter Seven

It seemed to Sarah that hours passed as she crouched in the shadows of St. Paul's. Disappointment grew in her like a palpable thing. She had not realized how much she was hoping the Demon of Alsatia would not abandon her. She had avoided Mr. Travis completely the night before. She had been too raw, too emotional, to expose herself to another of his gentle assaults. He must think her a complete idiot for running from him, for telling him that she feared being with him and could never surrender. Good heavens! All she wanted in the world was to be able to surrender! She finally squared her shoulders and resolved to find Dicken. She would not sleep if she went home anyway.

A light touch on her shoulder made her gasp and whirl to face Ethan Travis. "How do you do that?" she asked. "I did not even hear you."

"It comes with practice." He looked her up and down, noting her compliance with his rules, nodded his approval and then reached across the distance to rub her lapel between his fingers. "This is finer trim than you could buy from a ragpicker, Sadie. Where did you come by them?"

"I…know people, Mr. Travis."

He gave her a sardonic grin. "You do indeed, Miss Hunt. Quite a few of them, if I understand correctly."

"Wh-what I said before, about preferring many, Mr.

Travis, was not meant as an insult to you. It is…it is…
who and what I am." Words failed her. How could she
explain an irrational fear? How could she confess to the
absolute and unreasoning terror that there would be nothing left of her if someone used her so again?

He released her lapel and stepped around her. "Never
mind, Miss Hunt. I have been rejected erenow. I shall survive it."

"But I—"

"Forget it, Miss Hunt. Now pay attention, and keep up.
I do not have time to coddle a novice tonight. I have had
one of my men locate our target again."

Effectively cut off, she fell into step behind him. If she
had thought he was driving a relentless pace before, she
now had cause to think he had gone easy on her. Although
he never ran, his long strides outpaced her easily. Thankfully, the soft leather heels of Andrew's worn riding boots
made little sound on the cobbled streets.

He stopped across the street from Ye Olde Cheshire
Cheese and, although she knew her brother was attending
the prince regent at a private party, she was about to tell
him she'd wait outside when the door flew open and Harold Whitlock stumbled out. If they had not arrived that
very moment, they would have missed him completely.
"Game's begun," he whispered over his shoulder without
breaking stride.

She nodded and pressed her lips together, determined to
remain silent according to his instructions. Over the en-
suing hour, she imitated his every move, followed his
every step. Twice he glanced over his shoulder and gave
her an approving nod. Those nods were like gold, to be
held and treasured—all the more so because she knew she
had earned them.

The fog thickened, muffling sound as well as sight and
forcing them to follow Whitlock more closely than they
had before. When Whitlock disappeared into a small tavern in a narrow lane, Ethan turned and whispered, "He's

carousing tonight, Miss Hunt. It is not likely anything important will happen.''

She shrugged. Dawn was hours away and she did not want to go home to lie awake until light. ''Just the same, I think I'll stay. You may go, if you wish.''

''No,'' he said. ''I've begun to wonder if there is a pattern in his meanderings. I wanted to go to the roofs, but I do not think you are ready for them.''

''The roofs?'' she asked, her interest piqued.

''When the lanes are long and narrow and the buildings are joined, one can follow by walking along the eaves. People seldom look up, especially at night. You need a good stride, Miss Hunt, and the ability to jump a fair distance if you must.''

She wet her lips. The endeavor sounded wonderfully dangerous and exciting. She wanted—no, *needed*—to challenge herself. ''I am ready, Mr. Travis. Lead on.''

''I have not observed your balance. Some women are afraid of heights and become dizzy. We should work the roofs in daylight before attempting it at night.''

She lifted her chin defiantly. ''I will never meet you in daylight, sir.''

He regarded her somberly, as if he wanted to ask her a question but decided against it. ''It will be at your own risk.''

''Has the risk not always been mine?'' she asked.

He ignored her question. ''The fog has made the roofs slippery. Stay as far from the edge as possible. At the first sign of dizziness, sit down. Wait for me. I shall come back for you.''

''Sir, I walked on eaves this very night. I am not likely to have a dizzy spell now.''

''I hope this is not another of your little stories, Miss Hunt.''

He showed her how to use a drainpipe and the uneven surface of bricks and half-timbers to climb. Most important, he told her, was that she never use the roofs when there was rain or ice. Heavy fog could prove dangerous as well. Tiles and shingles were slippery and the eaves could be treacherous.

When, at last, they stood on the roof opposite the tavern, he studied her face as if looking for any sign of fear. She shook her head and smiled, loving the vantage and the freedom of the roofs. To demonstrate her ease, she spread her arms like wings and twirled, but the toe of her boot caught the edge of a shingle and she teetered precariously on the edge.

He grasped her hand and pulled her back from the precipice. She landed against his chest with a solid thump and looked up into eyes darkened with anger.

"Poorly done, Sadie! Your recklessness nearly killed you. This is not a lark, and I will not be a party to your suicide."

Amazed by his reaction, Sarah frowned. "You are not responsible for me or my behavior in any way, Mr. Travis. You are not my father, my brother or my husband. You needn't answer for me or excuse my behavior."

He loomed over her like some dark avenging angel. "You are female, and I am male. Nature itself has decreed that the survival of the species depends upon my instinct to protect you. While you are in my care, Miss Hunt, I am still enough of a gentleman to take that seriously."

"Have mercy, Mr. Travis. *We* are responsible for the survival of the species?" She chuckled merrily, completely disarmed by the thought of Ethan's unwilling chivalry. "What a pretty explanation. I think you and Reggie would get on well."

This time he did not stop himself. "Reggie?" he asked with the lift of an eyebrow.

She smiled and wagged one finger at him. "Uh-uh, Mr. Travis. Rule Two."

Ethan was saved the necessity of a reply when the door to the tavern opened and Harold Whitlock exited. He paused only long enough to pull his coat tighter, glance in both directions and begin walking north.

Ethan took the lead again. Every few moments he paused to glance back, as if afraid that she had fallen to the cobblestones below and not made a sound. She smiled, pleased in spite of herself, that a man such as Mr. Travis was taking such care with her. Survival of the species, indeed. What a sorry world it would be if it depended upon her to propagate.

Not a quarter of a mile further, Whitlock halted before a private residence and rapped sharply on the door. A dim light grew brighter through the transom window before the door opened to reveal a man in a heavy woolen robe, his nightcap askew.

The voices were muffled over the distance, but Sarah caught the last words as Whitlock snarled, "Make the brat ready. I'll be back for her in the morning."

Her heart bumped painfully. Those were the very words Mr. Whitlock had used in reference to Araminta at the orphanage! He was going to move the child yet again!

She glanced at Ethan's face to see if he understood the significance of the interchange. He seemed more intent on Whitlock's behavior than his words.

"He is not being invited in," he whispered. "Be ready to move."

"I think I shall stay here," she said, praying he would not quote one of his precious rules—the one about doing as she was told without question. Was that Two or Five?

He studied her through the darkness. "Why?"

"I would like to see what his business is at such a place."

"I thought we only cared where he went. 'Following,' I believe you call it."

He had her there. "Yes. But you were late tonight, and it will be growing light soon. I will have to be home."

"Miss Hunt, there is a difference between surveillance and interrogation. You cannot simply knock on that door and ask the occupant what business Harold Whitlock had with them.''

That was a sobering reminder. Still, she had a second chance at saving Araminta, and she would not squander it. She would get the lay of the land, memorize the address and see if there were any other ways into the house. She could return at dawn with Mr. Renquist. She would be prepared this time, and she would not be too late.

She looked up into Ethan's eyes and lied without conscience. ''Then I suppose I shall go home.''

''Perhaps you'd like to have a pint of ale with Dicken and Joe first.'' He nodded toward a recessed doorway in the street below, a cynical look on his face.

Sarah could barely make out a figure in the shadows. ''How long have they been following us?''

''They are not following us, Miss Hunt. They are following Whitlock. They have been on Whitlock's coattails from the beginning. Why did you set them on him?''

''I did not. Perhaps they are following me,'' she said, praying he would believe that subterfuge.

''They are not on to us, Miss Hunt. If you value their lives, warn them off.''

''I will,'' she said, grasping at any excuse to escape Ethan. This must be the reason he preferred to follow on rooftops—the advantage of watching all directions at once. ''Tomorrow?'' she asked as she made for a corner drainpipe.

He nodded. ''I will expect a report.''

She crouched on the eave until Whitlock snarled something at the man in the nightcap and stumbled off down a side street. The minute Ethan resumed his hunt, she scrambled down and sneaked up behind Dicken and Joe.

''Blimey!'' Dicken exclaimed as he grasped his heart. ''Ye gave me a scare to end me life! Where ye been?''

''Close by,'' she told them. After Mr. Travis's warning, she had decided not to tell them about her forays with him. Dicken, like Annica, would only warn her against dealings with the likes of Mr. Travis, and she had no intention of heeding those warnings. "Araminta is in that house. I overheard Mr. Whitlock talking about her. He intends to move her again tomorrow."

"What d'ye think we should do, Sadie?" Sticky Joe asked.

"Go 'round back and see if you can pick the lock." When there was a window to creep through or a lock to be picked, Sticky Joe was always their man. "Psst," she whispered after him. "Softly, Joe. Araminta will be frightened and might balk at going with a stranger in the middle of the night."

"I've got sisters, I 'ave," he grinned. "I'll bribe 'er wi' a sweet."

She and Dicken crouched at the end of the mews to wait.

"Now what?" Dicken whispered.

"We will take her to Auberville's at once. Mr. Hodgeson will protect her. Once Araminta steps through Auberville's door, we needn't worry about her ever again."

"An' then?"

"Then?" Sarah repeated numbly. "Then we find Teddy and Benjamin."

Anxiety ate at Sarah's nerves as they waited for what felt like an eternity. She stood and straightened her jacket. "I will go around front and knock on the door. Joe may be able to use the distraction to spirit Araminta out the back."

The sound of running footsteps came to them through the fog and a moment later Sticky Joe materialized, holding the hand of a young girl. Her hair was tangled and she wore nothing but a nightgown. Tears streamed down her cheeks and she looked terrified, but she did not make a sound.

Exhilaration raced through Sarah. They had done it! They had found Araminta! She tried to give a reassuring smile as she took the little girl's other hand and began running again.

A scream pierced the heavy air. "''Elp! Police! Kidnappers! 'Elp!''

The shrill pitch of a whistle sounded in the distance.

Ethan did not follow Whitlock for long. The man turned on Ludgate, headed for the wharves and disappeared into an opium den. No sense waiting until dawn. Whitlock would be occupied and insensible until then. He made a quick motion and was joined by his man, Peters.

"Keep him safe, Peters," he said.

"Aye, sir, but the man's a rotter."

Ethan looked back. He had to be certain that Peters understood the importance of his task. "I am repaying a favor, Peters."

"I know that, sir, but—"

"My honor depends upon it." Ethan turned to go.

Peters nodded. "And the lady, sir?"

Ethan froze. Sadie had no part in this and he wanted to make sure she never did. "The lady is my business. Now settle in. I'll send a replacement in a few hours."

"Aye, sir."

He hailed a passing coach and gave the address of his warehouse in the old Alsatia district—the one believed to be the hub of his criminal activities. Warehouse "R."

He had not been able to devote more than token time to his business since accepting Lord Kilgrew's request. This business of guarding Harold Whitlock was taking more of his time and resources than he could spare. Add to the mix his preoccupation with Miss Hunt, and it was a wonder he had any time at all for business. It had taken all his resources tonight to keep from asking her the fatal question yet again. *How much, Miss Hunt?* Dear God, how he wanted her! More than he'd ever wanted Amelia.

His former fiancée had been untouchable and ephemeral and all he'd thought a woman should be. But Sadie was life and vitality and grit and laughter. She was earthy and honest and a survivor at the most fundamental level. Sadie

Hunt, for all her odd prudishness, was passion personified. He doubted she would ever betray him, as Amelia had.

The coach drew up and Ethan pulled himself back to the present with a start. Momentary inattention could jeopardize everything. He surveyed the surroundings, looking for movement in shadows or anything out of place. Nothing.

The driver's voice called down to him. "'Ere we are, gov'ner. One schilling, six pence. An' watch ye'self. This ain't the best part o' town."

Ethan tossed the coins up to the driver and smiled when the man snatched them out of midair without missing one. Native caution made him wait until the coach was well away before he unlocked the reinforced warehouse door and bolted it again behind him. The sharp sound of his footsteps echoed in the silence as he crossed the long open room to a flight of narrow stairs leading to the second floor.

Bales of Egyptian cotton were stacked floor to ceiling, front wall to back wall, in half the structure. The other half contained wooden casks and crates bearing exotic spices and dyes for use in the wholesale market. Valuable, but nothing to draw unwarranted attention. The strong smells of the spices masked other odors, merging into a confusing but not unpleasant blend. There was nothing to betray the secret the warehouse held and the urgent business that awaited him.

Upstairs, in his office, he lit the wick of a small oil lantern. Removing a book from the shelves behind his desk, he tripped a hidden spring that swung the shelf outward. Not original, he acknowledged, but effective. He stepped around the hidden door to the other side and pulled it closed behind him.

He was now in an identical office, the mirror image of the one he'd left, but with a window overlooking a space below. The atmosphere on this side, however, was decidedly different.

A soft murmur of voices and the warm glow of lanterns greeted him. He looked down over the scene, thinking how like an exotic hotel lobby it appeared instead of a way station for returning hostages. The few men and women were dressed in everything from English garb to Algerian caftans.

He sat at his desk, removed a bottle and glass from the bottom drawer and poured himself a stiff whiskey. God knows he needed it after the episode with Sadie. Then, to work.

"Ah, here you are, Travis. I had begun to think you'd shun us again this evening."

Ethan glanced to the doorway at his second in command, Robert McHugh. "Have I been negligent, McHugh?"

"Our agent is due back from Algiers tomorrow night. Will you be here?"

"Ayers? Is something afoot?"

McHugh shrugged and stepped into the office, taking the chair opposite Ethan's. "There was a time when you wouldn't have asked that question. Does this have anything to do with the little prostitute you've been sporting with?"

Ethan pinched the bridge of his nose, trying to ward off an impending headache. "Do not prick me tonight, McHugh. I am not in the mood."

"Nor am I," McHugh said, his brogue heavier than usual. He reached for the bottle and took a healthy swig.

"Very well, McHugh. I am not 'sporting' with the woman in question. She asked my assistance in a matter, and I agreed to give it, as it does not take me out of my way or divert my attention from my task. There is no recreational involvement whatsoever. She has not distracted me from my business. Kilgrew did that when he diverted me to guard Harold Whitlock's back. If there ever comes a time when 'the little prostitute' jeopardizes our operation, you may rest assured that I will put her out of the way posthaste.''

McHugh raised the bottle in a salute before drinking again. ''I shall hope it does not come to that.''

There was more on McHugh's mind, Ethan knew. After a moment, the man rubbed his left arm where a ball meant for Ethan had ripped through it. That was an old argument—who had saved the other's life. Rob had stepped in front of a bullet meant for Ethan, but Ethan had risked his life, and yes, even the mission, to save the wounded Scot. Rob was his staunchest friend and had stood by Ethan through scandal and disgrace.

''I trust you with my life, Travis,'' Rob began. ''''Tis just that I'm terrified at the snail's pace with which we are moving and our lack of results. I'd give my life and all I own to buy back the day I put Maeve and Hamish on a ship bound for Venice. I *knew* the waters were dangerous, and that the Barbary pirates were out of control. But she begged to visit her sister, said some fortune teller 'saw' that her sister needed her, and I could not dissuade her. We should have found them within a few months. 'Tis near two years now, and we are no further ahead.''

Ethan sighed, familiar with that frustration. The Dey, the ruling official of Algiers, had got wind of their activities through the same unknown man for whose treason Ethan had been accused. And still, the driving question had not been answered. Who had informed the Dey of the impending British attack? Who had framed Ethan for leaking that information? And who was still feeding the Dey information? Ethan would give everything he owned for that name.

In their search for Rob's wife and son, they had come across a handful of British men and women. Wherever and whenever they encountered them, they had rescued them and brought them home, making them swear to keep their operation secret. Even those few were becoming scarce.

Rob shook his head. "Blast Kilgrew," he muttered. "His little assignment is a complication we did not need."

"I had no choice, Rob. I owe him my life."

"Owe him? Are you mad? He damned you with his silence." Rob looked down at his boots and sighed. "Is he not Cedric Broxton's uncle? I've never liked that little weasel."

Ethan ignored Rob's digression. "Kilgrew kept me out of court. Without evidence to clear me, I'd have been convicted." He put his glass down and raked his fingers through his hair. "Kilgrew saved me from hanging." He watched as Rob took another deep drink from the bottle. The Scot could hold his liquor, he'd give him that.

Rob gazed into the candle flame. "Aye, you cozy up to Kilgrew, then, but when Maeve and Hamish come home, we'll go back to the Highlands. I want to sit in my castle, drink a decent malt whiskey, watch my son grow and pat my wife's arse. Maeve and Hamish will be in the lot tomorrow. Aye, tomorrow."

"Tomorrow," Ethan raised his glass. He permitted himself a small smile. He'd wager there was still more than one Highland lass who murmured Rob's name in her sleep from the days before he and Maeve said their vows. Aye. Bonnie Laird Robert McHugh.

Although Ethan had no duty to launch this search—or to continue it—he had a moral imperative. And, without the structure Ethan imposed, Rob would have slashed his way through Algiers in search of his family and been killed for his trouble.

He shook his head to clear it of the past. "So, Ayers is due tomorrow night? Are we prepared for him?"

"Providing he does not have too many in tow. This lot," he nodded to the group below, "will be gone tomorrow. I've banked them all fifty pounds, and they are headed home with the story of their miraculous escape. All but Miss Ballard. She swears she cannot go back to Yorkshire a tarnished woman. She has no trade but that of lady's maid. Her former employer has died and, without references, she cannot obtain another position. What do you say? Cut her adrift or let her stay on?''

Ethan shrugged. ''Does she have any other skills?''

''I gather the position of lady's maid requires some rather specialized skills, but none she can use in another trade. She has made some delicious pastries since her arrival, but I cannot find a position for her in a bakery. Her choices are limited, Travis. I fear she will have to become a prostitute if we put her out now. 'Tis all she has known for the past two years.''

Ethan thought of Sadie. What had driven *her* to the streets? Why had no one helped her? How might her life be different if someone had? ''Buy Miss Ballard a bake-shop,'' he said, ''and let her stay until she can begin making it pay. We will find the money somewhere.''

McHugh grinned. ''Travis, the reluctant hero?''

Ethan ignored him. ''As for tomorrow, McHugh, I will be here. I want to know what Ayers may have discovered.''

''And I still want to know who really betrayed the Algerian mission two years ago,'' McHugh said.

Ethan lifted his glass in a silent toast.

Chapter Eight

Sarah stepped out of her bath and toweled herself dry before shrugging into her wrapper. She sat down at her vanity and tugged at the tangles in her wet hair. If she did not hurry, she would be late meeting Charity and Grace for the Gordon affair. She was anxious to tell them that Araminta was safely ensconced at the Aubervilles'.

And perhaps tonight she'd see Mr. Travis again. Annica's words came back to her in a heated rush. But Annica had to be wrong. Love, the kind of love that involved marriage and intimacy, had not been possible for her since that long ago night in Vauxhall Gardens.

She dropped her brush on the vanity and stood, her mind in turmoil. In fact, she had not felt peaceful since meeting Ethan. Why did he unsettle her so? Could it actually be love?

No. Absurd. Completely ridiculous. Out of the question.

The memory of his words prickled at the back of her mind. *How much, Sadie? How much to sate my hunger? How much to taste your charms? How much to…satisfy my curiosity?*

How much? What was the price for her pride? Was she willing to risk his scorn? Was she willing to undergo the humiliation of any man's physical attentions at any price? One thing was certain. She had better decide how to handle the situation before it got entirely out of hand. The tension between them was becoming unbearable.

She shrugged out of her damp silk wrapper and stood in front of the tall cheval looking glass. She had not looked at her body since the attack. Glimpsing herself naked reminded her of what those men had done, so she always turned quickly away from mirrors.

But Ethan wanted her—had been willing to pay for her—if only for one night. What had *he* seen in her? She turned from side to side, studying her reflection, trying to see what Ethan saw. She judged her form to be a trifle slender. Her breasts were adequate to her size and well shaped; her waist was little more than a man's hand span; her hips were softly curved and her legs were long and shapely. On the other hand, she lacked the voluptuousness of a Rubens model; she was neither pale nor fair haired as was currently in vogue; she was too short to be statuesque, and her hair had a mind of its own.

She flattened her hand against her heart and slid it downward over her belly. The bruises had faded years ago. The scars had healed and were gone now. No trace of the attack remained. No trace, that is, that was visible.

What scars still lurked beneath the unblemished skin? What had those men taken from her that she had been unable to reclaim? Could anyone who saw her as she saw herself now ever understand the depth of the wounds that had been inflicted? Because of those wounds she dreaded and feared intimacy.

And yet…of late, she had begun to wonder if she could be wrong about the marriage act. Would so many people do it if it were so awful? The keen edge of desire in Ethan's kiss had awakened something long dormant and stunted, almost as if her frozen emotions had begun to thaw and grow.

She shivered in the cool air and her nipples firmed. She touched them and was startled at the bittersweet aching that action evoked. What would Ethan's hand brushing her

flesh cause in her? She closed her eyes to see his face and
a sweet throbbing began at her core. Her knees went suddenly weak and spongy, but guilt squelched the sensations
as quickly as they had come.

She swept her wrapper up and shrugged into it, pulling
it tightly around her with a vicious jerk of the sash. She
could not think straight where Ethan was involved. He
would eventually give up his interest in her, just as all her
other suitors had. She prayed it would be soon.

"Oh, Sarah! You are a marvel!" Charity exclaimed
when the Wednesday League was able to hold a hurried
conference during the orchestra's intermission. "To have
found Araminta and spirited her out of her captivity in the
middle of the night! It takes my breath away!"

Grace nodded. "What can we do to help?"

"Nothing, really," Sarah said. "'Tis all very boring. I
just follow Mr. Whitlock and see where he goes."

She dared not involve them in the following because
she did not want to explain her relationship with Ethan
Travis. She needed him. He had taught her more about
following people unseen in a few short nights than she had
gleaned by herself in the past two years. Dicken and Sticky
Joe were rank amateurs next to the Demon of Alsatia.

Annica cleared her throat. "As you know, Auberville
and I are hosting a ball in two weeks. We sent an invitation
to the Whitlocks and Mr. Whitlock has sent his acceptance.
I intend to call upon Mrs. Whitlock to express my delight
in their acceptance. I would be glad of company."

"You mean actually go in that house?" Charity gasped,
her voice catching on a tiny sob.

Sarah studied her. This was the first potentially dangerous case the Wednesday League had taken since Constance
had been killed. She wondered if Charity had the fortitude
for what lay ahead. Annica caught her eye and nodded.
She was thinking the same thing.

Grace lifted her chin and waved one gloved hand. "Yes,

Charity, we must actually go inside. Mr. Whitlock must be made aware that his wife has allies. He'd never dare harm any of us in his own home, but if the uncertainty is too much for you—"

Charity looked pensive, as if she wanted to confess to a lack of nerves but was afraid to risk the good opinion of her friends. "I keep thinking of Constance Bennington and how she was killed while investigating your case, Sarah."

The group fell silent until Annica finally spoke. "Constance made only one mistake, Charity. She did not tell us what she was doing. None of us knew where she was bound that night, or who she set out to meet. Had we known, we could have taken precautions. We could have kept her safe."

That was what Sarah was doing! Working without the full knowledge of the group. Keeping secrets from them. Venturing forth with a man known to be dangerous and disreputable.

Soon after, Sarah pleaded a headache and Charles escorted her home. She had hoped she would have time to meet Sticky Joe and Dicken before meeting Mr. Travis, but the latter was waiting on the steps of St. Paul's. Her heart did a weak flutter, and she gave him a tentative smile.

"Good evening, Miss Hunt. I am glad you had the sense to come early. I cannot spare much time tonight. There is somewhere I must be later. One of my men has followed Whitlock to Vauxhall. Shall we?" He gestured toward the street.

Vauxhall! Surely he meant the district of Vauxhall, not the gardens. She hadn't been back there since…since the attack. Just the thought of it caused her heart to pound. She could not catch her breath as she followed Ethan down Creed Lane toward Black Friars Bridge.

When they reached the bridge, he hailed a coach and propelled her through the door, calling directions to the driver. Pure, unreasoned fear raced through her mind. She thought of Constance and wondered if she were being abducted. She slid across the leather seat and cowered in the far corner.

As Ethan settled himself beside her, he took his cap off and ran his fingers through his hair. "We shall save some time by taking a coach, Miss Hunt. I hope you do not mind."

"No. No, I..." Sarah took a deep breath and tried to steady her raw nerves. "Where are we going, exactly, Mr. Travis? Are we going to the gardens? I did not bring the price of admission. In fact, I cannot pay for the coach. You may have the driver pull over and leave me. I shall find my own way back," she offered in a rush, praying the coins in her pocket would not jingle and give her away.

"I have enough for both of us," he said.

On the other side of the Thames, the coach turned right and proceeded westward.

"Perhaps we should wait until another night. I would not want to make you late for your appointment."

He peered at her through the dim light of the coach's interior. "Is something amiss?"

Sarah clenched her hands into fists to steady them. She knew her panic was showing. "I do not like Vauxhall, Mr. Travis," she confessed. "I cannot go there."

"Why is that, Miss Hunt?"

The speculative tone of his voice annoyed her, as if he found something interesting. Good Lord. Could she ever explain her fears to a man who was fearless? "Do I need a reason, Mr. Travis?"

His pause set Sarah's nerves on edge. When he finally spoke, his words suggested that he knew more than he was saying. "Not for me, Miss Hunt, but I find it curious that you could be daunted by something so mundane as geography."

"I did not say I was daunted," she grumbled. "I said I do not like Vauxhall."

"Hmm," he said.

She gritted her teeth. She hated his *hmm*s. They suggested disbelief.

"Then you are prepared to continue?" he asked.

No, she was not, but Teddy and Benjamin were at stake. She squared her shoulders and fought a spike of panic. She was being silly, and she would not allow an event that had taken place years ago to control her now. "'Lay on, Macduff,'" she said with a determined lift of her chin.

Ethan laughed. "'And damn'd be him that first cries, *Hold, enough!*'" He finished the quote from *MacBeth.* "I see you are a scholar, Miss Hunt. Very well, then. I shall wait for you to call 'Hold, enough,' before I turn back. For the moment, you owe me a report of last night."

Sarah cursed herself for not remembering that he had asked for a report. Too late to cook up a likely story now. An abbreviated version of the truth would have to suffice. "Mr. Whitlock was making inquiries in regard to the householder's new scullery maid."

Ethan puzzled this for a moment. "Why should a reprobate like Whitlock fret over a mere scullery maid? Why would he concern himself?"

Sarah shrugged. "Perhaps he had some use for her."

Ethan's face set in grim lines, and Sarah realized what he must be thinking. As far as Ethan would know, there could be only one purpose for a man like Harold Whitlock to display an interest in a waif in the middle of the night. She could not correct him without betraying Whitlock's true connection to Araminta, so she remained silent.

He turned to face her and fixed her with a piercing gaze. "Miss Hunt, I do not want you approaching that man under any circumstances. Do you understand?"

A tingle of warmth rushed through her and settled in her chest. "I understand," she said, avoiding giving agreement.

In the end, it was not Vauxhall Gardens that was their destination, but a street of disreputable houses on Vauxhall Row. She nearly wept with relief when Ethan knocked sharply on the roof to signal their driver to stop, then stepped down and tossed him a coin. He turned to help Sarah, but she ignored his hand and hopped down on her own.

As the coach pulled away, she teased him. "Mr. Travis, do you want people remarking upon your courtesy to a boy?"

He laughed. "Nicely done, Miss Hunt." He peered into the darkness and whistled softly.

A man stepped out of the alley near the end of the row. One of Ethan's minions, no doubt. He pointed to the end house and then disappeared into the night. Ethan led her to the corner of Vauxhall Row and Glasshouse Street, where he found a darkened crack between houses.

They waited, Ethan standing close behind her. The heat of his body against her back was comforting. Within moments she forgot about Harold Whitlock and could only think of Ethan's clean scent, the warmth of his body so close to hers, his strength as evidenced by his utter stillness and the fact that she was surrounded by him. She did not speak, because speaking was against the rules. And anyway, she did not want to break the spell.

She shifted her weight from one foot to another after a quarter of an hour, and Ethan placed his hand on her shoulder, as if to caution her. He leaned forward, his breath a tickle in her ear. "Softly, Sadie. That is not an opium den or a bordello. He cannot be much longer."

The tickle of his breath fanned her neck and gooseflesh rose in response. What would his lips feel like there? She tilted her head to one side to invite his attention, and heard a soft exhalation of breath along with a muffled curse. He moved around her to block her vision.

"We had better come to an understanding, Miss Hunt. You cannot continue to tempt—"

The door across the street opened and Harold Whitlock rushed out, pulling on his gloves, his hat slightly askew. Sarah heard the sound of a child crying before the door closed completely. Teddy or Benjamin! She lunged forward, but Ethan caught her around the waist. His hand clamped over her mouth as he dragged her back into the shadows.

He whispered in her ear again. "Not so anxious, little one. We are following him, not attacking him. Do you want him to see us?"

She glanced from Whitlock to the house he had just left. She could just make out the address in the darkness. Number 8 Vauxhall Row. As soon as she could win clear of Ethan, she would find Dicken and Sticky Joe and come back. It was now becoming apparent that Mr. Whitlock was moving the children about, never leaving them in one place for long. Any rescue would have to come tonight.

"Damn!" Ethan exclaimed, watching helplessly as Whitlock hailed a passing coach and disappeared in the direction of the bridge. He took several steps into the street, no longer concerned that they'd be seen.

Thunder rumbled overhead and a few drops splattered on the cobblestones as a cold wind blew up from the river. Sarah groaned. She did not relish going home cold and wet, nor climbing to her bedroom window in the rain. "What a wasted night," she complained, hoping to rid herself of him.

"There are no more coaches. We shall have to find a place to wait the storm out. C'mon," Ethan ordered, heading down Glasshouse Street away from the river. At the corner, he entered the Black Dog Tavern and approached the publican.

Sarah stood beside him, keeping her head down while her mind whirled out of control. One of the Whitlock children was within her grasp, but she could not get to him. Dicken and Joe would have taken shelter from the storm, so she would have to wait the storm out and look for them later. Oh, pray it would not be too late!

"Ale?" the publican asked.

She lowered her voice as she had practiced. "Naw,

gov'ner. I'll 'ave a whiskey.'' She'd never tasted whiskey before, but she knew her brothers partook of it regularly. It seemed a very masculine thing to drink.

Ethan's eyebrows shot up in surprise. "I do not think—"

"Whiskey it is, lad," the publican said.

Ethan fixed her with narrowed eyes while speaking to the publican. "And a private room, if you have it."

The man paused, looking from Ethan to Sarah and back again. "Upstairs to your right. That's a guinea."

Ethan slid two coins across the counter, seized the whiskey bottle with one hand and Sarah with the other, and led her up the narrow stairway. He threw the door open to a tiny room with a fireplace along the outer wall, a small table, two chairs and a cot in one corner. Once they were safely shut away, he turned to her with an expression somewhere between amusement and anger.

"Are you mad? You are not supposed to speak unless I tell you. And where did you acquire a taste for whiskey?"

"You are more careless than I," she accused, still trying to think of a plan to separate from him. "Twice tonight you have given the appearance of having a taste for young boys."

"One takes one's pleasures where one can find them," he snarled. "And do not think your clothing fooled anyone, Sadie."

"Pleasures!" She gave him a cynical laugh. "Is that what you call it? I have never been able to puzzle that out." The small room was oppressively hot so she shrugged out of her jacket and threw it over a chair in a reckless gesture that spoke more of her mood than her words. "Seems more like pain to me. A bother at best."

"Come now, Miss Hunt. Are you telling me you have never taken pleasure from your occupation?"

"'Tis just business," she covered quickly.

He grinned hugely, as if he were beginning to solve a

puzzle. "Have you ever taken pleasure from the act at all?"

Dear Lord! How had they got into this conversation? Sarah drank her whiskey in a single gulp and winced as it burned its way down her throat. "Pleasure is a male concept, Mr. Travis. Any woman who says otherwise is lying."

Now he guffawed. "Do you think so, Miss Hunt? Care to wager upon it?"

"No, I do not." She eyed the whiskey bottle on the table. "How would you ever prove your point?"

Ethan walked around her in a wide circle, looking her up and down, as if measuring her for human sacrifice. "Well, well, well," he chuckled. "Now it begins to make sense. Of course you would deny me pleasure when you have never experienced it yourself."

"I do not know what you mean," she muttered, edging toward the table. The whiskey had hit bottom and kindled a toasty little fire in her stomach before seeping downward. One more drink, and then she'd sit before her knees gave out.

"Yes, it is now quite apparent that you do not know what I mean," he agreed good-naturedly. "So, I think we should level the playing field, Miss Hunt. Would you not agree?"

She shrugged. "How would you propose to do that?"

He laughed again, giving every appearance of being unaccountably pleased with some notion. He took her glass from her hand and filled it to the halfway point. "Easy, Miss Hunt. You will not be needing much more when I am done with you."

"Oh!" she taunted. "We are quite full of ourselves, are we not?" He reminded her of Andrew when he thought he was going to win some harebrained wager.

"With reason," he bowed. He drank straight from the bottle. Two swigs, if Sarah counted right.

She watched with the first faint stirrings of misgivings

as he hung his hat on one corner of a chair and shrugged out of his coat. He took a pocket watch from his vest pocket and set it on the little table. His gaze never left her as he removed his cravat, unbuttoned his vest and undid the top three buttons of his shirt. When he rolled up his sleeves with the air of someone preparing for a challenging task, a frisson of excitement raced up her spine.

A smile tugged at the corners of his mouth as he stepped closer. "I regret that my time is somewhat limited tonight, Miss Hunt, but sufficient time remains to lay the groundwork. Are you ready to begin?"

What amused him so much? "Lay on, Macduff," she said.

Chortling, Ethan stepped forward, removed her cap and sent it sailing across the room. Next he pulled the pins from her hair and let it fall loose to her waist, fanning it out across her shoulders and back. He captured a single curl and wound it around his finger. "I've never seen your hair like this. You should wear it thus more often instead of trying to tame it in a prim little bun." His head bent to drag a tantalizing kiss down the column of her throat. Then he reached for the buttons of her shirt.

"Hold," she gasped, covering his hand with her own. "I—"

"Hold? Are you saying, 'Hold, enough,' Miss Hunt?"

"No, I…yes. I mean, I—"

He gave her a slow, honeyed smile that never failed to bring her up short and then placed her hand upon his shoulder. "I know what you are going to say. *Lay on, MacTravis!*"

The whiskey had hit bottom and she giggled in spite of herself. "Macduff," she corrected. She had never seen Ethan in a playful mood before, and it charmed her so completely that she was not quite certain how to deal with him. "But I—"

"Did not bring any money? That's quite all right, Miss Hunt. There'll be no charge tonight."

"Charge?"

"For my services," he explained. In a quick movement, he had the buttons of her shirt undone to the waist. He raised his eyebrows when he saw the bindings over her breasts but it did not deter him for long. He removed the pin and pulled the binding away with a small tug.

Astounded, Sarah opened her mouth to protest just as Ethan's mouth came down to cover it. He pulled her against his broad, warm chest and cupped the back of her head. She grew dizzy when his tongue moved along the line of her lips.

"You taste of whiskey, Sadie," he murmured, "but you are twice as potent."

She could not catch her breath, nor did she want to. What she wanted was for that kiss to go on forever. She did not want to draw breath unless it came from Ethan. She did not want to step away if it meant she would be deprived of the support and warmth of his arms.

He bent slightly and lifted her off her feet. She clung to him, tangling her fingers in his hair, holding his mouth to hers. She did not want this moment—this one perfect moment—to end. He must have sensed her fascination because he stilled, giving exquisite attention to the kiss.

When, a moment later, she found herself reclining on the cot, she fought a surge of panic. She pushed against his chest, trying to dislodge him. "No! No, I told you I will not—"

"Do you not understand, sweet Sadie? I know you will not serve me, but I intend to serve you. Tonight I will add to your education. You will learn pleasure."

"I do not want to learn," she gasped.

"You are lying, Sadie. Your every response tells a different story. And the most interesting element is this—you do not yet know what you want. You will not know that until I am finished here tonight. Only then will I trust you to tell me how much is enough."

He kissed her again, and his warm, callused hand slid

past the opening of her shirt. His fingers stroked her breasts and circled her nipples and she caught her breath with a groan. Her eyelids fluttered and she closed them, the better to experience the sensation. Her mind returned to the moment, in front of the looking glass, when she had touched herself and wondered what Ethan's touch would do to her. Now she knew.

Ah, no terror here. No pain. Only delight. Could he be right? Could there be pleasure in this?

"Very nice, Sadie. Cannot say I've ever encountered better," he praised.

Better what? she wondered. Breasts? Reactions to his touch? Or a better kiss?

He lowered his head to nuzzle her neck and found a spot at the base of her throat that made her moan when he kissed it. He lingered there with patient attention.

"Christ," he sighed after a long moment, his hot breath in her ear causing her to shudder. "You defy logic, madam. It is not as if you are frigid, or slow to take fire. You respond as sweetly as an angel. I cannot believe no man has taken the proper time with you. Have you ever allowed it?"

"N-no," she confessed.

"Then you should learn, my dear. You do not yet understand your own power," he said. He lifted his head to look down into her eyes. "Tonight, Sadie, you become a woman in full."

A log fell in the fireplace and crackled as it adjusted to a new position in the grate. He smiled at her little start of surprise. "The door is locked, sweetling. We will not be disturbed. May I undress you?"

"No!" She was certain she could go no further than her unbuttoned shirt.

"Too vulnerable, eh? No matter, I can do this without undressing you." He nibbled her earlobe and his palm rubbed over her tender areola.

"You can...do what?"

But it really did not matter. By now, she would have let him do anything he wanted. She was burning for his touch. She was arching against his hand like a kitten to its master. And she was breathless with anticipation for his next move.

"Mmm," he intoned as his head moved lower, his stubble rasping against the tender flesh of her chest as he kissed and licked his way toward her breasts. "You even taste sweet, Sadie. Like the lilacs you smell of."

Then his mouth covered her breast and his teeth scraped against the hardened nipple, causing her to shiver with exquisite sensitivity. Fire licked through her veins and she whimpered in a voice she scarcely recognized as her own. This was beyond anything she had ever imagined! Shocked, she heard herself say, "Yes!"

"Yes," he affirmed, his lips moving on her skin. "Talk, Sadie. Tell me what you like, what you want."

He appeared to know the answer to that better than she. There were no words she could think of to tell him what she wanted. She only knew one. "More," she moaned.

The rumble of his laugh vibrated along her nerves. "I shall trust you to tell me when you've had enough."

She ran her fingers through his hair again and curved downward to kiss the shining cap of chestnut brown, then slipped one hand beneath his shirt and glided it across his back. His breath caught on a choke and he jerked back from her touch.

"No, Sadie. Not tonight. Do not encourage me or I will forget my promise. Lie back, sweetling, and open to me. That is all I want from you tonight."

His hand skimmed her belly and unfastened the waistband of her brother's trousers, folding the sides back to form a wide V ending just above her nether hair. Something deep inside her fluttered to break free and ached for deeper contact. He stroked her from her navel to the opening of the trousers with the back of his hand, his knuckles giving a deeper pressure.

She shuddered and arched, catching her lower lip between her teeth. "M-Mr. Travis, I…"

"Ethan," he corrected.

"Ethan," she repeated, her mind going blank when he gave attention to one firmed nipple.

"What, little one?"

She gasped as two fingers found their way past the V and curved over her mons. Oh, yes! That was what she wanted! *That* was the touch she'd been craving. How could he have known that? Her hips arched and tilted to give him better access. "Yes," she moaned.

"Yes?" he asked. "Yes what, Sadie? What do you want?"

"I…do not…know."

"Then 'tis a good thing that I do," he chortled, nuzzling her breasts.

She was panting now, truly unable to catch her breath. Coherent thought kept escaping with his every move. Each time she gathered the resources to be shocked, to stop him, he went a step further and she could not think of anything but how sensitive and strong his hands were, how hot his lips, how terrified she was, yet how safe and cherished he made her feel.

None of what Ethan did bore any resemblance to what Farmingdale and the others had done. None of the gentleness and consideration shown by this man had been evidenced on that long-ago night. And, her feeble protestations aside, she knew she could stop Ethan if she became desperate to do so.

She desperately did *not* want him to stop. In fact, when his hand cupped her again and two fingers stroked past the exquisitely sensitive little nubbin to make a shallow entry, she uttered an involuntary sound like a keening animal and twisted toward him.

He groaned. "You are ripe and ready, dear Sadie. God! You are so hot and tight." He eased his fingers into her again, and then out, clearly waiting for her response.

She gave it in the form of an angry squeal as she thrust toward him again, seeking to find and deepen the contact.

Both of his hands skimmed her trousers down over her hips to her knees. He cupped her buttocks and his head went down to circle her naval with his tongue. She gripped handfuls of his dark hair, frantic to hold on to something beside the edge of the cot. The curls lying against his forehead and neck were damp, as if he was under a great strain.

"You are close, Sadie. So close. Breathe deep and let me guide you."

Speech was beyond her. She nodded and whimpered instead, long past dissembling. His head moved lower, still trailing kisses downward, until it reached the spot his hand had so recently vacated. She nearly swooned at the sensation. A pleasure so intense that it set her every nerve to throbbing began to pulse over her. Rapid, shallow breaths could not keep pace with the demands of his mouth.

Just when she thought she would burst into flames, Ethan relented and eased upward, the heat and texture of his skin unbearably intimate as it slid along hers. He murmured nonsensical words in her ear and she had the distinct impression that he was gentling her, soothing her, as one would a skittish mare. His hand returned to her passage and he stroked slowly, gradually increasing both depth and pace, until Sarah was ready to weep with the unbearable pressure building at her core.

"Oh," she sobbed, holding him so close that he could barely move. "Oh, Ethan! Please!"

And he pleased her very much indeed.

"Yes, Sadie. Yes," he whispered. "My God, you are so beautiful. I can feel you close around me, I can feel your muscles contracting. You are more than I ever expected. I cannot wait until 'tis me inside you—"

But Sarah heard no more. Wave after wave of shimmering heat and pulsating electricity washed through her, drowning her in the sensation. She was only dimly aware of Ethan's hand, gentle and evocative, his mouth nibbling her flesh in the most delicious ways, and then the utter peace as she slowly surfaced from the swirling maelstrom of passion.

Faint chiming broke the peace and quiet of the room, and Ethan turned toward the sound, muttering darkly under his breath. When he turned back to her, his eyes, now a deep greenish brown, softened. He cupped her face and wiped her cheeks with his thumbs, a look of concern darkening his eyes. "Sadie, was I clumsy? Did I hurt you?"

She could not think of what to say. How could she put pure energy and beauty into words? How could she tell him what she felt? Her voice quavering, she said the only thing that made sense. "Thank you."

He laughed, throwing his head back with pure animal pride. "You are very welcome, Sadie," he said, and then returned his attention to the tender spot beneath her ear.

After a moment, he smoothed her hair back from her fevered cheeks and studied her, his touch warm with shared intimacy. "I am proud to have been your teacher in this."

A second wave of chimes began, and Sarah glanced toward the sound—Ethan's pocket watch. She pulled her shirt together and tugged her trousers up. Guiltily she realized that she had not thought of finding Dicken once since Ethan began his lesson in pleasure.

"Bloody goddamned hell!" He stood and buttoned his own shirt. "I must go, Sadie. I am sorry to leave you so. Here." He dropped a sovereign on the table as he retrieved his pocket watch and thrust his arms into his jacket. "Take a coach home when you are steadier. It is still raining, and I do not want you wandering the streets in your present condition."

A sovereign? Public coaches could not cost so much. Sarah frowned. "H-how much—" she began.

He pushed his cravat into his jacket pocket and grinned. "No charge, Miss Sadie. 'Twas my pleasure. Next time, however, it will cost you dear."

He was teasing her. An unfamiliar heat crept up her cheeks. The memory of what they—*he*—had just done swept over her and she had a vague recollection of her pleas and whimperings. She recalled, too, how his hands had felt and the sensations they evoked. She could not meet his gaze.

He returned to the cot and knelt by her side. "My goodness, Miss Sadie, is that a blush?" He stroked her cheek with the back of his hand. "I do not believe I have seen you do that before."

"You are mistaken," she murmured. "I never blush."

"Hmm. Then it must be the afterglow of—"

"Stop!" she said, mortified.

His lips twitched as if he were fighting another of those crooked grins. "As you say, Sadie. Please keep safe until we can meet again. Tomorrow?"

"St. Paul's," she murmured, a thousand questions crowding in on her muddled mind. Foremost among them was whether or not she would have the nerve to face him again.

He nodded and went to the door. "I regret leaving now more than you will ever know. We will have to talk seriously about our unlikely friendship very soon. Do you understand?"

She nodded, still holding her shirt together with one hand. "You…keep safe, too, Mr. Travis."

He came back to her, lifted her chin and dropped a light kiss on her lips. "Sadie, we are past formality. Ethan. Or Travis. Even scoundrel, rake or ne'er-do-well. But there are now things I know about you that you do not know about yourself. Do not dismiss me with a formality."

Dismiss him? How would she ever think of anything *but* him, ever again? When she looked up again, he was gone.

Reality dropped with a sudden thud and tears blurred her vision as she struggled to sit up. Ethan had done her no favor in teaching her the power of passion. He had shown her what was possible. But she could never again know the sheer joy of surrendering to Ethan. Had they gone any further, he would have known the worst. And he would have been filled with disgust.

Her gaze dropped to the table and the single sovereign. Had Ethan just paid her for that incident? Had she actually become a prostitute?

Which was worse, she wondered.

Chapter Nine

Sarah did use Ethan's sovereign to take a coach back to St. Paul's, but neither Dicken nor Sticky Joe were anywhere to be found. She suspected they were at the King's Head Tavern waiting out the weather, and debated the merit of risking a meeting with the lads there. Would anyone note her in the crush of people taking refuge? Likely not. A quick inspection of her garments revealed nothing untoward.

Not so her emotions. She could not drag her thoughts away from the room above the Black Dog Tavern. Nor could she make any sense of it. She and Ethan had crossed some invisible threshold, and now she felt somehow bound to him. Nothing would ever be the same between them again. She could still see his tender smile and feel his soft persuasive touch. The very strength of her emotions frightened her. She dared not need him so. Needing him could only end disastrously.

She put those thoughts from her mind as she opened the door to the King's Head. She ducked and pushed her way through the crowd with her shoulder, knowing Dicken and Sticky Joe would be at the benches along the back wall. They were young and would have little money for ale.

Dicken's eyes grew round when he recognized her. "Gor! What're ye doin' here?"

"I think I have found one of the boys," she whispered. "We must go there at once."

Dicken studied her with a frown. "Tell us where, Sadie, an' we'll go after 'im. You look a mite bedraggled."

She could not possibly look more exhausted or unsettled than she felt, Sarah thought. But Dicken was right. She would only slow them down. "Number 8 Vauxhall Row. I cannot be certain that it is Teddy or Benjamin, but I heard a child's cry, and Whitlock had been there for a short visit."

"Number 8 Vauxhall," Sticky Joe repeated. "We'll look into it, Sadie. Then report back to you?"

"No. Whitlock is moving the children every few days. We must seize the opportunity when it presents itself."

"An' what'll we do with 'im once we got 'im?"

"Take him to the kitchen door at 11 London Square in Mayfair. Tell the cook that she should make a place for him. If she has any questions, she should speak with Lady Sarah."

"Mayfair? Blimey!" Dicken looked impressed. "That's the Hunter mansion, ain't it? D'you know them, Sadie?"

Well enough to know they'd lock her in a closet if they knew the half of what she was doing. "Better than I'd like," she admitted. She pulled her cap down over her eyes and pushed her way out of the King's Head. She would have to sneak in her window, put on her nightgown and go wake Cook to tell her to expect a knock on the kitchen door.

The storm had ended and dawn slashed a violent pink across the warehouse skylight before Ethan finished debriefing Ayers. Thank God Rob had busied himself with settling the three hostages who had returned with Ayers. The Scot would not like what their agent had to tell them.

Ethan tossed his pen down and pushed the chair back from his desk. His back ached and his eyes burned from the tedious work of recording the information he'd gleaned. He stretched, wishing himself home in bed. Better than that—back at the Black Dog, in bed with Sadie.

Just the thought of her brought a smile to his lips. What a contradiction little Miss Hunt was! He would swear that her responses to his attentions had not only surprised her, they had shocked her. She was such a delightful little Puritan for one engaged in her profession. And new to it, unless he missed his guess. All the more reason to find a way to save her from it.

"What has you so amused, Travis?" McHugh asked, leaning against the doorjamb and rubbing his eyes wearily.

"Myself, McHugh. I scarcely know myself anymore," he admitted.

"That would make two of us," McHugh sighed wearily. "Christ, Travis. The stories these hostages tell! It sets my teeth on edge. Maeve…" He shook his head and cleared his throat.

Ethan glanced down at the notes he had made. He simply could not bear to see the pain in Rob's eyes again. "Ayers says the others will never be found. Only a scant handful left in all of Algiers, if any." He paused and glanced upward at the approaching dawn again. Anywhere but at Rob's tortured eyes. "We're finished, McHugh. 'Tis time to call it a day."

A low growl built in Rob's throat. "No. No, damn it. There has to be something we missed, somewhere we didn't look."

Although he knew he was signing Rob's death warrant, Ethan could not withhold the last piece of information. "Ayers only came up with one more lead. It is whispered that a pasha from the interior desert bought several fair-skinned women to enhance his harem. Nothing about a lad."

"God's eyes!" the Scotsman cursed and slammed his doubled fist into the wall. His knuckles came away bloody. "If she's been violated…"

Ethan tightened his jaw. He knew from bitter experience

that nothing he could say would lessen his friend's self-recrimination.

"One last mission," McHugh muttered, calmer now. "I have to be sure. I have to *know* it is not her."

Ethan nodded. He knew the futility of pointing out the practical impossibility of finding the specific pasha, and then looking into the man's harem. "One last mission," he agreed. "We'd best make it count."

"I'll go myself. I know all the right people, all the right places."

"No, Rob," Ethan said. He could not even contemplate what the Algerians would do to Rob McHugh if they caught him. "They've got your name and face carved on every gate to the city, not to mention posted in every inn, tavern and brothel within five hundred miles of Algiers. You are the legend Algerian mothers frighten their children with. *'Behave, little Abdullah, or the McHugh will come for you.'"*

"I shall grow a beard."

"Excellent," Ethan grinned. "You are dark enough to carry that off, and speak the language like a native, but I've yet to meet an Arab with green eyes. They will be watching for you. Enough hostages are missing to have alerted them. Aside from that, I need you here."

"Peters can manage for me. Or I can trade duties with Ayers."

Ethan studied Rob. His friend has been drinking too much, living too much on the edge, trying too hard to push the pain away. The ghosts and the guilt had taken their toll. He could never put the past to rest until he'd seen for himself that Maeve and Hamish were lost to him forever and that there was nothing further he could do. Still, because of Kilgrew's assignment, and his connection to the Foreign Office, there was an unacceptable level of risk that someone could inform the Dey of their mission. Unless…

"Wait until this new lot is gone home. Give me another week or two while I put other matters aside and ferret out the blackmail evidence against Kilgrew. Once he is out of the picture, the risk of exposure will ease.''

''How do you propose to find the evidence?''

''I am to guard Whitlock, keep him safe, but not to pursue any evidence. Kilgrew said he would handle that end. He admitted he was 'keeping an eye' on me, but if I can recover the evidence and hand it over, Kilgrew will have no interest in me.''

''What do you think he has done to get himself blackmailed?'' Rob posed the question with a hint of relish.

Ethan tilted his chair onto the back two legs. ''An indiscretion with a married woman? I doubt Kilgrew's wife, or his paramour's husband, would wink at such a thing. Kilgrew is a bit long in the tooth to be fighting a duel at dawn.''

McHugh gave him a dark smile. ''A fortnight, Travis. Then, suicide mission or not, I'm bound for Algiers.''

As if to taunt her, fate delivered Mr. Travis to Sarah the very next evening. He was standing in the foyer of the Hobart manor at the foot of the stairs, deep in conversation with their host. He looked the very picture of haute ton, dressed in elegant, expensive black, but for his burgundy waistcoat. She was perversely pleased to see that he had not cut his hair for the occasion. She rather liked the feel of the soft clean curls at his nape. He did not see her arrive with her brothers, and she was quick to separate herself from them after promising a dance to James later.

She turned down a corridor and ran for the ladies' retiring room, desperate to delay the moment when she would have to speak to him. Completely disconcerted, she realized she had thought her chance meeting with Mr. Travis at the Websters' crush was an aberration, unlikely to ever occur again, but now she suspected she had made a total miscalculation. Was he following her?

She was playing a dangerous game of cat and mouse. It was only a matter of time before Mr. Travis asked someone about her. That prospect unsettled her. She could not imagine what he might do with such knowledge.

In the ladies' retiring room, Mrs. Hobart's maid helped her put her hair to rights and repaired a small tear in the hem of her emerald-green gown caused by her flight down the corridor. She primped before the mirror, pinching color back into her cheeks. When she began chiding herself for the depth of décolletage, she realized she cared more than she should about what Ethan Travis thought of her. Heavens! He thought she was a prostitute! Could anything be worse than that?

She squared her shoulders, lifted her chin, took a deep, bracing breath and stepped into the corridor. By the time she reached the drawing room, Annica had seen her. She was standing in a small circle with the Wednesday League and waved Sarah over to the group. Sarah gave them the happy news that Teddy was safely ensconced in Cook's apartments at Hunter Hall, and then moved on before Ethan could see her with them.

She could not risk anyone addressing her as "Lady Sarah" in front of him, so she spent the next half hour moving about the Hobart affair to keep Ethan at bay until he was alone. If he even suspected who she was, he would never help her. His begrudging confession to being enough of a gentleman to feel protective of her convinced her of that. She would just have to keep him at bay until he was alone.

Bloody Hell! The last he'd seen of Collin, he'd been standing on the staircase of Linsday Manor, warning Ethan not to darken the door ever again. Ethan hadn't been back to Wiltshire since. He'd thought London a good place to avoid such encounters. But then, he hadn't planned to mix in "polite" society. So when had his brother come to town? And why? All the possibilities for such a visit crowded into Ethan's mind.

Reconciliation? He had a brief flash of his indulgent

older brother comforting him at age eight when their mother died, teaching him to ride and helping him with his Latin lessons. In those days, he'd believed Collin was his best friend and staunchest ally. But that was before Collin had realized that Ethan was their father's favorite. The day of their father's funeral, Collin had banished Ethan without so much as the blink of an eye. No, his reason would not be reconciliation.

Money? Also not likely. As eldest, Collin inherited the bulk of the Linsday fortune while, as the younger son, Ethan had been left the equivalent of a stipend. Ethan had done quite well investing his share, and had made a respectable profit in the import business he had started to shield the search for Maeve and Hamish McHugh and the hostage recovery effort. Collin, with his larger share, must have done even better.

Social standing, then? Collin must want to carve a place for himself and his wife amongst the haute ton. They would want to come to town now and then, and prepare their children to take their places when Collin had his heir.

His gut twisted when Amelia turned and her profile, perfect and serene, was outlined against the glow of candlelight. *Amelia.* His former fiancée—now his brother's wife. She was still as beautiful, as perfect, as a portrait. Elegance defined her every move, her every gesture. Men literally stopped to watch her glide through a room or sip a cup of tea.

Amelia had sworn her eternal love and fidelity to him, but she had not reckoned with scandal. A woman of Amelia's gentle birth and standing could not withstand the censure of society. But damn if her defection didn't still sting.

To compound his hurt, she had delivered the jilt at his father's wake. Her parents were compelling her to break their engagement, she said. They would not permit her to waste herself on a man who would forever live with the stain of treason, and her duty was to obey. From that day to this, he regretted the ugliness the scandal had caused her.

For Amelia's sake then, and no matter the reason they were here now, he would leave them in peace.

He halted and prepared to retreat when Collin's aquiline nose twitched as if he smelled something rotten. "Ah, Ethan," he said, his hands clasped behind his back in military fashion. "I hoped we might run into you."

Ethan stopped a few feet away and performed a perfunctory bow. "Did you? I thought you might prefer not to."

"I'd heard you were keeping clear of society. Engaged in trade, I believe?"

"Import," Ethan permitted himself a slight smile. Collin would never understand the jest.

"Yes. Well." Collin stepped back as if afraid of close proximity to one "engaged in trade." "I would prefer to have this unpleasantness behind us."

"Are we going to be unpleasant, Collin?"

Collin's upper lip curled in a sneer. "Cannot avoid it. You are here, and have the incredible bad judgment to mix in polite company. You had best understand straightaway that Amelia and I have every intention of taking our place in society. Thus, you will have to give over your place. We can scarcely continue such uncomfortable meetings."

Though not astonished at Collin's arrogance, Ethan was highly entertained by the notion that Collin thought he would force a relationship. "Indeed?"

He turned to Amelia. A flicker of fear passed quickly over her serene countenance. Her voice, soft and musical, came to him above the faint strains of the orchestra. "Collin is simply concerned that people…society…that is, he fears that your, ah, past will prejudice the ton against us."

"Some of these people do not credit gossip. They require evidence, and in the lack of it, they think none the less of me." He turned again to face his brother. "I am afraid, Collin, that if you think I will slink away and give over London to you without a fight, you are very much mistaken.''

''We shall see who garners invitations,'' Collin sneered. ''Once I make it plain that I do not care to attend the same events as you, your entrée will end.''

Ethan froze, scarcely breathing. He would not rise to the bait and allow Collin to provoke a scene. How had he gone from leaving Amelia in peace to defying his brother?

Amelia broke the silence. ''Can we not find some grounds for agreement?''

''Do you really believe that is possible?'' he challenged.

Long black lashes swept downward to veil her china-blue eyes, then upward to meet his gaze. ''I am sorry, Ethan. I would change it if I could.''

Collin moved closer to his wife in a possessive gambit. ''We must go pay our respects to our host. You will excuse us, of course,'' Collin said. ''Do not speak to us again.''

Amelia's little gasp drew his attention, and as he turned to look at her, he glimpsed Sadie approaching. Damn the timing! If forced to introduce a demimondaine, Collin and Amelia would think him utterly debauched and beyond redemption.

Just as he warmed to that idea, James Hunter intercepted her and dragged her toward the dance floor. He could not decide whether to be relieved or disappointed.

Collin took Amelia's arm. A pained expression, quickly masked, passed over his face. ''Stay out of my way, Ethan.''

''Accustom yourself to seeing me from time to time, Collin. London is *my* town, and I'll be damned if I'll hide when I see you coming just to ease your way.''

Collin's face suffused with color, as if holding his temper in check with great difficulty. ''Your town, eh? We shall see about that.''

Ethan set his jaw in grim determination. They would see about it on Lincoln's Inn Field at dawn if Collin interfered in his private business. His reputation, his honor, his entire future depended upon that. Nothing could jeopardize that. *Nothing*. He bowed curtly before turning and striding away.

Sarah spotted Ethan with a couple she had never seen before and decided it was time to press her advantage. The man was as dark as Ethan and a fraction shorter, and the woman was…well, breathtaking. Her blond hair was gathered at the crown to fall in shining ringlets to her nape, and her eyes were the color of summer cornflowers. She tilted her head to one side, exposing the slender column of her neck as her gaze lowered demurely. Ethan appeared to be wholly distracted by her.

The burden of an introduction to this unknown couple would fall to Ethan, and a look of consternation passed over his face as he noted her approach. She perceived she was not altogether welcome and she wondered if he was trying to think how he would introduce her. The thought brought a wicked smile to her lips.

She went forward to greet him, but before she could utter a word, her brother's voice came from behind her. "Ah, here you are, Sarah! I've come to claim my dance. 'Tis a reel, and no one dances a reel as well as you," he said.

She whirled, accepted James's hand and dashed to the dance floor before Ethan could intercept them. If Ethan spoke to her in front of her brother, James would want to know where and when she had met him, and she was not prepared to answer questions about the Demon of Alsatia.

To tax her patience further, Lord Cedric Broxton was waiting on the sidelines to take her hand as the reel ended. She had thought she was safe from such a meeting since she had noted Cedric and Lady Jane Perrin with their heads together earlier. Her brother handed her over with a knowing grin. The rascal had no doubt planned this "coincidence" with Lord Cedric. "Play nice, children," he told them.

She detected a slight change in Cedric's attitude. Together with Reginald's urging to wed and James's assistance in putting them together, she began to see a pattern emerging. Oh, why had she been cursed with matchmaking brothers?

Cedric smiled and led her toward the gardens instead of the punch bowl. Thinking quickly, she fanned herself and sighed deeply. "I believe I am quite exhausted by my brother's exuberance on the dance floor, Lord Cedric. I really would like to go to the ladies' retiring room and rest for a bit."

His grip on her arm tightened fractionally and he continued to lead her toward the garden doors. "Perhaps a dose of evening air will restore you, m'dear, and you cannot put me off forever. We will have this conversation tonight, or tomorrow, or the next night. Do not doubt it, and do not think to escape it. Why, 'tis your very coyness that makes me more determined."

She halted on the threshold to the terrace. That single last sentence was enough to convince her that Lord Cedric's pursuit had gone too far. He had become too bold, too insistent. A hint of panic began a tickle at the nape of her neck. She tapped his hand with her lacquered fan. "Let loose, Lord Cedric. I do not like being manhandled."

He smiled. "You know I would never manhandle you. 'Tis that very distance you seek to put between us that intrigues me so. That, together with your reputation—"

Her reputation? She swallowed hard, the panic building. Did he mean the attack? Or had someone seen her roaming the streets after dark? How had it got out? Who told? Ethan? *Please Lord, not Ethan.*

"M-my reputation?" she squeaked. "What do you mean?"

"For virtue and decorum. You are the pattern by which all other ladies measure themselves. Now, however, you are gaining a reputation for being left upon the shelf. I would be honored to save you from spinsterhood."

Relief at not being found out tempered her anger at his tactlessness. "Lord Cedric, I am flattered by your generous offer, but can we not discuss this another time? I really am not up to it tonight."

"That has been your consistent request, Lady Sarah. 'Another time' is now. I assure you, this will not take long."

Dear Lord, he would not relent! To make things worse, Ethan Travis was coming toward them, a grim set to his jaw. Again she tried to loosen Cedric's grip on her arm, but he held fast, ignorant of Ethan's approach.

Would Ethan call her Sadie? Would he unwittingly give her away to the worst possible person? It was too late to escape!

Halting behind Lord Cedric, Ethan gave her a polite society bow and a look that said they would be discussing this later. The tension was a palpable thing and she could not breathe.

"Broxton," Ethan acknowledged. The single word fell with the force of a large stone in a still pool.

Cedric froze for a moment, then turned to face Ethan. She gasped when she saw the look that passed between them. She had never witnessed undiluted hatred before, but there could be no mistaking it now. Oddly, the thought cheered her. She did not like to think of Ethan having much in common with Cedric.

"Travis," Cedric returned the single word in kind.

She glanced between them, fear sending little tentacles down her spine and setting her nerves in a jangle. The animosity between these two had nothing to do with her. There was more at stake here than her little secrets.

"Um, I...ah," she stammered when it became apparent that Cedric had no intention of performing an introduction.

His hand on her arm loosened and she stepped away.

"Ha-have you two met?" she asked, seeking to fill the void.

"Long ago," Cedric said, his voice barely more than a

whisper. ''What are you doing here, Travis? Can you really think your presence in society is welcome?''

Ethan's dark eyes barely flickered. ''I am here by invitation, Broxton.''

Another long silence stretched between them. Finally, as if he had lost some unspoken battle, Cedric bowed and excused himself. Her relief was short-lived, however, as Ethan took her hand and led her onto the terrace. ''Sadie, I warned you to stay away from Broxton.'' He lifted her arm to inspect the reddened mark Cedric's grip had left. ''Did he injure you?''

''No. Of course not.'' She smiled, anxious to reassure him. The last thing she needed was for Ethan to defend her nonexistent honor. ''I…I bruise easily.''

He shook his head. ''You are as tough and tenacious a woman as I have ever known.''

She wished he would tell that to her brothers. Oh, no! She certainly did not! Her confusion must have shown because Ethan chuckled.

''I worry about you, Sadie. What would happen if the other ladies here discovered who and what you are. That would be very unpleasant for you. Must you come to these events?''

''Yes, I really must,'' she sighed. That much was true, and she, too, worried that the other ladies would discover who and what she really was, though not for the same reasons.

''You like danger, do you not?'' he guessed.

''It makes me feel alive,'' she admitted.

''Perhaps we can find other ways to make you feel alive,'' he whispered, leaning closer.

Sarah shivered with the memory of his hands stroking her body, coaxing those wild little tremors from her very center. His voice was as warm as a caress when he said, ''Keep well until we meet later.''

She was incapable of an answer as heat seeped into her

cheeks. He released her hand and was gone without another word.

When she stepped back into the ballroom, she saw the
exquisite blond woman Ethan was so taken with standing
alone near the foyer. Curiosity got the best of her. She
strolled toward the foyer, glanced back over her shoulder
as a ploy, and bumped into the woman.

"Oh! I beg your pardon," she gushed.

"Quite all right," the woman said, rearranging the puff
of her gold tissue sleeve.

"Are you certain? Lady Hobart's maid is a miracle
worker. If I tore—"

"No. Truly, I am fine." The woman managed a sweet
smile.

Sarah affected sudden recognition. "Did I not see you
speaking with Mr. Travis earlier? Are you a friend of his?"

"No! I mean, not…actually. That is, it has been years
since our last meeting. I…scarcely know him."

"Ah, then he is an acquaintance of your husband's?"

"Acquaintance? I would not say that, precisely."

Puzzled, Sarah began to wonder if she'd been mistaken.
"Please forgive my rudeness and allow me to introduce
myself. I am Lady Sarah Hunter, Lord Lockwood's sister."

The woman offered her hand and smiled. "Lady Linsday. You may call me Amelia. My husband is fetching my
wrap."

"Oh! Are you leaving so early? Are the entertainments
not to your liking?"

Lady Amelia shook her head and set the blond curls to
bouncing. "We are fresh in town, and Linsday has accepted too many invitations. I fear we are expected elsewhere."

"Do not give that too much thought," Sarah advised.
"'Tis doubtful your host will recall seeing you at all. The
exception, of course, would be dinner parties. Bad form to
dodge those once you accept."

Lady Amelia giggled. "I suspected as much, but Linsday is a stickler for proprieties."

"Men." Sarah shrugged sympathetically, as if the single word explained all life's mysteries. She wished subtlety was more a part of her nature, but it was beyond her at the moment. She forged ahead. "Where did your husband meet Mr. Travis?"

"*Mr.* Travis? Oh, yes. Well, we have not seen him in quite some time. There was a falling-out, you see, and...well, nothing has been the same ever since."

"Lord Linsday carries a grudge?"

"They both do, I fear. I wish there were some way to mend it, but it has gone beyond that. I suspect I am part of the problem. Eth—Mr. Travis is so intractable and Collin will not even try."

"Hmm," Sarah replied, having gleaned no real information. But she could draw some conclusions. Lord Cedric Broxton was not the only enemy Ethan had made. Add Lord Linsday to that growing list. And how could Lady Amelia be part of the problem? Had Ethan seduced her? He must have done some very questionable things to earn the title of the Demon of Alsatia. Odd, how she had never really wondered what Ethan might be capable of. By reputation, everything.

"And you, Lady Sarah? How do you know Ethan Travis?"

She waved her fan in a vague arc. "Oh, I cannot recall. I believe one of my brothers must have introduced us."

"How very liberal of them. What was your impression?"

What an odd question. "I found him quite agreeable," she said. "Very pleasant, indeed."

"Did...did you dance?"

"Dance? Why, no. Does he dance well?"

"Quite well," Lady Amelia admitted in a soft sigh. "I recollect his skill at the waltz, in particular. But it has been a very long time since we...waltzed."

"The waltz," Sarah mused, an unfamiliar annoyance rising in her. "I shall have to remember that, should he ever ask."

"Oh, here is Collin now." Lady Amelia said with a sweet blush when she saw her husband take her wrap from a footman.

"Do have a pleasant evening, Lady Linsday," Sarah said. "We shall run into one another again, now that you are in town."

Lady Amelia gave her a smile that would dazzle every single one of her brothers and three quarters of the ton. "I should like to introduce you to my husband when next we meet."

"And I should be delighted." Sarah distanced herself from the couple and watched Lord Linsday drape a brilliant blue cloak affectionately over Amelia's shoulders. The color matched her eyes to perfection, no doubt. Not only was she beautiful and fashionable, she was sweet-natured and well-mannered. And she had waltzed with Ethan.

Sarah disliked her. Intensely.

Chapter Ten

Hidden in the shadow of a chimney on the opposite side of the lane, Ethan watched Sadie slip down a row of shingles to reach the narrow edge of the roof opposite him. He breathed relief when her boot caught the gutter and held.

So, these were the chances she took when he was not with her! She could have plummeted to the cobblestones below. She was too inexperienced to negotiate such a risky tactic safely. He wondered at the cause of her recklessness, and how she could have so little regard for her own safety.

Below, Whitlock rounded a corner, and she crossed over a steeply pitched roof to keep sight of him. When her quarry entered a tavern, Sadie edged to an iron drainpipe and shinnied down to the alley below, apparently deciding to wait on the ground after her close call on the rain-slick shingles. His anxiety eased and he sank into a squat, resting his weight on the balls of his feet. He suspected they would have upward of a quarter of an hour before Whitlock was on the move again.

Sadie crouched beneath a window, using a rain barrel to shield her from view. She hugged herself for warmth as the slow drizzle continued. Ethan watched for any sign that she would give up, go home or seek shelter, but she was persistent. Driven. If she was this committed to a mere exercise, then the best of the Bow Street Runners, Francis

Renquist, would have got himself a dedicated "follower" when she was finally trained.

But there was another job for which Ethan would like to train little Sadie. Ever since their interlude at the Black Dog Tavern, he had been puzzling how to make Sadie give up her various professions in favor of just one. His mistress.

He relished her responses to his handling, and damned near drowned in the sultry depths of her eyes. He could still see the tears sparkling on her lashes and feel the weight of surrender in every line of her sweet body. He knew her as no other ever had, yet he did not know her at all.

And that was just one more cause for regret! When Sadie surrendered, she surrendered everything. Her entire being had been in his hands. But now it was eating him up inside to know that she would take her new knowledge, along with her sweetly yielding body, to innumerable nameless, faceless men. The thought that she might experience that passion with another man made his stomach clench.

He must find a solution before that happened. There had to be some way to prevent any further degradation to her body and spirit, and to salvage her pride at the same time.

He shifted his weight slightly, easing a cramp in his thigh. An uneasy feeling raised the fine hairs on the back of his neck. He had learned to trust his years of experience in Algiers and glanced around, careful to make no detectable move. No sign, no trace, betrayed another presence. Perhaps he'd been mistaken. He glanced back to Sadie, still in a crouch, still focused on the tavern across the street. Still an enigma.

He had waited at St. Paul's a full half hour. He thought she'd been detained by an assignation with some simpering dandy she had met at the Hobart ball. But no—he'd found her, one step ahead, following Harold Whitlock without him. Did she think she no longer needed him?

From the corner of his eye, he caught another stealthy movement. There, in the alley below, a dark figure was inching toward Sadie's back. No sound betrayed the intruder, and Ethan hesitated, wondering if it could be Dicken or Joe, playing some cat-and-mouse game of surprise and pounce.

Another critical moment or two passed until Ethan realized that neither Dicken nor Joe were equal to the intruder's bulk. Whoever was stalking Sadie, it was not a friend.

He slid to the edge of the roof on his stomach, caught the eave as he went over and swung outward to drop with a controlled, bone-jarring force to the cobblestones. In that fraction of a second, Sadie turned to find the source of the noise and the intruder swung a small cudgel.

Sadie crumpled to a shapeless heap. Ethan staggered to his feet, and the intruder dashed for the street with a glance over his shoulder at Ethan.

Bloody hell! Here it was—the first sign that Kilgrew had been right to worry that Whitlock needed guarding. Had Sadie not stumbled into this trap, it would be Whitlock on the cobblestones. This, then, was what he was honor bound to do. Guard Harold Whitlock. He made a mad dash to the street and caught a glance of the intruder disappearing around a corner.

Sarah became aware of the sound of liquid being poured into a glass and the rustle of cloth as someone sat nearby. Then came the realization that she was lying on something wonderfully soft and warm, and that it smelled of Ethan. Lime and expensive soap. She smiled as the picture of Ethan stole into her mind.

"Sadie?" The voice was hushed, tentative.

"Mmm," she murmured. She stirred and her hand grazed crisp linen sheets. Bed. She was on a bed that smelled of Ethan!

Her eyes flew open and she sat up so quickly her head

spun. Dim light from a fireplace flickered unnaturally bright and she winced, closing her eyes and falling back onto the pillows. The mattress beside her dipped with the weight of another person, and a cool hand smoothed the hair back from her forehead.

She sorted through what she'd seen in the scant second her eyes were open. A dark room lit by a fireplace, wood-paneled walls, masculine dark blue draperies and bed hangings, a deep chair drawn close to the bed, and…Ethan Travis.

He had looked tense, his forehead creased with anxiety. Now his hand skimmed over the crown of her head and found a spot exquisitely tender to his touch. "Thank God you turned in time. Do you have a headache?"

She had to think about that for a moment. The sudden light had hurt her eyes but, aside from the tender spot, she could not detect a headache. Cautiously she opened her eyes again. "N-no. I am a little bewildered. I…I was following Mr. Whitlock, and then I heard something—someone—behind me. The rest is a blur. I cannot recall…"

"I did not see him until it was too late to prevent it."

She pushed herself up again. "Who was it?"

Ethan's voice dropped to a bone-chilling cold. "I will find out, and put an end to his interference."

Sarah did not think he meant to reason with the man. She shivered and rubbed her arms against the imagined cold. She noted that her jacket was thrown over a chair next to the fire and her boots were standing on the hearth to dry.

She stood and stumbled to the window. It was raining still, and the sky was a dark leaden-gray. She glanced around for a clock and found one on the fireplace mantel. Quarter past five o'clock! If she did not hurry, she would meet her brothers as they returned from the night's entertainments. When she turned back to look at Ethan, he was watching her intently.

"I waited." His voice was more a question than a reproach.

Her heart did a quick little skip as she looked at him. In shirtsleeves, an open leather vest and dark brown trousers, he was the picture of relaxed masculinity. A shock of chestnut hair fell over his forehead and dark stubble shadowed his cheeks. He was, in that moment, the most beautiful man she'd ever seen. And he wanted to know why she had not met him at St. Paul's. What could she say? That she was afraid she would fall into his arms? That following Harold Whitlock had become less of a threat than the danger of her nights with him? "I was late. I assumed you would have gone on without me, Mr. Travis."

"Mr. Travis? Are we back to that?" he asked, his voice heavy with angry sarcasm. He stood and poured a glass of wine.

"No," she said, refusing the glass. "I must go now. I—"

"Do not lie to me, Miss Hunt. I have known you long enough to know that your nights are your own."

"The night is gone. 'Tis morning."

He lifted her hand and wrapped it around the glass of wine. "You are not steady, and it is still raining."

In truth, her knees were a little wobbly. She took the glass and knelt by the hearth. "I do not mean to seem ungrateful, Mr. Travis, but I am feeling somewhat awkward at the moment. I have never been in a man's bedchamber before."

"Only rented rooms and whatever private spots are convenient at the moment? Alleys? Stables? Back rooms?"

Sarah turned to face him, momentarily stunned by his bald accusation. Dear Lord! She'd forgotten her guise and nearly given herself away! "Yes," she covered. "I...I am not the sort of girl one takes home, am I?"

The anger seemed to drain out of him. "And yet here you are," he said, coming toward her.

"Y-yes. Here I am."

"In my home."

His home. The thought unsettled her when she realized she must be in his bedchamber. "I shall try to behave myself," she said, taking a nervous swallow of her wine. A small droplet clung to her lower lip.

He knelt beside her and smiled. "Allow me to assist you." Leaning forward, he kissed her, paying extraordinary attention to the little droplet. "I swear 'tis sweeter from your lips than from any decanter, Miss Hunt," he murmured.

She could not catch the little moan that escaped her, and when he pressed her back on the deep rug she did not have the will to resist. He cupped the back of her head in his palm to cushion her bump, exquisitely gentle as always.

"Will you yield?" he asked, trailing kisses from a point behind her ear to the hollow of her throat.

Would she yield? Oh, how sweet the thought! But she could not. Dawn was within a heartbeat. She had to go. To her horror, she realized that she did not even know how far she was from Hunter Hall! "I...I must go," she insisted again, pressing halfheartedly against his chest.

"Not yet, Sadie," he whispered tantalizingly in her ear.

The unshaven stubble of his beard abraded her cheek. Oh, what a dark and murky heart she had, obscuring both reason and good sense, leaving only desire in its wake. She *wanted* to stay. She *wanted* to yield as she'd done the night before. God help her, she wanted...*him!*

"I want—" she began. But she could not say it. She was too afraid of what those words would bring. She could not change the pattern of her life on nothing more substantial than the sound of Ethan's voice or the promise of unknown pleasure.

He must have sensed her hesitation because he began to tell her what *he* wanted. "I want you naked in my bed, your arms out to welcome me." He nibbled one earlobe. "I want you writhing in ecstasy beneath me. I want to

hear your soft voice calling my name, begging for more."
His voice, a hot whisper, vibrated along her nerves and
awakened the same sweet ache in her middle that she'd
felt last night. "I want to be deep inside you, feeling you
close around me, quivering with the sweetness of your
release." One hand traced a light, teasing line across her
breast and her nipple firmed in response.

Sudden panic set in. Fear that had nothing to do with
reason brought her upright, tugging the gap of her shirt
closed. "No! No, I cannot. I must go. It will be light
soon."

He sat up and watched her put her clothing to rights. "I
wish to God I knew what terror dawn holds for you, Sadie.
Stay. Be my mistress. If you will not, then be my cook or
my housekeeper. I will keep you safe from whatever
threatens you. I care about you, little Miss Hunt."

Fighting tears, she staggered to her feet. Why was she
so afraid? Ethan would not hurt her. Not deliberately. She
was as certain of that as she was that the sun would rise,
but her fears controlled her, not reason. Those fears were
her dearest allies now, more comfortable and safe than the
unknown risk of loving. "I…I cannot explain, Ethan. I
simply cannot."

He stood and went to the window as if searching for the
intrusive dawn. Her sense of loss was overwhelming, and
she was nearly sobbing by the time she pulled her boots
on and shrugged into the woolen jacket.

"Ethan," she began.

"No explanations necessary, Sadie," he said, turning to
her, his face a calm mask and an air of firm resolve surrounding him like a cloak.

There was nothing she could say—no way to make up
to him for her inability to overcome her own fears, her
own inadequacy. The least she could do was set his mind
at ease on one point. "It is not you, Ethan," she said
before slipping through his bedroom door.

* * *

From his vantage behind the carriage house, Ethan watched Sadie climb a rose trellis rising from the garden to the full height of the four-story chimney. At the second floor, she stepped onto a ledge and inched toward an open window.

Sadie had been in such a desperate rush on her way home that she had not bothered to look over her shoulder—not that she would have seen him if she had. He had been very careful about that. Not even the slightest twinge of guilt at his tactic bothered him. He had known for some time that Sadie Hunt was not what she seemed. It simply hadn't mattered before tonight. Now, with her between him and Whitlock, it mattered.

The sound of hooves clattering on the cobblestones as they turned off the street and proceeded down the mews propelled her through the window with barely a glance over her shoulder. The coach drew up at the carriage house behind the mansion and two men stepped out, leaving their driver to stable the horses.

He edged along the opposite side of a boxwood hedge in an effort to hear their conversation.

"Did you see that, Reggie?" the younger of the two said. "I swear I saw someone going in Sarah's window."

Ethan glanced back up at the window. All that remained of Sadie's assent was a lace curtain billowing in the window.

"Absurd," the other man said. "'Twas just that lace folderol. She always sleeps with her window open. Likes the fresh air, she says. Helps her headaches, poor dear."

"Must she leave it open so wide? There's a chill in the air. She'll catch her death."

"I shall speak to her about it, Charlie, but I do not expect our sister to change her ways. You know how delicate her health is, and we have all spoilt her rather badly."

The younger man chortled. "I do not envy you trying to find a man she'll wed. And I shall miss her once she's wed and gone. She brings a certain grace and refinement to our lives that will be lacking without the presence of a woman.''

The eldest nodded. ''I've solved the first problem, Charlie. We shall host a fete at which we shall have a little surprise for our Sarah.'' The conversation grew faint as they made their way to the terrace doors.

Ethan frowned, gazing again at the second-story window with a sinking feeling. He closed his eyes and pinched the bridge of his nose as facts began to fall into place.

Sadie—a pet name for Sarah. Lockwood's fondness for Sadie at the Carter soiree. Sadie's slip of the name ''Reggie.''

Sadie, then, must be Lady Sarah Hunter, the most elusive of the haute ton's favored few. The eagerly pursued and never-caught heiress. Indeed, she was the possessor of one of the most blameless, pristine reputations in England. And only he knew that she was not all that she seemed.

What was her game? The night prowling, the courting of danger, the inexplicable appearances and disappearances? Despite her recklessness, he was certain she had a purpose. But what was that purpose, and what could possibly drive her to take such extraordinary risks?

Using him had not been too difficult a task. He'd been too willing to act the fool. The way she dressed and acted, the way she refused his offer to buy her services. It was clear now that Sadie Hunt could not be a prostitute. Not in this life or any other. Christ! Why hadn't he seen it before? But, innocent or not, she had wanted him in that room above the Black Dog Tavern. There could be no mistake about that, at least.

He quickly squelched a flash of guilt at having handled a noble-born woman as he'd handled her. After all was said and done, *she* had used *him.* A sharp stab of betrayal ran through him, then the cynicism of experience took hold. Well, why not use him? Hadn't Kilgrew? Hadn't his brother?

Hadn't Amelia?

He ran his fingers through his hair and sighed as the fragile threads of newborn hope frayed and snapped. *It is not you, Ethan.* Was it not, indeed? If not him, then who?

Oh, yes. It was him. And he would find a fitting way to make Lady Sarah Hunter pay.

Chapter Eleven

Sarah hurried down the wide staircase to the first floor as the tall grandfather clock struck nine times. Her brothers were rarely awake this early, but the message brought by Sylvie had sounded urgent. Reggie must see her at once.

She said a quick prayer that he and Charles had not caught sight of her diving into her bedroom window. Last night had been too close a call. She would have to make a concerted effort to be home no later than half past four in the future.

And now she had another worry. Ethan's house was just around the corner from the Aubervilles and scarcely five blocks from Hunter Hall. When had he become a neighbor? It had to be a recent development since she had managed to avoid encountering him during the day. Or had he been near to her all along, merely in the background? The thought that he was more a part of her circle than she had suspected unsettled her.

Turning right off the foyer, she headed for the library— Reggie's private sanctum. Her heart grew cold when another possibility occurred to her. Had one of her brothers indulged their quick tempers and got in an ill-advised duel at dawn? She could not bear to think of one of them hurt. She paused with her hand lifted to knock on the library door.

"Come in, Sarah," Reggie called, as if he could see through doors. His voice was tired.

"Reggie, dearling," she said as she swung the door open, "is something amiss?"

He was sitting at his desk, a sheaf of papers in front of him, and he looked as if he hadn't yet been to bed. She clasped her hands tightly in front of her. *Please, please God, do not let it be one of my brothers.*

"Sit down, Sadie." Reggie gestured at a stiff little chair in front of his desk.

Sadie. He hadn't called her that in years. Not since she was twelve and skinned her knee jumping from a swing. She perched on the edge of the chair, braced for bad news. Tears stung the backs of her eyes. "Say it quickly, Reggie."

He shrugged, dropped his pen on a stack of papers and leaned back in his chair. "I need your help with a fete."

She blinked. "Fete? This is about a fete?"

"What else?" he asked.

She giggled with relief. "What else, indeed?"

"Father has been gone a year now, and 'tis time we began paying back our invitations. Society has been quite patient with the Hunters. I would not have them thinking us shirkers."

"Of course not," she agreed. "How can I help?"

"You will be my hostess," he announced, just as if he were bestowing some great honor.

"I have little experience in that, Reggie. I only served once for Papa before he—"

"I know, sweetling, but Lady Auberville will help you once her party is over."

Sarah recalled that the Auberville grand ball was barely five days away. The real problem was her search for Benjamin, and her social obligations. "Nica is always helpful," she hedged, trying to organize her mind. "What sort of fete, Reggie? Shall we start small with an intimate dinner party?"

"Not a crush, m'dear, but larger than a dinner party. Perhaps a buffet? An orchestra for dancing. I should think…what, two hundred and fifty?"

"Two hundred and fifty?" She gulped. "I…suppose we could open the summerhouse in the gardens and string lanterns. That, in addition to the dining room, ballroom—"

"Yes, yes. I shall leave that all to you," Reggie interrupted. "How soon can you make the arrangements?"

"A month would allow sufficient time—"

"Sooner."

She frowned at the urgency in his voice. "How much sooner, Reggie? There are things I simply cannot rush. Arranging for an orchestra, ordering invitations, flowers, wine and food, hiring additional staff—"

Her brother's handsome face wrinkled in disgust. "S'blood," he murmured. "I had no idea. If we simplified, could we move the date up?"

"My goodness! You *are* anxious. Is there a reason? Mayhap a female reason? Are you set to court, Reggie?" she teased.

He flushed and changed the subject. "Have you thought 'pon what we discussed? You know that Cedric—"

"No," she hedged. "And I shan't have time if we're to have a fete. One thing at a time, Reggie. Which is most important at the moment?"

He sat forward, resting his arms on the desk. "Our social responsibilities. I dislike owing invitations to half the ton."

"Well then, give me a week and we shall do this up red! 'Tis short notice, but I've no doubt we shall draw a crowd."

"I'm counting upon that," Reggie murmured under his breath.

The shop bell above the door rang as Sarah let herself into Madame Marie's exclusive dress shop. A seamstress came from a back room and dropped a little curtsy. "Good afternoon, Lady Sarah. Lady Annica is with Madame."

Sarah followed the girl to a large fitting room. Annica was just redressing as Sarah opened the door and stepped in. "I am so glad you've arrived," Annica said. "Charity and Grace are due soon, and I feared you'd miss your appointment."

"*Oui,*" Madame said. "Your gown for Lady Auberville's ball is 'anging behind the screen. 'Urry, milady, before the others arrive, eh? Shall I send for the 'elp?"

"No, Madame. I can manage," Sarah said, tossing her reticule and bonnet aside. She disliked having strangers see her naked, nor did she want unfamiliar hands touching her. She supposed that was just one more way in which the attack, that single event, influenced her everyday decisions. It was her fear again. The bloody stupid fear that controlled her life!

She undressed quickly, talking over the screen to bring Annica up-to-date as she did. "Reggie wants to host a fete in ten days. Will you help, Nica?"

"I should love to," Annica called over the screen. "I am delighted that the Hunters are coming out of mourning. This will definitely be perceived as good news to half the marriageable men in London."

"You exaggerate," Sarah chuckled. "And you know that will go nowhere. But do you think I should invite the Whitlocks?"

"Indeed! Let Mr. Whitlock think he is advancing in society. 'Twill play into his vanity and keep Mrs. Whitlock safe a little longer."

Sarah slipped her new gown over her head, being careful of the few remaining pins. The fabric billowed to the floor in a graceful drape, the light silk as cool and soft as a caress against her skin. When she came around the dressing screen and stepped onto the stool, Annica tilted her head and sighed.

"Oh, Sarah! That color! The shade matches your eyes exactly. You must wear more of it."

"There! *C'est vraie!* Did I not tell you, chérie?" Madame said, pinning the hem quickly and allowing for a small train in back. She stood and walked around Sarah, evaluating her work. "I think…yes, the décolletage should be lower—*oui?*"

Sarah looked down at the dark violet, a shade so deep it was nearly plum. "Oh, I do not think—" but a few quick snips of Madame's scissors made disagreement impossible.

Madame stepped back, a triumphant smile on her face. "*Voilà!* I trim with ribbon, yes? And embroider green silk leaves? At Lady Annica's ball you will outshine everyone, little Lady Sarah. Now put on your clothes, eh?"

Sarah stepped down from the stool and ducked behind the dressing screen. When she heard the door close, she whispered, "Nica, how can I wear that dress now? I will feel so…so exposed. And Reggie—"

"Reggie will be very much encouraged that you are baiting the hook, Sarah. You looked stunning. Were I a man…"

A little frisson of tension ran up her spine. Making a quick decision, she sat beside Annica and forged into unknown territory. "Nica, I was wondering if…well, Mama died when I was very young, and—"

"Ah, I see," Annica nodded. Her lips curved in a slight smile and she studied the cuticles of her left hand intently. "Of course, Sarah. You may ask me anything."

"Well, ah, I wondered if…men—I mean marriage—is entirely distasteful. I know you avoided it as long as you could, but you seem quite content now that 'tis done."

The color in Annica's cheeks deepened. "Actually, Sarah, it is not distasteful in the least." She looked up, meeting Sarah's gaze. "Is Reggie pressing you to marry again?"

"I must know, for my own peace of mind, whether the

marriage act is painful and degrading every time, or if one becomes used to it. Or if it simply comes to matter less."

Annica's eyes widened. "I should have guessed what you've been thinking! I am so sorry I did not set your mind at ease sooner." The sound of the shop bell followed by happy chatter reached them. Annica leaned forward and lowered her voice. "Sarah, I actually look forward to my private time with Auberville. He is most gentle and kind, and has never caused me the least little pain or discomfort. To the contrary, he…he brings me great joy."

She glanced over her shoulder toward the door and rushed on. "What Farmingdale and the others did to you is not what husbands and wives do. But, that said, I cannot imagine ever, ah, lying with anyone but Auberville. I collect you must bear affection for the man for it to be truly enjoyable."

Enjoyable? The best she had hoped for was that she could endure such an encounter without panicking. And yet…and yet Ethan had done things to her that set her every nerve to quivering, and left her yearning vaguely for more. Could Annica be right? Could there be enjoyment in such circumstances?

Ethan waited patiently while Sarah danced a quadrille with his grace, the Duke of Dunsmore, attempting to fully comprehend the enormity of her lies. After his discovery last night, his every instinct demanded retribution. What would satisfy his pride? Public exposure? A cautionary word to her brother? Private or public denouncement?

Her willow-green gown flared at the hem as she made a quick turn and her rose-tinted lips curved in a smile. Black lashes swept cheeks flushed with excitement, and the remarkable violet eyes sparkled in the candlelight. Tendrils of rich brown hair escaped the green ribbon and curled around her face.

He envisioned her as she'd been last night, vulnerable and innocent as she lay in his bed. He had actually thought he could offer her his protection, the security of a safe, warm place to live, and the comfort of affection. And all along, she'd had a reputation and position in society that put her above his reach. His pride had taken some bitter blows these past few years, but this was the worst—Sarah had been slumming when she'd come to him.

The dance ended and he watched as she dropped a chaste kiss on his grace's weathered cheek. Lord Nigel grinned widely and returned the favor before removing a handkerchief from his vest pocket and mopping his brow. Had he not known her for the deceitful little chit she was, he'd have sworn Sarah was genuinely fond of the old man.

Dunsmore said something and she laughed, the same genuine, unaffected amusement that had first drawn him in the King's Head Tavern, and he knew he could not ruin her, or expose her deceits. Ah, but he could, and would, have his pound of flesh. 'Twas only fair, after all.

His patience paid off when she bobbed a quick curtsy and turned toward the hallway in the direction of the ladies' retiring room. He moved from the shadows in a line to cut her off. When he took her arm and pulled her into a curtained alcove, she gasped in surprise. Breathless, she searched his face for a clue as to his intent.

"Sadie," he whispered, keeping his expression completely neutral, "I watched you with Dunsmore. You could be hanged if you put your hand in his pocket."

She looked momentarily confused, then a flicker of chagrin crossed her features. "And you, Mr. Travis, must be very careful at these soirees. Think how embarrassed you will be if you are caught talking to the likes of me."

How deftly she had turned the tables on him! *Well done, Sarah,* he silently acknowledged. He responded, "And what *are* 'the likes of you'?"

"I, ah." She glanced over her shoulder. "You know what I am, Mr. Travis. Do not ask me to speak it aloud."

He grinned, enjoying her discomfort. "Ask one of your...patrons to introduce us. Once that formality has been breached, we may be seen to talk without causing comment.''

Chagrin played across that lovely face. "If we are seen together, and should anyone ask you, who shall you say I am? An acquaintance of his grace, Lord Dunsmore? A light skirt? A common demimondaine?''

"Is that not how Dunsmore and the others know you?'' He could not help but grin when he saw the trapped look cross her face. He could afford to show mercy now that he'd caused her considerable discomfort, but no. She was still deep in her lie, and he had just begun.

The little baggage frowned. "Then how shall I tell others that I know you?''

"Who will ask, Sadie?'' He shrugged. "Does anyone think you are aught but what you are?''

"Well…''

"Have you assumed a false name for society?''

"They do not know me as…Sadie Hunt,'' she admitted.

"Suppose you tell me what story you have cast about, and I will swear to it,'' he offered.

Her cheeks infused with a deep pink, and she gazed at her slippers rather keenly. "I, um, think we should avoid one another in public, Mr. Travis. That is the best way to forestall any awkward questions.''

Oh, of course she would prefer that. How could she ever explain her relationship with the Demon of Alsatia to her haute ton friends, let alone her hotheaded brothers? He gave her a wicked smile. "If you wish, Miss Hunt.''

Ah, but he had no intention of abandoning her to her own devices on her nightly prowls. He had yet to discover what she was up to, and he was still too much of a gentleman to ignore the risk that she would fall victim to another cudgel-wielding villain. He was likely one that Kilgrew had hired to find Whitlock's blackmail evidence. He had no doubt that Kilgrew's men would be every bit as ruthless as his. Yes, he acknowledged with a sigh, he was still obliged to save Sarah—even from herself. He released her arm and stepped back, allowing her room to escape. "I shall expect to see you tonight at half past two. Our usual place?"

Her head popped up, and her pansy eyes were filled with gratitude. "Yes, thank you. I feared, after last night, that you would not want to help me ever again."

"What?" He laughed. "Did you think me so conceited a lout that a simple refusal would cause me to withdraw my friendship? We've been through that before, Sadie."

"You are a better friend than I deserve," she said.

She did not know the half of it, he thought. He could not resist one final gibe. "I enjoy your company more than any of these brainless little society creatures. I've yet to meet one worth common table salt."

She gave him a weak smile before stepping out of the alcove and continuing down the corridor.

Dressed in Andrew's castoffs, Sarah sat hunched over her tankard of ale in a dark corner of the King's Head Tavern. Mr. Renquist droned on about the dangers of capering abroad dressed as a boy. As if she did not know the danger well enough after being knocked on the head last night! She could not even think of it without a stab of fear slicing through her.

Ethan was making her very nervous, too. Something had changed. His manner at the ball earlier had been cooler, less concerned. Challenging. She was feeling edgy, almost bubbling with anxiety. Like a moth flirting with flame, she was drawn to Ethan, compelled beyond reason to come closer, yet fearing it would be the end of her. *And not caring!* Her heartbeat sped as she remembered his kiss—the softness of his lips, the sweet urging of his tongue, the heat of his breath on her skin as he dropped his attention to her neck, her throat...

She was terrified of taking the risk of loving Ethan, unwilling to chance her hard-won peace and self-confidence. And yet...and yet she knew that she'd come to an end of some sort. She dared not go forward, but she had gone too far to turn back. It was time to make a decision.

"…and furthermore, you are in over your head. You cannot know how dangerous this is."

Sarah came back to the conversation with a guilty start. Any thought of telling Mr. Renquist that she'd been hit over the head was quickly discarded. She raised her eyes from her tankard and sighed. "I understand your apprehension, sir, but I am seldom alone. Dicken and Joe are never far, and Mr. Tr—that is, there are others who are looking out for me."

"Others?" Francis Renquist's eyes narrowed.

"People who are expert in this sort of thing."

"*I* am expert in this sort of thing. Leave this investigation to me, Lady Sarah, before disaster overtakes you."

Sarah blinked in consternation. "Of course, but…" Disclosing Ethan's identity would only provoke another long lecture. "I simply want to assure you that I am not alone."

Renquist lowered his brows in a scowl. "What have you done, milady? Who have you got yourself mixed up with?"

She suppressed her anxiety and refused to meet his gaze. "I have been very careful, Mr. Renquist. I offer as proof the fact that we have recovered two of the Whitlock children. Only Benjamin's whereabouts remain unknown. Time is our enemy. Mr. Whitlock will discover that Araminta and Teddy are missing and, when he does, he will seize Benjamin and hide him where he will never be found. Thus we must find Benjamin at once."

"The more I learn, the less I like it. This Whitlock is a villain and has got himself involved in some nasty business." He paused as if to measure her determination and sighed, abandoning his lecture. "I have one lead. One of my men reports that a workhouse in Cheapside has got a few new lads. He is looking into the matter."

She was almost afraid to hope. "I pray he is there and

safe. Meantime, I shall continue my strategy of following Mr. Whitlock. That has worked rather well.''

Mr. Renquist glanced over his shoulder and then leaned forward, dropping his voice in earnest. ''You are putting yourself in disaster's path.''

''If I could recover Benjamin without waiting for Whitlock to lead me to him I would do so, but your information could take too long. Can you not see that the situation is critical?''

''Aye, critical indeed. And that is why you must stay out of it.''

''Where is this workhouse, Mr. Renquist? Do you have an address?''

''Not yet. I'll send word to you once I have the details.''

She heard a church bell chime twice. She needed to meet Ethan soon and would have to run the whole way if she could not catch a passing coach. No time for further argument. ''When shall we meet again, Mr. Renquist?''

''I need a few days to gather the necessary information and verify the report. I will send for you if I have news sooner.''

''A few days?'' Her heart dropped. She could not wait that long to search for Benjamin. Despite the danger, she would have to proceed on her own. She nodded. ''Day after tomorrow. Covent Garden at three in the afternoon. By the flower market.''

''Aye, Lady Sarah. Be careful until then.''

Ethan watched Sarah take the wide steps of the west porch two at a time. She glanced around quickly, missing him in the shadows, and ducked behind a column on the far right. She bent slightly to peer around the base and her snug trousers molded to her decidedly feminine bottom. Ethan's breath caught in a soft groan. Knowing who she was may have put her out of his reach, but it couldn't stop him from growing tight with need. He cursed himself and struggled for self-control.

She fidgeted, obviously waiting for him. If she had any sense at all, she would be nervous from the attack last night. She drew her jacket tighter and shivered in the damp night air, and he wondered what would drive a pampered society darling to masquerade as a boy and brave the elements to prowl London streets? How far was she willing to go to gain her ends?

Ah, but the real meat of the matter was this—how many lies would she tell to keep her secret, and were there any risks she would not take? Any lengths to which she would not go?

The answer to that question was almost as important to him as repaying his debt to Lord Kilgrew and putting that part of his life behind him. Lady Sarah Hunter would not give him satisfaction between the sheets, but she would damn well give him satisfaction in the answers to those questions.

He straightened and took a deep breath, a plan forming in his mind as he stepped out of the shadows and went toward her.

The man who was currently following their quarry had just sent word that Whitlock was comfortably ensconced at a corner table at Ye Olde Cheshire Cheese.

"Ready?" he asked with a note of challenge in his voice. "My man has located our target in Holburn."

She turned, the excitement of the chase dancing in her eyes, and nodded. "Lay on, Macduff."

She really was incorrigible.

He set a brutal pace, knowing she would have difficulty keeping up. She did not complain, but he slowed slightly when he heard her footsteps falling farther behind. He did not want to make this easy for her, but neither did he want to lose her rounding some dark corner.

Deciding on a shortcut, he headed down a narrow alley and smiled when he saw a stone wall. Ah, this would confound his little dilettante. He hitched himself up and swung his legs over the wall. Sarah's dismayed face was the last thing he saw as he dropped to the street on the other side.

Grinning, he whispered, "C'mon, Sadie. Whitlock will leave before we get there."

After a moment of scuffling, he heard her reply. "I cannot reach. And I cannot swing my legs over."

He leaned against the wall, laughing silently. When he could trust his voice, he replied, "I will meet you half-way." He pulled himself up to the top again and reached one hand down to Sarah. "Grab hold, Sadie. You will have to learn this technique if you are going to work for Mr. Renquist."

She reached up and put her hand in his. The warmth and softness of her flesh caused him a momentary twinge of conscience, quickly ignored. He gripped her wrist, not trusting the strength of her hand, and pulled her up until she was able to straddle the wall. He dropped to the street and turned to her.

Fearless. That's what she was. She was braced to push off from the wall and follow him. She'd break her ankle landing on the cobblestones from such a height. He moved to block her and cushion her fall and she fell directly into his arms. He allowed her to slide slowly down the length of his body. Her little gasp told him she was as stirred by the experience as he. Her eyes closed as she lifted her lips, inviting—nay, *expecting*—a kiss.

Gaining control over his own baser instincts, he bent his head to within inches of hers and whispered, "Having fun, Sadie?" He knew *he* was enjoying having the advantage for once.

The long lashes fluttered open. "You are a difficult task maker tonight."

"You did not think 'following' would be all rooftops, alleys and taverns, did you? We've barely scratched the surface of what you need to learn."

"H-how much more?" she whispered, her lips still inches from his.

"There are fences, walls, thoroughfares, crowds, day-light and more. Can you ride astraddle? Hire a coach? Have you ever entered a gaming hell, an opium den, a bawdy house?" He paused meaningfully. "Oh, of course you have been in a bawdy house, but it looks different from the customer's side. I should think you would not be able to hire a woman, but then there is much I do not know about you, eh?"

Sarah gasped and stepped back from the circle of his arms. Her face registered a quick flash of fear before it smoothed over again. "Lay on," she said.

Although he'd deliberately inspired it, the knowledge that she feared him angered him. He turned away and set off for Ye Olde Cheshire Cheese at the same relentless pace, listening for her footfalls behind him.

Chapter Twelve

Ye Olde Cheshire Cheese! Dear Lord! She glanced up at the sign and then at Ethan as he reached to open the door. "I...I cannot go in," she said. What if Reggie was inside?

He shrugged. "Then wait out here. Try to find shelter. Looks like rain." He stepped inside.

Sarah peered over her shoulder and shivered. The air had grown heavy and humid and she pulled her jacket collar up to shield her neck against the wind. A spike of fear stabbed through her when she heard a rustling sound from around the corner. Anxiety sent her across the threshold and into the dim interior on Ethan's heels.

His lips twitched suspiciously and he nodded toward a table near the fireplace. "There's our man. Find a place where we can watch him. I'll get us a bit o' the barley."

She headed for the back of the main room where an empty table was pushed against the wall. Sitting facing the door, she pulled her cap a little lower to hide her features and then studied the room. Several smaller rooms adjoined the main room, and a corridor led toward the rear of the establishment. There were, perhaps, thirty men in various states of inebriation at tables and on benches along the walls or in front of the fire. None of them were her brothers.

Breathing a little easier, Sarah turned her attention to

Harold Whitlock. His hunched posture indicated that he was either drugged or drunk. He spoke in a slurred mumble to a man who sat with his back to Sarah. There was something familiar in the set of the man's shoulders. Where had she seen that before?

Ethan joined her, carrying two overfilled tankards. "The publican says he has been drinking steadily. Who is he with?"

She shook her head. "He has not turned. I believe they are arguing."

"Do you?" Ethan asked, interest quirking one eyebrow. "Why?"

She tilted her head toward their quarry. Mr. Whitlock pounded the table with his fist. The other man grew still, then shook his head emphatically. She and Ethan strained to make out the words, but Sarah had chosen a table too far away to hear hushed tones. Another mistake.

Two men burst into the tavern, laughing uproariously. Sarah cringed. *Reggie and James!* Could it get any worse?

Ethan noticed her distraction and followed her line of vision. "Ah! The Hunter brothers. I believe I have seen you dance with them. Shall I ask them to join us?"

"No!" she gasped. "They must not know I am here."

"Afraid they might not find you so appealing in boys' clothes? Aye." He appraised her with a critical eye. "Not as fetching as when you are all done up like a lady." Ethan lifted her to her feet by her shoulders and reseated her in a chair with her back to the center of the room. He took the chair she had vacated and settled himself in comfortably. After a deep drink from his tankard, he crossed his arms across his chest and leaned back, watching the room.

The fire in her stomach flared up and nearly doubled her over with a stab of pain. She'd find herself in a convent by sundown tomorrow if Reggie recognized her. She hunched lower and watched Ethan's face for any clue as to what was going on.

"Well, that is interesting," he murmured in an undertone. "Our friend is quite agitated. I believe you are correct. There is a disagreement, and Whitlock appears to be winning. Now, where have I seen that man's back before? Did you recognize his companion, Sadie?"

She shook her head, afraid to use her voice lest Reggie or James hear and recognize it.

"Hmm. Guess we will have to wait until he turns around. His collar is up and his cap is down though, so it may not be possible to get a good look. Go stand by the door, Sadie, so you can have a clear line of sight."

She swallowed hard, shaking her head. She was too terrified to even stand, let alone walk past Reggie and James. They would know her for certain! At the very least, they might recognize Andrew's old jacket.

"What happened to 'Lay on Macduff'? I thought you were game for anything. Why so timid, little sparrow?"

"Tired," she whispered, gritting her teeth.

Ethan's deep hazel eyes glittered in the dim light. "Yes, you are looking a little peaked. Are you feeling well, Sadie?"

"Just tired," she repeated.

"Shall I hire a private room?"

She considered that invitation barely more than three seconds before shaking her head. If she thought she was in danger now, there was greater danger in being alone with Ethan, and with the potential to be even more devastating.

Ethan's gaze shifted slightly in acknowledgement of someone. He nodded once, cordial but cool. A flicker of annoyance passed over his face and he murmured, "Lord Reginald looks as if he will come over to pay his respects."

Sarah felt dizzy. She pictured herself as Reggie would see her, unchaperoned, bent over a tankard of ale, sitting across the table from the Demon of Alsatia, dressed in Andrew's old clothes, and was appalled.

Ethan stood quickly and came around the table to block

her from Reggie's view. "'Lo, Lockwood," he said, addressing Reggie by his title. "Out gaming?"

Reggie's speech was slightly thick. "Aye. I haven't seen you in a good long while. Keeping well, Travis?"

"Well enough."

Sarah concluded that they had an acquaintance but were not friendly. What did Reggie have against Ethan? Or was it the other way around? Did Ethan bear her brother some grudge?

"Who's your friend? I like to know trouble when I see it coming."

Panic clogged Sarah's throat and she braced herself for exposure. She had better start accustoming herself to black and white robes and learning the mass.

"No trouble here, Lockwood," Ethan said. "We were just waiting for a friend, but it looks as if he will not make it tonight." The toe of his boot tapped the leg of Sarah's chair. "Allow me to offer my regards to Lord James."

A slight rustle and the fading of their voices indicated that Ethan had taken Reggie by the arm and was leading him away. Sarah waited for a count of five, stood, and walked briskly for the door, looking neither right nor left.

None the worse from her flight from Ye Olde Cheshire Cheese, Sarah hummed the newest little ditty about the Prince Regent and Mrs. Fitzherbert on her way to the kitchen. As she passed the morning room doors, Reggie called out to her.

Confident that he had not recognized her the night before, she peeked around the corner. "Yes, Reggie?"

Eyes reddened and looking a little haggard from lack of sleep, Reggie squinted in the morning light streaming through the east windows and gestured to the chair across the table from him. "Sit a moment, Sadie. We need to chat."

The hair on the back of Sarah's neck prickled. Not that Reggie never wanted to talk to her—just that he was so obviously suffering the consequences of last night's carousing. Yes, he had something specific in mind, and she feared she knew what it was. She kept her smile in place as she slipped into the chair opposite him and poured a cup of tea.

"No eggs, Reggie?" she asked, looking pointedly at his empty plate. "Shall I ask Cook to bring a black pudding?"

He groaned and his complexion took on a greenish cast. "No, sweetling. Toast will do me well enough. I just wanted to have a word with you."

She searched for a diversion. "What a happy coincidence. I needed to talk to you, too, Reggie."

"Good. I shall go first, then you shall have your turn."

Sarah shook her head. "Please let me go first. You know how easily I forget things." She stirred a small spoonful of sugar into her tea, speculating on how quickly she would have to leave the room once she had him properly diverted.

He raised one hand in surrender and let it drop to the table. "You first, Sarah."

"Um, I needed your advice about your event. I was on my way to the kitchen to discuss menu with Cook when you called to me. I cannot decide upon a theme. Help me, Reggie."

"Theme? Why do we need a theme?"

"'Tis all the rage. Have you not noted how Henrietta Fletcher decorated with palm trees and fronds and then served pineapple ladyfingers and coconut cakes?"

"No, I—"

"And I have yet to decide upon a theme, let alone a menu. Perhaps we could arrange an Egyptian theme. We could rent four or five mummies from the museum, some statuary, but I cannot think of any Egyptian foods. Do you know of any? Did they not invent bread and beer?"

As she had hoped, Reggie looked slightly bewildered. "Mummies? Oh, I think you have gone too far, Sadie. Surely there must be something more simple."

"Shall we go at it from the other side?" she asked, leaving Reggie to figure it out.

He knit his brow in a frown. "You mean…menu?"

"Exactly! Menu. Let us decide upon food, and the decorations can be chosen to fit that."

"Wine. Punch. And a light cider?"

Sarah grinned. How like a man! "Food, Reggie."

"Fruit and cheese?"

"Hmm, would that be provincial France? Or Switzerland?"

"Does it matter?" Reggie asked, looking ill at ease.

"Of course. Oh! Greece! Mutton, olives, baklava—"

"And Grecian statuary and columns," he finished. "Rent a ruined temple for the gardens. That should complete the list."

She judged Reggie to be nearly misdirected. One last gambit should do it. "I wonder if the orchestra I've hired will know any Greek arrangements. But do the men not all dance with each other?"

"What is Lady Annica's theme?" He sighed, fatigue showing.

Sarah could almost taste victory. "She said she wanted it to be a surprise, but I saw her shopping for potted flowers and greenery. What do you think she will do with them?"

He smiled warmly, the dimple in his chin deepening. "I knew you were equal to the task, Sadie. You always accomplish everything with such style and grace."

"Did you find the time to go over the guest list?"

"Oh, about that." He rubbed his temples as if to ease a headache. "I've issued one or two invitations to people who were not on your list. Andrew and James have done likewise. I apologize for not informing you."

"Not Charlie?" she asked in feigned surprise. "Well, never mind. I suspect there will be a good many guests without invitations. Do not worry, they will not be turned away."

"Wouldn't want a scene." Reginald tapped one finger against the side of his cup thoughtfully. "It must be a very special night. No breath of scandal must mar the event."

"Certainly not," she agreed, wondering why this was so important to Reggie. She stood, breathing relief. She was seconds from escape when little Teddy, squealing with laughter, ran past the window, chased by the cook's daughter. She took another step toward the door when Reggie blinked and came back to himself with a start.

"That's the new lad, is it not? Teddy? What does he do?"

She cleared her throat. "He helps clean the pots and—"

"Where did you get him?" he interrupted.

"He...he had been abandoned," she said truthfully.

"And you could not leave him on the street with the hundreds of other children abandoned by mothers sunk in blue ruin? Or did you find him at that orphanage where you help?"

Sarah chose her words carefully. "No, Reggie. Not at Saint Anne's. But he was alone and crying. How could I leave him in such dire straits? He is so small and...and vulnerable."

His brow cleared as if he had remembered something. "There. You see. You have such a tender heart, m'dear. You will make such a good little mother."

A pang of suppressed yearning made her heart ache. How she would have longed to be a mother had things been different. "Do not put the cart before the horse, Reggie."

"Exactly, Sarah. 'Tis time to harness the horse. The question is, which horse?"

She almost groaned as the trap sprang shut. After all her care and preparation, and after being so close to escape, she had walked right into it. "No, Reggie. I am not about to choose a horse, let alone harness one."

"You cannot put it off any longer," he said. "The blush is nearly off the rose, if you catch my drift."

"Spare me the clichés, Lockwood," she said, giving her brother his title.

"Sit down. We are not done here."

"We are quite done," she contradicted.

"Sit down," he said again with cold emphasis.

Sarah narrowed her eyes and perched on the edge of her chair, ready to bolt if things got out of hand.

"We've had these discussions before," Reginald began, "and I have been remiss in not bringing it to a conclusion. Father would have had you wed by now, and I will have failed in my duty if I allow this to go any further. I have been sensitive to your mourning of our father's death, and tried to honor your maidenly modesty, but you must make a choice, and make it now."

"Now?" Quick tears stung her eyes. *"Now?* I have so much to do at the moment, so many details to attend, how can I give proper attention to this now, Reggie?"

"You must, Sarah. I want your future settled."

She had never seen her brother so resolute. She had come to the end of her amnesty. Reggie would have to know about that night in Vauxhall Gardens. He would have to know that there was no honorable way for her to ever marry. But not yet. Please, God, not yet. She could not face hostessing a party with the stain of ruination and scandal tainting her in Reggie's eyes. "Reggie, you have my oath I shall give you an answer soon."

"By the night of our soiree?"

"Yes. Yes, by the soiree," she agreed, desperate for any reprieve at all. But, the night of their soiree, after all the guests had departed, she would sit down with Reggie and tell him her secret. Her chief—nay, her *only*—consolation was that she had not left anyone for her brothers to challenge on the field of honor. They might be disappointed, but they would be alive.

Reggie cleared his throat, reclaiming her attention. "Very well, Sarah. I will not bring this up again. But if you do not make your choice by then I shall make it for you.''

There was no choice to make. There would be no marriage for Lady Sarah Hunter.

Ethan led the way east on Cannon Street toward the Tower. He had no time to indulge the little adventuress. He needed to find Whitlock's blackmail evidence so he could eliminate the risk to Rob McHugh's coming mission and pay his debt of honor to Kilgrew. Sarah would just have to keep up or go back to one of her fancy dress balls.

"What happened after I left last night?" she asked as she followed him into the night. "Did Lockwood quiz you about me? Where did Mr. Whitlock go? And who was the man he was with? I vow I knew the set of his shoulders. Did—"

Ethan waved her to silence, not wanting to slow down to answer her questions. She deserved to suffer a little uncertainty in view of her deception.

He kept track of the soft tread of her boots behind him though he did turn to check on her. He did not need to. Ever since she'd been attacked, Ethan had assigned Peters to watch their backs. The man was so good at his job that Sarah hadn't the slightest notion he was there. If, for some reason, she fell behind, Peters would follow her until she got safely home. Likewise, if Ethan and Sarah were diverted in another direction, Peters would continue the Whitlock chase.

Within ten minutes they came to one of the many small taverns dotting the lanes off main thoroughfares. Ethan gestured her to silence and stepped into the shadows to wait. She followed his lead, careful to take a position that would not put her in physical contact with him. She did not have to touch him for him to be uncomfortably aware of her nearness. And he despised himself for that weakness.

Unbelievably, his desire had grown since learning her

true identity. Knowing now that she was completely un-
attainable, and that he would never stroke that soft, warm,
silken flesh again, only served to intensify his lust. He
could smell the subtle scent of lilacs and something green,
the soap she had washed with. He could feel the heat of
her body. He could hear her soft sighing and the easy rise
and fall of her breathing, and he remembered the sweet
little mewling sounds she made when he had taught her
the secrets of her own body. She surrounded him, envel-
oped him, without even touching him. He clenched his jaw
and forced his mind away from Lady Sarah Hunter.

Twenty minutes lapsed before Harold Whitlock exited
the pub and paused to turn his collar up against the rising
wind. After glancing right and left, he headed eastward,
and Ethan suspected he would visit the opium dens of
Whitechapel near the London Docks. Another wasted
night. Another night Whitlock did not give up the secret
of where the blackmail evidence was hidden.

He gave the man a slight lead as he entered Rood Lane.
The street was narrow and dark, lending a claustrophobic
feeling to the chase. When lightning slashed the sky overhead and thunder broke almost on top of it, he heard a
frightened squeak behind him. Sarah's footsteps did not
falter, and he fought the impulse to turn to her and gather
her beneath his coat. She might be a liar, but she had no
deficit of courage.

As they turned onto Fenchurch Street, the sky opened
and loosened a violent torrent of cold drops that shattered
against the cobblestones and stirred the dirt into a slick
mud. Ethan looked back in time to see Sarah slip and land
on one elbow with a sickening crack. Instinctively, he
turned in midstep to hurry back to her side. The cold feeling of fear surprised and annoyed him. He was prepared
to see to her safety, but he was not prepared to care so
damned much.

He tilted his head toward Whitlock's route and caught
a flash of Peters's coat as he stepped into the chase. If he

could not get Sarah into a coach for home, he would be finished for the night. There would be no way to catch up to Peters or find Whitlock among the bordellos and opium dens.

Cupping her left elbow in her right palm, Sarah staggered to her feet. A little frown knit her brow as she gingerly tried to flex it.

"Are you injured?" he called above the wind and rain.

She shook her head. Rivulets of rain trickled down her face and disappeared beneath her shirt collar. Her woolen jacket hung heavily from her shoulders and one dripping chestnut tendril had escaped her soft cap. She looked like a drowned kitten.

"I'll go back to Cannon Street and find a coach," he said.

"No! I shall manage on my own. You go on."

"Do not be a fool. I will pay the coachman. I cannot leave you out here."

Sarah frowned and pointed in the direction Whitlock had gone. "Mr. Whitlock—"

"Has already got away," he finished. His hopes dimmed, and he fought the resurgence of frustration. "Come on, then. I think I saw an inn nearby. We'll get you out of those clothes and look at that arm."

Fifteen minutes later, Ethan found himself standing in the center of a little room very similar to the one at the Black Dog Tavern. He watched Sarah peel away her sodden jacket and drape it over the back of a wooden chair. Her cap went next to hang off the corner of the mantel of the tiny fireplace. She knelt before the fire and rubbed her hands together to warm them, looking small and vulnerable. And very desirable.

Bloody hell! Was he so weak that he could not resist the little liar more than ten minutes? He sent up a silent prayer to maintain his distance long enough to send her packing.

She sighed and glanced over her shoulder at him. "I...I

am sorry to put you to this trouble, Mr. Travis. If I were a man, I could stand before the fire in the public room and you would not need to hire a room.''

''Ethan,'' he corrected, shrugging out of his own jacket and hanging it on a hook on the back of the door.

Her voice was subdued, almost apologetic. ''I will pay for the room, but I do not have enough with me. Next time—''

''Next time?'' he asked.

''I may not be able to come tomorrow. I have another obligation. The night after?''

Her face, lit by the warm glow of the fire, was heart-breakingly beautiful. Before he could think better of it, he held out his hand to her and she reached to take it. When his fingers closed over hers and he pulled her to her feet, a surge of warmth swelled in his chest.

The rain had soaked through her jacket and trickled down her neck, and now the threadbare linen shirt clung to her, revealing every curve, hollow and tint. It was obvious that she had not bound her breasts tonight by the tempting little dots pressing against the cloth. His body was instantly hard.

Sarah stepped closer and tilted her chin upward, inviting a kiss. Her black lashes fluttered and settled in a soft fan against her cheeks. Her lips parted ever so slightly, giving him an inner glimpse of the dark honeyed heaven of her mouth. Lord, how deeply he wanted her!

Why now, when he finally knew he could never have her, did she seem ready to accept his advances? He dropped her hand to break the physical contact, his only hope of maintaining some semblance of self-control. She was startled by his withdrawal, and he studied her face for a moment before he spoke.

''I'd advise you to strip and hang your clothes from the mantel to dry but, given our history, that wouldn't be wise.''

She glanced down at herself, then at his groin, and a

soft pink swept her throat and cheeks. "No. Not wise at all."

He went to the bed, pulled a blanket away and took it to her. "See what you can do with that." The words came out more gruffly than he intended—a result of his body's betrayal.

Unnerved, she wrapped the blanket around herself like a cocoon, and he took some small amount of pleasure in that.

"I'm sorry," she murmured.

He smiled. "*I* am sorry. I enjoyed the view."

"Then you are welcome."

Ethan's quick laugh surprised them both. He shrugged. "Just when I think I have you pegged, you surprise me. You were all maidenly modesty, and now you are all sass and wit."

He pulled another wooden chair close to the fire and sat, gesturing her back to her comfortable position on the hearth. The more distance between them, the better. Some inner demon drove him to ask, "How's business, Sadie?"

She opened her mouth, but no sound came out. Her brow furrowed, as if she were wrestling with some difficult decision.

Unless he missed his guess, and he rarely did, she was on the verge of confession. He'd never make that easy. A confession would ruin his fun, and he'd barely begun taking his revenge. "I do worry about your means of support," he volunteered. "Most women in your profession earn their livings after dark, yet here you are spending your nights in nonpaying activities. Surely business must be suffering."

She would not meet his eyes. "I am doing well enough."

"Hmm," he said. "Then your tonish clientele pays well for day work and does not require you past midnight?"

Her eyes flashed before she turned away. "I do not think that is any of your business, Mr. Travis. Unless you are considering entering the trade yourself and asking for professional advice.''

''Now that would be interesting, would it not? But in point of fact, Miss Hunt,'' he said evenly, ''I've offered to make it my business, and to turn your evenings into profitable endeavors. On several occasions. But you are evidently more discriminating than most of your 'sisters.'''

Her full lower lip trembled—the one he loved to nibble—just slightly more delicious than the upper lip. ''It was not that, Mr. Ethan. 'Tis just that I thought it best not to mix business and…and business. But, of late—''

''Do not fret,'' he interrupted. He grinned at her confusion. ''Were I you, I would not serve me either. I've been told I am quite demanding and require no small amount of stamina. Not to mention that I have rather odd tastes.''

Her eyes grew round. ''I find you most appealing, and I cannot think that you would be so difficult to please.''

Ah, a small sop to his pride. Here was the sweetness that had fooled the entire ton. Lady Sarah Hunter knew her social graces. ''I would have liked to put that to the test, Sadie. Would you have felt the same afterward, I wonder?''

Her color deepened to a bright pink. That was part her charm, he supposed, and the likely result of having been raised with boys. Ethan had never cared much for hothouse flowers, and Sarah's quickly covered flashes of temper intrigued him.

''I think we had better change the subject,'' she said.

''You choose. I have a talent for embarrassing you.''

She turned to face the fire, and he knew her well enough now to know that she was regrouping. His rebuff had surprised her. Hell, it surprised *him!*

''I am curious, sir. Why did you agreed to teach me to follow? I asked on impulse, and I fully expected you to refuse.''

Good question, he thought. Why *had* he agreed? Looking back, he knew it had been more than just keeping an eye on her while he followed Whitlock. He'd have helped her anyway. Ah, but why? The memory of his first awareness of her at the King's Head came to him strong and clear. "Your laugh, Sadie. 'Twas your laugh."

"I do not understand." She tilted her head to one side.

"It was a genuine laugh without bitterness or cynicism—the first of its kind that I'd heard in many years. But once I knew what you were, I knew you would lose it, sooner or later. I hoped, if I helped, you would be able to keep your laugh."

"You are..." She paused and cleared her throat. "You are very kind. Kinder than I deserve."

"Keep that to yourself, will you?" he asked. "I would not want it widely known."

"You enjoy your reputation as the Demon of Alsatia, do you not? You encourage it."

His smile deepened and he rocked his chair back on the two rear legs. He was not about to allow the conversation to focus on him. "Speaking of trades, Sadie, tell me what you have gleaned from 'following.'"

Her shoulders sagged. "I confess it is more complicated than I'd thought. Still, I will be able to master it in time."

"I've no doubt of it," he said. "You have the coordination and the stealth necessary, but there is much work to be done before you are ready to go out on your own. Depending upon your level of commitment, of course."

"I am completely committed," she vowed. "What else must I learn?"

"Following is only the beginning. To excel at your task, you must draw conclusions from what you observe and be able to separate fact from illusion. I am curious, Sadie. What have you learned about Harold Whitlock?"

"That he is rarely at home of an evening."

He smiled again. She had a way of provoking that. "And why is he never home of an evening?"

"Because he is gone to a barroom, brothel or opium den."

"Think, Sadie. Take your information to the next step."

She pursed her lips in a delightful little pout as she thought. "I do not think he is a nice man. I think he ill-treats his inferiors. He behaves like a man with a secret."

Well, well. Little Sarah Hunter was as shrewd a pupil as any of His Majesty's finest. He nodded approval. "I believe you may be right. Can you guess what his secret is?"

"Jewel theft." She smiled and paused for a moment before adding, "Or blackmail."

Ethan feigned a mild curiosity to cover a sharp stab of fear for Sarah. How could she have suspected such a thing? Such knowledge could put her in grave danger. He had to steer her away from that suspicion. "Blackmail? Hardly. More likely he is hiding an *affaire d'amour*," he offered.

Sarah's eyes widened in disbelief. "Who would ever—that is, are you suggesting he has a mistress?"

"Or a particular favorite among the demimonde. So, perhaps I should ask *you* 'who would ever?' Do you not have friends amongst that group? Surely they talk. I would think you have a wide range of resources open to you that other, more genteel, women would not."

"I...I suppose," she allowed.

Color swept her cheeks again and her lashes fluttered as she looked down at her lap, unable to meet his gaze. "Do you think you could use your resources to learn more about Harold Whitlock?" he asked with a straight face. "When next you find yourself in the company of your...er, colleagues, you could find out who he favors." He turned the screw. "You might even be able to *be* that person."

"Be?" She furrowed her brow again. "Are you suggesting that I—oh!"

"Ah. I see I have overestimated your commitment."

"You have not, Ethan. I could not be more committed."

He cocked his head to one side and swept her with an

appraising gaze. "Then do you lack the necessary talents?"

Sarah looked startled by the question. "Talents?"

"Of seduction."

Something sparked in the pansy eyes. She rose to her feet and glided to his chair. Little tendrils of polished chestnut curls framed her oval face and the hint of a smile curved her mouth. Her hand cupped his cheek and she leaned toward him, the lilac scent of her perfume wafting around them. Her lips brushed his ear as she whispered, "By your previous invitations, sir, I cannot think I lack anything of great importance."

Her breath in his ear, hot and moist, brought his blood up, thickening in his veins. He gripped the edges of his chair, hands trembling, knuckles white. "Are you playing with me, Sadie?" he asked. "Because if you are, I advise against it. I will consider the next such episode an invitation and will react accordingly."

Her slender index finger trailed down his jawline and came to rest beneath his chin. She tilted his face up to hers and gave him such a provocative smile that he could almost believe that she was an accomplished demimondaine. She leaned even closer, her lips brushing his as she spoke. "Ah, then my intentions *are* clear. This *is* an invitation, Ethan."

Of all the things Ethan could think of to say, none of them were acceptable in mixed company. Had she spoken those words a week ago—when he hadn't known who she was—he'd have fallen on her like a ravenous wolf, matching her kiss for kiss until she was weak and pliable to his passion. It was all he could do not to seize her and ravish her on the bare floor in front of the fire. In fact, he could not even stand and walk away for the swelling ache in his groin.

Worse, he honestly did not know whether he'd strangle her or plunder the soft secrets of her body if he laid his hands on her. "You had better get yourself out of harm's way, Sadie, or I will not be responsible,'' he said between clenched teeth.

She straightened and stepped back from the chair, a wounded look in her soulful eyes. ''I believe I shall take you up on your offer of a coach.''

''A good idea,'' he agreed.

Chapter Thirteen

Excitement bubbled in Sarah as she handed a footman her shawl and waved her brothers to go on without her into the foyer of the Aubervilles' London home. She smoothed the cool silk of her new plum-colored gown as she glanced around. Annica had outdone herself! Glittering chandeliers sent shards of bright light dancing across the ceiling and walls. The strains of the orchestra tuning up carried from a distant room, and the heady scent of roses in full bloom filled the air. Footmen carried silver trays laden with wine glasses and maids offered delicacies on tiny china plates, biscuits or mint leaves.

Too excited to nibble, Sarah hurried toward the reception line at the wide double doors to the ballroom. She was supposed to wait in the reception line with Annica until the Whitlocks came. Then she would distract Mr. Whitlock while Annica whisked Mrs. Whitlock away for a reunion with little Araminta. She prayed the visit would give Mrs. Whitlock new hope and the strength she needed to see this thing through.

The press of the crowd slowed her and she glanced ahead to see if her friend was watching for her. To the contrary, Annica was deeply involved in conversation with her husband and a guest he had just introduced. Sarah halted and stepped out of line to hold back. How, she wondered, had Tristan introduced Ethan? *Annica, my dear, may I present the Demon of Alsatia?* Or perhaps, *Ethan, old boy, you must tell my wife how you came by your nickname. Quite a story, that.*

Her heart skipped a beat. Ethan was dressed in dark gray with a forest-green waistcoat. His pristine cravat was intricately tied in the height of fashion and secured with an emerald stickpin. He was far and away the most handsome man she had ever seen. But she dared not approach Annica for fear of being introduced! Just the thought of it made her light-headed with anxiety. Still worse, Harold and Gladys Whitlock had just entered the foyer! How could she distract Mr. Whitlock without Annica's help? Was it too much to hope that Ethan was an uninvited guest and would be shown the door?

As if intercepting her thought, Ethan glanced up and caught her eye. His slow smile lifted the corners of his mouth and he gave a nearly imperceptible nod in her direction. Then he winked! Actually winked! Oh, what brazen taunting!

Or was he attempting to remind her of her unwelcome advances of the night before? Humiliation washed over her at the memory of his rejection. Oh yes, he was laughing at her. The cad! She promised herself that he'd never know that invitation was the bravest thing she had ever done.

She had long despised herself for letting her fears control her but, until last night, she hadn't known what to do about them. Then, when she realized that Ethan was teasing her as she dried herself in front of the fire, she had known in a flash of uncommon clarity that she had to face those fears if she was ever to be free of them. And she thought she knew how—have it done with! Beard the lion! Breach the gates! Brazen it out!

Open her legs.

She'd been ready to yield. And why not? He had been preparing her for that almost since the night they met. She had nothing to lose that had not already been stolen in

Vauxhall Gardens so long ago. Nothing but her pride. She had lost that last night.

Ethan met her gaze again as she hardened herself with resolve. The hint of a cloud passed over his face and he took his leave of the Aubervilles. Without another glance in her direction, he disappeared into the ballroom.

Just in time! The Whitlocks had made their way to the front of the reception line. Sarah squared her shoulders and pressed through the crowd to join them.

Annica turned to her with almost comical relief. "Mr. Whitlock, have you met my dear friend, Lady Sarah Hunter?"

With a reassuring nod in Gladys's direction, Sarah offered her hand to the man. "How do you do, Mr. Whitlock. I must tell you how very much I have enjoyed making your wife's acquaintance at the Ladies' Assistance League. Indeed, she is quite an inspiration." There was no such league, but the Wednesday League certainly assisted women.

Harold Whitlock bowed low over her hand, and she feared he would kiss it. Straightening with an obsequious smile in place, he spoke his first words to her. "You are no stranger to me, Lady Sarah. I feel as if I know you quite well."

Sarah froze and the noise of the party faded. Gladys Whitlock covered the awkward pause. "I have been telling my husband how devotedly you work on behalf of the less fortunate."

"Oh," Sarah said. "Yes, well...."

"You must do me the honor of a dance, Lady Sarah." He smoothed his thinning hair back.

She braced herself for duty. "I believe I may be able to manage that, Mr. Whitlock. In fact, I know I shall be occupied later, so if you have not promised your wife, this would be an excellent time. Otherwise, I shall have to consult my brother Reggie to be certain he has not made other arrangements for me."

"An obedient, dutiful woman." He smirked and turned to his wife with a triumphant smile. "You see, Gladys? Some women still know their place."

Sarah blinked. The man was an absolute maggot! A sideways glance at Annica caused her a moment of concern. Though the smile had frozen on her face, her eyes betrayed her anger. Auberville's mouth quirked and he took a small step back, as if giving Whitlock over to Annica's not-so-tender mercies.

Watching the interplay, Sarah knew that Annica was about to risk their plan with ill-advised words. The burden of social diplomacy had fallen to her by default. Sarah disengaged her hand from Mr. Whitlock's grip and waved it airily. "You give me too much credit, sir. I am certain that, should you ask my brother, he would tell you that I have a mind of my own."

It warmed her heart to see the slightly muddled expression on the man's face. He was socially astute enough to realize he had said something wrong, though he was not entirely certain what.

Annica took a deep breath. "Mr. Whitlock, will you permit me to steal your wife for a few moments? She has admired my maid's fine handwork, and I have promised to introduce them. We should be no longer than half an hour."

"Half an hour? Should you be gone from your guests so long, Lady Auberville?" he queried in a petulant tone.

She took Gladys Whitlock by the arm and laughed. "Oh, Mr. Whitlock. *I* shall not be gone. Once I have introduced her to Mary, I shall excuse myself so that Mary may teach Mrs. Whitlock a fancy lingerie stitch. Unless— would you like to join us, Mr. Whitlock? Are you handy with a needle?"

Sarah held her breath. Annica was taking Gladys to see Araminta. If Mr. Whitlock accepted the invitation—

"Oh, I—I th-think I shall just…" Whitlock stammered. "Yes, I shall claim my dance with Lady Sarah."

Auberville coughed to cover a laugh. "You go on, my dear," he said to Annica. "I shall greet the guests until you return."

With that, Annica led Mrs. Whitlock away in the direction of the staircase, chatting in low, casual tones. Sarah was nearly giddy with the knowledge that mother and daughter would be reunited in a matter of minutes. She prayed for a reel so she would not have to suffer Mr. Whitlock's hand on her waist.

The strains of a waltz began and Sarah wondered if she was going to have rotten luck all night. First Ethan, and now the waltz. She glanced toward Reggie and James for reassurance, but they were engaged in conversation with Cedric Broxton.

"You are nervous, Lady Sarah," Whitlock said as he took her hand and led her into the ballroom. "Have you waltzed before?"

He was so deucedly condescending! "Dozens, perhaps hundreds, of times. Why would you think I am nervous?"

He pulled her into the steps, his hand biting into her waist to indicate each turn. "I am mistaken, my lady. But I think I am not mistaken that we have met before."

Sarah swallowed hard. "I am certain we have not."

"I know your face. Perhaps we have bumped into one another at another soiree?"

Had she not been as stealthy as she thought? Was there something familiar to him in her shape or bearing? Was there the remotest chance that he would unravel it?

"Hmm. No. I think I would recall such a thing. When Lady Annica and I dropped by for tea last week, Mrs. Whitlock pointed to your portrait in the parlor. I distinctly remember commenting that you looked very distinguished. I assure you, I would have recognized you on sight from that moment forward, sir."

Her answer flattered him, and he preened. "I would not look so high for recognition, Lady Sarah."

"Nonsense," she said. Here was an opportunity too

good to waste. ''I have not seen you at these affairs before. I wonder why our paths have not crossed erenow?''

''Oh, ah, perhaps we have been at the same affairs, but were not introduced.''

''Perhaps. What affairs do you attend of an evening?''

''I am here and there, Lady Sarah. 'Tis difficult to remember day to day.''

She shrugged at his vague explanation. ''And what do you do during the day, sir? Are you a member of parliament?''

''I am assigned to the Foreign Office.''

''How fascinating,'' she said, just as if she hadn't known it. ''That must be very interesting. I collect you must be a very important man, Mr. Whitlock. Not just *anyone* is qualified for that sort of work, are they?''

''No, indeed. Why, we are privy to information that could bring down entire governments.''

There was a frightening thought! But how could she encourage him to discuss his nightly activities? Was there any way to induce him to share his rounds of opium dens, brothels and, more important, the place where he had hidden Benjamin?

The dance ended and she was still in midcurtsy when a hand cupped her elbow and a voice spoke from over her shoulder.

''Lady Sarah,'' Cedric Broxton said above the murmur of conversation. ''Your brother tells me you have not reserved the next dance. Would you honor me?''

''Oh! But of course, Lord Cedric,'' she answered, glad of the opportunity to gather her wits and plan a strategy for questioning Harold Whitlock. Only then did it occur to her that she'd been rude. ''Mr. Whitlock, have you met Lord Broxton?''

''Er, yes,'' Cedric said. ''Good to see you again, Whitlock.''

''And you, my lord,'' Whitlock bowed.

Sarah caught a hint of something veiled in the greeting,

but neither of them seemed inclined to comment further. Again, the social niceties fell to her. "I shall look forward to seeing you again, Mr. Whitlock. Please tell your wife that I will see her Thursday next at the Ladies' Assistance League meeting."

He bowed and turned toward the buffet. Annica appeared to intercept him, sacrificing herself to keep him occupied and prevent him from going in search of his wife.

Cedric looked mildly annoyed. "Where have you met the likes of Harold Whitlock?"

"Here, Lord Cedric. Nica introduced us a moment ago. We know his wife from the Ladies' Assistance League."

"I doubt the Whitlocks are the sort Reggie would want you associating with."

How had he managed to annoy her so thoroughly and so quickly? "Then Reggie may tell me so." She snagged a glass of wine from the tray of a passing footman, taking a quick swallow before setting it down on a side table.

He gave her a surprised look. "Have a care, Lady Sarah. That is not very ladylike."

"Perhaps not, but I need the fortification," she said.

"Come, now. I am not so bad a dancer as that," he laughed.

Sarah smiled. It was easy to see why Cedric was so popular when he forgot to be pompous. "Of course not. 'Tis just that it promises to be a long evening, and I am tired already."

"Would you like to sit this dance out, Lady Sarah?"

"Never! As long as I am dancing, I will not fall asleep."

"Then I am glad to be of service." Cedric grinned and offered his arm and led her to the dance floor.

This time the dance was a lively reel, and she did not have to keep up a conversation—just smile each time they met or bowed. The dance ended, and the orchestra took an intermission. Cedric led her toward the sidelines. "I must say that you are looking stunning tonight, my dear. That purplish color becomes you and makes you look quite exotic. Almost…almost sultry,'' he murmured thoughtfully. He turned to face her and took her other hand in his. "You quite take my breath away."

When she tried to free one hand, Cedric looked wounded. "Have I made you uncomfortable, my dear? 'Twas not my intent."

"I collect that you have paid me a great compliment, my lord, but I did not mean to draw attention to myself. I do not like to feel that people are watching me."

"It does you credit that you do not recognize how your beauty has made you the North Star to many a compass. I have been meaning to have a talk with you. Shall we adjourn to the gardens, or would you prefer to find a private spot?"

Panic lapped at the edges of Sarah's reason. She *never* walked in gardens with men after dark! Not since… Vauxhall. "N-no," she said, glancing toward the French doors.

Cedric smiled. "Auberville's library is likely vacant. We can be private there." His fingers tightened around her hand.

There was something unbearably intimate in his touch and Sarah resisted. "I have forgot myself, Lord Cedric. I promised Lady Annica I would help her with introductions as I know most of her guests. Later, perhaps."

His voice was a low plea. "I cannot keep trying to catch you between dances, Sarah, or to find you at home. We have matters to settle, and I would see it done tonight." In a mercurial change of strategy, he flashed her his best boyish grin. "Come. 'Twill not be too painful. If I do it right, you are certain to enjoy it." He reached for her hand again.

If she continued to resist they would draw attention. Reggie would not like that. Reggie did not like anything that hinted at a scene. She was trapped!

A burst of male laughter gave her the excuse she needed to delay. She turned around to find the source of the merriment and saw Lord Auberville standing with a group of men, Ethan among them, tossing down the contents of their glasses. Evidently Auberville had made some risqué toast.

She caught Auberville's attention and sent him a silent plea. He disengaged himself from the circle of men with a few pats on the back and came toward them.

"Ah, Broxton. Here you have claimed the notice of the uncontested beauty of the ball. You will have to share. At least three young bucks have begged introductions. I am afraid I must claim her to do the honors."

"This is not a good time, Auberville."

"'Twill have to be," he insisted.

The two men faced each other, neither giving over the contest of wills. Sarah inched closer to Tristan, making her choice subtly clear.

Cedric stepped forward again, reaching to take her hand, a look of grim determination hardening his boyish features. There was going to be an unpleasant confrontation.

"I see you have finally caught her attention, Auberville," a familiar voice came from behind them.

"Lady Sarah, here is someone I would like you to meet," Lord Auberville said.

Her heart sank and her stomach twisted in a knot. Ethan. She was about to be exposed right there in Auberville's ballroom. Reggie's disappointment, Cedric's shock, Auberville's scorn, all loomed on the horizon. Life, as she knew it, was over. She composed herself and turned to face her Waterloo.

"Have a care, Auberville," Cedric said. "There are some scoundrels a lady should not have acquaintance with."

"I quite agree," Auberville said. "But I gather Hunter has already introduced you."

The barb took a moment to find its mark. When it finally registered, Cedric released her and lowered his voice to a deadly growl. "Hunter will hear about this."

Sarah watched in dismay as Cedric stormed away. She took one deep breath and turned back to her rescuers, straightening the little puff sleeve of her gown while she composed herself.

Auberville's voice gentled as he said, "Lady Sarah Hunter, may I present Lord Ethan Travis?"

Her head snapped up to meet Ethan's eyes. "Lord? *Lord* Ethan Travis?"

"Merely a courtesy title, Lady Sarah," he said smoothly. "My older brother is the heir to the Linsday lands and title."

Sarah frowned. So *that* was his connection to Lord Linsday and the lovely Amelia! Linsday was his brother, and Amelia was his sister-in-law. And they had...*waltzed.* "V-very nice to meet you, Lord Ethan," she said and offered her hand.

He accepted, lifting it to his lips. "My pleasure," he murmured into her palm. "Believe me."

It occurred to Sarah that Ethan had not been in the least surprised by *her* title. She glanced sideways at Auberville to see if he understood the implications of their exchange. If he did, he was not inclined to mention it.

"Will you excuse me," he asked with a crooked grin. "I see Annica is embroiled in conversation with Lord North. I should extricate her before she says something unforgivably honest."

"Of course," Ethan nodded. "I shall escort Lady Sarah to the punch bowl."

Auberville halted and turned back with another smile. "It is good to see you back in society, Ethan."

"Yes, Ethan," Sarah mocked in a whisper as they strolled toward the long sideboard that held hors d'oeuvres and a bubbling citrus punch over sliced fruit. "So good to see you back. And how long have you been gone from society, prithee?"

His low laugh sent a little thrill up her spine. "A few years. Since before I...went abroad."

"You *knew*," she accused in an undertone. "How long have you known? What game were you playing?"

"Hold up, *Sadie Hunt*. Think before you speak. Who was playing with whom?"

"You—"

"I? No, Lady Sarah. I have not deceived you in anything important. I have never pretended to be other than I am."

"The Demon of Alsatia?" she scoffed. "I thought you were some disreputable merchant eking out a living in stolen goods."

"Precisely."

She eyed him suspiciously. "But you knew who I was and did not tell me."

"I thought I was being a gentleman by allowing you your little subterfuge. If you choose to be an adventuress, who am I to say you nay?"

"When did you find out?"

"I followed you home after you were hit over the head."

Tears stung the backs of her eyes. "All this time…you've been toying with me. I thought—"

"What did you think?"

I thought you liked me. I thought you enjoyed my company. "I thought you wanted to help me."

He held a crystal cup beneath the punch waterfall and offered it to her with a slight smile. "And so I did. But who is the injured party here, *Sadie?* You have played me for a fool since we met. You told one lie after another, and tricked me into playing whatever game is afoot without teaching me the rules." His expression did not change, but his voice lowered dangerously. "You will tell me what your game is, Lady Sarah Hunter. Just why the hell are you prowling the streets of London, tempting disaster, playing at 'following,' keeping company with street urchins and Bow Street runners?"

"I…I—"

"Do you know how close I came to relieving you of your maidenhead? Were *you* laughing at *me* when I offered to buy your services and make you my mistress? Did you think you could tempt and tease me with impunity? Do you know nothing of the nature of men? You are lucky that you are not ruined."

That sobered her. She was ruined, though he could have no way of knowing that. "I never laughed at you, Ethan. And I know more than I care to about the nature of men."

He filled his own cup from the fountain and raised it to her. "To lies, and the freedom they give us to live our fantasies. One wonders, Lady Sarah—what fantasies could lead you into London slums in the middle of the night?"

Fie—he was right! When he hadn't known she was Lady Sarah Hunter, she'd had the freedom to be anything she wanted, to do what was forbidden for a woman of her station, to give rein to her hidden passions. Shame filled her.

"*You* are angry at *me?*" he asked. He gave a mirthless laugh, as brittle as ice. "Try to imagine what I felt when I realized who you were, and how you'd been using me in a selfish pursuit of excitement or adventure. It wasn't a game to me, Lady Sarah. There was risk involved. If you wanted excitement, I could have provided you with all you could possibly want."

"Expose me, then! Take your 'pound of flesh.' You have earned it." She swallowed her punch in two gulps, wishing it were wine or some other alcohol.

He gave her a smooth smile that was somehow threatening. "I will, Sadie, but not yet. I intend to make you squirm."

Chapter Fourteen

Ethan watched the little harridan walk away, the luscious plum silk gown clinging to the sway of her hips, her dark hair falling in ringlets from a coronet of amethysts. She was disturbingly beautiful, and far too vulnerable. He cursed under his breath when he realized how intensely he wanted her.

Harold Whitlock was making his way toward her again, and he gritted his teeth. Ethan recognized that he was nearly wild with jealousy. That scum was not fit to touch the hem of her gown. Almost as soon as she saw him, she flirted and cajoled Whitlock onto the dance floor. By the time she turned loose of him, he was looking like a moon-faced lad. Then she turned her formidable charms on Cedric Broxton.

Broxton was the bitterest pill to swallow. Watching her laugh at Broxton's jokes, respond to his teasing, allow him to touch her, had threatened his reason, particularly when he'd learned that Lockwood had selected Broxton for Sarah. He'd been on the verge of doing some serious damage to Broxton's face when Auberville had interceded.

He supposed there would be no more midnight meetings with Sadie on the porch at St. Paul's. He would miss her, but he would accomplish more without her. He'd made no progress in finding Whitlock's blackmail evidence, probably because Sarah had proved too much of a distraction. Peters was growing tired of covering for him, and Rob was just growing impatient.

He took up a position near an entry to the corridor for the next half hour and watched Sarah down another glass of wine—her third—when he saw his brother and sister-in-law. He had been skirting them all night, but now they were making a straight line for him. Something was afoot, and he knew he wouldn't like it by the grim expressions on their faces.

"You have God's own nerve to show up here," Collin said.

"Collin, hush," Amelia pleaded. She turned her china-blue eyes to Ethan, but the pleading look that used to win her way was strangely ineffective. "Ethan, please do not cause a scene. We are new to London. I could not bear it if we were made a subject of gossip."

Ethan struggled to maintain a neutral expression. "I've done nothing to cause a scene, Amelia," he said.

"*Lady* Linsday, to you, Ethan," Collin insisted.

Ethan realized that it chafed Collin's pride to know that Amelia had first loved Ethan. "*Lady* Linsday," he repeated, allowing his gaze to sweep Amelia's form in an intimate study he knew would enrage Collin.

His brother rose to the bait. His voice climbed in both tone and intensity. "Your insolence astounds me, Ethan. You will show my wife the respect she deserves."

"Or what, Collin? You will disown me? Disinherit me? Denounce me? Hmm. Too late."

"Why you—"

"But, as it happens, I meant no disrespect to Lady Amelia. Indeed, I applaud her choice and allow that it was the correct one. God knows I could never have given her what you have."

Collin's mouth moved as if he were trying to frame a reply to a remark he did not fully understand. "Just…just the same, you would do everyone a favor if you would leave quietly."

Ethan clenched his jaw to hold back the explicit words struggling for expression. He glanced to the side and found Sarah standing perhaps ten feet away as if she had halted in midstride on her way to the corridor. Her head was tilted slightly to one side, and he wondered how much of the conversation she had heard.

Though she thought him a thief and a purveyor of stolen goods, he did not want her to witness a scene that was certain to lower him even further in her esteem. He wanted this meeting over before she could witness more. "Do not push me, Collin," he said between gritted teeth. "I had my invitation from Auberville. I do not need your permission to be here."

"You might consider Amelia," his brother snarled.

Ethan turned to Amelia and studied her sweetly bewildered expression. "Am I an embarrassment to you, Lady Amelia?"

"Ethan." She expelled in a sigh. "I wish it were not so, but your reputation is such that…"

Her voice trailed off and he glanced to the side to see if Sarah was still listening. She had pivoted on one heel and taken another step toward the corridor when Amelia followed the direction of his gaze and straightened. She evidently saw in Sarah a way to diffuse the inevitable fight between him and Collin, because she called out to her. "Lady Sarah! Oh, I was so hoping to run into you tonight."

Sarah's back stiffened. She halted and turned slowly back to them. An odd little smile curved her lips as she affected surprise to see them. "Lady Amelia, what a surprise."

Ethan tried not to groan. Here was Sarah's chance for revenge for his earlier taunt. On her way to join them, she stopped a passing footman, lifted a glass of wine—her fourth—downed it in two gulps, and placed the empty glass back on the tray. He suspected he was in for a rough ride.

"Lady Sarah, how glad I am to find you. I promised to introduce my husband when next we met, and here we are."

Innocently Sarah looked down at herself, then let her gaze sweep Lady Amelia. "Why yes, so we are." She waited, but Amelia did not detect the sarcasm.

Ethan glanced again at Amelia with detached interest. She was as stunning as ever. She was everything he remembered and had longed for. She was the walking symbol of what his life had been and what he hoped to reclaim. Now, standing next to Sarah Hunter, she quite literally paled to insignificance.

After the requisite introductions and pleasantries, Sarah turned to arch an eyebrow at his brother. "Travis? Travis is the family name? Why, that would make you cousins— or would it be brothers?"

"Brothers," Lord Linsday acknowledged.

"We have not seen Ethan for quite some time, Lady Sarah," Amelia explained. "As you know, we have just come to London."

"How happy to renew family ties." She smiled and a devilish gleam lit her eyes. "I should have guessed something of the sort from our previous conversation, Lady Amelia." She turned to Ethan. "I have heard that you are quite skilled at the waltz, Lord Ethan. Is that not correct, Lady Amelia?"

Amelia's complexion deepened to a tone near that of a pomegranate. "I believe I may have said—"

Collin glared at his wife and Ethan found some satisfaction in that. He wondered if Sarah had deliberately set them at odds. He would have to remember to thank her.

"Then you have met Mr. Travis?" Collin asked Sarah, purposely slighting Ethan the courtesy title. He was on the verge of denying an acquaintance for Sarah's sake when she answered for them both.

"Oh my, yes. Lord Ethan is quite a wit. Or is he a wag? I vow, there are some days I cannot decide. He sets me on a roll with the greatest ease, and I quite literally *squirm* with anticipation of his next jest."

Ah yes, Sarah was going to have her revenge. He accepted her offered hand and bowed over it, prepared to endure whatever little justice she decided to mete out. "Lady Sarah, how nice to see you again so soon."

"Ethan?" Lady Amelia asked, her blue eyes blinking in disbelief. "A wag? Why I cannot conceive—"

"Oh, *conceive,* Lady Amelia," Sarah urged. "Lord Ethan is quite beyond amusing."

Ethan laughed outright. He had to admire Sarah's flawless skill in delivering insults with a smile—so adept that she'd managed to insult both him and Amelia in one thrust, and even more so because one of them did not realize it.

Collin scowled. "Mr. Travis is my brother, Lady Sarah. We know him better than you and therefore we must warn you that—"

Without missing a beat, Sarah bestowed an angelic smile on his brother and interrupted. "Better, Lord Linsday? Or merely longer?"

Collin flushed. Amelia stared in horror.

Had it been anyone else standing there risking their reputation to defend him, Ethan might have laughed, but he could not permit Sarah to face social ruin because of a misdirected desire to make *him* squirm. A strategic retreat was in order. "If you will excuse me," he said with a slight bow, "I believe I have another engagement."

"For shame! Have you forgotten your promise of a waltz?"

Sarah grinned hugely and Ethan felt the cold to the bone. She'd thrown down the figurative gauntlet. He had thrust the introduction from Auberville on her, and she had riposted with a waltz. It was bad enough for a paragon like Sarah to have a public acquaintance with a man of his dishonored past, but quite another to allow society to witness a closer relationship as evidenced by a dance—and not just any dance—a waltz!

He was confounded. He could not call her a liar, but neither could he risk the scandal in picking up the gauntlet. "I would not want to disappoint, Lady Sarah, but—"

"Good," she said, parrying his excuse. "I believe a waltz is next on the program." She offered her hand.

Outmaneuvered, Ethan was trapped. A rebuff would make her look a fool. Acceptance would risk her reputation and standing in society. He was still trying to decide which of the two evils to choose when Sarah went one taunt too far.

"Come now, Lord Ethan. Surely you would not leave me jilted. Shall I be forever deprived of divine waltzing?"

He narrowed his eyes, seized her hand and nearly dragged her to the dance floor without giving her the chance to deliver another insult in her goodbyes to his brother.

The orchestra began the smooth strains of a waltz and he turned to face her on the perimeter. "This is your last chance, Sadie. Curb your recklessness before it is too late."

She tilted her chin upward like a soldier marching into battle, glanced slowly, deliberately, right and left to be certain they were being noted, and then gave him a little nod that said she was ready. She took one step closer to fit within the circle of his arms and placed her left hand on his shoulder.

He nearly groaned. He was truly damned if he did, and damned if he didn't. There was no saving Sarah now.

Ethan's right hand at the small of her back burned through the light silk of her gown, and with the slightest pressure of his fingers, he guided her into the measure. Sarah followed his lead, feeling almost as if she were a part of him. He began slowly, increasing his step until he reached the limit of hers. The same grace and assurance she had admired in his breathtaking balance on rooftops was evidenced in the dance, and the world created by the circle of his arms was so intimate that the rest of the room seemed to fade away.

Gentle pressure from his fingers guided her, and her hand in his looked insignificant and fragile. But most disturbing of all was his mere *presence*—his size, his warmth, the faint clean scent of lime, and the intensity of his hazel eyes. Everything combined to remind her of their night in the Black Dog Inn. She knew what those hands could do. She yearned for him to pull her the remaining inches that would land her against his chest and allow her to feel the warmth and intimacy of his entire body.

She looked up at him as he guided her into another turn. "Lady Amelia did not lie. You do waltz divinely."

"She actually said that?"

"Yes, but there was something in the way she said the word that made me wonder if she meant 'waltz,' or was speaking of something else entirely. How much *waltzing* did you and your sister-in-law do?"

He laughed at her outrageous interpretation. "You've had too much to drink."

"I have, indeed." She tilted her head and smiled in a relaxed friendliness. "And I'm feeling simply wonderful. Denounce me on the spot, and I would not care in the least."

"More recklessness, Lady Sarah? Have you not learned your lesson?"

"I most seriously doubt it, my lord," she said agreeably.

"Then you are foolhardy. This dance is little more than social suicide. Whatever possessed you to—"

She could not have him taking responsibility for her decisions. "You overestimate your consequence, Lord Ethan. My reputation will survive the dance. 'Tis when you expose me to my brothers after you are done making me squirm that will finish me. Aside from that, I overheard a part of your conversation." He winced and she shook her head. "I was not eavesdropping, Lord Ethan. I was on my way to…repair myself when your brother's voice stopped me. His demand that you leave made me angry, and I decided that those provincial little nobodies would not speak for London society. And anyway, he put me in mind me of all the 'P' words. I do not like the 'P' words."

Grinning, he asked, "'P' words?"

"You know, presumptuous, pretentious, pompous, priggish—"

"Pretty," he countered.

"Parsimonious, penurious, petty, promiscuous," she continued, just warming to the challenge.

"Passionate." He chuckled. "Priceless."

She blinked, finally understanding that he was describing her. "Yes. Well. I did not like that he was treating you with such disrespect."

A shadow passed over his face and his smile faded. He frowned as he asked, "If you fear that I am going to expose you, why did you intercede on my behalf?"

Because she could not bear to see him hurt? Because she wanted to be certain that society understood that Lord Ethan Travis was acceptable? How could she say that? She opted for truth of another sort. "Because I wanted to waltz. Just once, to…waltz."

He lowered his voice. "I've seen you waltz before, Sarah."

"Not with you, Ethan. I hear 'tis different with you."

"I can bloody well guarantee it is different with me. My God, is there no end to your recklessness? Do you have any idea how close I am to living up to my reputation? And do not affect the wounded look. Try to remember that I am the injured party."

Sarah shrugged. "That is open to argument, Lord Ethan."

The waltz ended and he stopped abruptly, causing her to cling to him for support. "I've had enough of your taunting for one night. Shall I see you back to your friends,

Lady Sarah, or shall I just prop you in a corner with another glass of wine?''

She lifted the little train of her gown and turned her back on him with a look that could wither flowers. ''I shall see to myself, as I always have. Thank you.''

For the next hour, she caught glimpses of him in the crowds. She was like a hare with hounds at her heels, watching left and right for Cedric, Reggie, Harold Whitlock, Lord Auberville and Ethan.

The prospect of another encounter with Ethan sent her heart racing. Their waltz had been more devastating than she had wanted him to know, and she was wholly ashamed of the intensity of her desire. God help her, she needed to escape any proximity to Ethan at all.

Most unsettling of all, she would have to formulate a new plan for finding the children. She could no longer count on Ethan's help. His tightly contained anger was not likely to fade soon. But, oh, how she would miss those wildly exciting nights of breathtaking leaps from roof to roof, anticipating Ethan's smile, his touch.

All she wanted tonight was to escape to the quiet solitude of her own bedchamber, sit in her warm bed with a cup of tea and try to sort through her confusion. She felt inexplicably wounded, and needed time to regain her balance and heal. She found a temporary respite by slipping into the library and using Annica's desk to send messages to Mr. Renquist and Dicken to go on without her.

When Mr. Whitlock made his excuses and departed, Ethan followed suit. She took comfort from the happy radiance on Gladys's face. The reunion with Araminta, at least, had gone well. She began to breathe a little easier until she noticed Cedric circling like a vulture over dead meat. Just as he appeared ready to approach, Lady Jane Perrin intercepted him. Sarah made a mental note to thank Jane later.

Pleading a headache, she said her goodbyes to Lady Annica, called for the Lockwood coach, and went to join the queue of departing guests. The effects of the wine had worn off, leaving her slightly embarrassed by her behavior with Ethan but not in the least embarrassed by her anger over Linsday's treatment of him. Her sense of fairness recognized her part in the failure.

Her behavior *had* been reckless. And she had been unfair to embroil him in her scheme to follow Mr. Whitlock and find the children. She had told one lie after another, tricked him into helping her and teased him mercilessly. Yes, she had taken advantage of him and put him at risk. If he had been harmed, it would have been her fault. Her conscience would never let her rest until she made amends.

Chapter Fifteen

What a colossal waste of time. Whitlock had actually gone home with his wife. Ethan waited outside nearly an hour, but the man had not reappeared for his nightly round of drinking, gambling and whoring. Peters, looking disgusted, volunteered to stay, allowing Ethan to make an early night of it.

As he unlocked his front door, he wondered briefly what it would be like to be Auberville, with a lovely, loyal wife, a gracious home, an heir and the promise of yet more to come. Surely that must be heaven and, sadly, he would never achieve it. But, for one brief moment as he danced with Sarah Hunter this evening, it had not seemed so impossible.

By waltzing with him, she had been protecting him, showing the ton that she found him acceptable. And she had demonstrated clearly where her loyalties lay. When was the last time anyone had put their reputation on the line for him? Sarah had more courage than half the ton, more than his own brother. She could not know how grim the consequences could be for such a grand gesture. He had no doubt her brothers would chastise her tomorrow over the breakfast table. But that was typical of Sarah— rash and impetuous. And he was nonetheless grateful.

Some of the women that he'd been with were, like Amelia, beautiful, witty and charming. Lord knows some were practiced and expert in the arts of making love. But they were not what he wanted. He wanted…what? Love? Loyalty? Honesty? Yes, he wanted all the things his money could not buy. He wanted Sarah.

When Ethan pushed his door open, Wiley set up a deafening noise as he ran upstairs from the kitchen to the foyer, slipping on the planks as he rounded the corner of the landing. A light from that direction told him that Mrs. Grant had not yet departed for home. He offered up a quick prayer that she had not cooked him dinner.

When Wiley saw Ethan, he stopped barking and wagged his tail so hard that he knocked the umbrella stand over. "Here now, precious," Mrs. Grant called. "What's the fuss?"

"It's me, Mrs. Grant," he said, dropping his coat and key on the mahogany side table and retrieving his mail from the silver tray. He looked through the envelopes until he came to one that bore only his name in a graceful script but no address. It must have been personally delivered. He dropped the other envelopes back on the tray and headed for the kitchen, Wiley at his heels. The dog pushed his head beneath Ethan's hand, begging a pat.

"'Tis late, Mrs. Grant. What kept you?" he called ahead.

"I've been havin' a fine visit with yer little friend, Mr. Travis. We didn't expect ye home so soon."

"My little—" He entered the kitchen and stopped in his tracks. There, in a chair at the polished wooden table, sat Lady Sarah. She watched him with a hint of…fear? Surprise? What the hell was she doing here anyway?

Warmth filled him at the sight of her. Despite her gown and the amethyst coronet, she looked at home in his kitchen. This, then, was the way Auberville felt when he came home.

She stood and smoothed her gown in a nervous gesture. "I expected you to be out, Mr. Travis. I came to leave you a note, but Mrs. Grant found me at the door as she was leaving and insisted I come in for a cup of tea.''

''Aye.'' Mrs. Grant nodded. She took the kettle from the hearth and got another cup from the cupboard. ''You so seldom have company, sir, that I knew you wouldn't want me to let this one get away.'' She chuckled at her own joke.

He looked down at the envelope in his hand. So, it was Sarah's handwriting. Mrs. Grant was right. It would never do to let her get away. ''Thank you for your diligence, Mrs. Grant,'' he said with a little bow in her direction.

She beamed. ''He's a real gentleman, this one,'' she said to Sarah. ''I've worked for all sorts, but Mr. Travis is tops.''

''Indeed,'' Sarah said, her expression undecipherable.

Mrs. Grant put the cup on the table and poured a dark tea into it.

He sat and placed the envelope beside the cup. He kept his gaze fastened on Sarah, afraid she might disappear if he turned his back. At his gesture, she sat down again.

The housekeeper picked up her own cup and put it in the basin. ''I'll just clean these things up in the morning, sir. Can I get you anything else before I leave? There's some stew left. Miss Hunt said it was very tasty.''

''Did she, now?'' He smiled, knowing that for a blatant lie.

''Aye. Says as how she'd have had more but dined earlier. Says they have the same recipe in her family, but they use more salt and herbs instead of spices. Gave me her recipe, she did.''

Sarah met his gaze and gave a little shrug. ''My brothers prefer salty to sweet. I thought Mrs. Grant might like to try that variation.''

Ethan leaned back in his chair and folded his arms across his chest, feasting on Sarah rather than on an insubstantial stew. ''Thank you, Mrs. Grant, but I ate whilst I was out.''

Mrs. Grant wiped her hands on her apron and retrieved her coat from a peg by the back door. "Next time I'll try Miss Hunt's recipe. Always willin' to try new things, I am."

"That is a great virtue, Mrs. Grant," Ethan said.

"Well, I'm off," she said, halfway out the door. "Nice to meet ye, Miss Hunt."

"And you, as well, Mrs. Grant," Sarah acknowledged, standing again—whether in deference to the housekeeper or in preparation to go he could not tell.

He shook his head and pointed her back to her chair as the door closed behind the housekeeper and the room fell silent. Unmoving, he studied Sarah for a long moment. Wiley, sensing the tension between them, padded softly to Sarah's side and placed his head in her lap. She began stroking the setter's head in soothing rhythms. She had made a conquest of his dog. He had long suspected Wiley was a good judge of character.

He drummed his fingertips against the envelope on the table and smiled when Sarah's face registered horror. Prolonging the moment, he gestured at her bowl. "Tasty, eh?"

"Well, um, yes."

"In truth, Sarah, only Wiley eats Mrs. Grant's culinary accomplishments with enthusiasm."

"She was very kind, Mr. Travis, and I—"

"Ethan," he insisted.

"—could not tell her that clove and cinnamon are not considered standard seasoning for stew."

He was pleased that she had cared enough to spare Mrs. Grant's feelings. "I shall pray she likes your recipe," he said. He picked up the envelope and tapped the edge against the table's surface.

She stood again, looking more desperate this time, and her gown made a soft sound as it settled around her hips and legs. "I did not expect to find you here. I intended to put that—" she gestured at the envelope "—through your mail drop and go back to Nica's. I was unaware that you had servants. I do not recall seeing anyone the night you brought me here.''

''Mrs. Grant does not live in,'' he said, not certain why he felt a need to explain himself. ''And my groom lives above the carriage house. But why did you come in? You could have refused Mrs. Grant's invitation.''

''She does not accept refusal well. I tried. I think she intended to discover my purpose in coming here.'' She retrieved an embroidered silk shawl with a deep fringe from the back of her chair. ''I'll be going now.''

''Oh, not yet, Sarah.'' He inserted his index finger beneath the envelope's flap and lifted, drawing the moment out. ''I confess to a certain curiosity, myself.''

''I believe the note is self-explanatory.''

''Bear with me.'' When he unfolded the single page, he was surprised to find several paragraphs. ''Well, what have we here? Hmm.

> *''Dear Mr. Travis,*
> *It is my most fervent hope that you will accept my*
> *apology for the many wrongs I have done you. You*
> *had a right to know who I was, and I deliberately*
> *deceived you as to my identity.''*

He looked up. Sarah was studying her fingernails rather intently, flushed, but not yet blushing. He read on.

> *''I further compounded my error by allowing you to*
> *put yourself at risk as a favor to me. No true friend*
> *would have permitted that, and I am deeply ashamed*
> *of my selfishness.''*

Deeply ashamed? No more so than he for using her vivacity and appetite for life to stir his own dormant emotions.

Sarah edged toward the door. "I really must be getting back. Nica will be looking for me."

He held one hand up to stay her. He was nearly done and wanted to wring the last possible drop of revenge out of this situation before he tendered his own apology.

"I pray that, in time, you will forgive me and remember me kindly.
Your Most Remorseful Friend, Sarah Hunter."

He stood and dropped her note on the table. "It may interest you to know that I forgave you the instant you disregarded the opinion of society to defend me against my brother's vilification."

Her eyes widened. "But you were so angry."

"I am still angry."

"I wanted to tell you weeks ago, Ethan, but I was afraid."

"Of me?" That prospect sobered him. He had deliberately cultivated a dangerous reputation to keep snoops away from his warehouses, but he had never wanted Sarah to fear him.

"That you would refuse to help me. Or tell my brothers out of a misguided sense of chivalry."

"Chivalry? Me?"

Her gaze came up to meet his full on. "Was it not you who lectured me on the future of the human race depending upon the male's instinct to protect the female? And was it not you who attempted to reform me by offering better positions at every turn? Time and again, and given every opportunity to the contrary, you have proved that you are a gentleman."

He stepped closer and stroked the line of her cheek with one finger. "The cost to me has been greater than you can possibly know."

"No greater than the cost to me, I think." She retreated

until her back was against the wall. She glanced toward the hallway and front door as if measuring her chance for escape.

He followed, pinning her in place with a firmly planted hand to the wall on each side of her. "Do you realize the torture it was—wanting you, needing you and knowing I could never have you? Try to imagine what being with you did to me."

"Never have me?" Sarah looked up at him with those luminous eyes and he felt as if he had fallen off a precipice. "But I told you...I invited you to...I did not know how to make it more plain."

To his shame, he gave lie to his good intentions with a firming in his nether regions. Gathering strength, he held her at arm's length and shook his head. "How could I ruin your future for my own pleasure. One day you will want to marry—"

"I shall never marry." She expelled the words quietly as if she had said them countless times before.

"You say that now, Sarah, but someone worthy of you will come along. Someone you can love."

"Stop it!" Tears welled in her eyes and she shuddered with some deep emotion Ethan could not identify. "I am not a virgin, Ethan."

Her words stopped him. If what she said was true, what unconscionable rake had damaged her and left her without a future? She still had a full complement of brothers, so he had to surmise that she had been successfully avenged.

In the wake of his silence, Sarah pushed against his chest and ducked beneath his arm. "That did not matter when you thought I was a fallen sister. What is the difference now? Do you want me less because I am titled?"

Her anger and hurt confused Ethan. "Would you have me cast your future to the winds, Sarah? Shall I show as little regard for you as the man who dishonored you?"

"*Dishonored* me?" Sarah's voice was closer to hysteria

than Ethan had ever heard it. She spun on her heel and headed for the door. "Would that it were that simple!"

Suspicion grew as he watched her reaction. Sarah's disregard for her safety, as if she had nothing more to lose, her odd mix of innocence and fear, her accusation that pleasure was a male concept, her certainty that she would never marry—all could be accounted for if…but it could not be. Sarah would have fought tooth and nail if a man had attacked her. But if it had not been a single man? "Sarah, how many were there?"

She stopped and her shoulders sagged. A long moment passed and Ethan thought she would not answer. He knew she was considering denial. But when she turned, the proud tilt of her chin told him she was telling the truth.

"Four." No explanation. No excuse. No appeal for sympathy or hint of weakness.

Afraid he would do or say something that would send her running, he did not reach out for her, but neither did he retreat. He held his ground and hoped for the best. "When?"

"Does it matter?"

"To me."

The defiance seemed to drain from her and she closed her eyes and shuddered. "It was years ago, Ethan. I cannot…if you must know more, you will have to ask Auberville."

"Auberville? Not your brothers?" This was a surprise.

She touched his arm in an earnest plea. "You must not say anything to my brothers! Swear it, Ethan."

They did not know! Dear Lord! Sarah had endured the worst that fate could deal a woman, and had kept it from her own family. He looked down at her hand on his sleeve, small and fragile and trembling with fear that he would expose her to her brothers. "Who are they, Sarah? I will kill them."

"Auberville," she said again. "Ask Auberville."

He nodded his agreement, determined to return to the

ball and pull Auberville aside for a private chat this very night.

Sarah sagged against him in relief, her cheek against his chest. He closed his arms around her and dropped a comforting kiss on the top of her head.

"Ethan, my brothers must never know. But I am so tired of keeping secrets, so tired of being afraid and living a lie, pretending to be whole. Being with you made me believe—"

"What? What did you believe?" he asked, tightening his arms with the very *rightness* of feeling her, soft and pliant, against him.

"That you might not care that I wasn't whole. That you might want me anyway. And that I might be able to conquer my fear of...of being with a man."

And suddenly Ethan realized why Sarah had made innocent little attempts to seduce him, and what it was that she needed from him. He lifted her chin with one finger and studied her face. "Sarah, is that true?"

Her dark lashes fell to shield her eyes and a delicate hue of pink swept upward from her bodice until her cheeks burned with it. "Yes," she said in a voice so soft that he nearly missed it.

He crushed her against his chest and murmured, "God help me, Sarah, I want you enough not to warn you about me."

She gasped with the force of the current that shot through her. Ethan's arms, his touch, were like coming home after years of absence—foreign, but somehow right.

He scooped her off her feet, left the kitchen and carried her up the wide staircase. She gave a soft, breathless laugh. "I can walk, Ethan."

"Not a chance. I'm not letting loose of you this time." He kicked the door of his bedroom open and deposited her on her feet next to his bed. The door rebounded off the wall and slammed shut again.

The room was as she remembered it, but someone had

turned down the covers, placed a log on the fire, drawn the curtains and lit a candle by his bedside.

Ethan hesitated, his hands cupping her shoulders, his eyes burning into her. "Yea or nay, Sarah?"

"Y-yea," she said. Anxiety feathered the edges of her consciousness, but she attempted to fight it back. Once and for all, she needed to rid herself of the fear.

With a smile so vulnerable that she began to realize how important this was to Ethan, too, he leaned forward and fit his mouth to hers in a tentative kiss, requesting permission. Not his usual challenge, nor an invitation. The kiss was a tribute. The offering of a supplicant.

"Sarah," he whispered in her ear, "are you certain?"

"Utterly," she said on a shaky sigh. The silk shawl slipped from her shoulders to puddle at her feet.

He tangled his fingers through her hair, dislodging the amethyst coronet. As it clattered to the floor, he tugged gently to tilt her face up to his in a soul-shattering kiss. He held nothing back. His response was so strong, so transparent, that she felt the power of his hunger.

A muscle jumped along his jaw and he stepped back. "I am going to need a drink." He went to the table in front of the fire and seized a decanter of brandy and two glasses.

Disappointment filled her. "You've changed your mind."

"Dear God, no!" He laughed and came back to place the glasses on the bedside table. "I just need to slow this thing down before I disappoint us both."

He removed his jacket and threw it in the vicinity of a chair before he leaned toward her again to kiss her neck. When she reached for him, he stepped away. "Patience, Sarah. This is going to take some time."

He poured two brandies and snuffed the candle, dimming the room to an intimate glow. He brought her a glass and pressed it between her hands. "Sip. Brandy deserves respect."

She nodded and took a sip, anxious for anything that would quiet her nerves. He took the glass from her hand and put it back on the nightstand. Coming up behind her, he leaned down to nibble delicately at her earlobe. She felt a little tug, and the sash of her gown slipped to the floor to join the shawl. His hands worked at the buttons down her back to free them of their loops and he peeled one little puffed sleeve off her shoulder before pressing a kiss there, too. Her other shoulder received a similar gift. "Ready?" he asked.

She nodded, glad of the warmth that had begun to radiate outward from her stomach. It took every ounce of courage she possessed to fight her fears back into the ether.

He released her gown and it slid to the floor in a whoosh. She shivered in the sudden cold. Her silk shift fell to just below her knees and afforded no protection for her modesty. She wished she had worn the new French drawers Madame had made for her. Then Ethan released the little straps over her shoulders, and the shift, too, fell to the floor, leaving her in nothing but her white slippers and stockings, and pink garters.

He came around to face her, his eyes darker than she'd ever seen them. "You shame the moon," he said reverently before lifting her and placing her on his bed. One leg at a time, he pulled off her slippers and tossed them over his shoulder, then removed her garters and rolled her stockings down to her ankles and threw them, too, into some far corner.

Completely naked, Sarah shivered. She reached for the coverlet but Ethan shook his head. "Please, Sarah, give me this much for the sleepless nights you have caused me."

Warmth of another kind flooded her, and she reached for the brandy instead. As the liquid burned its way down her throat, Ethan began disrobing. His gaze never left her, and she was frozen with fascination. For the sake of modesty, she wanted to look away, but fear would not let her.

With four brothers, she knew enough to know that Ethan was a fine specimen. The muscles in his chest, shoulders and arms were hard and well-defined. A light matting of dark hair on his chest spilled downward in a sharp V past his abdomen to disappear into his trousers. And there, when he pushed his trousers down his narrow hips, her eyes widened. She had never seen Ethan so…distended. His organ appeared rigid and swollen, and standing at attention. Her heart stopped and her gaze snapped upward to his. Her panic must have shown, because he smiled and shook his head.

"Do not worry, Sarah. Everything will fit when the time comes. Trust me in this."

And then he, too, was naked. She reached for the brandy again. Because she had brothers, and had endured a brutal attack in the night-dark gardens of Vauxhall, she was not completely ignorant of the equipment. But how could she have guessed Ethan would be so generously endowed? She wondered if it was too late to change her mind.

It was. The bed creaked as he added his weight. He reached for her, his hand gentle and warm, and she melted into him. There was nothing yet to fear. The sensation of his skin against hers was the most sensual feeling she had ever experienced. She liked this infinitely better than when he'd kept his clothes on. Under her fingertips, he was a blend of hardness, heat and velvet smoothness. She was fascinated with the texture of his skin and the ways his muscles moved beneath it.

He brushed her hair back from her face and kissed her eyes. "I love your eyes, Sarah. They remind me of violets and pansies in the spring."

She smiled, welcoming the languor of the new infusion of brandy and the addition of Ethan's warmth against her. She touched his cheek and sighed. "Ethan, you do not have to do this."

"Oh, but I do," he said, and lightly traced the seam of her lips with his tongue, urging her to open.

When she did, he deepened his kisses and slipped his knee between her thighs, then pulled her leg up to ride his hip. "I want to feel your heat, Sarah. I want you to feel mine."

His steel velvet shaft pressed against her mons, and her breath caught on a gasp. She was not shocked. To the contrary, she was deeply and instantly aroused. The slight pressure against her awakened a need for deeper contact. She moved her hips forward, seeking that contact, and Ethan groaned.

"Slowly, Sarah. Anticipate. The longer the delay, the sweeter the release."

"Have we…not anticipated…long enough already?" she asked, unable to catch her breath.

"Almost, sweetling." He laughed quietly, the sound sending little chill bumps up her spine. "Almost."

He blazed a trail of kisses down the line of her neck to the hollow of her throat, and she trembled with the memory of the Black Dog Tavern, and how Ethan had worked some kind of magic on her. His hands cupped her breasts and he shifted his attention there. She thought she would jump out of her skin when, in a series of nibbles and kisses, her breasts became so sensitive and the pleasure so powerful that she whimpered.

"Sarah?" Ethan mumbled, his mouth still against her skin. "Shall I stop?"

"No!" She grabbed a handful of Ethan's dark hair and held him in place. She would die if he stopped! She needed more. More of that, and more of…of that exquisite pressure at the soft core of her. Thinking that, she opened her legs a little wider and slid her inner thigh up Ethan's hip.

"Almost," he murmured again, returning his attention to the firm little buttons her nipples had become.

When the tingling sensation spread to every extremity and she thought she could bear no more, he lifted his weight off her and rolled her onto her side. Before she could feel his absence, he began kissing the nape of her neck and whispering in her ear.

"I do not want to neglect a single part of you, Sarah. I've waited too long to miss a thing."

With that, one hand came around her to cup a breast, and the other hand came around her to dip lower. Even as he kissed her shoulders and began a descent down her spine, her attention was riveted on that other hand. It slid over her mons and his middle finger separated the petals shielding her passage. The heel of his hand pressed enticingly against her as his finger made a shallow entry.

"Oh!" Heat swept through her, and a new need sprang to life, a need for more of everything. More pressure, more entry, more movement. She trembled with anticipation and arched her hips to give him better access.

"Nearly," Ethan coached her. "Almost." And his fingers began a rhythmic stroking.

She was wild when his kisses finally reached the small of her back. Her entire body felt as if it would burst into flames. Her hips twitched and began to match the rhythm he set with his stroking.

"Yes, Sarah," he muttered against the curve of her buttock. "You're close. We're almost there...." He released her long enough to turn her around again. Abandoning kisses, he trailed his tongue in a little circle around the dip of her navel.

She shivered and closed her eyes, the better to experience the sensation. And when his mouth went lower still, she was burning for it, no longer shocked by what he might do next.

By the time his tongue touched the little nubbin, Sarah was panting, literally gasping, for air. Her chest heaved and little keening sounds emitted from somewhere deep in her throat. All sensation was inward now, concentrated in her center. Eyes still closed against unwanted, unneeded distractions, she felt as if she were jumping out of her skin. She could not remain still. Her head thrashed on the pillow, and she arched in instinctive response to his skillful manipulations. She was frantic within minutes.

She seized a handful of Ethan's hair and tugged him upward. "Ethan! My god! End it...end it, please."

Slowly he slid up the length of her, letting her feel him, accustom herself to his contours. Her knees bent to hold him between them, and then, for one breathless moment when the fear took control, everything stopped as she gulped air, feeling as if she were going to faint.

"Open your eyes, Sarah," he demanded in a tightly controlled voice.

Poised above her, Ethan watched her with somber intensity. His eyes did not reflect her, but seemed to swallow her. She could not look away, nor could she close her eyes again and separate him from what was happening.

His first probing was tentative, as if seeking, testing, stretching her to his size. Fear stirred with the discomfort and licked at the back of her mind, struggling to come forward and assert itself. But, still lost in Ethan's eyes, she felt too safe, too cherished, to give them credence.

He hitched her knees a little higher and slid forward at the same time, deepening his entry in a slow, sure stroke. She let her breath out in a long sigh that was voiced as a moan. She felt swollen, filled with him. There was a thickness inside her, discomfort, but no pain, only an ache for more, for any and all of him that he would give her.

"Sarah?" he whispered, his muscles straining above her. "Are you with me?"

She didn't know what he meant, but she nodded in the affirmative.

He withdrew barely an inch or two, and then slid into her again. Chill bumps covered her body in response. The sensation was so completely torturous but illogically satisfying that she knew she needed more. She ran her hands down his sides to his narrow hips, then around to his buttocks. She lifted to him awkwardly as he began to withdraw again.

"No, my love," he said, a smile curving his lips. He took her hands, one at a time, and laced his fingers through hers. When he pressed them against the pillow on either side of her head, he said, "Let me do the work."

That seemed so unfair in view of the fact that he looked as if he were in pain. His breathing was labored and his chest was heaving. "But—"

"You've trusted me so far, Sarah. Trust this, too."

"Yes," she said, anxious to end it. With the pause had come a resurgence of her fears. She closed her eyes to shut them out.

He began moving again, a slow, shallow rocking against her that brought her back to a fever pitch, and then he lifted, almost to the point of withdrawal and slid back in. She whimpered.

"Sarah!" he demanded in a hoarse voice. "Open your eyes."

Ethan, showing the strain, was searching her face with a desperate look. "It's me, Sarah. Only me. Say it."

"Ethan. Only Ethan," she murmured. The fears receded.

He shuddered and began moving again, slowly at first and then faster, and all the while he held her gaze. There was something unutterably intimate about that, as if he were looking into her very soul, seeing things in her that no one else had ever, *could* ever, see. The pressure that had been building since he had carried her up the stairs was nearly unbearable. She was on fire.

And, just when she thought there could be no more, Ethan moaned and came into her with one final thrust. Every nerve was zinging, every muscle straining. Suddenly, and without warning, tremors erupted at her core. She arched and cried out as wave after rapturous wave washed over her in devastating completeness. She finished as he rasped her name like a prayer.

As her heartbeat slowed, she closed her eyes again, swallowed by the *petit mort*, the little death, as she had heard Madame Marie call it. She was dimly aware that Ethan had separated from her and fallen to her side. He pulled the covers over them, and still she could not drag herself from the delicious lassitude.

Gentle hands smoothed the hair back from her face and a voice murmured in her ear. "Sarah? Are you there?"

She gave a breathless laugh. "No, I am somewhere between heaven and earth."

"Are you still afraid?" he asked with an anxious catch in his voice.

"Terrified."

There was a long pause before he asked, "Of me?"

"Yes. Petrified that you will never do that again."

He laughed and pulled her over on top of him. "I am at your disposal, madam. Do with me as you please."

She rested her cheek against his chest and felt the rumble of his laughter. His laugh! That's what was different about him. His laugh had always been slightly detached, partly cynical and partly self-deprecating. But since carrying her up the stairs, it had been the laugh of a young man living wholly for the moment. Is that what he had heard in *her* laugh?

Her hair tumbled over her shoulders and fell across his broad chest. She liked the sight of it there. She traced a circle around one brownish nipple and watched in fascination as it firmed. He shivered and tightened his arm around her.

The mantel clock chimed three times and reality came back to her with sobering suddenness. "I...I must go." She stood and looked around frantically for her clothes.

"Sarah, come back to bed. 'Tis too late to salvage the situation. I shall go to your brother first thing in the morning, and we will work this out."

Her heart sank with a sickening thud. "You are going to tell Reggie? But you will be dead by evening! Every one of my brothers delights in defending the family honor. 'Tis why I had to hide...oh, why must you tell Reggie?"

''I love you, Sarah.''

Ethan's words startled and unnerved her. But she could not just surprise her brother with this news. ''R-Reggie does not need to know that, Ethan. I do not want him to know.''

Ethan went to his wardrobe and tossed her a shirt, trousers and a cap to hide the tangles of her ruined coiffure. ''Very well, Sarah. Come to me on the morrow and we shall work this out. Promise?''

''Promise.''

Chapter Sixteen

Everywhere Sarah looked, life was more vibrant today and anything seemed possible. Ethan loved her and she loved him. Last night she had been too befuddled to know how to respond to his declaration, but today she knew. She would tell him how she felt tonight.

She walked along, peeking into stalls offering goods of every kind, amused by the gaudy colors and wares. The hubbub distracted her maid, Sylvie, and Sarah told her to wait by a puppet show while she made her purchases.

She examined a selection of pralines, candied nuts, sugared plums and dried fruits. Reggie had a sweet tooth. She had left a message for him that she needed to talk to him before he went out that evening. She intended to tell him the truth—that she was not virgin, and why, and that she had found a man who did not care, who loved her anyway. And that she thought he might ask her hand. Fearing his objection once he knew the man's name, she chose the largest tin of his favorites and paid the vendor.

She caught sight of Mr. Renquist wending his way through the crowds. He stopped at a flower cart and she headed that way, affecting bored indifference. With Sylvie watching the puppet show, Sarah knew she'd be safe for at least ten minutes.

When she stood beside him inspecting a display of roses

and lilies, she murmured, "Has Dicken told you that we have not found a lead on Benjamin?"

"Aye," Mr. Renquist said. "The lad at the workhouse was too old. Benjamin is barely more than a babe. I fear we shall have to look for him amongst chimney sweeps and the like, where smallness is a virtue."

Sarah's heart twisted with fear. "Oh, but that is so dangerous, Mr. Renquist! We must find him soon."

He lowered his voice and said, "Lady Sarah, the ship I have arranged to, er, take Mr. Whitlock on his tour is scheduled to sail Sunday, just before dawn."

Sunday? "But that leaves only tonight, tomorrow and Saturday to find Benjamin! Reggie's party is tomorrow night. That is not enough time, Mr. Renquist."

Mr. Renquist leaned down and pulled a yellow day lily from a flower bucket as if examining it for flaws. "We are doing our best, milady."

"I am certain of it, sir, but— "

"The more I learn, the less I like it. Whitlock is a nasty piece of work. Leave the investigation to me, Lady Sarah, before disaster overtakes you."

She shook her head, staring down at a posy of violets. "Pray continue and, time being short, I must do the same."

"Give me tonight, Lady Sarah. If I do not come up with little Benjamin's whereabouts, I will not impede you," Mr. Renquist conceded with a heavy sigh.

Sarah nodded her agreement to his terms, but she still needed one more piece of information. Knowing which scandal had tainted Ethan's reputation had never seemed important before, but now, in view of the news she was about to give her brother, she was desperate to know. "Do you recall introducing me to a man named Ethan Travis?"

Renquist turned to look at her directly. "I did not introduce you, milady. He introduced himself."

"'Tis a fine distinction, I am sure. Either way, we were

introduced, and you referred to him as the 'Demon of Alsatia.'"

"That is what people call him."

"Speak, Mr. Renquist. You cannot shock me, nor can you prevent me from finding out more about the man. Whatever it is, I know him to be a man of character and—"

"No, milady. You must not trust him."

"Why?"

"He keeps turning up in our investigation. Just when we think we're closing in on Whitlock, Travis shows up and queers it. It's almost as if he's protecting the bastard."

Sarah smiled. She really should have warned Mr. Renquist that Ethan had been working with her. "I know it must seem that way, sir, but a week or so after I became involved, he began lending a hand—"

"No. Travis has been showing up from the first. It was no coincidence—him being at the King's Head that night. I've been running afoul of him ever since you put us on this case, at least a week before."

Sarah pressed her temples where a dull throbbing began. Had Ethan contrived their meeting? Had running into him the following night outside the orphanage not been happenstance? Surely not. When she picked Mr. Whitlock out of the crowd at the Swan as their target for following, had that, too, been engineered by Ethan? A sick feeling settled in her stomach.

"I...I cannot believe it," she managed to say.

"He is a criminal. A thief. Like as not, a murderer. 'Tis common knowledge he is a traitor."

She suspected Ethan might have skirted the law, but murder? Treason? "You are mistaken, Mr. Renquist."

"No, milady." Renquist shook his head emphatically. "Why, when he first came to these parts, he bought a warehouse. Immediately after, dead bodies started showing up thereabouts."

Sarah frowned. "He is an importer?"

"Importer! That's a corker! 'Tis just a fancy name for stolen goods. Did you hear me, milady? I said *dead bodies!*"

"Coincidence."

"Seven of 'em, milady?"

"Well—" she swallowed "—that does seem excessive, but there must be a logical explanation."

"Aye—Travis did not want anyone snooping around his warehouses! He's got stolen goods in there or my name is not Francis Renquist. For certain, there's blood on his hands."

Ethan's hands? Those strong, gentle hands that could drive her into a frenzy? How could that be? She glanced over her shoulder, praying they could not be overheard. She trusted Mr. Renquist implicitly. She knew him to be a man of honor. He would not lie about such a thing, nor would he slander another man's reputation.

Struggling to comprehend, she seized on the only thing that made no sense. "T-treason? Did you say treason?"

Mr. Renquist explained. "He gave military secrets to the Moors, Lady Sarah, so they could hide British hostages. The whole operation went for naught. There was no trial. 'Twas whispered they could not get the proof on him. British ships, British sailors, British subjects, sacrificed for naught, because of one man's betrayal. Travis's betrayal."

She recalled such an engagement shortly after the Wednesday League had uncovered a white slavery scheme. Englishwomen had been kidnapped and sold at auctions held in Algiers and Tunis. The Wednesday League had discussed possible strategies for locating and freeing those women.

Scant months later they received news of the bombardment of Algiers. The Royal Navy had sailed into the port demanding the release of all Christians and foreign hostages and slaves. Unbeknownst to the British admiral, someone—Ethan?—had alerted the Dey before the engagement. Dutch, German, French, Italian and Spanish hostages had been released, but not a single British man or woman. England had been outraged.

She had been outraged! "No," she murmured. "He cannot have had anything to do with that."

Not that he was not capable—he was. More than capable—adept. She had not the slightest doubt he could command an army of thieves and deceive the entire constabulary of London. Yes, he was capable of cutting down anyone who got between him and his goal, and she was quite certain he was as dangerous as she'd been warned. But treason—this *particular* treason?

"My information is reliable, Lady Sarah."

"But, had there been proof, he'd have been charged."

"'Twas said he was well-connected, and only his family alliance saved him from public trial."

A quick picture of Ethan's brother and his wife flashed through her mind. Is that why they did not want to acknowledge him? If his own family believed him guilty—heavens! She could have forgiven murder and thievery easier than this particular treason. *This* treason was personal, almost as if it had been committed against her. Because, in a way, it had. The men who attacked her in Vauxhall Gardens had been kidnappers and suppliers of Englishwomen to the Dey. *And Ethan, too, had been in the employ of the Dey—selling not women, but information.*

If he was capable of misleading her about following Mr. Whitlock, then he was capable of almost anything. And if that was true, everything she had believed about him was based on lies and deception! She had trusted her instincts, her heart, when she should have given credence to his reputation and the warnings from Mr. Renquist and Dicken.

Oh, the villain! He had coaxed kisses from her with no more than a honeyed smile and a lowered head! There were dukes, and yes, even a prince, who had not accomplished as much with considerably more effort. And Ethan had accomplished so much more. She moaned as she recalled lying in his arms, arching to his hand, wrapping her legs around him like a wanton hussy!

With a crescendo of drum and cymbals, the puppet show ended and Sylvie clapped gleefully. She whirled and headed in Sarah's direction, waving as she came. "Lady Sarah, are ye done?"

Tears stung her eyes. *Completely done,* she thought. Thank heavens she had never confessed her love to him!

Once home, Sarah instructed Sylvie to draw a hot bath while she took her flower purchases to the kitchen.

Reggie appeared in the doorway of the library as she headed down the corridor toward the kitchen. "Ah, here you are," he said, taking her burden from her and going back into the library. "I've been waiting on tenterhooks since reading your note. Have you news for me, Sarah? Who have you chosen?"

Sarah bit back a curse. She had forgotten the note she'd left her brother. "N-no, Reggie. I have not chosen, but I am narrowing the field."

"Who is left?" he asked, laying the bundle on his desk. "I've been watching, dearling, and I cannot tell who you favor."

Sarah fell into a chair and folded her hands in her lap. "Reggie, you are assuming I could have any man I fancied. That is rather vain, do you not think? It is not as if I have amassed a pile of proposals."

"Cedric has asked permission to pay you court, and I have given it. There are three or four others who, with the least encouragement, would make an offer. If you do not want Cedric, encourage them."

His face, so handsome and hopeful, was a reproach to her. She should tell him why she would never marry now and end it. But how could she bear to see his disappointment? She stood and retrieved the tin of sweets from the pile on his desk. "Look what I brought you, Reggie."

He grinned as he opened the tin and popped a candied

nut into his mouth. "I shall miss you, Sarah, when you have your own home. Who will take care of me then?"

"I will, Reggie." She sighed deeply. Yes, she would grow old in Hunter Hall, barely tolerated by whatever wife Reggie took, pitied by her nieces and nephews, and ignored by her brothers. "I will take care of you as long as you need me."

"Thank you, dearling, but you will be too busy taking care of your husband and children. I am pleased that you would sacrifice so much for me, though."

"'Tis no sacrifice, Reggie."

His smile faded and he came around the desk to kneel by her chair and take her hand earnestly. "I've said it before, but it is important to me to know that you believe it. Your rowdy brothers and I love you. We have always wanted what is best for you. I am not anxious to lose you, but I know that a family of your own will complete you. Trust me in this, dearling."

Trust me in this.... The very words Ethan had said to her last night. And look how *that* had turned out.

Well, the time had come for Reggie to know the truth. It was time to trust *him.* "Reggie, were you aware that, several years ago, Richard Farmingdale paid me court?"

"Farmingdale? Faugh! The man was a villain. Had I known, Sadie, I'd have put a stop to it. Did Father know?"

"No. You see, the rituals and manners of society were all so new to me that I did not know what to expect. I thought he might be serious, but I could not be certain, and—"

"He broke your heart," Reggie finished with a nod. "Which explains why you have been so reticent. My dear Sadie, your heart will heal. Farmingdale was not worthy of it, and Father would never have approved such an unworthy match in any case."

Sarah shook her head emphatically. "He did not break my heart, Reggie. He broke my—"

"Here you are," Charles said as he entered the library.

He spotted the heap of flowers and the tin of sweets on Reggie's desk. "Ordering flowers for the gala tomorrow? Good to see you have it under control, Sarah." He opened the tin and removed a praline. "What time do you want us in line to receive guests?"

Sarah looked from Charles to Reggie and back again. She could not tell them both. Not now. Not like this. She stood and headed for the door. "Eight o'clock."

"Sarah," Reggie called after her. "I noted your waltz with Lord Ethan Travis last night. Please do not encourage his interest. I do not think he is the man for you."

She could not agree more.

Somewhere in the distance a church bell rang twice. Ethan pulled the curtain aside and glanced out at the darkened street. Where was Sarah? She had promised to meet him tonight, but she hadn't been at St. Paul's and she hadn't come here. He poured a glass of claret and took it back to his chair.

His blood thickened as he thought of the previous night. He had struggled with his conscience before he'd made love to Sarah. He was well aware that such an action would change their lives forever—Sarah's not for the better. But her softly voiced plea had so surprised and enchanted him that he could not have resisted even if the house had caught fire. Finally he'd made love to her because she wanted him—despite his reputation, his dishonor, his relentless taunting when he'd found out she had deceived him—she'd wanted *him*. Ethan Travis. Not the fops who surrounded her at galas and balls. Not idle rich gentlemen with sterling reputations like—

Cedric Broxton. And yes, to his shame, he'd made love to her in part because he couldn't bear the thought that Broxton was literally being "groomed" for the task. The mere thought had eaten at his vitals every second until, scarcely twenty-four hours ago, she had looked at him with her heart in her eyes and said that she had hoped he might not care that she wasn't whole. That he might want her anyway.

Ethan laughed, the sound echoing in the empty parlor. Want her anyway? Not much. Just with a wildfire in his veins that threatened to burn out of control every time she looked at him. Just with the same single-minded purpose that had kept him awake every night since meeting her. And he fully intended to marry her at the first opportunity.

The fly in the ointment was the chaos in Ethan's personal life. The timing could not be worse.

With the luxury of time, he would court and cajole her, woo and win her. She deserved that much. But, in view of last night, Sarah required immediate attention. He could not have her roaming the midnight streets in search of adventure, nor could he expose her to the risk of an early pregnancy.

He glanced at the side table next to his chair where a small parcel wrapped in brown paper and string rested. The light, almost liquid, silk of Sarah's gown, petticoat and shawl had folded around her coronet into a parcel no thicker than an inch or two. If she was not able to come tonight, he would seek her out tomorrow at her brother's gala. And then he would settle matters with Lockwood.

Chapter Seventeen

Sarah stared down at her green satin slippers and noticed the slightest hint of a scuff. The reception line was growing shorter, and Cedric was waiting to claim her first dance.

"Ah, so kind of you to have me, my dear," Lord Nigel Dunsmore said, claiming her attention.

Sarah glanced up and smiled. He was looking tired tonight, and his lips had a bluish tinge. "Your Grace," she said, and curtsied. "How could we ever forget you? I vow, we'd have rescheduled if you had sent your regrets." She really must remember to tell Nigel how very dear he was to her.

"Sweet girl." He squeezed her hand warmly. "I looked for you before I left the Aubervilles' the other night. Wanted to say goodbye, but you'd gone on. I'd like to talk to you tonight. Save me a dance? Early, if you please."

"Of course, Your Grace," Sarah said. She would request a slow, stately dance from the orchestra. If Nigel wanted to speak with her, he must have a reason.

"You look enchanting this evening, m'dear. No longer a girl, but a woman in full. Your papa would have been proud."

Sarah looked down at herself. Her white underdress was of silk, and the overdress that fell only as far as her knees was of a fine white lawn with a green embroidered border.

Madame Marie had assured her it was in the very height of fashion. Could Lord Nigel be referring to the low cut of her décolletage? Or, good heavens, was there something about her that betrayed that she now a woman of "experience?"

Next in line came Lord and Lady Carter. They exchanged pleasantries and Sarah was feeling almost relaxed when an uneasy feeling made the hair on the nape of her neck stand on end. The faint scent of lime tickled her nose and her heartbeat sped.

When she turned and found Ethan Travis standing there, she was not surprised. Although she had suspected he would come, she could not catch her breath, and hysteria seemed mere seconds away. Would he expose her? Confront her? Ask her why she had not come for her things yesterday?

"Ah, Lord Ethan," Reggie said. "Glad you could make it. I wasn't sure you'd remember the invitation."

Ethan gave a polite bow in acknowledgement. "I never forget the things I *want* to do," he said with a pointed look in Sarah's direction.

"I believe you have met my sister?"

Ethan's hazel eyes flashed at her, his emotions visibly deepening. "Met? Has Sarah not—"

"A-at the Aubervilles', night before last," Sarah filled in before he could betray them.

"Ah, yes. Aubervilles'," Ethan repeated. He accepted her offered hand, bowed over it and turned the palm up to kiss her wrist where her pulse beat close to the surface.

The heat of his lips and the memory of what that mouth could do nearly caused her knees to buckle. Time stopped for one breathless moment as Ethan straightened and his gaze met hers. There was an angry challenge there and she knew he would demand answers when he found her alone.

Reggie had not seen Ethan's gesture and was saying something about hunting in Scotland by the time she regained her senses. She reclaimed her hand, resisting the impulse to clasp it behind her so he could not unnerve her like that again.

When Reggie was finished with his story, Ethan turned to her and bowed again. "Lady Sarah, I shall see you again this evening. You *will* save me a waltz?"

"I…I may have promised all my dances, Lord Ethan."

Ethan stared at her a long moment, and a hard look settled over his features. "Yes, well, one of those would be mine. If I recall correctly, you promised me a waltz."

"When did she promise you a waltz?" Reggie asked, looking as if he had missed something.

"Night before last," Ethan murmured. "At the Aubervilles'. Just after our last…waltz."

Sarah felt heat suffuse her cheeks. Ethan was not referring to a dance. "I…I had forgot," she faltered.

Reggie studied her closely, and she knew he suspected that there was more to Ethan's conversation than was apparent.

"I can see that I credited myself with more importance than I deserve," Ethan said. He clenched his jaw and a muscle jumped along his cheek. Sarah recognized it as an angry response.

"I did not mean to give offense, Lord Ethan, but the duties of a hostess are very demanding, and—"

Reggie furrowed his brows again. "'Tis just a dance, Sarah."

Her heart sank. How would she ever be able to keep a polite smile in place as she danced and told Ethan that she never wanted to see him again? She would have to find a way. "I shall look for an opportunity, Lord Ethan."

"I am at your disposal."

Yet another reminder of…no, she couldn't think of that. She had to cut him from her life.

Ethan shot her a look that said he was not finished with her, bowed again and moved on to greet her other brothers.

* * *

Playing Reggie's hostess was an exercise in diplomacy and management. One moment she was charming a sulking guest or smoothing over an argument that threatened to come to blows, and the next she was visiting the kitchen to leave instructions for more punch or to replenish the buffet. And all the while, she kept an eye on Ethan. He was watching her, waiting to find her alone for a few moments. She had a bad moment when, seeing him in deep conversation with Lord Auberville, she recalled telling him to ask Auberville for the details of the attack on her. Well, that was of little consequence now.

She was on her way to the kitchen with instructions when Reggie intercepted her. He linked his arm through hers and led her toward the ballroom.

"Come with me, Sadie. 'Tis time to address our guests and thank them for coming."

Something secret in his smile made her uncomfortable. Fighting the instinct to break away and run, she followed Reggie's lead. When they reached the dais, Reggie nodded to the musicians and they played a small crescendo.

The guests halted their conversation in midsentence and turned to give them their attention. Sarah's heart raced and her feeling of alarm deepened. Something was afoot. She caught Lord Nigel's glance and he shrugged in helplessness.

"Dear friends," Reggie began. "I would like to thank you all for coming tonight. And now that our official mourning is at an end, it is fitting that we begin anew by sharing good news with you. I have accepted an offer for my much-loved sister—"

Sarah grew dizzy with shock. She looked up at Reggie's handsome face, unable to close her slack jaw. She began a protest, but Reggie put his arm around her in a gesture of filial devotion and continued in a carrying voice.

"—to wed Lord Cedric Broxton."

Even when Cedric stepped onto the dais to join them,

she could not comprehend the words. He took a position beside her and lifted her hand to his lips in a gesture she suspected was calculated to please the crowd. She gritted her teeth to keep from snatching her hand away.

Annica and Grace were glancing between Sarah and Cedric with astonishment. Auberville appeared dismayed. Ethan's eyes narrowed and his jaw set in a hard line. James and Andrew wore silly smiles and Charles winked at her.

Married? Married! Her stomach turned and she slipped her hand from Cedric's the moment his grip loosened. Trying her best to hide her astonishment, she whispered up to Reggie, "I must see you in the library at once."

"Dearling, this is not a good time."

"It had better be, Reggie, because if I do not talk to you at once, I am apt to make a scene by refusing Cedric publicly."

"Sarah, we are out of mourning, and 'tis time for you to get on with your life." The applause had died down and Reggie returned to his address. "Thank you once again, and please join us in our celebration."

Footmen, who had obviously known about this announcement before she had, came forward bearing trays laden with glasses of champagne. Outraged at her brother's ploy, Sarah nodded to the crowd and stepped down from the dais. Looking neither right nor left, she made straight for the library.

She heard a multitude of footsteps behind her, but she did not look back until she was safely inside the library and had poured herself a large unladylike glass of brandy from the decanter on Reggie's desk. They were all there—Reggie, Charles, Andrew, James—and Cedric.

Looking at Cedric, she pointed to the door. "Out."

"I have a right—"

She shook her head. "This is between me and my brothers. I will talk to you later, Lord Cedric. But for now—out."

Her brother nodded and Cedric departed on cue. Reggie

turned back to her and folded his arms across his chest. "You had your chance to choose, Sarah. You cannot say I did not give you ample time and opportunity."

"I do not know how, Reggie, but you will undo this at once. You cannot force me to stand before a minister and say words I shall never utter."

"I cannot 'undo' this. Cedric would look a fool, and you would look a jilt. You would make the Hunters a laughingstock."

"I am sorry, but that is your fault."

"You will marry Cedric. It is an excellent match, and I vouch that he is fond of you."

Sarah gulped half the brandy in her glass to the shocked expressions on her brothers' faces. She knew she was going to need the fortification. "Sit down. All of you."

Reggie remained standing, but Charles, James and Andrew all found seats in a grouping of chairs around the fireplace. She looked at their faces, so handsome, so dear, and...and so confused. Oh, if only she didn't have to do this.

But there was no hope for it now. The fat was in the fire. On the verge of tears, she began pacing as she talked. "Do you recall, several years ago, when Richard Farmingdale was paying me more than the usual amount of attention? Well, one night in the autumn, when we all went to Vauxhall Gardens for the entertainments, Mr. Farmingdale prevailed upon me to stroll with him down one of the darkened paths."

"Ah!" Charles said. "I recall. That was the night we looked all over for you until we got the note from Lady Annica saying that you were staying with her."

Her chin began to tremble and she struggled to control her voice. "Yes. That was the night."

James frowned. "We feared there was some chicanery afoot."

She sighed. "There's an interesting word for it."

"An interesting word for what, Sarah?" Charles asked.

Slow tears trickled down her cheeks. She finished the brandy and set the glass down on Reggie's desk with a bang. "Rape," she pronounced, and then felt oddly relieved, as if a great burden had been lifted from her. She went to look out the window, unable to face her brothers.

"Richard Farmingdale and three other men raped me that night. When they were finished, they discarded me in the mews behind Annica's house. Her driver found me when he was bringing her carriage around back. He brought Nica and she helped me to her room, took care of me and swore she'd keep my secret."

She had expected an angry outcry, denial, denunciations, exclamations, gasps—anything but the heavy silence that followed. The warmth of a hand on her shoulder nearly caused her knees to buckle, and when Reggie turned her to enfold her in his arms, she let her tears flow freely.

Reggie gave her his handkerchief. "Why did you not tell us, Sadie? Why have you carried this secret alone for so long?"

"I…was afraid you would think it was my fault. That I invited it by walking down that path with Mr. Farmingdale."

"No!" The cry was a single word from all her brothers.

"And I was afraid you'd seek to avenge me, and that you would come to injury on my account," she finished.

"Oh, Sarah." Charles shook his head. "We know you better. It could never be your fault." He led her to a chair while Reggie poured her another glass of brandy.

James handed her his handkerchief as he knelt beside her. "'Twill come a'right, Sarah. You've told us now, and we shall take care of it."

Andrew, expressionless, but with eyes as cold as ice, asked, "Who else, Sarah? I know Farmingdale is dead, but who else was involved? There are three more, and we shall draw straws for the honor of disemboweling them."

"Thank you, Andrew, for not disappointing me. But I fear I left none for you."

"What?" her brothers said in one voice.

She held up one hand, palm outward to quiet them.
"Later. For now, we must deal with this mess."

"If they're all dead, Cedric needn't know," Charles began. "You could still marry."

"He may not care," James chimed in.

"I could never deceive him. Nor could I...bear to have him...that is—"

"Never mind," Reggie comforted her. "I shall speak with Cedric and tell him that you—"

"No! I do not want him to know."

"—have convinced me of the unsuitability of the match. We shall concoct some likely story to whisper about. Perhaps we shall say we could not reach agreement as to the settlements."

"Thank you, Reggie." She blew her nose and heaved a sigh.

"Be kind and respectful to Cedric in the meantime. Allow society to think you are fond of him, and perhaps even honored by his offer. That will go a long way in soothing his pride."

"How long will this draw on, Reggie?"

"A week. No longer than two. We must give society enough time to believe that we have been haggling the details."

She nodded. The delay was a small enough price to pay for her freedom. She sniffled again and dabbed at the corners of her eyes. "Could you make my apologies to our guests, Reggie? I am completely overset by events."

"Of course," he agreed. "But tomorrow, we shall talk. I need to know about Farmingdale and the others. I need to know that there is nothing more to fear from that quarter. The men who did that to you must be dealt with."

She nodded, stood and went to the library door, wanting nothing more than to escape her brothers' questions.

Cedric was waiting outside the library door, and came forward. "Sarah? You have been crying. Are you well?"

Remembering her promise to be kind and respectful, she smiled at Cedric. "'Twas just such a shock, m'lord. I really had no idea what was afoot."

"Quite all right, m'dear," he said in a clipped voice. "We shall go back to the ballroom and seal our bargain with a dance for all to see."

"I have a crushing headache, my lord. I must go to my room to lie down with a cold compress. Tomorrow?"

An expression of annoyance crossed his face, quickly replaced with a bland smile. "I have some business I should take care of tonight, anyway. One little detail to be put out of the way so that we may enjoy our wedding."

She forced herself to remain still as Cedric leaned forward to skim her cheek with a proprietary kiss. Just over his shoulder, she caught a glimpse of Ethan's face as he passed in the corridor. Controlled fury looked back at her, and she swallowed hard. He was not going to be an easy enemy.

Ethan gritted his teeth. Less than forty-eight hours ago, he and Sarah had lain in each other's arms. She had wanted him. He could have sworn she hadn't just used him to conquer her fear. What they had done went deeper than that.

And now he could not tell if her hand on Broxton's chest was a gesture of affection or to hold him at bay. Her eyes were red and swollen. She had a look of expectancy about her, and he realized she was waiting for him to denounce her. Well, she could relax on that score. If Sarah regretted their interlude, he would not force her to acknowledge her momentary weakness.

But what of the vows her body had made to him? Sweet heaven, what of her greedy little moan when he had tried to withdraw before spilling his seed within her? She had clutched at his buttocks and held him inside, and he had gloried in it! He'd been fool enough to believe she'd never let him go.

Ethan's stomach clenched. His seed! Bloody hell! How

had he forgotten that? The possibility that she could be breeding even now threatened his sanity, and the mere prospect that Broxton could play father to *his* child enraged him. He took a step forward, an objection on his tongue, but the desperate plea in Sarah's eyes stopped him.

As he stood there, frozen with rage, he saw Cedric release Sarah's hand and she backed away. She spun on her heel and fled down the corridor toward the back of the house. She could not escape him so easily. They would discuss this debacle in private. Soon. Very soon. Tonight, if he had anything to say about it.

Heading up the servant's stairs at the back of the house, Sarah wavered between screaming her frustration and crying. Ethan had witnessed her darkest moment. He knew her weakness, her every secret, and he knew how to destroy her. Her standing in society and her reputation were all she had left, and he could end it all with a few well chosen words.

She slipped through her bedroom door and locked it behind her. For good measure, she pushed the back of a chair beneath the knob. Safe at last, she felt the tension drain out of her. The light of a single candle lit her room and she crossed to her bedside to blow it out. The glow of the fireplace was all she needed to accomplish her purpose.

She unwound the ribbons from her hair and removed her emerald ear bobs. Her overdress was next, and then the silk sheath beneath it. She went to her wardrobe and removed her brother's castoffs: shirt, trousers, jacket and boots.

She had to finish what she had started. She had meant to find a moment with the Wednesday League to tell them that Mr. Renquist had failed to find Benjamin last night.

And since Mr. Renquist had failed to find Benjamin, she only had tonight and tomorrow to find the lad. As she changed her clothes, the enormity of that task hit her with breathtaking suddenness. By the time she could button her shirt and push her hair into the soft cap, a deep prickling of fear and self-doubt raised the fine hairs on the back of her neck. She had been over and over her strategy for finding Benjamin, and she could only think of one remaining source of information.

It was a measure of her desperation that the activity in the stables and carriage house did not even cause her to hesitate as she lifted the sash of her window. As she climbed down the trellis, the distant music from the ballroom floated through the night air. A couple was strolling along the path beneath her, and she held her breath. Ethan was right—people never looked up. When they were out of sight, she lowered herself the rest of the way and made a mad dash across the lawns for the safety of the shadows.

The Wednesday League believed that if their investigations went wrong, it was always best to go back to the beginning. That was where Sarah headed now, but this time she would make the conscienceless woman tell her what she'd done with Benjamin.

Sarah wasted precious time looking for Dicken and Joe. They were not at any of their usual haunts. She suspected she should go home rather than continue on her own, but time was of the essence. She would be safe enough dressed as a lad.

She glanced toward St. Paul's as she skirted Cannon Street on her way to the orphanage. It was past midnight, and Ethan would not be there in any case. She could still see the look on his face when Reggie had made the announcement of her engagement, and the fury in his eyes when he saw Cedric kiss her cheek.

She turned her jacket collar up as she passed Saint Bartholomew's Hospital and veered down a side lane. The buildings were closer together now and the lane was narrow. She thought she heard a sound behind her and stopped, fading into the darkness of a recessed doorway.

Scarcely daring to breathe, she waited. The moments

lengthened while she watched the sinister shadows cast by the moonlight, but no movement or sound betrayed another presence. She released her breath in a long sigh and stepped into the lane again. When she came to the gate of the orphanage, she paused to look over her shoulder. She saw nothing, but she could not shake the feeling that something was wrong.

Footsteps echoed on distant cobblestones, retreating, not advancing. She breathed a little easier.

At the orphanage, she slipped through the gate and made her way across the narrow courtyard. The kitchen door was ajar and a faint light shone from within. A shiver raced up her spine. Why would the kitchen door be open this time of night? Was Mrs. Carmichael expecting someone?

Sarah announced her presence with three soft raps, and waited impatiently. When no one answered, she called out. "Hello? Is anyone there? Hello? Mrs. Carmichael?"

She pushed the door open with one finger and peeked around it. A woman wearing a nightgown and nightcap sat before the dying fire with her back to the door, her head tilted to one side. The old woman must have fallen asleep. She would have a stiff neck in the morning.

"Mrs. Carmichael?" she called. No answer.

She advanced a few more steps and tried again, louder this time. "Mrs. Carmichael? I believe you know the whereabouts of boy I have been looking for. I am willing to pay…"

Over the woman's shoulder, she caught a glint from the edge of a knife on the stone hearth. She swallowed her rising terror and tiptoed around the chair to face the woman.

A wash of red covered the front of the woman's white nightgown and still trickling down from her neck to collect in her lap. Buzzing filled Sarah's ears and she grew dizzy with shock. Her knees turned to butter. She sank to the hearth attempting to comprehend the horror of what was before her. Her cap fell off and her hair tumbled over her shoulders. She reached out to brace herself, and her hand grazed the handle of the knife. She picked it up and stared at it as if it held the answer to this incomprehensible riddle.

"Christ's blood!"

Sarah's gaze snapped up to the doorway. A tall stranger, a man possessed of a desolate dark beauty, stood there, studying her with eyes the color of glacial moss.

"What were you thinking, madam?" he asked in a faint Scottish brogue.

She looked down at the knife in her hand, at Mrs. Carmichael and back to the stranger. Heavens! He thought *she* had killed the woman. She dropped the knife with a clatter and shook her head. "No," she said.

The man came into the room and circled them. He knelt and felt Mrs. Carmichael's wrist for a pulse, then dropped it. "She's dead, madam, and you were holding the knife. There is blood on your hands. What would you have me think?"

"But I..." She shook her head helplessly and looked down at her hands. They were red and sticky with Mrs. Carmichael's life force. Gagging, she tried to wipe her hands on her jacket. "I found her this way," she choked. "I've only been here a few minutes."

"Did you see anyone?" the man asked.

"I heard footsteps. I think, yes—footsteps."

The shrill sound of a watchman's whistle carried from down the street. Sarah stumbled to her feet and glanced up into the cold green eyes. "How...did they find out so fast?"

"That is a question worth posing." He held out one hand to her. "I do not want to be here when the charleys arrive. If you're smart, you won't be here either."

She hesitated, not knowing whether to trust the stranger or the municipal police. The realization that the evidence would point to her and the knowledge of what her arrest would cost her brothers decided her. She took his hand. He led her out of the kitchen and headed southwest at a full run, pulling her along with him. Half a mile later, muscles burning and out of breath from trying to keep up with the stranger's long stride, she pulled her hand away and doubled over, her hands upon her knees.

"I have a stitch in my side," she panted. "I cannot go on. Please, save yourself."

His low laugh gave her his answer. "Save myself? Too late for that, madam." He bent, threw her over his shoulder and continued at the same brutal pace.

She braced her arms against his back to keep her stomach from bouncing against his shoulder. By the time he finally stopped and put her on her feet again in front of a warehouse door, she marveled at his stamina. While he fumbled with the key, she noted the lapping of water against wood—the only sound in the still night.

The gravity of her situation struck her, and she couldn't believe she had trusted a stranger. He could be a murderer. He could be planning to... "Who are you and where are we?"

"Too late for second thoughts now, miss."

As if to punctuate his words, the echo of a penetrating scream from a nearby street rent the air. He opened the door and stepped inside. "In or out?" he asked, opening the door.

She glanced over her shoulder. A lock of hair brushed her cheek and she reached up. Her hat was gone. She had a quick flash of running from the authorities—dressed in Andrew's clothes, covered in blood, and her hair falling down her back in a bold proclamation of her gender. "In," she said, stepping across the threshold.

A narrow band of windows high along the outside wall afforded them scarcely enough light to prevent them from bumping into boxes and bales of cotton.

"Shh," he warned her. "Follow me."

Tensed to bolt at the slightest cause for alarm, she followed him through the maze of rows and stacks and then up a narrow stairway. He opened another door and stood aside. She entered the room, temporarily blinded by the light. She squinted and blinked, trying to focus.

''The Carmichael woman was dead—throat slit ear to ear—and this little pigeon was holding the knife,'' the stranger said. ''The watch was coming. I thought I'd better bring her to you.''

Chapter Eighteen

Ethan glanced up to see Sarah standing in front of his desk, her glorious chestnut curls tumbling about her shoulders, rubbing her eyes and shrugging Rob's hand off her shoulder. Well, well. The worm had turned. How convenient to have the little charlatan delivered to his doorstep, as it were. Now he would not have to climb through her window to get some answers.

He dropped his pen on the ledger and sat back in his chair. "Sit down, Lady Sarah. I think 'tis time we had a chat."

Focusing, her gaze snapped up to meet his. He could not say who looked more dumbfounded—Sarah or Rob McHugh.

Rob was the first to recover his composure. He laughed and looked meaningfully at Sarah. "And would Lady Sarah also be known as Sadie Hunt?"

"Aye," Ethan admitted.

"Well done, Travis," Rob said, sizing Sarah up with an appraising glance. "She's a gritty little baggage. She killed the Carmichael woman. Not that the woman didn't deserve it, selling children and all, but murder is murder. She'd be sitting in Newgate right now if I hadn't dragged her away."

Just when he thought Sarah could no longer surprise him— "Is that so, Sarah?" he asked.

She shook her head and narrowed her violet eyes at him. "I did not murder Mrs. Carmichael. I had only just got there, and then this great hulk of a man came immediately after." She turned to Rob and glared at him. "Were you following me?"

Rob raised his hands and laughed. "No, Lady Sarah. You will have to forgive my conclusions. I walk through an already-open door and you are standing over a body holding a knife dripping blood. What else should I think?"

"I was not standing. I—"

"Enough!" Ethan commanded. "Rob, could you go back and find out what is happening? Lady Sarah will tell me her part in all this, and we shall look for a way out later."

"Leave it to me. There's bound to be a charley who'll sing for a pint," Rob said. He bowed in Sarah's direction. "A pleasure, Lady Sarah. And you're welcome."

Sarah looked slightly abashed. "Oh. Yes, thank you. I do not think I would like Newgate."

"I can guarantee that," Rob said, touching his finger to his brow in a salute.

When the door closed, Ethan folded his arms over his chest and turned his attention to Sarah. "Last I heard of you, Lady Sarah, you had gone to bed with a headache. I am told they can be murder."

"Very amusing," she said. But she did not look amused.

"Where shall we begin?"

"I…I do not know what you mean."

"What were you doing at the orphanage?"

She sat in the chair in front of his desk and leaned forward with an ingenuous look on her face. "And what is *this,* Lord Ethan? Your lair? Is this what the proceeds of treason can buy?"

A cold, steely anger rose in him, and he did not speak

until he had it well under control. "We shall get to that, Sarah. Believe me, I have my share of grievances. For the moment, we have more immediate concerns. Shall we discuss what could land you in Newgate or at the end of a rope?"

Sarah's whole body shuddered. "It was ghastly," she murmured. "I've never seen anything like it. Oh!" She glanced up with a stricken expression. "The children! How dreadful for them to discover her that way. We cannot allow them—"

He pressed his fingertips together, anything to prevent himself from going to her and comforting her. "Easy, Sarah. The watchmen and municipals will take care of it. Now, back to the subject at hand. What were you doing at the orphanage?"

"I wanted to question Mrs. Carmichael about where she sent the children."

"What children? The orphans in her care?"

She glanced at him, a wary set to her features. He now recognized that look. She feared she had said too much and was considering a lie.

"The truth, Sarah. Not another of your convenient fairy tales," he cautioned.

It took her a moment to mull that over before sighing deeply and admitting, "Mr. Whitlock's stepchildren."

So he'd been right. Sarah had her own agenda. Could *she* be the danger that he was supposed to guard Whitlock against? Almost as soon as the thought came to his mind, he dismissed it. Sarah was certainly not a professional "follower" or an assassin. He could not think of a more unlikely candidate, and he knew Renquist would never condone such a matter. He studied her more closely, watching for any sign of deceit.

"Then you've been following Whitlock all along? That first night, when I intercepted you with Dicken and Sticky Joe, you'd been following him?"

"Yes," she admitted.

"And what makes you believe Whitlock's stepchildren are at that orphanage?"

"He took them there to have Mrs. Carmichael dispose of them. We…I promised Mrs. Whitlock that I would find her children and take them to a safe place before we…"

"What, Sarah? Before you what? And who are 'we'?"

"Mr. Whitlock commits violence upon Mrs. Whitlock."

"That is unfortunate, but it does not surprise me. What did you think you could do about it? You have no right, legally or morally, to interfere in their marriage."

"Not until Mrs. Whitlock asked our…my help. Since then I have had every right to help her. He stole her children, Ethan. He took them away and said she would never see them again if she did not obey him in all things. *Holding her babies hostage, Ethan.* That is too cruel to be borne."

"If this is true, why were you following Whitlock? Why not search every workhouse, orphanage and sweat house for the children? Why waste your time at brothels, opium dens and taverns? Are you certain you don't just have a taste for the low life, Sarah? Could that account for your behavior of late?"

Color high, she tilted her chin defiantly. "I felt my best chance of finding the children was to follow Mr. Whitlock."

"Have you had success?"

"Some."

"I am happy to hear that, because you will no longer follow him. Do you understand?"

"He has led me to two of the three children. He has proved our…my best lead."

That was one too many slips for Ethan to ignore. If he was to keep Whitlock safe, he needed to know how many people were following the man, and if they presented a danger to him. "Who is helping you, Sarah? Who else is in on this scheme of yours?"

"D-Dicken, Sticky Joe. And Mr. Renquist. He used to

be one of Bow Street's finest thief takers, and I thought if he could find thieves, he could locate three small children.''

She wouldn't meet his eyes and he mistrusted her answer. At the moment, he wondered if he could trust anything she said. "Be that as it may, do not follow Whitlock again. If you do, there will be consequences."

She squirmed in her chair, then tightened her jaw with determination. "I shall follow Mr. Whitlock for as long as it takes to find the last child. Consequences be damned."

Bloody hell! Sarah Hunter was the most aggravating woman he'd ever known. "*Grim* consequences," he told her in a threatening tone. "Are you certain you want to risk that?"

"Absolutely."

If threats were not going to work, he certainly could not keep her under lock and key until McHugh located the blackmail evidence. There was only one solution. "If I find the child for you, Sarah, will you stop?"

She hesitated, uncertainty in her eyes. "I…I suppose. I mean, *I* would have no further reason to follow him."

Relieved, he nodded. "Then tell me who I am looking for."

"Benjamin. He is the youngest. He is five years old but small for his age, and we have speculated that Mrs. Carmichael may have apprenticed him to a chimney sweep. We have not been able to find a trace of him in any of the usual places, and Mr. Whitlock's nightly ramblings have not led us to any likely sources."

"And that is why you went back to talk to Mrs. Carmichael?" At her nod, he continued. "How will I know him?"

"He is so high." She held her hand up to measure three feet. "Blond, with blue eyes, and thin. Mrs. Whitlock says he has a dimple in his right cheek. I have seen a miniature portrait of him. I will recognize him."

"Then I shall bring you every dimpled, blond, blue-eyed sweep in London, and you may choose the right one."

A tiny smile curved her lips before a veil fell over her features again. "We are out of time. I shall go with you."

"Be here at seven in the morning." He called her bluff, knowing she could never get away in daylight. "I'll send out my best men. We shall have him within the week."

"Week? I need him tomorrow."

Surprised at her urgency, Ethan frowned. "I will do all I can, but I can promise nothing. In fact, it would be best if you keep out of it. My men could move faster without you."

She clasped her hands together and the knuckles turned white with her intensity. She seemed to be struggling with her pride, then looked up at him and nodded. "I shall wait for word from you until evening tomorrow. After that, I shall have to join the search. If Benjamin is not delivered to my door, should I meet your man here or at St. Paul's?"

"St. Paul's. Why the urgency, Sarah?"

"M-Mrs. Whitlock is beside herself."

"What will prevent Whitlock from stealing them away again? Have you thought this out?"

"Thoroughly." She shrugged. "I have a plan."

The mere thought of that gave him pause. He leaned forward and rested his forearms on his desk. She met his eyes and did not waver. "Very well. I shall find Benjamin, and you shall leave Whitlock alone."

"Why are *you* following Mr. Whitlock?" she asked.

He had known that question would come and had decided to tell her as much of the truth as he could without endangering her. "Like you, Sarah, I am doing a favor for a friend."

"Then you know the level of my commitment."

Yes. He knew. His commitment, his honor depended upon the repayment of his debt to Kilgrew.

She tilted her head. "So you arranged everything, down to finding Mr. Whitlock at the Swan? What would you have done if I hadn't chosen him as the subject for my 'following lessons'?"

"I'd have guided your choice."

"Guided?" she asked, arching her eyebrows in scorn. "Was I so easy to manipulate? I begin to doubt you were ever honest with me, Ethan. Yet you have the temerity to take me to task for lying to you."

"Enough," he snapped. "I have more than my share of grievances. Shall we keep to the subject at hand?"

"I think we are finished." She stood up and glanced around. "I believe I can find my way out."

Ethan stood, too. Was Sarah so rattled that she had missed the obvious? "Did you lose your cap when Rob brought you here?"

She became still and stared at him thoughtfully. "I...I think it fell off at the orphanage."

"Good God," he muttered. "Was there any mark, anything about it, that could lead the authorities to you?"

"I don't know. It was the one you gave me."

Ethan ran his fingers through his hair. He was safe enough. He never tagged or marked his clothing for just such reasons. "I will take you home. We cannot have you roaming the streets with half the authorities in London looking for a murderer." When Sarah shook her head, he grabbed his jacket from a peg on the back of the door and ignored her. "You are important to one of the few friends I have left."

"Reggie?"

"Auberville."

Her voice was soft. Uncertain. "You spoke with him?"

Recalling the things Auberville had told him caused Ethan a momentary flash of discomfort. "I hoped for a clue as to why you would suddenly decide to marry Cedric Broxton. God knows, the last time I saw you, you were entreating me to free you from your fears, and then you were avoiding so much as a single dance with me. What was it, Sarah? Remorse over having allowed me to make love to you? Or did Reggie persuade you that I was not worthy of you? That I am a thief and a murderer?''

She looked up at him and the pain in her eyes was startling—and unexpected. ''Should I have ignored the evidence of my own eyes and ears? But you were always a gentleman to me, and so I did not care until I learned *what* placed you under a cloud, sir. Treason. You were in league with those who employed Mr. Farmingdale and the others. And one does not earn a title such as 'Demon of Alsatia' without cause.''

He twisted her words this way and that, trying to make sense of her reasoning. She had not cared when she thought that he was a thief or a murderer, but could not forgive treason? Then the hidden meaning in her words hit him full force. He blinked in astonishment. Sarah had believed the worst of him all along. She simply hadn't cared. And he had been naive enough—nay, *eager* enough—to believe that she saw through the lies and aspersions to the truth of who and what he was.

The realization was deep and painful. He could deny her charge, of course, but to what purpose? People believed what they wanted to believe unless they had solid, undeniable proof to the contrary. He had no proof.

He took Sarah's arm more roughly than he intended and turned her toward the door. ''Time you were in bed, Lady Sarah.''

The next morning when Grace, Charity and Annica were present, Sarah went to her parlor door and peeked into the hall. No lurking brothers, thank heavens. She closed the door to insure their privacy. The servants were far too busy cleaning from the party last night to eavesdrop, and her brothers would stay far away from what they assumed was a Saturday meeting of bluestockings for the purpose of discussing literature.

''Last night,'' she began as she took her seat again, ''I

found Mrs. Carmichael dead. She'd been killed where she
sat. I doubt she even saw it coming.''

Shocked gasps met this announcement and Sarah rushed
on, glossing over the things she did not wish to discuss.
''Someone said she was selling the children in her care.
Money. I wonder if that was not Mr. Whitlock's motive
for stealing the children rather than keeping Mrs. Whitlock
under his control. His nightly activities do not come
cheap—tarts, opium, drink. And did Mrs. Whitlock not say
he'd been blackmailing someone?''

''I recall something like that,'' Charity mused. ''It does
appear he is a man in need of money. But what happened
last night? Did you report the murder to the magistrate?''

''I fled,'' she admitted. ''I heard the watchman's whistle
and ran for all I was worth. I could only think of what
Reggie would say if I was caught at a murder scene
dressed in Andrew's clothes. I had picked up the knife,
and there was blood on my hands. It would have looked
as if…'' She glanced down at her hands, trembling with
the memory.

''Did you see anyone?''

''No. But I heard footsteps when I arrived.'' She shivered. ''It must have been the murderer.''

''Lord,'' Grace muttered. ''What next?''

''Tonight,'' Sarah said, ''I shall rejoin the search for
Benjamin.''

Annica gestured airily. ''If Mr. Renquist cannot find
Benjamin, 'tis unlikely you will be able to do so.''

''Tonight is all we have. If we do not find Benjamin
tonight, we could miss our chance to put Harold Whitlock
on that ship. I think we should have him conscripted
whether we find Benjamin or not. I fear 'twas Mr. Whitlock who dispatched Mrs. Carmichael—to prevent her
from telling. If he would do that to an ally, what might he
do to Mrs. Whitlock if he suspects her of treachery?''

''I see your point, Sarah. Yes,'' Grace said. ''I think

you may be right. We should get rid of Harold Whitlock at once whether we find Benjamin or not."

"Those in favor?" Annica called for a vote.

"Aye," they said unanimously.

"I shall send word to Mr. Renquist to intercept Mr. Whitlock tonight," Annica volunteered.

"Without delay, please, and as early as possible. I would hate to come across him tonight should I have Benjamin in tow." Her conscience troubled her for a moment. She had promised Ethan she would not interfere with Mr. Whitlock if he found Benjamin for her. Still, Benjamin had not been delivered to her, and Mrs. Whitlock's safety was more important than anything else. If Mr. Whitlock was committing murder now, she could be next.

In an effort to reassure the Wednesday League, Sarah said, "Dicken and Joe are much more clever than you may think. They are children, so people say things in front of them that they would never tell anyone else. We will come up with Benjamin sooner or later." She pressed her temples where a nagging ache began. "The worst is that I know there is something I should remember—something that could help—but it keeps eluding me. It is there, in the back of my mind—something I know, but do not know I know."

Grace smiled. "I fear that actually makes sense."

Annica lifted her teacup and took a sip. "Relax, Sarah. You are trying too hard. It will come to you if you do not force it."

"You are right, Nica. But I shall meet the others tonight to see if any progress has been made in finding the boy."

Charity nibbled a piece of butter cake. "I do not think you should, Sarah. Now that you're to become Broxton's bride, he will have something to say about how you spend your nights."

Nights! With Cedric! She shuddered.

As if reading her mind, Annica said, "I was dumbfounded at Reginald's announcement last night."

"No more astonished than I," she admitted. "Reggie thought to surprise me with the news. He has been urging me to make a choice for some time, and I have been putting him off because it meant I would have to tell him about Farmingdale and the others. So when I did not make a choice, he made one for me."

"Not the result you were hoping for, I gather," Grace said.

She shook her head. "Heavens, no! I...actually, I am not betrothed to Cedric, but that is a secret."

Everyone stopped what they were doing to look at her.

"I told my brothers last night. About the attack," she clarified. "Reggie says he will make things right with Lord Cedric, but he has asked me to be patient a fortnight while he thinks of a way to get clear and smooth things over."

"Ah." Annica nodded. "I wondered where you went after the announcement. I looked for you to find out what had happened, but you had disappeared. Then Reggie said you'd had too much excitement and went to lie down."

"They think I am delicate." Sarah said.

Chapter Nineteen

The midnight streets were unusually quiet for a Saturday, and Sarah feared she would be conspicuous alone. She had waited fully one half hour past the appointed time when the man who had thrown her over her shoulder last night bounded up the steps of the west porch of St. Paul's.

He gestured to her and called in a hoarse whisper, "Hurry! No time to spare."

She skipped down the steps to meet him halfway before he spun on his heel and headed off at a brisk pace. The church clock chimed once, taunting her with the arrival of Sunday. "Where is he? Have you found Benjamin?"

"You must have a great deal of influence with Travis," he said as he set a course for Spitalfields. "He put everything else aside and put all his men on a search for one small boy."

Out of breath from matching his long stride, she smiled up at him. "I think he is just anxious to be quit of me."

"Somehow, I doubt that, Lady Sarah. Whatever the reason, it has worked. Travis is on his way there now to keep watch lest someone try to move the boy. He said he would wait for your identification before trying to…er, liberate him."

Hope lifted her spirits. How had Ethan found Benjamin in a single day when Renquist, his runners and she had been unable to find a single trace of him? All his unsavory connections, no doubt. "If this is so, sir, you and Lord Ethan will have my eternal gratitude."

"I shall give my share to Ethan. I think he will find more use for it than I."

Sarah glanced sideways at the Scot. His expression did not change, but those remarkable green eyes gave him away. She smiled in spite of herself. The man was teasing her!

"Then I am safe. Lord Ethan will tell me to take Benjamin and be gone from his life."

He shook his head and led her down a side street toward a dark, cramped-looking structure with high windows and a heavy door. It sat back from the street to provide a small paved yard barred by a fence and gate.

He turned to her and squeezed her arm in a friendly gesture. "Life is brief, Lady Sarah, and full of ironies. You may think you have all the time in the world, but the course of your life can turn in an instant. Try to waste as little of it as possible, eh?" he whispered before pointing to a darkened alley across the street. "Travis will be waiting there. I'd best get back to guarding Whitlock."

Sarah watched him disappear into the shadows with a feeling of regret. If her plan had gone well, Harold Whitlock would be aboard a ship about to set sail for Java. Would he still think her amusing when he discovered her role in that?

She dashed across the lane into the alley. Ethan was crouched by a wall, waiting.

"Sarah," he whispered. "I think the lad is the one you are looking for. I heard the head sweep call his apprentice Benny-boy. They were working late and arrived home just a half hour ago. I could not tell if the lad was blond or not. He was covered head to toe in soot."

"How shall we get him out?" Sarah asked.

Ethan peered at her through the gloom. "I thought you had a plan."

"I...not actually," she admitted. "Do you?"

There was a long silence, as if Ethan were biting his tongue. Finally, in a low growl, he said, "I suppose I could offer to buy his apprenticeship."

"I will reimburse you."

He stood from his crouch. "Wait here," he instructed. He left the alley and went to rattle the iron gate to the small yard.

A tall, lanky man dressed in a black coat and dark trousers opened the door and came to the gate. His sharp voice carried across the distance. "'Erenow! 'Tis late. What d'ye want?"

"I need an apprentice sweep," Ethan said. "How much training does yours have?"

"'Ow much? Well, not so little as to come cheap. You could 'ave 'im for twenty quid."

"I'll give you twelve."

The man affected outrage. "'E's a right small one. Got a lot of good years before 'e's too big. A new 'prentice would cost me."

"How do I know he's worth it?"

"'E took down twenty bushels just today. Light some straw under 'im, an' 'e works real fast, 'e does."

"Straw, eh?" Ethan's back stiffened. Sarah saw his hands clench into fists and prayed he would not hit the man before they had Benjamin. "Fifteen quid."

"I dunno," the man hedged. "Trainin' a new one'll set me back."

Ethan shrugged and turned away as if withdrawing his offer.

"Wait! Gi' me seventeen an' 'e's yours."

"What is his name?"

"Benny. 'E's about five years old. Slight frame. You'll get four years out of 'im before you need another. 'E's a bargain at twice what I'm askin'."

"Bring him out and let me have a look." Ethan said.

The lanky man scrambled back to the door and disappeared within. Sarah joined Ethan at the gate. "I'll nod if it is Benjamin. Then you can pay the man and we can leave."

He did not turn to look at her. "Something isn't right. Go back to the alley and wait for me."

"Ethan—"

"Go, Sarah."

She caught the urgency in his voice and dashed for the alley. Within a few moments, the lanky man was back, dragging a small boy by his shirt collar. The lad was struggling and flailing his arms wildly. Sarah recognized panic when she saw it, and the poor child was in the grip of it. A lump formed in her throat.

"'Ere 'e is," the man told Ethan. "Right small, 'e is. Give me my seventeen quid, and you can 'ave 'im."

Ethan stepped forward as the man opened the gate to push the lad through.

From the corner of her eye, Sarah caught a movement in the shadows across the street. Was it the Scot, come back to help? There was a small flash of light from that direction, and then a sharp crack that echoed down the narrow street.

The sweep flew backward with a loud grunt and Ethan fell on top of him, dragging the boy with him. The child screamed as another shot rang out. Sarah staggered to her feet, fear tripping her heartbeat at a rapid pace. She started forward as the shrill sound of whistles carried from a nearby street. The watch! Every instinct she possessed drove her toward Ethan's side, but before she could reach him, he rose to his knees and gathered the boy against his chest.

"Run!" he yelled, and Sarah knew he meant her.

She was desperate for reassurance that he was uninjured. She wanted to ignore him and go to him, or shout her question across the distance, but her instincts told her that Ethan knew what he was doing. She pivoted and headed back the way she had come at a dead run. More whistles and shouting, growing louder, converged on the sweep's house. She hadn't gone more than a quarter of a mile before she realized she did not have a destination.

Dodging down a side lane, she came upon Ludgate Hill and realized she'd been heading for the safe familiarity of St. Paul's. Her lungs were burning by the time she collapsed against one of the smooth white columns of the porch. Panting, her back against the column, she slid down to a crouch. Tears stung her eyes as she began praying for Ethan's safety. She had seen that Benjamin was uninjured, and that Ethan had thrown himself between the boy and danger, but that was not altogether reassuring. Ethan's back as a shield was still Ethan's back.

She covered her mouth to muffle her sobs, her heartbeat still hammering in her ears. "Please, Lord, oh, please," she wept aloud, "let them be safe. Keep them from harm's way, I entreat Thee. And—"

"You must have God's ear, Sarah," a hushed voice said in her own ear.

She squealed and jumped, so caught up in her fear that she had not heard his approach. Before she could prevent herself, she threw her arms around him and hugged him tightly. "Ethan! Thank heavens! Where is Benjamin? *Is* it Benjamin?"

"It had better be, after all of this," he said with a hint of humor. "He's in the coach. Come on."

"How…how did you know I'd come here?" she asked.

"You have good instincts, Sarah, when you use them."

Good instincts? Like the one that had led her to walk down that darkened path with Richard Farmingdale? Or the one that had led her to give herself to a traitor? Oh, yes. She could trust her instincts—to be wrong! She released him and stepped back, embarrassed by yet another bad instinct. She was far better off to rely upon reason and intelligence.

Ethan's face registered a flash of anger before he said,

"Hurry, Sarah. The watch may be in pursuit. Pray the son of a bitch with the pistol is not."

She braced herself and followed him down the steps and into a waiting hired coach. Huddled in a corner with his knees drawn up to his chest, the small boy from the sweep's yard sniffled and wiped his nose on his coat sleeve. She recognized the crystal-blue eyes sparkling with unshed tears from Mrs. Whitlock's miniature.

Sarah took a seat beside him, facing Ethan, as the coach started off again. "Hello," she said. "My name's Sarah. Are you Benjamin?"

He nodded, his lower lip trembling.

"Your mother sent me to find you. She misses you very much, you know."

"M-Mama? She didn't d-die?"

Sarah caught Ethan's glance and guessed that they would both like to punish Mr. Whitlock for what he'd done to this small child. She took her handkerchief from her jacket pocket and wiped at the dirt and grime on the boy's face. "No, Benjamin. She is quite well but for missing you so terribly."

"Can we go see her now?" he asked hopefully.

"Not tonight, dearling. Tomorrow."

"I've made arrangements for you tonight," Ethan contributed. "Somewhere you will be safe and no one will think to look for you. You wouldn't want your mama to see you this way, would you? We are taking you to a nice woman named Mrs. Grant. She has a warm tub and clean clothes waiting for you."

"B-but I want to go home." The tears finally spilled over and ran down his cheeks, leaving clean streaks in their wake.

"Tomorrow, Benjamin," Sarah promised. Ethan smiled and nodded at her. "Mr. Travis will bring you to me, and I will take you home."

"What about 'Minta?"

"Araminta is safe with a friend of mine, and Teddy is

at my home. You will all be together with your mama very soon.''

His lower lip trembled when he looked up at her, as if afraid to believe. Sarah opened her arms and, after a moment's hesitation, he threw himself into them. She held the small warm body against her chest and didn't mind the smell of smoke and soot at all. After a brief storm of relieved weeping, the child grew silent and relaxed against her. Worn-out with despair, fear and now hope, he'd fallen asleep.

She noticed that Ethan was looking down, his jaw tightening in anger. When she followed his line of sight, she saw that the bottoms of Benjamin's trousers were singed. Lord, she could not even imagine the horror this little boy had endured. If she had not felt completely justified in sending Mr. Whitlock away before, she certainly did now.

Within a quarter of an hour, the coach stopped outside a small house in a quiet neighborhood. Ethan took the still-sleeping Benjamin from her arms and brushed a lock of hair away from the boy's forehead. His lips curved into a small smile when the child swatted at his hand in his sleep. Ethan's unaffected smile touched Sarah's heart. She remembered that gentleness quite well.

Mrs. Grant answered his knock at the door and made sighing and clucking sounds over the boy. After a hushed conversation, Ethan handed the lad over and returned to the coach.

''Thank you, Ethan,'' she said after he gave the driver the address of Hunter Hall, along with instructions to drive once around Hyde Park before going there. ''I will not ask you how you found him so quickly.''

Ethan settled back in the facing seat, his arms crossed over his chest. ''Just as well. I don't think you'd like it.''

She could only imagine. ''Mrs. Whitlock will be very grateful. She will want to thank you in person.''

''I'd much rather you kept my name out of it.''

''If you wish.''

"I do. And now that you owe me yet another favor, Sarah, shall we talk about Broxton and your impending nuptials?"

Ah, so this was why he wanted to detour around Hyde Park. She would have to account for herself. "I'd rather talk about the favors I owe you and what I must do to repay you," she said.

His lips quirked, but she would not have called it a smile. "Of course. Wouldn't want to carry that debt into your new marriage, would you? Have you told him about us?"

"There is nothing to tell."

"I do not remember it that way. I wonder if we were in the same place, Sarah. My bed, I believe?"

She felt the heat steal up her cheeks. "Reggie arranged the marriage. I do not know what he told Cedric."

"Did Reggie know about us?"

"No."

"Hmm. Then he cannot have told Cedric, can he?"

"I suppose not."

"You *suppose* not," he repeated slowly, as if tasting the evasion on his tongue. "Have you always been so ambiguous, Sarah, or am I just now noticing?"

She shook her head and a tendril of hair slipped from her cap to tickle her cheek with a touch as light as Ethan's finger. "I do not know what to say to you, Ethan, or how to talk to you. I fear I did not know you at all. You are a stranger to me."

Before she realized what he was doing, he was beside her on the seat, holding her arms in a firm grip, his lips mere inches from hers. "You think you do not know me? You are wrong. You know everything that you need to know."

Uncertainty clouded her mind. What did she need to know? His mouth lowered the rest of the way and the soft urging of his lips caused a bittersweet burning at her core. His clean, provocative scent, his primal masculine energy, overwhelmed her. The heat, taste and intimacy of his mouth compelled her and she begged for more by wrapping her arms around him and fondling the curls at the back of his neck. She wanted him despite her fears, despite her disillusionment. His mouth moved lower, finding a spot, low on her neck just to the right of her collarbone, that made her gasp with pleasure.

"Tell me," he murmured against her flesh, "how you can marry Broxton when you take fire in my arms. A few nights ago I was inside you, Sarah, loving you, cherishing you, teaching you not to be afraid. Does Broxton's kiss ignite you? Will he—"

Cedric's kiss? The very thought worked like ice water on her passion-fogged brain. "I've never—" She stopped herself, but it was too late.

Ethan gave her a sardonic smile. "I thought not. Yet that is what lies ahead. *He* will kiss you. *He* will be inside you. *His* seed will ripen in you. Your babies will look like him."

She shriveled inside at the thought of carrying Cedric's child. Thank God Reggie would get her out of that mess.

"I want to know why, Sarah. Why would you agree to wed Cedric Broxton when the mere thought of him disgusts you? Think what you will of me, but do not fall into Broxton's arms to spite me."

"I won't," she whispered, more to herself than to him.

"See that you do not. I do not like to think how Broxton would abuse that privilege."

Something dark in his voice gave her pause. "Why do you hate Lord Cedric? What has he done to you?"

Ethan seemed about to answer and then shrugged. "He is a dangerous man. Do not trust him."

"*He* is a dangerous man?" she asked. "Yet you are called the Demon of Alsatia. You are the one under suspicion of treason. You have warned me about him before, but you have never said why. What should I believe?"

His hesitation was longer this time before he spoke. "Believe what you will, Sarah."

His curt refusal to answer cut her deeply. "Then what of Mr. Whitlock, Ethan?"

"Your duty is done now that you have Benjamin. Mine will not be done until I have found the threat to him, and kept him safe from it. My honor depends upon it."

Sarah's stomach twisted and she scooted away from him. "Your honor? Safe? You are to keep Mr. Whitlock *safe?*"

"Of course. Did you think I meant to kill him?"

"I...I did not think at all," she admitted. She had been so focused on her plan, so single-minded in purpose, that she had not even questioned Ethan's goal beyond his doing a favor for a friend. "Is Mr. Whitlock in danger?"

"More than he knows," Ethan snarled. "Do you think you were hit over the head because someone wanted to pick your pocket? Or that the gunman tonight was taking aim at me because I'd just gotten a shipment of olives?"

Sarah grew cold with the memory. "What has he done?"

"Aside from abusing his wife and children? I do not know, Sarah. That is none of my business. I am simply to keep him from harm until he can be...dealt with."

Ethan's words caused a shiver up her spine. "You must have some idea."

He leveled his gaze at her. "I believe it may have something to do with blackmail. My...friend is looking for the blackmail evidence."

"What is it?"

He frowned at her, his eyes narrowing in suspicion. "Do you know something about this, Sarah?"

She recalled her conversation with the Wednesday League. Mrs. Whitlock had told them she suspected he was blackmailing someone, but they had never discussed who or why. Could the victim be Ethan's friend? Still she knew nothing for certain. "No, Ethan."

''Then stay clear of it, and out of my way. That was our bargain.''

Yes. But at the very moment that Ethan was rescuing Benjamin, she had been working against him, breaking her promise. There would *be* no Mr. Whitlock for Ethan to keep safe. What would happen to his friend now? How would he ever redeem his honor?

''What time is it?'' she asked. Perhaps it was not too late to stop Mr. Renquist!

Ethan removed a pocket watch from his vest. ''Half past four.''

Half past four. Too late. Whitlock's ship had sailed.

Chapter Twenty

Sarah knelt on the window seat in the parlor overlooking the private back garden. Tears stung her eyes as she watched Gladys Whitlock embrace her children. Earlier that morning, Annica had brought Araminta, and Ethan's coach had delivered Benjamin minutes later. Within half an hour, Mrs. Whitlock and her children would be home together, with a limitless future ahead of them. But Sarah's moment of triumph was bittersweet.

She glanced down at the folded letter on her lap that told her of the success of the Wednesday League's plan. Harold Whitlock had been intercepted on his way to his favorite pub, dragged into an alley, bound and gagged and carried aboard an anonymous vessel bound for Java. Mr. Renquist had waited until the ship had hoisted anchor, entered the Thames and caught the current— "Once burned, twice shy," he'd said. A failure to be certain when investigating Lady Sarah's case had cost a member of the Wednesday League her life and had nearly cost Lady Annica hers, as well.

Whitlock was gone—no longer a threat to his wife and stepchildren. She should feel elated, or at least some satisfaction in a job well-done, but all she could think of now was that Ethan had failed because of her betrayal. And why did that thought sadden her? Why did she still care about a traitor?

Mrs. Whitlock looked up at the window and waved at Sarah, an expression of pure joy on her face. Sarah waved back, tears filling her eyes. Mother and children disappeared around the side of the house where a coach was waiting to take them home. Tonight, at the Thackery musicale, she would give her final report to the Wednesday League.

Sarah felt suddenly empty. The chase, the nights of danger and the excitement of being with Ethan, had so completely consumed her that she did not know how she'd spend her time now. Society—*everything*—seemed so pointless.

"Sarah?" Reggie called.

"In the parlor," she answered. She wiped her tears away with the back of her hand.

Reggie came through the door, his face registering deep sadness. He took her hand and led her to a settee. "I see you've heard."

"Heard what?" she asked.

"About Lord Nigel."

Foreboding squeezed her heart. "Tell me, Reggie."

Reggie's voice was gentle. "You looked so sad, I thought you knew. He died last night."

She bowed her head and let her tears flow. Reggie offered her his handkerchief and slipped his arm around her. "It is not unexpected. He had been failing for quite some time."

"I shall miss him."

"Did you know he made an offer for you?"

Surprise and pleasure made her smile through her tears. "He did? When?"

"After I announced your engagement to Cedric. He came to me later and said that he thought you and he were more compatible than you and Cedric. He was prepared to be quite generous with you."

She snuggled against his broad chest and stroked the soft fold of his cravat. "Reggie, he did not suffer, did he?"

"It was sudden, Sarah. I am certain he was at peace."

Nigel's kindly face rose to her mind. His gentle prodding for the truth just weeks ago, his sympathy and acceptance, had been quietly reassuring. His response had given her the courage to tell her brothers what had been done to her. Oh, if only she'd made the time to tell him how much he meant to her!

The Scotsman had said, *Life is brief, Lady Sarah...you may think you have all the time in the world, but the course of your life can turn in an instant. Try to waste as little of it as possible, eh?*

She heaved a shaky sigh. "Nigel was a good friend. I loved him dearly. I wish I had told him that. I fear I shall live with that regret for the rest of my life."

"He knew," Reggie said with quiet certainty.

She wiped at her eyes again and sat straighter. "I wish I could believe that."

"Believe *me,*" her brother said. "He knew."

"But how do you know?"

He lifted her chin with one finger so that she was looking into his face. "Some things you just know, dearling. They defy reason or explanation. You just *know.*"

"I dare not have that sort of faith," she murmured. "I have been wrong too many times."

"We are bound to be wrong occasionally. Instinct, Sarah. Women pride themselves on that. Surely you've drawn conclusions from observations and feelings?"

Instincts? Yes. Knowing Nigel, and him knowing her history, she could well believe he had tried to rescue her from a loveless marriage.

You have good instincts, Sarah, when you use them, Ethan had said. So, then, how could she reconcile Ethan the traitor with Ethan the man she knew? One had to be a lie. "I—if you had to choose between your instincts or popular opinion, Reggie, which would you rely upon?"

"Why, my instincts, of course."

"Yes," she said, wincing and pressing her temples. "I suspected you would say that."

"What is wrong, Sarah?"

Wrong? Just that she'd turned her back on a man who had been nothing but kind to her. Just that she'd denied her heart because of the gossip of people she neither knew nor cared about. "I am a fool. I've done a friend a grave injustice and I do not want to waste my life in regrets. I must find a way to make it right."

Sarah, Annica, Charity and Grace all lifted their glasses in a discreet toast in one corner of the Thackery music room while the low tones of conversation swirled around them. The drone of the musicians tuning their instruments provided a warning that it would soon be time for them to take their seats.

"Justice," they all whispered as they touched the rims of their glasses.

"What next?" Charity asked. "Have we any other cases at the moment?"

"None," Annica said. "I think we have earned a well-deserved respite."

Sarah smiled with a nervous glance at the other guests. Would he be here tonight? No respite for her yet. She had a confession to make, and amends, if possible. But that was personal. The Wednesday League had no part in how conscienceless she had been in her use of Ethan Travis, and it was up to her to right that wrong.

A discreet bell rang, and the guests began taking seats facing the piano. She and her companions claimed chairs in the back row as the musicians arranged themselves for the piece they would perform.

Grace leaned toward the group and whispered, "I have hired a companion. She should be arriving from the country in the next few weeks."

"Did you check her references, Grace?" Annica asked.

"I do not need to. She was my husband's niece. I am afraid her family has fallen on hard times, and she is too proud to accept my help. She was very firm that she wants employment, not charity."

"We shall have great fun showing her the sites," Sarah offered. "Perhaps she will want to join the Wednesday League."

"Hmm," Grace hedged. "We must first be certain of her discretion. 'Twould never do to..." Grace let her words trail off as her eyes traveled upward behind Sarah's chair.

Sarah turned and found Ethan in the process of bending near her ear. "I must speak with you at once, Lady Sarah. The matter is of grave import," he said in a hushed tone.

She glanced at her companions. Ethan must be desperate indeed to approach her like this. Annica covered a slight smile behind her fan, but Grace and Charity could not hide their astonishment. "Of course, Lord Ethan," she murmured.

"Now. Privately."

Standing and stepping around Annica's chair to join him, she pointed toward a curtained alcove along the back wall. If they whispered, they would not be overheard. Just then, the musicians struck a chord and began their first selection. All attention was focused upon the dais, and no one noticed as Ethan seized her hand and led her to the terrace doors.

Once outside he dropped her hand and turned her to face him. "I cannot find Harold Whitlock. We've been looking for him all day. Last night, whilst McHugh and I were liberating Benjamin, someone knocked my man, Peters, unconscious. When he came 'round, Whitlock was gone. I remembered that you said you had a plan for Whitlock. Would you know anything about this?"

Sarah swallowed hard and braced her courage. A clean split would be best for her breaking heart. "Harold Whitlock will not be found, Ethan. Not for several years, if my plan goes well. I arranged for him to be conscripted. He was put aboard a ship bound for Java last night.''

''Why the hell would you—''

''To buy Mrs. Whitlock time to escape and build a new life before Mr. Whitlock could stop her. I did not know until it was too late that your purpose was to keep him safe.''

Ethan ran his fingers through his hair—a sure sign of frustration. ''You swore you'd leave him alone if I helped you find Benjamin. Because of you…''

Sarah's heart dropped. ''How can I make it up to you, Ethan? I will do anything you ask.''

''My friend, Sarah,'' he said angrily. ''How will you make it up to my friend? Now the blackmail will surface, and he will be ruined. He was depending upon me, and I let him down.'' His wounded eyes met hers and he shook his head. ''You've made a liar of me.''

She swallowed her little moan of despair. ''I shall tell him it wasn't your fault. I shall confess all I did to get in your way, Ethan. I will not let him judge *you* for this.''

''You will do nothing of the sort. Such a confession would ruin you, and would not help me. It was my responsibility to see that the task was faithfully performed, and I was the one who allowed you to get in the way.''

''If I could take it back, I would.''

He stepped closer, forcing her to tilt her head back to meet his tortured gaze. ''I expected too much of you. I forgot who you were.''

Too much? Had it really been too much to expect honesty from her? A lump formed in her throat. ''There is more.''

He groaned. ''What more could there be?''

''I…I was wrong about you, Ethan. I am so sorry. I was wrong to have judged you by what others said or thought.''

His eyes bored into her soul, but he said nothing. She could see his distrust and suspicion, and did not know how to repair the damage she'd done.

"You were much better than I ever deserved," she confessed.

He gave a choked sound that was half laugh, half ridicule. "How could you possibly know such things?"

She lifted her right hand and placed it over his heart. The heat and the steady, rhythmic thumping against her palm brought tears to her eyes. "This is the truth, Ethan. It is all the truth I need. It is all that matters."

"Is this some sort of new trick? A new game for the spoiled little dilettante?"

She ignored the insult in her desperation to make him understand. "It was *me* I doubted, Ethan. I see that clearly now—my own fears, my own distrust of myself—and never really you at all."

"How have you found proof for that?"

"You are proof enough." She placed her left hand over her own heart and felt it skip a beat as a little shock of electricity raced through her to connect with his. *"Le coeur a ses raisons que la raison ne connaît point,"* she quoted. The heart has its reasons which reason does not know.

"God, what I would give to believe you," he said with a quick shake of his head.

"I love you. I cannot say it any plainer than that."

He pulled her into his arms with a low moan.

She lifted her face to his. "I'll do anything to make this up to you, Ethan."

He lowered his lips to hers. "Will you…"

"Yes?" she asked breathlessly.

"Not help me?"

Sarah frowned, trying to collect her wits. Not help? "But—"

"No, not another word," he rasped as he released her and stepped back. "You and I will settle accounts in full when this is done—you can count on that. But not now. Now I need to see if I can salvage anything from your machinations."

* * *

In her darkened room, Sarah pulled her reading chair to the window and drew her knees up, hugging them against her chest. She gazed out at the moon-dappled lawn toward the willow tree.

An almost desperate need to make amends burned in her. Ethan's honor had suffered enough, and she had made it worse. She tried to imagine how she would feel if she had failed Annica, Charity or Grace. *Devastated.*

But what could she possibly do? Ethan had been quite explicit about not wanting her help. Ethan's honor would be beyond redemption once the blackmail surfaced, and his friend would be finished.

Blackmail! *That* was the thought that had been troubling her since last night in the coach with Ethan! She pressed her fingertips to her temples and closed her eyes. An image of Mr. Whitlock with Mrs. Carmichael, holding a locked metal box, rose before her. *The box, now, that's a separate matter. Keep that safe, mind you, and keep your mouth shut. I'll be back for it one day soon.*

The box had been of the size that would hold a packet of letters or even a pouch filled with jewelry. Reggie had a strongbox just like it where he kept their mother's jewels and emergency cash. Could Mr. Whitlock have hidden his blackmail evidence in that box and given it to Mrs. Carmichael to hide? Could that be the reason she was murdered?

She hurried to her writing desk and pulled a sheet of paper from the drawer, intending to write a quick note to Ethan. He should know about this. But then she recalled how distrustful of her he had become. She left her desk and went to her closet. She would have to do this herself.

Well past midnight, Sarah rapped on the kitchen door of the orphanage. She lifted the collar of her jacket and hunched into the woolen warmth. Her heart hammered nervously. She had no idea what she'd say to whoever answered the door, but she knew she wouldn't give up until she'd looked for that metal box.

A pretty miss in a shawl and nightgown opened the door and the light of a single lantern shone behind her. "Who is it?"

Sarah looked closer. The girl's waist-length red hair tumbled down her back and it was obvious that she had been wakened from her sleep.

"Are you Bridey?" Sarah asked.

"Aye, mum," she answered. "An' 'oo are you?"

"I am Sadie Hunt. Sticky Joe's friend. I was here with him several weeks past. Do you remember?"

The girl blushed. "I remember."

"May I come in? I'd like to talk to you."

The door opened wide enough for Sarah to slip through. She glanced involuntarily toward the chair before the fire, unable to shake the memory of the last time she had been in this room. "Bridey, did the constables question you about Mrs. Carmichael?"

"Aye, miss. An' they put me in charge until they can find a replacement," she said with a proud lift of her chin.

"Did they search for clues to her murder?"

Bridey frowned. "Aye. They took away anything they thought might have something to do with it."

"A box, Bridey? Did you see a small metal strongbox with a lock?"

"No, miss. Nothing like that. They took a cap, a knife, the account books, and all Mrs. Carmichael's personal papers, but I didn't see a strongbox."

"About so big?" she asked, indicating a small rectangle with her hands. "It belonged to me. I only want what's rightfully mine," she lied, and she'd lie again for Ethan.

"I'm sorry, miss." The girl shook her head. "If that's what the murderer came for, he likely took it with him."

"Maybe he couldn't find it," Sarah said. "If the killer didn't know where Mrs. Carmichael hid the box, maybe he didn't find it. The watch came very quickly, I'm told."

She shivered. If she had interrupted the murderer, there was still a chance that the strongbox was hidden somewhere. "Please, Bridey. May I look? I promise I won't be long. Besides, 'tis after midnight. No one will ever know."

The girl shrugged. "I suppose it could not hurt." She led the way down a short hallway with a single door. "I don't want to go in. I think her ghost is still there. That's what folks say—that the spirit stays where sudden death happens."

Sarah nodded and opened the door. A small bed stood in one corner and a bureau and wardrobe lined the far wall. The fireplace was upon a raised stone hearth, but the ashes had long grown cold since Mrs. Carmichael's death. A small rocking chair sat near the fireplace, as if to catch the light for reading.

It did not take much time to search the meager contents of the room. As she suspected, nothing. She searched for any hidden panels or secret drawers in the wardrobe, then focused on the bed, turning the mattress up on end to see if anything lay hidden beneath. But—

"Nothing." Her heart sank. She turned around slowly, scanning the room for any clue, any indication of anything out of place. She couldn't give up. The authorities hadn't found the metal box, and it was unlikely the murderer had found it so quickly.

Beginning at the wall behind the bed, she rapped the wooden panels on the wall, seeking a hollow spot. She worked her way around the room knocking and running her fingertips along the joints and raised panels. And still nothing.

She studied the pattern of blocks that formed the hearth, noting one block around which the mortar appeared to be crumbling. She wedged her fingertips in the crack and rocked it back and forth, working it until she could get a grip and lift it away.

Sarah didn't want to put her hand into a dark hole where anything might be lurking, but she had no choice. Her fingers closed around something cold and smooth. She almost jumped when she heard the scraping of metal against stone, and then it was visible. The strongbox! The same one she had seen in Mr. Whitlock's hands.

She examined it more closely. It did not weigh as much as she expected and, when she shook it, she heard paper shifting, but no rattle of coin or jewelry. She glanced over her shoulder. If this was the blackmail evidence, someone had already been killed for it.

Sunk in introspection, Ethan sat in the dark, warming his brandy between his palms. He had failed Lord Kilgrew. His honor and reputation were now beyond redemption. He had played the fool with Sarah Hunter. The trickle of hostages from Algiers had dried up entirely. Tonight Rob McHugh had boarded a ship bound for North Africa where he would launch his search for his missing wife and son. How had it all gone so wrong?

Wiley lifted his head from his paws and cocked it to one side. His ears twitched back and a low growl rumbled in his throat. He stood and looked toward the front door.

Ethan put his brandy aside and strained to hear whatever had alerted Wiley. A moment later, the faint sound of a timid thumping carried to him. Wiley started for the door at a run, his paws slipping as he rounded the corner into the hallway.

By the time Ethan came around the corner himself, Wiley was sniffing at the threshold and wagging his tail. Whoever was at his door had been here before. He glanced at the hall clock as he approached the door. Three in the morning. Not a time for a friendly call.

He opened the door to find Sarah, her hand raised and trembling as she prepared to knock again. He was angry at himself for the leap of excitement he felt at seeing her there, dressed in her usual disguise. True to form, a rebellious lock had escaped her cap and curled like a vine around her slender neck. A neck, he mused, that he alternately wanted to throttle, or nibble and kiss.

"Why am I not surprised?" he asked as he rubbed the stubble on his jaw.

Sarah took a deep breath and launched into quick, nonsensical speech. "I know you told me not to help you, Ethan, but I remembered seeing Mr. Whitlock with a strongbox when I first followed him to the orphanage. I—"

He leaned forward to glance into the street, checking for any followers or nosy neighbors. Seeing none, he seized her by the arm and pulled her inside, then closed the door with a sharp thud. "Have you no sense at all? Christ! Standing at my door at this time of night! You could be seen."

Her violet eyes were enormous at his reaction, and she looked down at herself and frowned. "Who would know me?"

He backed her against the door until only the strongbox she held and an inch separated them. "Me."

"Then I am in no danger."

He almost laughed. She really had no idea of the force of his desire. He could easily ravish her standing up, pressed against the door. "Greater danger than you know," he growled.

"Th-that is silly," she said. "You've had ample opportunity to harm me before. Why would you do so now?"

He lowered his head to look in her eyes. "Why? A better question might be, why *not?* God knows I'm angry enough. I should devise a different torture. I've had you in my bed before. Perhaps I didn't get enough. Perhaps I'll carry you up there again." He indicated the stairs to the second story with a nod of his head.

"Empty promises," she murmured, and shouldered past him. She placed the strongbox on the hall table.

"By God, you tempt fate, Lady Sarah." He shook his head and fought to hide his amusement. He wondered if she'd be so saucy if she knew how close he was to doing what he'd threatened. "What is this about?"

She gestured toward the strongbox. "I remembered seeing Mr. Whitlock give that to Mrs. Carmichael for safekeeping. I recovered it from Mrs. Carmichael's bedchamber tonight. It was hidden beneath a stone in the hearth."

Ethan lifted the box to examine it more carefully. He turned the lock and tugged experimentally. "What is in it?"

"I think it may contain the papers you thought could incriminate your friend."

He shook it. His eyes glittered in the dim light. "Why didn't you open it? Were you not curious?"

"No," she said, then smiled. "Well, yes. But I did not want to violate your trust any further."

He breathed a little easier. "Good. I would not want to go after you because you learned something you shouldn't."

She backed away, rubbing her arms as if suddenly chilled. "I hope your friend will forgive you, Ethan. And I hope you will forgive me someday."

He turned toward her, forgetting the metal box in a deeper hunger than mere curiosity. Forgive her? His need was strong enough to swallow her whole. But forgive her? That was a stretch.

Loving her was another matter. When had that happened? When she had screamed his name in the throes of rapture? When she had made certain that the entire ton witnessed Lady Sarah, the paragon, waltz with him? Or was it the first time she had challenged him with Sticky Joe and Dicken at her back? No, it went further back than that. He had loved Sarah ever since she had laughed and reminded him that life can be joyful. And when she placed her hand on his heart earlier tonight at Thackery's musicale and said, "This is…all the truth I need. It is all that matters," he knew his heart was lost forever. But could he trust her to be faithful and steadfast in the face of opposition? To trust him when all odds were against him?

Sarah's eyes were enormous and she gazed at him with a wounded look. Something of the fierceness of his emotions must have reached her, because her hand came up to her throat and she stepped back.

He opened his mouth to speak, then shook his head and turned back to the strongbox. When he looked up again, Sarah was gone.

Chapter Twenty-One

"Where did you find this?" Lord Kilgrew asked as he studied the lockbox on his desk. "Does it have a key?" he queried.

The image of Sarah standing at his door just hours ago flashed through Ethan's mind. He shook his head. "The key, I gather, has disappeared with Whitlock."

Kilgrew licked his lips nervously and glanced at the closed door of his office. "Have you looked inside?"

"No, sir. I brought it to you as it was delivered to me last night."

"Who—"

Ethan held up one hand. "A confidential source."

Kilgrew nodded. "Have it your way for now, but if this should become evidence of some kind, we will need the testimony of the finder as to the circumstances surrounding its recovery. We will have to establish authenticity."

"I understand," Ethan said. He would just have to make certain it never came to that.

Kilgrew nodded and turned his attention to the strong-box.

Ethan went to look out the window to a busy street washed in sunlight, thinking how far he'd come since that night Kilgrew had summoned him. "If it is all the same to you, I shall wait. If this is not the evidence you seek, I shall return it to Whitlock's wife. She would be the rightful owner.''

"Of course, Travis. I…I cannot tell you how much this means to me.''

"No need, sir. I gave you my oath that I would keep Whitlock safe until you could find the evidence. Given that Whitlock has disappeared, bringing you the evidence is the least I can do. If this is not it, I shall continue the search.''

Lord Kilgrew went to his door and made a whispered request. Within two minutes, a balding secretary with hunched shoulders rushed in with a folded felt pouch. Kilgrew dismissed him with a wave of his hand and, once the door was closed again, took a set of picks from the pouch and began picking the padlock.

Ethan returned to his musings as he watched the people in the street scurry about their business. He wondered what Sarah would be doing this morning, and then it occurred to him that he'd never seen her by daylight. By all that was holy, he knew her as he knew no other, and yet he did not know her at all.

He heard a click, the scrape of metal as the padlock opened, and the rasp of a hinge as Kilgrew lifted the lid. There was a shuffle of papers, then a long silence. The next sound was a deep exhalation of breath.

When he turned, Kilgrew's face was ashen.

"Sir?'' Ethan asked.

"My God,'' the man muttered, looking up from an unfolded letter. "I never expected…''

Ethan stood still, waiting.

"He…he lied.''

"Who, sir? Whitlock?''

Kilgrew gestured at the open strongbox and shook his head. He seemed beyond speech.

How had Lord Kilgrew been deceived? Ethan took a few steps toward the desk and the page and envelope scattered there.

Kilgrew looked up, a bewildered expression on his face.

"I should have seen it. My God, all the signs were there, but I did not see it."

Brandy seemed in order. Ethan poured half a glass from the decanter on Kilgrew's desk and offered it to the man. "Is it the evidence you sought?" he asked.

Kilgrew downed the brandy in a single gulp. "Have a look."

It was Ethan's turn to shake his head. "This is none of my business."

"'Tis very much your business, lad. Very much, I fear." Kilgrew poured himself another brandy. "You see, *I* wasn't the one being blackmailed."

With mingled feelings of misgivings and fascination, Ethan turned the envelope over. *Lord Lieutenant Cedric Broxton to Mr. Harold Whitlock!*

He glanced up at Lord Kilgrew's stricken face and recalled that Kilgrew was Broxton's uncle. Bloody hell. No wonder the man was stunned. Well, he'd best know the worst. He unfolded the sheet and read.

July 1, 1816

My Friend Harry,
What a sweet little setup I've found here. The Dey of Algiers wants to buy information. He suspects the British are preparing an attack on the port and wants warning enough to remove and hide slaves and hostages. Use your position at the Ministry to discover what you can. Meantime, my unit is posing as French merchants while Captain Travis is trying to locate the British captives. I have paid the innkeeper a pittance to intercept his mail. Advance news of the attack should earn a tidy sum. Should you learn anything, you may post me by way of the Gibraltar courier.
Yrs. C.B.

Ethan had always suspected Broxton of treachery, but this was beyond his expectations. This letter had been passed mere weeks before twenty-five ships left Plymouth bound for Algiers. Pieces of a puzzle three years in the making began to fall into place. Here was the proof of Ethan's innocence.

And Cedric Broxton's guilt. So it was Cedric Broxton that Kilgrew had been trying to protect, and it was Broxton who was behind the attempts to find this very evidence. And, likely, Cedric who had knocked Sarah over the head, who had killed the Carmichael woman and who had tried to kill him at the chimney sweep's home.

He dropped the letters back in the metal strongbox. "What will you do with this, sir?" he asked.

Lord Kilgrew shrugged, still looking dazed. "I thought the scandal had died. I thought it was over. Now we shall have to dredge it all up again."

Oddly, Ethan was not jubilant with the prospect of clearing his name. For years, he had wanted exoneration more than anything else in the world. But now, clearing his name would require him to sully Sarah's. The cruel irony was not lost on him. He smiled. "Sir, I shall leave it to you to handle as best you see fit. The people I care most about never believed I passed information to the Dey—or that I committed treason. That is enough for me."

The old man smiled and sighed. "You are a good man, Travis. Not many men wouldn't jump at the chance for vindication." He stopped and waved his hand in dismissal. "I need to think. I need to talk to my sister about her son." He shook his head. "I need to talk to Cedric."

"Take all the time you need, sir," he said. The more time the better, because he had a more important score to settle before he settled privately with Broxton.

"I spoke with Cedric today," Reggie began as they rounded a corner on their way to the Argyle Rooms. The entertainment for the evening was a masquerade to raise funds for acquisitions for the British Museum. The theme was Ancient Greece, and attendees had been asked to dress in Grecian style.

Sarah wore a Grecian gown of saffron, wound with silken cords of purple, and her hair was in a style reminiscent of the statues currently on display at the museum. Reggie had opted for the garb of a Greek soldier, complete with brushed helmet. Sarah knew they'd be dressed conservatively by the standards of the evening. If she hadn't promised Reggie she'd accompany him, she'd have stayed home with a good book and a cup of tea.

She nodded now, afraid to ask the obvious question.

Reggie cleared his throat and offered another tidbit. "He is not pleased."

She smiled, imagining a temper tantrum of monstrous proportions. Cedric could forgive much, but not being made to look a fool.

"He demanded a reason for the cry-off," Reggie continued.

"What did you tell him?" she asked.

"That you had convinced me of the unsuitability of the match. When he demanded an explanation, I did not give one. I told him that, beginning tomorrow, I would put out the story that we were unable to reach agreement as to the settlements and that my announcement had been premature."

Sarah knew that society would interpret this in one of two ways—that Reggie was niggardly or that Sarah felt she was too far above Cedric's station. In either case, it would reflect poorly on the Hunters, and she was sorry for that. But worse was Cedric. "Was he…terribly angry?" she asked.

"'Terribly' does not do it justice." Reggie smiled. "I had not realized he was so smitten. And your settlements are not insignificant, you know."

"Papa left me well-situated," she acknowledged. "And Cedric wanted me, I knew that, but I never knew why."

Reggie regarded her with a long look. "Sarah, you know you were blessed with all the beauty in the family, do you not?"

She tapped his arm with her ivory-slatted fan. "The female half of the ton would disagree. I have heard more than one sigh when you pass by, Reggie."

"Hmm. Well, the point is, dearling, that Broxton has been a very patient swain, and his displeasure is in proportion to his wait. I had not realized how thoroughly unpleasant he could be when he is crossed. Please be very careful of him."

Ethan scanned the entrance hall of the Argyle Rooms for the third time. The light thrown by the elegant Grecian lamps provided a clear view of the crowd. Groups passed him on their way to the vestibule, and thence up the grand staircase. Ethan watched for any sign of Kilgrew. Perhaps he'd already gone in.

Ethan felt conspicuous in ordinary evening clothes, but it appeared he would have to brave it. He caught a flash of another uncostumed attendee. Cedric Broxton lurked in the shadows of the staircase, taking great pains to remain in the background. He had the look of a man with a purpose, and Ethan could well guess that purpose—to persuade his uncle to protect him from exposure. Would he succeed?

He handed the engraved invitation that had arrived by messenger from Lord Kilgrew that afternoon to a footman guarding the stairway. He climbed the elegant staircase to the first of several lounges. The festivities tonight would flow over into most of the larger rooms available, including the ballroom. He hoped it would not take long to find Kilgrew and find out why he'd been summoned. He had other fish to fry this evening.

And there, standing next to an ionic column holding a glass of frothy punch while her brother handed her wrap to a footman, was another of his fishes. She took a sip from her cup, put it on a passing footman's tray and walked into the Saloon Theatre.

The faint strains of an orchestra reached him as he claimed a glass of wine from a side table and continued his pursuit. He caught a flash of blue and gold in a far corner and turned to see his brother and the Lady Amelia glowering at him. He merely lifted his glass to them, shrugged and proceeded on his way.

The Saloon Theatre was lit by the radiance of six glass chandeliers and the orchestra played on a raised platform. Couples were scattered about the dance floor and lined the sides of the room. Ethan spotted his quarry standing in a group of women. Her brother had evidently deposited her with her friends and gone off to join his own.

He approached slowly, savoring the moment. He'd been less than pleasant last night when she'd brought him the strongbox. How would she respond now? He needed to know if she was prepared to honor her words, because it was not likely that Lord Kilgrew would clear Ethan's name at the expense of his own family.

Sarah stood with her back to him and was unaware of his approach. Only when her companions fell silent did she turn to see what had inspired their sudden reticence. He could see her tense as she acknowledged him with a smile and a proper curtsy—not too deep, and not insultingly small—just enough to accord him respect without being overt.

He bowed to the group. "Ladies," he said.

All eyes turned to Sarah. "Good evening, Lord Ethan. How nice to see you here."

Her companions followed her lead and offered like curtsies and greetings. Ah, yes. This was what it was like to be a paragon, he mused. He had almost forgotten how that felt. To have your peers waiting to mirror your reactions and take their direction from you. He could not help but smile wider when he wondered if Sarah's friends would follow her through London's seedy streets dressed in trousers, too.

"And you?" he asked. "I hope you have been well?"

"Quite well, thank you."

"And your family?"

"Thriving, Lord Ethan. My brothers are all the picture of health and high spirits. I came with Reggie tonight. I am certain he would want to pay his regards."

"Thank you, Lady Sarah. I shall look for him."

Another pause. How far would she go, he contemplated.

"I am wondering, Lord Ethan, if you will give me the opportunity to waltz with you tonight. I was sorry to have missed our dance at my brother's party and would be glad of the opportunity to make it up to you now."

He heard the soft intake of breath from the gathered women at this boldness, but Sarah pretended not to notice. "I am at your disposal," he said, realizing that she had just put society on notice that Ethan Travis was acceptable. Even desirable.

Sarah turned to her friends and said, "Should you have the opportunity, I would recommend Lord Ethan as a dance partner. He waltzes divinely. Lady Amelia Linsday first recommended him to me." She smiled brightly and waved to a point over his shoulder. He turned to see Amelia and Collin watching their little gathering.

Amelia flushed guiltily and waved back. There was little else she could do when caught in such a blatant study. He grinned and nodded a greeting, realizing that Sarah had just forced Collin and Amelia to acknowledge him. Even Sarah's banter with her friends had hinted at the nod of approval from his brother and sister-in-law.

"I should very much like to waltz with you, Lord Ethan," Grace Forbush said. "If not tonight, then soon."

"It will be my pleasure," he returned.

"Here's a waltz now," one of the young ladies announced as the orchestra transitioned from a quadrille into a waltz.

"Lady Sarah?" he asked with a slight bow in her direction.

She offered her hand and a shock went through him. The heat of her body, the scent of lilacs and the delicate hue of her blush enchanted him. When she placed her hand on his shoulder, he had to restrain himself from pulling her the rest of the way into his arms. That temptation doubled when he saw Cedric Broxton watching them from the safety of an alcove.

"Nicely done, Lady Sarah," he said as he led her into the measure. "To all appearances, you have approved me."

She smiled. "Not appearances only, Lord Ethan."

"What are you up to?"

"Making amends. 'Tis the night for that."

God, how he wanted to believe that. He led her into a quick turn and a lock of polished hair loosened from the purple cords and uncoiled down her back. She tilted her head back and laughed with pleasure. He could barely rip his gaze from the slender column of her throat and the spot there he knew could bring her to a boil.

"You did that apurpose," she accused. "That is why being with you is so exciting. I never know what you will do next."

She matched her step to his, reminding him of the little waif on the rooftops. She had always followed his lead with such grace and determination. "Whatever I do," he whispered, "I will keep you safe, Sarah." The words were out before he could think better of it. He had learned nothing if not that he had to be cautious when dealing with her.

She looked into his eyes and her smile faded, as if some burden had been remembered. "The...box? Was it what you needed? For your friend?"

"Yes."

He could feel some of the tension ease from her slender body as she nodded. "Thank heavens. Is it over, then?"

"Almost," he said. He glimpsed Lord Kilgrew on the sidelines, gesturing for Ethan to join him. "Just one or two loose ends to tie up. Afterward, I think you and I may have some things to discuss."

Her step faltered but she recovered quickly. "I have some loose ends of my own to tie up," she murmured. "I have made amends to you, but I still owe my brother a friend."

He did not like the sound of that, but he had no time to argue it now. He returned her to her group, bowed and turned away to go find Lord Kilgrew, but not before he overheard Sarah's next ploy to repair his reputation.

"Oh, Sarah!" one of the younger ladies said. "That was such a brave and daring thing to waltz with someone of Lord Ethan's reputation. I mean…treason!"

Sarah's laugh sent a thrill up his spine. "Treason? Oh, Beatrice, have you not heard? That rumor was just a ploy to draw out the real traitor. Lord Ethan, while undoubtedly mysterious, is quite a gentleman."

"And so handsome," another of the girls said.

Sarah, it seemed, was not finished repairing his reputation. He would speak to her about that once he'd met with Kilgrew and settled with Broxton.

Lord Kilgrew took the letter from an inner fold of his toga and tossed it on the small dining table in the center of the small private room. "It isn't good, my boy," he said. "I showed him the letter and demanded an explanation. He merely shrugged and asked where I'd got it."

Ethan knew Cedric Broxton's capacity for treachery well enough, but Broxton's uncle was new to the concept. It was bound to be a painful awakening.

"Sorry to use your name, lad, but you haven't told me who gave this to you or where it was found, so I told him you were the man I'd put on the job. A man has the right to know who his accuser is."

And he never *would* tell where the letter came from,

Ethan thought, but he'd have to find some way to prevent Kilgrew from finding out.

"My sister has taken to her bed. She begged me to reconsider exposing Cedric. Burn the damned letter, she said. Forget I ever saw it. I could not make either of them understand that you'd bear the taint of treason the rest of your life. Honor is apparently beyond Cedric."

"Sir, I've grown used to scandal and disrepute. Indeed, it has had some rather beneficial results."

"But you should not bear the blame for something you did not do. I shall make Cedric's letter public on the morrow," he said. "And Monday next, I shall read it in Parliament. That, with the testimony of the person who found the letter, will exonerate you. Then everyone will know you are innocent."

Ethan's stomach clenched. How would he keep Sarah's name out of this mess then? No, he had to end Kilgrew's plan without revealing who had found the letter. The less attention it drew, the better. "Please do not do that, sir."

"The public should know you did not—"

"Not necessary. I seem to be enjoying a resurgence of popularity." Ethan lifted the letter from the table and went to the small fireplace in one corner of the room. Before Kilgrew could protest, he dropped it into the embers and watched as it curled and blackened. Now Sarah was safe. With no letter and no authenticity to establish, there was no reason to pursue where they had come from.

"You've earned my gratitude, Ethan. I cannot hope to repay you. That you are willing to endure censure…"

Willing to endure that—and more—to protect Sarah, he thought. He cleared his throat and stood a little straighter. "I am glad I was able to return the favor."

Kilgrew cleared his throat and continued, "Anything you need…ever."

"Broxton and I have to settle accounts, but that will be in private. I will find him and throw down the glove. Before I leave you, sir, will you tell me what disposition you proposed to Broxton?''

Kilgrew nodded. ''I gave him a choice. Surrender to the authorities and confess, or leave England and never return. Australia or the Americas would be a good place for him, I said. I gave him twenty-four hours to make the choice.''

There was no telling the damage a cornered man like Broxton could do in that time. Broxton might have twenty-four hours to make a decision, but Ethan would settle with the man tonight.

Chapter Twenty-Two

Buoyant with relief that Ethan's honor was no longer at risk, Sarah watched him join a mature man dressed as Zeus, complete with a glittery cutout of a lightning bolt. They moved slowly toward the private dining rooms with every appearance of deep conversation. As soon as they disappeared, Cedric Broxton came up behind her and took her elbow.

"Do you have a moment for me, Lady Sarah?" he asked.

She turned and tried to hide her shock when she saw him. He looked wild-eyed and breathless, as if he had been running or exerting himself. She had never seen him so...undone. Reggie's earlier warning sprang to her mind, but she knew she could mend their rift.

"A moment," she answered.

"In private?" Cedric asked, glancing over his shoulder. Sarah frowned. "Shall we find an empty alcove?"

Cedric glanced toward the little alcoves placed between Grecian columns, some of which contained chairs or settees. "I would prefer more privacy than that." He indicated that she should proceed him with a sweep of his hand.

She entered the dim corridor between the succession of rooms and headed to her left, toward one of the larger supper rooms. As they passed the servant's stairs to an upper floor, Cedric jerked her sharply backward. When she tried to scream, he clamped his hand over her mouth and used his other arm to hold her hard against his chest.

She tried to twist away. Her robes tangled around her legs and prevented any effective defense. And, to her horror, her screams came out no louder than a sneeze.

"Stop it, Sarah," Cedric's moist breath against her ear sent cold shivers through her. "Struggle is useless."

Determined to break away, she continued to struggle and emit muffled squeaks as he dragged her backward up the stairs. Her panic took a toll. She was growing weaker by the minute.

"Damn," he snarled. He tightened his hand over her mouth and moved it up over her nose, cutting off her air. "I hoped I wouldn't have to do this."

What? Do what? she wondered, still thrashing and twisting. Her lungs burned with the need for oxygen. Her strength drained and the lights dimmed. Still struggling for breath, the darkness crowded in.

Her next awareness was of bursting up from deep water, gasping and clawing for air. She sat bolt upright and opened her eyes wide, blinking to focus.

"Ah," Cedric said. "Back with the living, Lady Sarah?"

Nausea gurgled low in her stomach. Cedric was standing near an open window in a small room. From the feminine decor, she thought it must be a ladies' retiring room. She was reclining on a green velvet chaise, and a side table bearing a washbasin and pitcher stood nearby. When she tried to push the hair from her eyes she realized her hands were bound in front of her with the purple cords from her coiffure.

"You've been crying in your dreams. Tell me, sweet Sarah, what terrors could such a prim little paragon be harboring?"

The sick feeling intensified. If there was any chance to get out of this, she would need to keep her wits about her.

They had to be somewhere in the Argyle Rooms. Should she scream? Even if they were in a vacant section of the immense structure, someone might hear.

Cedric chortled as he shrugged out of his jacket. "I almost gagged you, but no one will hear you. Still, a gag might be a nice touch."

The thought of being gagged brought Sarah back to her senses. She studied Cedric's face for any hint of madness. "What do you hope to accomplish with this tactic, Lord Cedric? Surely you know that Reggie will be angry."

He loosened his cravat. "Lockwood will come to heel soon enough when I've got his precious sister in tow. I am taking you to Gretna Green, where you will stand before an anvil and plight your troth to me."

Ah. So this was a simple case of anger at her rejection! "Please, Lord Cedric, I am honored by your offer of marriage, but I would abhor the married state and make a very poor wife, indeed. You are much better off without me."

"I've no doubt of that." He unfastened the buttons of his vest, a cruel quirk to his mouth.

"Then *why?*" She risked a glance at the knots that bound her hands and strained her wrists to loosen them. She realized with dismay that they were only tightening from her tugging.

"Because you, Lady Sarah Prim-'n-Proper, will be my salvation." He stepped toward her.

"Sylvie says I snore," she told him. "And my manners are not all they are cracked up to be. I have frequent headaches and assorted maladies. I...I am expensive to keep, and stubborn, too."

"Do you think I care about those things? He shook his head, grinned and popped the studs at his shirt cuffs. "Once I get an heir on you, 'twill not matter what you do."

"G-get an heir?" She cringed at the quaver in her voice.

Cedric's careful disrobing took on a sinister meaning. Oh, why could she not loosen the cords around her wrists?

"Once you are my wife, in fact and deed, Lockwood will come to his senses."

"This is a public place. You cannot drag me away, bound and gagged." She swung her feet off the chaise and stood.

"I have no intention of doing so," he said evenly, advancing on her. "We shall wait another few hours, and when everyone is gone home, we shall leave. My coach is waiting on Oxford Street. We shall take the northbound road to Scotland."

She backed toward the door, keeping her eyes on him. "Reggie will be looking for me. He would not leave without me."

"Oh, I think he would." Cedric grinned. "He is used to you leaving events early to go nurse a sick headache. By the time he even thinks to look for you, the deed will be done."

"Wh-what deed?" But she feared she already knew.

"We are going to have our wedding night just a tad early, Lady Sarah. That way, should Reggie find us, or catch us before we reach Scotland, he will have no choice but to consent to our marriage. Simple, really."

"He…he would kill you first." She bolted for the door and grasped the knob with her bound hands. Locked! She spun around to find Cedric grinning and holding up a key. She sagged in defeat.

"You will not escape. Do not even try."

"What do you hope to gain by this foolhardy scheme?"

"Respectability, Lady Sarah. Your reputation will save me. The Foreign Office cannot send me away, nor bring me up on charges once you are my wife. They will let Travis take the fall again."

Travis? "What have you done? What charges?"

"Just a little moneymaking enterprise," he said. "Selling information can be quite lucrative. but it can have

some unpleasant consequences. Let's not talk about that.''
He laughed. Actually laughed! ''You've made me look a
fool, and you will pay for all these months of careful courting. I should have just lifted your skirts and taken what I
wanted.''

Selling information? Had Ethan taken the blame for
Cedric's crime, just as Reggie had at Eton? A chill invaded
her bones and she strained again at the bonds around her
wrists. Oh, where was Ethan?

Cedric reached her and snaked his arms around her to
press a wet kiss on her neck. ''So come, little Sarah, and
lie down for me. 'Twill only hurt for a minute.''

The memory of Ethan's tenderness, his soft, slow seduction, caused her to moan softly.

Ethan! Yes. She glanced toward the window, a desperate plan forming.

She brought her arms up against her chest to act as a
wedge between her and Cedric. Using the leverage of her
hands against his chest, she pushed as hard as she could.

Cedric staggered backward, flailing wildly to regain his
balance. Without hesitation, Sarah lifted the water pitcher
from the small table and brought it down sharply on his
head. The porcelain shattered, sending shards of pottery
showering to the floor. He fell to his knees and toppled
forward. Sarah knelt and tried to push him over to gain
access to his pocket. She needed that key!

He moaned and shook his head. Good heavens! He was
not unconscious after all!

A puff of wind carried heavy fog through the window.
She stood and staggered toward it, trying to keep her balance. She sat on the sill and swung her legs over. The
ledge was not wide, but it was her only chance of escape.
Holding to the window sash, she pulled herself into a
standing position. She began edging toward the corner of
the building, with her back against the wall, praying for a
drainpipe, trellis, vine....

Her sandal slipped on fog-slick ledge and she struggled

to correct herself. She could hear Ethan's voice calming her, instructing her. *Slow and steady, Sadie. Heavy fog can prove dangerous....*

She could not use her bound hands to keep her balance or to cling to the stone facade. The wind was whipping tendrils of her untied hair into her eyes, obscuring her vision. Just when she thought it could get no worse, Cedric leaned out the window, emitted something closely resembling a growl and crawled out on the ledge after her.

Bloody hell! No Broxton. Ethan was nearly desperate to find him. Now that Broxton knew who had exposed him, the danger was doubled. He would be looking for a way to silence Ethan—and whoever had turned over the letters.

Failing to find Broxton, he'd gone in search of Sarah. He questioned her friends—discreetly, of course—with no concrete results. Grace Forbush said she'd seen Sarah heading for a refreshment room, but had not seen her in the past half hour.

He all but forgot Broxton in his search for Sarah. He went to the entrance hall to query the attendant at the cloakroom. Sarah's wrap was still there. Alarm building, he climbed the steps to the Saloon Theatre again, hoping he'd simply overlooked her in the crowds.

Going up, he bumped into Sarah's brother. "Sorry, Lockwood," he said.

"Quite all right, Travis."

At this point Ethan was desperate enough to run the risk of a set-down. "I hoped to see Lady Sarah again this evening. Do you know where I might find her?"

Lockwood hesitated only a moment. "No. I was just going to see if she had claimed her wrap or sent to have the coach brought 'round. 'Twould be unlike her to leave without giving me notice, but I cannot think of where else she might be."

The troublesome little thought that had been nagging at

the back of Ethan's mind came forward. "Sarah's wrap is still in the cloakroom. Have you seen Broxton?"

"Christ! Is he here?" Lockwood's eyes rounded in astonishment.

"I saw him briefly earlier. He was hiding near the staircase."

Lockwood checked his pocket watch. "She would not…I warned her to stay away from Broxton. He is angry over her refusal, and I would not put anything past him."

Ethan remembered Sarah's words earlier. His lungs constricted and he felt as if he could not breathe. "Sarah may have done something foolish," he murmured.

Lockwood changed direction and climbed the stairs at Ethan's heels. "I fear you are right."

When they arrived at the top, Ethan pointed. "You search right. I'll take the left. Meet me back here."

Anxiety heightened his senses and he scoured the public rooms for any sign of Sarah. He peeked in every curtained alcove, every private box and every unlocked room. To no avail. He recalled that Lockwood had been on his way to see if his coach was still waiting. He decided to eliminate that possibility and hurried downstairs and into the street. The queue of waiting coaches ran several blocks long. A light windblown rain began to fall as he ran along the line of coaches. Two blocks down, the Hunter coach was easily identifiable by the family crest emblazoned on the doors. Another bad sign.

Before going back inside, he decided to search all around the building. As he rounded the corner to the rear, a blast of wind caused a flutter somewhere over his head. Sensing danger, he looked up to see Sarah, her hair loose and plastered to her face by the rain and driving wind, fighting to keep her balance on a narrow ledge twenty feet above the street. And, barely eight feet away, Cedric Broxton was edging toward her. Fear built in Ethan like a living animal, clawing and scratching to gain control.

He positioned himself beneath her and called up. "Sarah? Can you hear me?"

"Ethan?" She stared straight ahead.

"I am beneath you, Sarah." He knew she was afraid to look down and wondered if she would have the courage, the trust, to do as he asked.

Broxton looked down and his mouth distorted in an ugly snarl. "Damn you, Travis. You think you've won, giving that letter over to my uncle. But I'll still beat you."

"Give it up, Broxton," Ethan yelled above the wind. "Back away from Sarah."

"She's my last chance, Travis. She's going to salvage what's left of my life."

The loud crack of splintering wood preceded the appearance of Lockwood in the window, a frantic look about him. "Cedric! What do you want? I'll get it for you. Anything."

Broxton looked back at Lockwood in the window, then at Sarah, trembling and unsteady as she neared the corner. "I want your sister. And I want things back the way they were."

Ethan knew the situation was out of hand. Broxton was a desperate man, and he was not going to surrender. Unless Ethan missed his guess, Broxton was spiteful enough to destroy anyone who had crossed him. Anyone in his way. There was one chance, and it was slim.

"Sarah! Stop," he yelled. "Steady, now. Take a deep breath." He was relieved to see that she followed his instructions. From the corner of his eye, he saw Broxton closing the gap between them.

"I am directly under you. Can you see me?"

She shook her head. Wind and rain had plastered her hair around her face and across her eyes.

"Don't jump. Just step off the ledge. I will catch you."

A little sob broke in her voice. "I am terrified."

"I know, love. I am, too. But it's the only chance we have."

Cedric's arms stretched out to seize her and he lunged. *"Now, Sarah!"*

She drew her bound hands against her chest, lifted her chin and stepped off the ledge.

Sarah understood with sudden simplicity how wrong she had been to keep Ethan at arm's length—how much time she had wasted letting her fears control her—and vowed that, if she lived, she'd never make that mistake again. How odd, that everything should suddenly became so clear when one's life was nearly over.

A man's scream broke off abruptly as strong arms closed around her. Together she and Ethan tumbled to the ground with bone-jarring force, Ethan cushioning her fall with his body. They rolled on the cobblestones and then everything stilled.

A moment later there was an outcry and voices shouting to one another. For a moment the words made no sense, and then she heard Reggie yell to someone below, "Broxton fell headfirst!"

Another said, "He's dead! Broken neck!"

Then her name was being called, and Ethan's, too.

All that faded to insignificance when Ethan's voice rasped, "Sarah? God! Say something."

She managed a breathless laugh. "All the time we spent on rooftops, and you never taught me that trick."

He stood, dragging her up with him, his right arm around her waist and his left arm dangling uselessly at his side. He crushed her against his chest and held her so tight that she could scarcely catch her breath.

"You are never," he whispered in her ear, *"ever* to go out on a ledge again, no matter the cause. Do you understand?"

"Oh, Ethan. We cannot keep doing this. 'Tis making me crazy."

"I can't give you up, Sarah. I won't."

"How much?"

"What?"

She wondered if he would recognize the words that had seared her heart and begun her rebirth. "How much, Ethan? How much to sate my hunger, how much to…satisfy my curiosity? How much to spend every day and every night with you?"

He gave a deep throaty laugh that Sarah had never heard before. The sound was joyful and he held her tighter all the while. "How much? Your heart and soul, Sarah. Your love, and all your tomorrows. Nothing less. Are you prepared to pay so high a price?"

She sighed, the last of her fears fading in the strong and steady beat of his heart as he followed his demand with a deep, tender kiss. It was fully a minute later before she could reply, "I already have."

Epilogue

London
December 10, 1818

Ethan leaned against the doorjamb, watching Sarah at her dressing table, brushing her hair into a semblance of an elegant chignon. He never tired of observing her at an ordinary task. She was such an extraordinary gift in his life that he needed the occasional reassurance that she was real—and his.

She glanced at her reflection in the mirror and smiled when she saw him behind her. "Ethan, stop lurking. Should you not be putting the finishing touches on your cravat? We shall be late to Reggie's supper party."

"My valet is pressing the folds, and Reggie will wait. He always does," he said. "Where is Sylvie?"

"I sent her to the kitchen." She smiled and her eyes sparkled like dew on spring violets when he stepped over the threshold, closed the door and turned key in the lock. In an attempt to divert him, she gestured with her brush to an envelope on her dresser. "You have not told me how you want me to respond to your brother's invitation. Yea or nay?"

He came up behind her and placed his hands on her shoulders. "I do not care, my love. You choose."

"Hmm." She frowned thoughtfully. "Well, Linsday *is* your brother. But I am still angry over his treatment of you."

"That's in the past," he said, running his index finger down the column of her throat and watching in fascination as little dots firmed beneath the fluid silk of her dressing gown.

"Has he groveled enough?" she asked, a delicate shiver raising tiny chill bumps on her arms. "Despite that he has realized he needs your approval to succeed in society, I frankly think he could do more. I must say, however, that seeing the Lady Amelia making cow eyes at you must humble him considerably. I almost pity him at those times. Oh, very well, then. I shall send our acceptance to his little soiree."

"Are you jealous of Amelia?" he asked hopefully. He was always oddly pleased when she displayed annoyance with any attention he drew from the opposite sex.

"Positively pea-green," she admitted.

He took the brush from her hand and dropped it on the dressing table. "'Twould never do to have you too sure of me."

"How could I ever be too sure of you?" She gave lie to her words with a smile that would melt stone. "You are society's darling these days. I cannot tell you how many of my friends have confessed to finding you incredibly handsome."

"But my former reputation—"

"Gives you a certain…*cachet*," she finished for him. "I count myself lucky that you stooped to marriage with a plain little mouse like me."

He laughed. *"Mouse?"* He bent and lifted her in his arms. "You cannot possibly see what I see."

"What do you see, Lord Ethan?" she asked, loosening the shirt studs at his neck as he carried her to the bed.

He placed her carefully upon the coverlet and untied the sash of her dressing gown. ''I see courage beyond imagining. I see strength, honor and determination.'' He pushed the fabric aside to lay her bare to his view. ''I see blinding beauty. And I see my entire future laid before me,'' he murmured against the soft beginnings of a swell at her abdomen.

She giggled as she reached up to him, the mere gesture causing an instant firming in his loins. ''Have I ever thanked you for saving me from a life of emptiness, my love?'' she asked.

Then the irony hit him full force and he threw his head back with laughter. From the day he first met her, he had been trying to save Sarah from real and imagined perils, and from herself—yet she had saved *him* in every way that mattered. He owed Sarah his honor, his reputation, his very soul.

''Are you ready, Miss Hunt?'' he asked, poised above her.

''Lay on, Macduff,'' she invited.

* * * * *

LOOKIN' FOR RIVETING TALES ABOUT RUGGED MEN AND THE FEISTY LADIES WHO TRY TO TAME THEM?

From Harlequin Historicals

July 2003

TEXAS GOLD by Carolyn Davidson

A fiercely independent farmer's past catches up with her when the husband she left behind turns up on her doorstep!

OF MEN AND ANGELS by Victoria Bylin

Can a hard-edged outlaw find redemption—and true love—in the arms of an angelic young woman?

On sale August 2003

BLACKSTONE'S BRIDE by Bronwyn Williams

Will a beleaguered gold miner's widow and a wounded half-breed ignite a searing passion when they form a united front?

HIGH PLAINS WIFE by Jillian Hart

A taciturn rancher proposes a marriage of convenience to a secretly smitten spinster who has designs on his heart!

Visit us at www.eHarlequin.com

HARLEQUIN HISTORICALS®

ITCHIN' FOR SOME ROLLICKING ROMANCES SET ON THE AMERICAN FRONTIER? THEN TAKE A GANDER AT THESE TANTALIZING TALES FROM HARLEQUIN HISTORICALS

On sale September 2003

WINTER WOMAN by Jenna Kernan
(Colorado, 1835)

After braving the winter alone in the Rockies, a defiant woman is entrusted to the care of a gruff trapper!

THE MATCHMAKER by Lisa Plumley
(Arizona territory, 1882)

Will a confirmed bachelor be bitten by the love bug when he woos a young woman in order to flush out the mysterious Morrow Creek matchmaker?

On sale October 2003

WYOMING WILDCAT by Elizabeth Lane
(Wyoming, 1866)

A blizzard ignites hot-blooded passions between a white medicine woman and an amnesiac man, but an ominous secret looms on the horizon....

THE OTHER GROOM by Lisa Bingham
(Boston and New York, 1870)

When a penniless woman masquerades as the daughter of a powerful marquis, her intended groom risks it all to protect her from harm!

Visit us at www.eHarlequin.com

HARLEQUIN HISTORICALS®

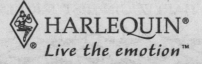

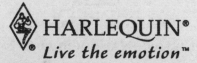

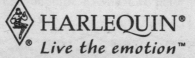

Want to be swept away by electrifying romance and heart-pounding adventure? Then experience it all within the pages of these Harlequin Historical tales

On sale September 2003

THE GOLDEN LORD by Miranda Jarrett

Book #2 in *The Lordly Claremonts* series

The best-laid plans go awry when a woman faking amnesia falls for the dashing duke she's supposed to be conning!

THE KNIGHT'S CONQUEST by Juliet Landon

When a proud noblewoman is offered as the prize at a jousting tournament, can she count on a bold-hearted knight to grant her the freedom— and the love—she ardently desires?

On sale October 2003

IN THE KING'S SERVICE by Margaret Moore

Look for this exciting installment of the *Warrior* series!

A handsome knight on a mission for the king becomes enamored with the "plain" sister of a famous beauty!

THE KNIGHT AND THE SEER by Ruth Langan

In order to exact his revenge, a tortured military man enters the Mystical Kingdom and enlists a bewitching psychic to summon the spirit of his murdered father....

Visit us at www.eHarlequin.com

HARLEQUIN HISTORICALS®